Palgrave Studies in Nineteenth-Century Writing and Culture

General Editor: **Joseph Bristow**, Professor of English, UCLA

Editorial Advisory Board: **Hilary Fraser**, Birkbeck College, University of London; **Josephine McDonagh**, Linacre College, University of Oxford; **Yopie Prins**, University of Michigan; **Lindsay Smith**, University of Sussex; **Margaret D. Stetz**, University of Delaware; **Jenny Bourne Taylor**, University of Sussex

Palgrave Studies in Nineteenth-Century Writing and Culture is a new monograph series that aims to represent the most innovative research on literary works that were produced in the English-speaking world from the time of the Napoleonic Wars to the *fin de siècle*. Attentive to the historical continuities between 'Romantic' and 'Victorian', the series will feature studies that help scholarship to reassess the meaning of these terms during a century marked by diverse cultural, literary, and political movements. The main aim of the series is to look at the increasing influence of types of historicism on our understanding of literary forms and genres. It reflects the shift from critical theory to cultural history that has affected not only the period 1800–1900 but also every field within the discipline of English literature. All titles in the series seek to offer fresh critical perspectives and challenging readings of both canonical and non-canonical writings of this era.

Titles include:

Laurel Brake and Julie F. Codell (*editors*)
ENCOUNTERS IN THE VICTORIAN PRESS
Editors, Authors, Readers

Colette Colligan
THE TRAFFIC IN OBSCENITY FROM BYRON TO BEARDSLEY
Sexuality and Exoticism in Nineteenth-Century Print Culture

Dennis Denisoff
SEXUAL VISUALITY FROM LITERATURE TO FILM, 1850–1950

Laura E. Franey
VICTORIAN TRAVEL WRITING AND IMPERIAL VIOLENCE

Lawrence Frank
VICTORIAN DETECTIVE FICTION AND THE NATURE OF EVIDENCE
The Scientific Investigations of Poe, Dickens and Doyle

Jarlath Killeen
THE FAITHS OF OSCAR WILDE
Catholicism, Folklore and Ireland

Stephanie Kuduk Weiner
REPUBLICAN POLITICS AND ENGLISH POETRY, 1789–1874

Kirsten MacLeod
FICTIONS OF BRITISH DECADENCE
High Art, Popular Writing and the *Fin de Siècle*

Diana Maltz
BRITISH AESTHETICISM AND THE URBAN WORKING CLASSES, 1870–1900

Catherine Maxwell and Patricia Pulham (*editors*)
VERNON LEE
Decadence, Ethics, Aesthetics

David Payne
THE REENCHANTMENT OF NINETEENTH-CENTURY FICTION
Dickens, Thackeray, George Eliot and Serialization

Julia Reid
ROBERT LOUIS STEVENSON, SCIENCE, AND THE *FIN DE SIÈCLE*

Ana Parejo Vadillo
WOMEN POETS AND URBAN AESTHETICISM
Passengers of Modernity

Palgrave Studies in Nineteenth Century Writing and Culture Series
Standing Order ISBN 0–333–97700–9 (hardback)
(*outside North America only*)

You can receive future titles in this series as they are published by placing a standing order. Please contact your bookseller or, in case of difficulty, write to us at the address below with your name and address, the title of the series and the ISBN quoted above.

Customer Services Department, Macmillan Distribution Ltd, Houndmills, Basingstoke, Hampshire RG21 6XS, England

The Traffic in Obscenity from Byron to Beardsley

Sexuality and Exoticism in Nineteenth-Century Print Culture

Colette Colligan

First published 2006 by
PALGRAVE MACMILLAN
Houndmills, Basingstoke, Hampshire RG21 6XS and
175 Fifth Avenue, New York, N.Y. 10010
Companies and representatives throughout the world

PALGRAVE MACMILLAN is the global academic imprint of the Palgrave Macmillan division of St. Martin's Press, LLC and of Palgrave Macmillan Ltd. Macmillan® is a registered trademark in the United States, United Kingdom and other countries. Palgrave is a registered trademark in the European Union and other countries.

ISBN-13: 978–0–230–00343–9 hardback
ISBN-10: 0–230–00343–5 hardback

This book is printed on paper suitable for recycling and made from fully managed and sustained forest sources.

A catalogue record for this book is available from the British Library.

A catalog record for this book is available from the Library of Congress.

10   9   8   7   6   5   4   3   2   1
15   14   13   12   11   10   09   08   07   06

Printed and bound in Great Britain by
Antony Rowe Ltd, Chippenham and Eastbourne

For my Mother

Contents

List of Figures	ix
List of Plates	xi
Acknowledgements	xii

1 The Traffic in Obscenity — 1
  1 Introduction — 1
  2 An 'extensive traffic': the print trade in nineteenth-century British obscenity — 9

2 Harems and London's Underground Print Culture — 23
  1 The unruly copies of Byron's *Don Juan*: harems, popular print culture, and the age of mechanical reproduction — 24
  2 Harem novels: the *Lustful Turk* to *Moslem Erotism* — 45

3 Sir Richard Burton, the *Arabian Nights*, and Arab Sex Manuals — 56
  1 'Esoteric pornography': Sir Richard Burton's translation of the *Arabian Nights* — 58
  2 'A race of born pederasts': 'Pederasty', *The Perfumed Garden*, and *The Scented Garden* — 73
  3 Collecting British obscenity: *Marriage – Love and Woman Amongst the Arabs* and *The Old Man Young Again* — 87

4 The English Vice and Transatlantic Slavery — 96
  1 The prurient gaze: the flogged slave woman among British abolitionists — 97
  2 Slavery obscenity in the 1880s: William Lazenby's *The Pearl* and *The Cremorne* — 104
  3 Slavery obscenity at the turn-of-the-century: *Dolly Morton* to *White Women Slaves* — 114
  4 Whipping in the twentieth century: the fugitive image — 122

5 Japanese Erotic Prints and Late Nineteenth-Century Obscenity — 125
  1 The traffic in Japanese erotic prints — 126
  2 Aubrey Beardsley's libidinal line: *Japonisme*, *Art Nouveau*, and obscenity — 129

3 Japanese prostitution: *Amorous Adventures of a Japanese
   Gentleman* to *Yoshiwara: The Nightless City*   162

Coda: The Obscenity of the Real   169

Notes   173
Bibliography   208
Index   227

List of Figures

1 Anonymous photograph using photomontage, 1895–1900. By
permission of the Kinsey Institute for Research in Sex, Gender,
and Reproduction, Bloomington, Indiana   17
2 Anonymous photograph of woman with erotic album, 1885.
By permission of the Kinsey Institute for Research in Sex,
Gender, and Reproduction, Bloomington, Indiana   18
3 [H. Heath], [*March of Mind*], [1826?]. By permission of the
British Museum, London   25
4 Thomas Rowlandson, *The Harem* [after 1812]. By permission of
the British Museum, London   33
5 Thomas Rowlandson, *The Pasha* [after 1812]. By permission of
the British Museum, London   34
6 J. L. Marks, *Sultan Sham and His Seven Wives* . London: Benbow,
1820. By permission of the British Museum, London   35
7 J. L. Marks, *Cuckold Cunning**m Frighten'd at his W − f 's
Caricature.* London: Benbow, 1820. By permission of the
British Museum, London   36
8 Don Juan [Isaac Robert Cruikshank], *The Libel Publisher Cut Up* .
London: J. Fairburn, 1825. By permission of the British
Museum, London   43
9 Anonymous, *Four Specimens of the Reading Public.* London:
J. Fairburn, 7 Aug. 1826. By permission of the British Museum,
London   47
10 Anonymous, 'The Barbarous Cruelty Inflicted on a Negro',
*Curious Adventures of Captain Stedman, During an Expedition to
Surinam.* London: Thomas Tegg [*c*.1805]. By permission of the
British Library, London   101
11 Aubrey Beardsley, *J'ai Baisé ta Bouche Iokanaan. The Studio* 1
(April 1863)   132
12 Aubrey Beardsley, *Enter Herodias*, uncensored version for Oscar
Wilde, *Salome*. London: John Lane, 1894. By permission of the
Victoria and Albert Museum, London   135
13 Aubrey Beardsley, *The Toilet of Salome* I, original version for
Oscar Wilde, *Salome*. London: John Lane, 1894. By permission
of the Victoria and Albert Museum, London   136
14 Aubrey Beardsley, *The Stomach Dance* for Oscar Wilde,
Salome. London: John Lane, 1894. By permission of
Harvard University Art Museums, Cambridge,
Massachusetts   137

15   Aubrey Beardsley, *A Platonic Lament* for Oscar Wilde, *Salome*,
     London: John Lane, 1894. By permission of the Victoria and
     Albert Museum, London   138

16   Aubrey Beardsley, *The Woman in the Moon* for Oscar Wilde,
     Salome. London: John Lane, 1894. By permission of Harvard
     University Art Museums, Cambridge, Massachusetts   139

17   Aubrey Beardsley, *The Eyes of Herod* for Oscar Wilde, *Salome*.
     London: John Lane, 1894. By permission of Harvard
     University Art Museums, Cambridge, Massachusetts   140

18   Aubrey Beardsley, *The Peacock Skirt* for Oscar Wilde, *Salome*.
     London: John Lane, 1894. By permission of Harvard
     University Art Museums, Cambridge, Massachusetts   141

19   Aubrey Beardsley, *The Toilet of Salome* II, altered version for
     Oscar Wilde, *Salome*. London: John Lane, 1894. By permission
     of the Victoria and Albert Museum, London   142

20   Aubrey Beardsley, *The Burial of Salome* for Oscar Wilde,
     Salome. London: John Lane, 1894. By permission of Harvard
     University Art Museums, Cambridge, Massachusetts   143

21   Aubrey Beardsley, Cover for Ernest Dowson's *Verses*. London:
     Leonard Smithers, 1894. By permission of the Victoria and
     Albert Museum, London   144

22   E. T. Reed, 'She-Note', *Punch* 10 March 1894   150

23   Aubrey Beardsley, *The Climax* for Oscar Wilde, *Salome*.
     London: John Lane, 1894. By permission of the Victoria and
     Albert Museum, London   151

24   E. T. Reed, 'She-Note', *Punch* 17 March 1894   152

25   E. T. Reed, *'The Woman Who Wouldn't Do'*, *Punch* 30 March 1895   153

26   Aubrey Beardsley, *The Kiss of Judas*, *Pall Mall Magazine* July 1893   154

27   E. T. Reed, *Britannia à la Beardsley*, *Punch's Almanack* 1895   155

28   Aubrey Beardsley, Bookplate Design for Herbert J. Pollitt,
     n.d. By permission of Harvard University Art Museums,
     Cambridge, Massachusetts   159

29   Franz von Bayros, *Salome with the Head of John the Baptist*
     (*c*.1907). By permission of the Kinsey Institute for Research in
     Sex, Gender, and Reproduction, Bloomington, Indiana   161

30   Anonymous illustrations from *Yoshiwara: The Nightless City* .
     Paris [Chicago?]: Charles Carrington [Targ?], 1907. By
     permission of the Kinsey Institute for Research in Sex, Gender,
     and Reproduction, Bloomington, Indiana   165

31   Anonymous photograph of lovers, *c*.1911–25. By permission
     of the Kinsey Institute for Research in Sex, Gender, and
     Reproduction, Bloomington, Indiana   167

32   Anonymous photographic sequence of women washing,
     c.1903–5. By permission of the Kinsey Institute for Research in
     Sex, Gender, and Reproduction, Bloomington, Indiana   168

List of Plates

1 William Blake, 'Flagellation of a Female Samboe Slave',
   John Stedman, *Narrative, of a Five Year's Expedition Against
   the Revolted Negroes of Surinam, in Guiana, on the Wild Coast of
   South America: From the Year 1772, to 1777*. London: n.p., 1796.
   By permission of Simon Fraser University Special Collections,
   Burnaby
2 Anonymous lithograph from *My Grandmother's Tale, The Pearl.
   A Journal of Facetia Voluptuous Reading* Unknown, reproduced
   from Patrick Kearney, *A History of Erotic Literature*. London:
   Macmillan, 1982. By permission of Pan Macmillan
3 Anonymous lithograph from *My Grandmother's Tale, The Pearl.
   A Journal of Facetia Voluptuous Reading* Vols 2–3. London:
   Printed for the Society of Vice [Augustin Brancart?], 1879–81
   [1890]. By permission of the British Library, London
4 Anonymous lithograph from *The Secret Life of Linda Brent, a
   Curious History of Slave Life, The Cremorne; A Magazine of Wit,
   Facetiae, Graphic Tales of Love, etc*. London: Privately Printed
   [Lazenby?], 1851 [1882]. By permission of the British Library,
   London
5 British Telecom Prostitute Cards, *c*.2000–02. London
6 Sazuki Harunobu, *Lovers with Rutting Cats* . 1765. By permission
   of the British Museum, London
7 Japanese Pillow Book, early nineteenth century. By permission
   of the Kinsey Institute for Research in Sex, Gender, and
   Reproduction, Bloomington, Indiana
8 Anonymous photographic postcard of Salome, *c*.1910. By
   permission of the Museum of New Zealand Te Papa Tongarewa

Acknowledgements

I am indebted to many librarians, archivists, and private collectors for their help with this project over the years. I would not have been able to undertake this kind of work on nineteenth-century obscenity without free access to rare materials at the British Library; the British Museum; the Victoria and Albert Museum; the National Archives; the Women's Library; the British Film Institute; the Bodleian Library; the Bibliothèque Nationale de Paris; the Kinsey Institute for Research in Sex, Gender, and Reproduction; and the Huntington Library. I wish particularly to thank Michael Goss, Jonathan Ross, Patrick Kearney, and Simon Brown for introducing me to their collections and sharing their specialised knowledge in the field. I am also indebted to a number of specialists in nineteenth-century studies for their helpful comments on this book in its various stages, especially Lisa Z. Sigel, Audrey Fisch, Lynda Nead, Joseph Bristow, Mark Turner, Mary Wilson Carpenter, and Maggie Berg. I conducted much of my research while a recipient of doctoral research grants from the Social Sciences and Humanities Research Council of Canada and the British Council. A grant from Simon Fraser University and a research fellowship from the Huntington Library helped me complete the project. Finally, I would like to express my appreciation for the support and mentorship of SFU's Centre for Studies in Print and Media Cultures.

The author and publisher gratefully acknowledges permission to reproduce material from the following: the Kinsey Institute for Research in Sex, Gender, and Reproduction; the British Library; the British Museum; the Victoria and Albert Museum; the Sambourne Family Archive, The Royal Borough of Kensington and Chelsea Libraries and Arts Service; Pan Macmillan; Simon Fraser University Special Collections; Harvard University Art Museums; and the Museum of New Zealand Te Papa Tongarewa.

Some of the material from this book was originally published elsewhere and reappears here, in revised form, with permission: 'The Unruly Copies of Byron's *Don Juan*: Harems, Popular Print Culture, and the Age of Mechanical Reproduction', *Nineteenth-Century Literature*, 59:4 (March 2005) 433–62. Reprinted by kind permission from the University of California Press. 'Anti-Abolition Writes Obscenity: The English Vice, Transatlantic Slavery, and England's Obscene Print Culture', *International Exposure: Perspectives on Modern European Pornography, 1800–2000*, ed. Lisa Z. Sigel (New Jersey: Rutgers University Press, 2005) 67–99. Reprinted by kind permission from Rutgers University Press. ' "A race of born pederasts": Sir Richard Burton,

Homosexuality, and the Arabs', *Nineteenth-Century Contexts*, 25:1 (2003) 1–20. Reprinted by kind permission of Taylor & Francis UK/Routledge. ' "Esoteric Pornography": Burton's *Arabian Nights* and the Cultural Discourse of Pornography', *Victorian Review*, 28:2 (2003) 31–64. Reprinted by kind permission of the editors.

1
The Traffic in Obscenity

Obscenity invades our homes persistently through the mail, phone, VCR, cable TV, and now the Internet. This multi-million dollar industry with links to organized crime has strewn its victims from coast-to-coast. Never before has so much obscene material been so easily accessible to minors.

The Internet is perhaps the most pernicious medium for obscenity. The Internet is a double edged sword: on one hand, it is an amazing tool that provides children a wealth of educational resources and gives them access to cultures and ideas that are beyond their everyday experiences. On the other hand, it also serves as a conduit for child exploitation and obscenity that respects no boundaries and recognizes no jurisdictional lines.

(Former US Attorney General John Ashcroft, Federal Prosecutor's Symposium on Obscenity, 6 June, 2002)

There are several classes of this indecent matter; there are indecent books and pictures and photographs, and then there are offensive postcards [. . .]. The indecent photographs and pictures, and all that kind of matter, which is of the most gross character, is almost entirely sent from abroad. I do not think there is much traffic in it by dealers in this country, comparatively; dealers abroad in Holland, Belgium and Paris deal largely in these things, and no doubt, despite everything that can be done, there is a certain amount that can be transmitted by post.

(*Joint Select Committee on Lotteries and Indecent Advertisements*, 1908)

1 Introduction

This is a book about obscenity and its most significant commercial, legal, and discursive formations in nineteenth-century Britain. Although it focuses

1

on the nineteenth century, it was conceived in the midst of neo-conservative eruptions of moral panic over Internet obscenity. A recent address by former US Attorney General John Ashcroft at the 2002 Federal Prosecutor's Symposium on Obscenity has driven this panic. His remarks, represented in my first epigraph, are striking for their concentration on the run-away circulation of obscenity. While this book does not examine the contemporary articulations of obscenity, it is profoundly aware that its current digital incursions of far-reaching global consequence started in the age of mechanical printing presses, worldwide postal services, and imperial trade routes. I have juxtaposed Ashcroft's remarks with testimony from the *Joint Select Committee on Lotteries and Indecent Advertisements* from 1908 to show how his panic about an onslaught of obscenity was anticipated almost one hundred years earlier. The fear that obscenity is crossing borders, circumventing media laws and aesthetics, infiltrating communities and homes, and becoming increasingly uncontainable is the legacy of the nineteenth-century global information economy and the emergent print traffic in obscenity.[1]

When I began this book, I intended to update Steven Marcus's classic psychoanalytic and thematic reading of obscene writing in *The Other Victorians* by giving greater attention to the historical circumstances of the nineteenth-century British trade in obscene publications.[2] It soon became apparent that the topic was not conducive to positivist historiography. The frontiers of obscenity, then as now, are never clear-cut. It has no stable definition: the surfeit of terms – obscenity, pornography, erotica, and smut – reveals the extent of the confusion and the problem endemic to the field.[3] It has no origins: it thrives on exchange, dissemination, reprinting, piracy, adaptation, translation, remediation, parody, simulation, and resurrection. It has no continuous tradition: obscenity is not institutionalised, but rather deracinated and disowned. It has no recognised influence: except perhaps for de Sade, authors and works are not eagerly embraced and imitated. It has no recognisable form: it is dispersed in print, aural, visual, and now electronic media. It has no fixed market: regulatory authorities continually break it up. It has no reliable readers and viewers: it is too dangerous and volatile for there to be a regular means of consumption. Its self-doubt is also sizeable. After all, the cultural value of obscenity is by no means secure: it is one of the world's most reviled and hunted forms.

This book therefore offers a history of nineteenth-century obscenity that explores its discontinuous trajectories and uneven developments, while recognising that it is one of the most ecstatic and unstable commodities of modernity. Michel Foucault's theory of the archaeology of history, which acknowledges the discursive layers, fragments, segments, and ruptures that make up the past, is helpful for the study of a cultural form like obscenity which defies the positivist pursuit for unity, connection, progression, and monument. However, his theory also immobilises history into a scholar's dig.[4] I instead examine the history of obscenity by showing how it gained meaning and existence in the nineteenth century in large part through its trafficking. In using 'traffic' as a model for understanding the formation of obscenity as a concept and trade in the nineteenth century, I draw on the word's complex discursive history. The etymology of the word is uncertain, but it arose in the commerce of the Mediterranean and came into use in the sixteenth century during the age of exploration and expanding trade. Over five centuries, the word has had multiple and interlaced meanings: the transportation of merchandise; the transportation of vehicles, vessels, and people; the transmission of messages through communications systems; trading voyages and expeditions; trade in general; illicit trade; and prostitution (OED). The word has thus encapsulated in its history overlapping modes of circulation and exchange. With its associations with commerce, communication, and transportation, it refers to the economic, spatial, and temporal dynamics of culture, which can be measured by flow, volume, speed, or current and hindered by intersection, congestion, or jam. The word also conveys the suggestion of illegitimate activity – the sex trade and drug smuggling. It even carries a lingering Orientalism from its commercial underpinnings in the Mediterranean. Although 'traffic' did not enter into nineteenth-century legislation against obscenity, the term was solidly linked to this new publishing phenomenon by the nineteenth century as morality campaigners and government commissions decried its 'extensive traffic'.[5]

My use of 'traffic' as a model for understanding this publishing phenomenon also draws on recent critical nodes in media theory, globalisation studies, and postmodernism. Print and media culture studies have opened up investigation into the circulation and transmission of material culture in relation to media technologies, hegemonies, and shifts. These include Robert Darnton's work on communication networks in the eighteenth-century French book trade, Jay David Bolter and Richard Grusin's broader theories of mediation and remediation, and the new MIT Press series on Media in Transition that encourages historical studies of media collision and congestion.[6] Globalisation studies, meanwhile, have turned our attention to the geographical scales and market logic of today's global culture, while forcing us to think about material culture in relation to space, time, and movement. In *Modernity at Large*, Arjun Appadurai describes the new global cultural economy in relation to different disjunctive flows along which ideas and objects move. Increasingly rapid and agitated flows of people, technology, finance, information, and ideology mobilise today's 'run-away world', an intensification of the Victorian industrial process.[7] Jean Baudrillard also offers one of the most innovative theories of circulation and movement with his breathtaking description of a postmodern consumer culture that has abandoned itself to the 'abject principle of free circulation' where there are no interiors, exteriors, boundaries, or borders. He provides an economic theory of unfettered circulation in capitalist societies increasingly preoccupied with the circuitry and velocity of exchangeable commodities. He even suggests the libidinal investment in these late capitalist cultural exchanges: 'Obscenity is not confined to sexuality, because today there is a pornography of information and communication, a pornography of circuits and networks, of functions and objects in their legibility, availability, regulation, forced signification, capacity to perform, connection, polyvalence, their free expression.'[8]

These critical perspectives on the dynamics of culture, variously explained in terms of technological change, geographical systems, and late-capitalist economics, come together to articulate a larger theory of cultural traffic. A theory of traffic, along with its historical associations with criminality, Orientalism, and even eroticism, is particularly useful for the study of obscenity, which has been on the move and dodging authorities since the nineteenth century. This is the first book to study obscenity in relationship to its trafficking. I show how it was mobilised by changing and interrelated cultural forces during a period of intense global interactivity and innovations in technologies of communication and information. More precisely, I am interested in how obscenity was caught up with the progress of print media, the expansion of empire and global economy, and the heightened disciplining of sexuality in nineteenth-century Britain.

Since the mechanisation of print in the early nineteenth century, obscenity has exploited almost every new medium of representation, communication, and transportation for its purposes. In the nineteenth century, these included the printing press, railway, post, and cinema, and they anticipated the more familiar technologies of obscenity of the twentieth and twenty-first centuries, such as the telephone, video, and Internet. Each new technological invention has transformed and accelerated the traffic of obscenity, until it has been stopped and diverted by a new regulation or prohibition. Because obscenity has often 'drive[n] new technology forward while also dragging it through the dirt', as Laurence O'Toole has observed, it has also become intimately associated with new forms of technological media.[9] Since the nineteenth century, obscenity has become so closely tied to its mediation that certain media forms have often acted as a sexual prosthesis, becoming an extension of the obscene, folded into its definition, and anticipating Baudrillard's sense of today's 'cool communicational obscenity' of circuits and networks.[10]

Expanding empire in the nineteenth century also crucially underpinned the development of obscenity as a concept and a trade. Edward Said dates the emergence of Europe's second empire, the sequel to its first empire in the Americas, with Napoleon's invasion and occupation of Egypt between 1798 and 1801.[11] This invasion was just the first-wave of European imperial incursion into Ottoman territories such as Sicily, Malta, the Ionian Islands, and Syria.[12] Informal empire in the guise of commerce and agents eventually gave way to a formal empire of protectorates, colonies, and globalised economies. Between 1875 and 1914, European nations began to engage in fierce rivalry over territories and spheres of influence in Africa and Asia. Since the Government of India Act of 1858, Britain administered India through a special department of government, but the escalation of British imperialism, some argue, began with the country's suppression of the Arabi Rebellion in 1882 and *de facto* rule of Egypt. Similarly, France had occupied and exploited Algeria since 1830, but its aggressive imperial policies began with the conquest of Tunisia in 1881.[13] New technology, such as the telegraph and the railway, crucially intersected with European imperial projects, shrinking time and space and globalising commercial and libidinal economies. According to Sir Richard Burton, this new empire 'did not improve morals'.[14] These dubious indulgences of British imperialists would lead one unnamed public servant to write an article in 1887 for the *Pall Mall Gazette*, 'Is Empire Consistent with Morality?' His answer was no:

> In general the men form relations of an immoral type with the natives, and they come to glory in so doing, or to justify it at any rate. [...] Morality – as the stay-at-home English understand it – they come to regard as a local English institution, which is to be left behind on quitting England [...]. They cap the precepts of the Sermon on the Mount by quotations from the Kama Shastra, and, in short, their minds become as the mind of Sir Richard Burton, that wondrous mind, which has 'informed' the appalling footnotes of the latest and unique translation of the 'Arabian Nights'.[15]

By the end of the nineteenth century, obscenity became fully implicated in the infrastructure of empire, which informed its fantasies and enabled its dispersal around the world via train, ship, and post. As Ronald Hyam observes in *Empire and Sexuality*, 'it can hardly be an accident that all the classics of British erotic literature were written by men who were widely travelled inside and especially outside Europe.'[16]

The heightened disciplining of sexuality in the nineteenth century also drove the traffic in obscenity. In the last 20 years, Marcus's repressive hypothesis has been challenged, albeit still not defeated, by more nuanced studies by Peter Gay and Michael Mason on Victorian sexual discipline and anti-sensualism.[17] The discursive explosion around sex in the nineteenth century, which led to the construction of Britain as a nation of prudes beleaguered by the vices of the French and other exotics, both produced and regulated obscenity. Its construction as a social problem that needed disciplining created an international underground traffic in illicit publications and helped circulate the idea of a deviant cultural form.

In proposing that obscenity was caught up in the global cultural traffic of print technologies, international trade, exotic fantasies, and sexual discourses that led from the farthest reaches of empire back to the metropolis, I offer a novel juxtaposition of nineteenth-century authors, publications, imagery, and events. One reason for this is to escape the limitations of many of the dominant histories and theories of obscenity. I stress the intersection of obscenity with larger cultural institutions and print markets, while shifting the existing scholarship on obscenity away from the language of 'other Victorians', 'Victorian underworlds', 'private parts', 'secret lives', and 'sexual subcultures'. I am instead interested in how obscenity became a transnational trade and concept dispersed across media, markets, and borders and dependent on new print technologies and complex commercial and fantasmatic global networks for its continuation and survival.

It is true that the field of obscenity studies has recently attracted compelling scholarship that has shifted the critical terrain from the notion of 'Other Victorians' that dominated the 1960s and the intractable feminist debates that dominated the 1980s. Linda Williams, Laurence O'Toole, and Frederick S. Lane importantly examine the relationships between obscenity and technological media, such as hard-core films and cyber pornography.[18] There has also been some recent groundbreaking work on historical obscenity. Peter Mendes's bibliographical study of clandestine erotic fiction, which builds on Patrick Kearney's work, has deepened our knowledge of the figures central to the production of obscene publications from the late nineteenth and early twentieth centuries.[19] Moreover, as the critical study of print culture and book history has consolidated in recent years, so have useful cultural histories of illicit literary relations and practices. Robert Darnton and Lynn Hunt have examined the French underground book trade in obscenity from the *ancien régime* and revolutionary France.[20] Iain McCalman's study of obscenity's emergence from underground political literature in early nineteenth-century Britain is also a pioneering work on the formation of obscenity as a print trade. His work has been even more recently supplemented by solid historical studies of British obscenity by Lisa Z. Sigel, Allison Pease, Lynda Nead, Bradford Mudge, and Julie Peakman.[21]

However, while obscenity studies has become a serious area of interdisciplinary scholarship, the field is dominated by bibliographical lists, legal histories, and Marcus's Freudian-inspired repressive hypothesis that obscene publications were the outgrowth of Victorian culture's abrogation of sexuality. Even more worrisome, though, is the prevailing assumption that obscenity is a fixed and obvious historical phenomenon when it is in fact volatile and continually changing – qualities that have been central to its survival and social menace. This is the problem with Pease's innovative explanation for how modernist writers like James Joyce and D. H. Lawrence wrote about explicit sexuality while avoiding the charge of pornography. In arguing that these writers destabilised the traditional binary between aesthetics and pornography, she overdetermines both categories and their complex and uneven histories. While McCalman's investigation into the transition from radical populism to obscenity among artisan publishers of the period is more sensitive to the irregular formation of the trade, his primary interest is in political history, and he peremptorily dismisses the 'counter-culture' pretensions of a trade that eventually 'popularised debased versions' of de Sade.[22] I believe a more relational approach to the study of obscenity, one inspired by Pierre Bourdieu's understanding about how culture is shaped by relational forces of power, helps break down preset ideas about obscenity as unambiguously sexually rebellious, or politically motivated, or masturbatory fodder, or nationally determined.[23] Such an approach instead reveals how obscenity emerged chaotically and moved widely in different, but overlapping print communities, which shared surprisingly consistent colonial and technological trajectories.

Therefore, in my book, I delineate four fields of cultural traffic that illustrate the larger formations of nineteenth-century British obscenity alongside the pressures and opportunities of developing print technologies, overlapping print communities, and intensifying globalisation. The method behind what may appear to be a selection of heterogeneous primary sources was largely experiential. It began with an examination of clandestine literary works in Henry Spencer Ashbee's three-volume bibliography of historical obscenity (1877–85).[24] The list readily revealed titles like the *Lustful Turk*, the *Kama Shastra*, and the *Khan of Karistan*, which underlined the exotic thematics of these underground works. Further investigation soon revealed clusters of publications that shared similar imagery and settings, underwent numerous reprints, adaptations, and remediations, and revealed frequent and sometimes parodic crossovers with mainstream authors, publishers, writings, and images. It soon became clear that there was sustained interest in the sexual capital of Oriental harems, Arab erotic handbooks, slave plantations, and Japanese erotic art. My interest thus turned to the fields of cultural traffic that mobilised and sustained these topics.

My study begins in Chapter 2 with the Oriental harem, the favourite landscape of Orientalist painters and purveyors of obscenity. Although the harem had been a European fixation since the eighteenth century, the rapid improvements in the mechanical reproduction of print in the early nineteenth century also made it one of the most repeated subjects of obscenity. In this chapter, I not only show that in the early nineteenth century pirated copies and spurious imitations of Lord Byron's harem episodes in *Don Juan* (1819–24) became a fulcrum for legal debate about obscenity, but I also demonstrate that by mid-century, many of the same radical publishers who pirated *Don Juan* for the common reader produced obscene harem novels for a wealthy clientele, a genre that fed fantasies of empire and survived until the end of the century.[25]

Chapter 3 draws attention to the traffic in Eastern literature that arose among the British elite, particularly Sir Richard Burton's circle and followers, and was likely influenced by the underground interest in the harem. An infamous explorer and linguist, Burton translated a series of Indian and Arabic texts that had an enormous impact on the British understanding of obscenity. I focus on how his translation of the *Arabian Nights* (1885–6), which had a limited run, caused a furore that introduced the term 'pornography' into British popular discourse for the first time. I also discuss how his privately published translations of Arabic sex manuals, including *The Perfumed Garden* (1886) and his burnt manuscript *The Scented Garden*, played an important role in theorising homosexual identity.[26] Not long after Burton's death in 1890, a series of pseudo-translations followed that imitated his style, prompted the collection of his publications, and continued the debates about homosexuality and pornography. The circulation of these translations over the last few decades of the nineteenth century shows how Orientalism was interrelated with discourses of obscenity and sexuality, a discursive formation that ultimately exposed for Burton's inner circle Britain's deficiencies in both fields.

In Chapter 4, I shift to the illicit transatlantic trade in obscenity over the century. More specifically, the image of the flogged slave woman underwent a series of literary and visual repetitions as it journeyed back and forth across the Atlantic. It was introduced by abolitionist print communities, but later exploited by hard-core smut peddlers who capitalised on the British fixation with the whip. I study the transformations of this racialised image in mainstream and clandestine print communities to show that the appropriation of slavery imagery was not simply part of an emerging commodification of sexuality, but also a parody of concealed and displaced transatlantic fantasies about racialised violence.

My last chapter focuses on how Japan's visual and erotic arts played an important role in the formation of British obscenity in the late nineteenth century. Japanese erotic prints circulated widely in Europe, influencing artists like Aubrey Beardsley who combined European and Japanese media aesthetics in his black and white drawings for Oscar Wilde's play *Salome* (1894).[27] While his detractors criticised his prints for their exotic perversities, others delighted in their obscenities. Moreover, I show that alongside this high cultural discourse about *art nouveau* aesthetic improprieties, a clandestine trade grew and peddled novels embellished with pseudo-Japanese prints and fixated on Japanese prostitution.

The four fields of cultural traffic that I examine bring together a distinctive configuration of non-canonical and canonical nineteenth-century publications that reveals the uneven developments of obscenity in the period. By bringing together different print media and communities, I make some striking discoveries about the changing global mediascape of nineteenth-century obscenity and sexuality. Obscenity became associated with Orientalist themes and pirated rip-offs in low print media. Translations of Oriental sex manuals explored theories of homosexual identity and English sexual prudery while igniting the emergent cultural discourse of 'pornography'. Classic English whipping fantasies were intertwined with the history of slavery in the transatlantic print marketplace. And finally, Japanese erotic prints reinvigorated the English sexual imagination. There are also larger implications to these discoveries. They illustrate that obscenity exploited worldwide systems of communication and representation, belonged to larger commercial and fantasmatic circuits of desire, engrossed some of the most sexually radical writers of the day, and participated in contemporary discourses about the possibilities and limitations of sexual identities and practices. As a commercial enterprise and a shared concept, obscenity was interleaved in the culture at large, intersecting majority and minority culture, circulating from home to empire, searching out new print and visual media, and readily globalising. A look back at the emergence of obscenity when it began to thrive on the technologies of globalisation helps us see how its modern-day incursions feared by Ashcroft and lyricised by Baudrillard are simply an escalation of its nineteenth-century print traffic.

2 An 'extensive traffic': the print trade in nineteenth-century British obscenity

In order to follow the traffic in obscenity in nineteenth-century British print culture, it would be useful to present some basic information about its circulation in the period. While the careers of Byron, Burton, and Beardsley will be familiar to many, the clandestine print communities with which their careers intersected will be less so. Except for underground catalogues, the occasional memoir, and the publications themselves, there is no record keeping on the trade in obscenity: little, especially the street material, has survived the test of time, library policy, or public tolerance.[28] However, crucial, albeit piecemeal, information about this metropolitan print culture is found in legislation, parliamentary debates, trial documents, newspaper law reports, investigative journalism, and Home Office papers – the documents that flowed from the exercise of jurisprudence. Mendes, McCalman, and Sigel have done the most sustained bibliographical and archival research in this field. McCalman shows how a well-defined trade in obscene publications grew out of the postwar political radicalism and republican dissidence of the 1820s. Mendes, meanwhile, explores how book clubs and private subscription lists were central to up-market publishers. This research has helped identify the major underground publishers, from George Cannon, John Duncombe, and William Dugdale in the first half of the century to William Lazenby, Henry Judge, Harry Sidney Nichols, Charles Hirsh, and Charles Carrington in the latter half, when the London business shifted to Amsterdam, Rotterdam, and especially Paris, where publishers such as Hirsch, Nichols, and Carrington ran a mail-order postal trade for its wealthier British clientele.[29] But, many of the judicial papers and newspaper reports, some of which I am examining for the first time, reveal a far less scripted print culture and offer insight into how obscenity began to be understood in relation to its trafficking, informing fantasies and fears of relentless circulation.

One of my main positions is that obscenity did not emerge as a complex publishing enterprise and print crime in Britain, Europe, and eventually North America until the nineteenth century. This claim needs some explanation. There is indeed a rich body of erotic writing and imagery in Britain from the seventeenth and eighteenth centuries. David Foxon, Roger Thompson, and Julie Peakman have helped uncover its history and cultural value. John Wilmot Rochester's *Sodom: or, The Quintessence of Debauchery* (1684), John Cleland's *Fanny Hill* (1749), and John Wilkes's *An Essay on Woman* (1763) are all British classics, their notoriety persisting through the nineteenth century.[30] The British also consumed, adapted, and translated French and Italian literature: 'Aretine's Postures' (1524), *L' Ecole des Filles* (1655), and Nicolas Chorier's *Satyra Sotadica* (c.1660).[31] Roy Porter and Lesley Hall also mention the circulation of popular sex manuals such as Aristotle's *Master-Piece* (1684) and Nicolas Venette's international bestseller 'Tableau de l'amour conjugal' (1686).[32] Other authors were also read specifically for their salacious content: particular favourites were Martial, Juvenal, Ovid, Catullus, Giovanni Boccaccio, and François Rabelais. Yet, despite the presence of these works, some of which even faced legal prosecution, obscenity was neither a significant enterprise nor volatile print crime.

Before the nineteenth century, the legal understanding of obscenity in Britain was uncertain and driven by common law. Britain's first Obscene Publications Bill was drafted in 1580 in order to 'restrain the licentious printing, selling, and uttering of unprofitable and hurtful English books', but it was never presented to Parliament.[33] Publications could be suppressed by the Licensing Act (1557–1695) or the Society for the Reformation of Manners (1692–1738), but these checks indiscriminately targeted blasphemy, political libel, and sexual indecency, and, in the case of the latter, focused mainly on theatrical performances.[34] Obscenity was not legally understood as distinct until 1727. The landmark case against Edmund Curll in that year finally made obscene libel a common law misdemeanour subject to punishment, subsequently becoming the basis of future British obscenity law. Found guilty of publishing two obscene libels – Jean Barrin's anti-Popish *Venus in the Cloister* and Johann Heinrich Meibomius's *Treatise of the Use of Flogging* – Curll was heavily fined, £16 13s 4d for each book, and sent to the pillory.[35] Donald Thomas observes, however, that Curll's publication of a seditious pamphlet during his trial did not help his case.[36] His indictment for obscene libel was likely influenced by his political indiscretion: obscene libel and political libel were still commensurate print crimes.

When King George III issued a royal proclamation targeting profane and indecent publications in 1787, obscenity became a more specific target of censorship, but still not an exclusive one. This proclamation aimed to prevent 'vice, profaneness, and immorality' by suppressing 'all loose and licentious prints, books, and publications dispensing poison to the minds of the young and unwary' and by punishing 'publishers and vendors'.[37]

From this proclamation emerged the Proclamation Society, which in 1802 was absorbed into one of the most vigilant public wardens of morality in England: the Society for the Suppression of Vice (SSV). Founded by the abolitionist William Wilberforce, the SSV aimed to suppress Sabbath breaking, blasphemous publications, obscene publications, disorderly houses, and fortune-tellers. Within a few decades, however, SSV reports show that the prosecution of obscenity, what it deemed the 'least excusable' offence, became its special target.[38]

A spate of legislation followed in the nineteenth century that targeted obscenity and shifted the terms of the crime from political dissent and public exhibition to circulation, distribution, and trafficking. The focus was increasingly on the volume and number of publications and the velocity and scale of penetration. In her study of obscenity in mid-nineteenth-century Britain, Lynda Nead makes the remarkable, though underdeveloped, observation that the legal understanding of obscenity rested on perceived notions of its unruly circulation in metropolitan urban culture, where it gathered in London's cicatrise of little streets, mews, and bottlenecks and congested people's minds and morals as they moved through the city. Early nineteenth-century legislation against obscenity thus attempted to break up the congestion of obscenity and reintroduce the right kinds of flows of people and commodities through the city. The Vagrancy Act of 1824 attempted to stop the viewing of obscene materials in the streets, making it a summary offence wilfully to expose 'to view, in any street, road, highway or public place, any obscene print, picture or other indecent exhibition'. The 1838 amendment to the Vagrancy Act widened the purview of the law to displays in shop windows, and the Metropolitan Police Act of 1847 extended the rights of metropolitan police to regulate the public sale and distribution of obscenity, concentrating again on the street distribution as it targeted 'every person who publicly offers for sale or distribution, or exhibits to public view, any profane, indecent, or obscene book, paper, print, drawing, painting, or representation, or sings any profane or obscene song or ballad'. By 1857, the Obscene Publications Act was passed, giving statutory authority to existing common law against obscene libel and newly authorising the police, who were formerly reliant on dubious informers supplied by the SSV, to search suspect premises as well as to seize and destroy obscene materials.[39] When Lord Campbell introduced and promoted the bill in parliamentary debates, he justified it by emphasising the increased circulation of obscenity: 'It was not alone indecent books of a high price, which was a sort of check, that were sold, but periodical papers of the most licentious and disgusting description were coming out week by week, and sold to any person who asked for them, and in any numbers.'[40] The intention of this law, he stressed, was not to prosecute Alexandre Dumas fils's *La Dame aux Camélias* (1848) or the fine arts, but rather the cheap, mass-distributed publications sold 'week by week' and 'in any numbers' at railway stations and in Holywell Street, the nucleus of the print trade in obscenity by mid-century and one of the city's famed sites of moral congestion.[41]

At the end of the century, obscenity legislation was rescaled and reflected the changing perception that it had grown into a problem of international dimensions. New statutes were introduced, shifting the terms of the crime from the streets to the information highways by regulating the expanding mechanisms of long-distance communication, such as postal services, new mail-order businesses, and private subscription catalogues. The Customs Consolidation Act of 1876 was passed to prohibit the importation of obscene materials. The list of prohibited imports included 'indecent or obscene prints, paintings, photographs, books, cards, lithographic or other engravings, or any other indecent or obscene articles', an indication that visual obscenity was increasingly viewed as a threat. Significantly, obscenity was not among its list of banned exports as it was deemed a foreign problem infiltrating Britain. The Post Office (Protection) Act of 1884 and the Indecent Advertisements Act of 1889 similarly focused on preventing the circulation of obscene materials, especially photographs and postcards.[42] In the late nineteenth and early twentieth centuries, there was also a wave of international legislation against the global traffic in obscenity. Canada and India both passed their Post Office Act in 1908. New Zealand passed its Post Office Act in 1893 and Post and Telegraph Act in 1901. Australia passed the Victorian Customs Act in 1883. France passed morality laws in 1898 and 1908. Meanwhile, America strengthened laws against the mailing of obscene materials with the Comstock Act in 1873. The twentieth century also saw international conferences on obscenity where nations met to discuss their respective legislation. An International Conference on the Suppression of Obscene Publication met in Paris in 1910 to coordinate information and operations, and the League of Nations held an International Conference for the Suppression of the Circulation of and Traffic in Obscene Publications in 1923 in Geneva in order to monitor the traffic and suppression of obscenity.[43]

In addition to the legislation that tried to regulate obscenity and its mechanisms of circulation, other records from the period reveal how it was increasingly understood and condemned in relation to its circulation. As early as 1817, George Prichard, a member of the SSV, reported to the Police Committee of the House of Commons on a *traffic* in obscene publications:

> The Society first entered upon their investigation into the state of this trade shortly after its institution in the year 1802; at which period prosecutions for such offences being almost unknown, so little disguise and concealment were used by dealers of this class, that, with no great difficulty, important discoveries were soon made as to its nature and extent. It was early ascertained, from indubitable testimony, that several foreigners (having their head quarters in London) of apparent respectability and considerable property, were united together in partnership for the principal, and almost exclusive purpose of carrying on an extensive traffic in

obscene books, prints, drawings, toys, &c. The agents, by whom the partners of this house disseminated their merchandise, were about thirty in number, chiefly consisting of Italians, under the assumed character of itinerant hawkers, by whom they established a systematic trade throughout the great part of the United Kingdom.

After initial successes with suppressing these publications, Prichard then describes the 'revival of the trade' in 1815 after the Napoleonic Wars. 'In consequence of the renewed intercourse with the continent incidental to the restoration of peace', he reports, 'there has been a great influx into the country of the most obscene articles of every description, as may be inferred from the exhibition of indecent snuff boxes in the shop windows of tobacconists.' His description of how the SSV secured obscene books and prints gathered for upcoming trials reveals the extent to which the society, early in its history, perceived obscenity as a distinct and extremely volatile cultural form, in desperate need of containment:

These specimens are kept in a tin box secured by three different locks; one of the keys of which is kept by the treasurer, one by a member of the Committee, and one by the secretary; so that the box can at no time be opened, but with the concurrence of these three persons.

Prichard's report situates the traffic in obscenity as a lower-class social problem imported by itinerant foreigners, whether Italian commercial travellers or French opportunists of postwar efflorescence, who circulated their wares across Britain at country fairs and boarding schools.[44]

Henry Mayhew's reportage on London street culture in *London Labour and London Poor* (1861) provides additional evidence about the traffic in obscenity: he investigates an ephemeral, less documented trade that developed alongside a more established one that operated out of printshops. He alludes to a street trade in indecent French snuff-boxes, cigar-cases, prints, and playing cards, sold by women and men generally to the 'rich', often gentlemen from Oxford or Cambridge who could spare 2s 6d for a snuff-box with a coloured picture of a naked woman. One of Mayhew's informants also described a common swindle, the 'sham indecent street trade'. Men would place themselves near shops on Holywell Street, Wych Street, or the Haymarket that displayed five-shilling 'shameless publications' in their windows, and they would offer to sell these items for sixpence in sealed packets which actually enclosed Christmas carols or religious tracts. He identifies the clientele as 'principally boys, young men, and old gentlemen'.[45] Mayhew is informative because he describes other patterns of circulation by revealing how opportunistic street peddlers drew off the business of more established bookshops that traded in obscene publications.

Later in the century, there was much consternation about obscene displays in shop windows that might corrupt innocent, vulnerable passersby, such as middle-class girls and women. An article from 1882 entitled 'Holywell Street Literature' from the magazine *Town Talk* discusses the dangerous print culture of the streets:

> It has been a still greater marvel to me that obscenity should be permitted to actually publicly display itself in the shop windows. It is nonsense to say that such a thing does no harm, for passing down Holywell Street the other day I observed two quite young girls, one of whom was pointing at the other, as they stood blushing and grinning at a shop window, a card bearing only one word, but which is only too frequently found in the shops of the thoroughfares.[46]

This passage from *Town Talk* emphasises the metropolitan geography of obscenity that Nead studies, where vulnerable middle-class consumers would mix with the lower classes while brushing up against obscene window displays, impeding the right kinds of flows through the city streets.

London 'Police' articles and 'Law Reports' from the *Times* provide more evidence about how obscenity was circulated and exchanged over the years. Perhaps most strikingly, the paper reveals that women and families participated in the trade. When Henry Vaux, a newsvendor and printseller, was charged for selling obscenity from his shop in Spitalfields, it was not actually he who sold the offending item, an illustrated three-shilling copy of the *Life and Intrigues of the Earl of Rochester*, but a female assistant.[47] The *Times* also reported that William Dugdale's family participated in the trade as he passed in and out of prison.[48] Obscenity was not the exclusive domain of men, but involved women and families, like many other artisan trades. The *Times* further documented how the police would occasionally sweep problem districts, such as Holywell or Wych Street, and focus on notorious booksellers and publishers. Dugdale, prosecuted at least five times for obscene libel, was sentenced and imprisoned for the last time in 1868, the year he died.[49] The *Times* duly recorded the seizure of his goods:

> The property thus condemned consisted of the pirated, but unbound, sheets of 35,000 volumes of obscene books and pamphlets, 46 lithographic stones (each to print six page-size illustrations to the above-mentioned books), with 318 printed impressions from the stones, 15 copper-plates, engraved with equally-disgusting designs, and between 700 and 800 impressions.[50]

It was not the content of the publications that caused concern, but rather the scale of production and possible circulation. Dugdale's more upscale publications, produced in small numbers and sold for two to three guineas, were never mentioned in the court proceedings. The kinds of publications that were typically prosecuted include cheap magazines and books such as *The Rambler's Magazine* (an illustrated weekly periodical that sold for six to eight pence), *The Festival of the Passions* (a popular book that sold for five shillings in 1831, but up to two pounds in 1890), *Venus's Album* (a book sold for 2s 6d), *The Ferret* (a penny magazine sold in the streets by teenage boys), *The Confessional Unmasked* (the anticlerical work that kept reappearing in court), *The Fruits of Philosophy* (a medical book on population control that sold for six pence), *Wild Boys of London* (penny 'trash' with stereotype plates sold by teenage boys), and *Modern Babylon* (a book that made its way to Eton College).[51]

The National Vigilance Association (NVA) papers, which are held at the Women's Library in London, give us yet another perspective on the traffic in obscenity toward the end of the century. The NVA replaced the SSV as moral watchdog in 1886, and its activities and publications reveal the growing anxieties about the global scale of the business and its growing outlay in images.[52] NVA correspondence shows, for example, extreme anxiety surrounding the immorality of port cities, where obscene literature and photographs surfaced to profit from sailors and travellers on stopovers. An Englishman, C. E. Barlow, wrote to a representative of the NVA on 19 January 1905 in order to inform him about the spread of obscenity in principal ports on trading routes to Port Said:

> The case of Port Said is no doubt more difficult; it does however seem incredible, when one remembers the very large proportion of British ships which pass through the Canal, and the overwhelming strength of British influence in Egypt, that nothing can be done to purge this moral plague spot of some, at least, of its accumulation of filth.
>
> It is not only that the monstrous abominations are committed in the foul dens of the city, but young Arab boys are allowed to approach Englishmen in the main street of the town, even when accompanied by ladies, and offer them obscene literature and pictures for sale.

Elaborating his claims a few days later, he adds,

> I can myself testify at Port Said the whole thing is so blushingly carried on in the open that I should think that you would have no difficulty in seeing it for yourself. I am told that it is very bad in Cairo and Suez, but at least English sailors and passengers to the East are not exposed to temptation at these places, at Port Said the vessels must stop for coaling. [...] Port Said is at present a perfect sink of iniquity, a vile plague spot, situated well upon the highway of all the intense shipping traffic to the East.[53]

Barlow's letter reveals growing worry that obscenity travelled with the extensive shipping traffic to the East, exploiting Britain's imperial infrastructure to become a complex global operation and regulatory problem.

Such fears about the traffic in obscenity not only grew in proportion to its globalisation, but also its associations with new advances in photographic media. From the beginning of the nineteenth century, obscene publications integrated graphic print technology, from wood engravings to steel engravings to coloured lithography; however, the 'media explosion' in photographic technologies led to obscenity's dramatic transition from print media to photographic media at the end of the century.[54] By the 1850s, there was already an emerging underground traffic in photographs that was almost immediately international in scope. Every technological variant of the medium was exploited for obscenity: daguerreotypes, stereographs, *carte de visites*, and postcards. Most commercial producers of sub-rosa photographs remained anonymous lackeys to the latest technological novelty: hard-core photomontage offered, in Jonathan Crary's words, a 'carnal density of vision' (Figure 1);[55] erotic postcards spread, according to Malek Alloula, their 'vulgar expression of colonial euphoria';[56] and stanhopes concealed microphotographs of nude women hidden at the base of everyday objects such as pens.[57] Much of the early hard-core and experimental visual obscenity that circulated in the mid-nineteenth century was stereographic, three-dimensional images that showed fellatio, cunnilingus, copulation, and threesomes.[58] There were a number of stereographs that situated women in provocative poses with books, images, and albums, an erotic illustration of the intersection of print and photographic obscenity through the course of the century. One stereograph from around 1885 shows a semi-nude woman masturbating while looking at a large album with sexually explicit images (Figure 2). The top image in the album includes a close-up of women's genitalia, while the bottom image shows a woman masturbating with her legs spread in virtually the same position as the woman in the centre of the image. The erotic album accentuates and repeats the image of the self-pleasuring woman, pulling the spectator further into the space as he or she searches for the image within the image, a Victorian erotic experience of virtual reality.

Underground catalogues also reveal a private, upscale traffic in obscene photographs, many of which shared the same colonial thematics as the print material I discuss more closely. *Catalogue of the Latest Photographic Novelties*, a Paris-based pamphlet from *c.* 1901, advertised cabinet photographs.[59] These small, hand-sized photographs were distributed to the wealthy by subscription catalogue, intended for private, secret consumption and often accompanied by a discretionary note regarding circumspect mail delivery. One series of 25 photographs entitled 'In Egypt' was directed at a European market and sold for a costly 30 francs or £1.50s.

Figure 1 Anonymous photograph using photomontage, 1895–1900. By permission of the Kinsey Institute for Research in Sex, Gender, and Reproduction, Bloomington, Indiana

18

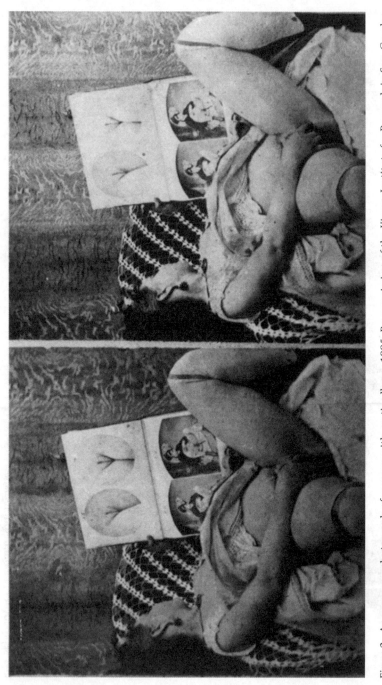

Figure 2 Anonymous photograph of woman with erotic album, 1885. By permission of the Kinsey Institute for Research in Sex, Gender, and Reproduction, Bloomington, Indiana

We are in an Oriental brothel – The walls are adorned with very lecherous engravings and before this decoration prepared for the carnal debauches, a man with a strong penis possesses at a time two enamoured women. This man is of unusual strength and the two women are of a perfect beauty. The mutual voluptuousness they enjoy together are rendered by ingenious poses of a downright obscenity.

The series turns to the familiar harem fantasy, remediating the allure of the exotic explored in obscene print culture with the latest, pocket-sized photographic novelty. Another clandestine catalogue entitled *Strictly Confidential*, also probably printed in Paris in the early twentieth century, listed 20 cabinet photographs of 'slave negresses' for 25 shillings or $6.25. The catalogue describes how the photographs visualise the sexual dominion of the slave owner over his female slaves:

A young planter orders one of them to take off all her clothes. He then seats himself on horseback upon her, clastifying [sic] her violently with a whip, and when the climax of his sensual evolutions has been reached, she has to pump his penus [sic] with her big lips whereby she finally receives as reward a full avalanche of her master's sperm in her mouth.

These catalogues show how photography had become an increasingly viable medium to mediate, stimulate, and record sexual feeling.

Erotic films also began to emerge at the end of the nineteenth century.[60] Some of these films include *Slave Trading in a Harem* (Méliès 1897), *Le Reveil de Chrysis* (Pathé c.1898), *Marché D'Esclaves en Orient* (Pathé c.1900), *Flagrant Délit D'Adultère* (Pathé, 1900), *Five Ladies* (Pathé, 1903), and *Eine Blume der Kasbah* (Italy c.1905). *Marché D'Esclaves en Orient* focuses on the much-loved harem fantasy; it dramatises the disrobing, inspection, and purchase of female slaves at a slave auction. One of the most sinister examples of early cinematic obscenity, the film depicts the Oriental despot accumulating women of various nationalities for his harem. Usually no more than a minute long, these shorts were marketed to a wide spectrum of the population. Pathé Frère dominated the trade; its well-mannered films had already secured the largest distribution network in Europe, America, and the colonies by the first decade of the twentieth century.[61] The company's catalogues distributed its erotic films under the category 'scène grivoises d'un charactère piquant'.[62] The catalogues also indicate that these films were distributed to England.

Authorities responded to the unprecedented circulation of visual obscenity. By 2 November 1871, the *Times* quoted the President of the SSV on the new problem with photographic obscenity: 'Our difficulties have been greatly increased by the application of photography, multiplying at an insignificant cost filthy representations from living models, and the improvement in the postal service has further introduced facilities for secret trading which were previously unknown.'[63] By the early 1890s, the British Home Office concentrated their energies on the trade in obscene photographs and early film such as mutoscopes and cinematographs as a major domestic and international juridical problem. Its internal correspondence on visual obscenity, as well as its correspondence with the Post Office, the Customs Office, the Foreign Office, rose exponentially with the development of new technologies that were increasingly incorporated into ever more complex global systems of communication. The Home Office monitored various clandestine operations, discovering 'brass finger rings containing photographs of nude white women' sold to the natives in Basutoland, stopping the trade of thousands of obscene photographs in Cairo by Lear & Co, or intercepting 'certain filthy photographs' entering the country through the agency of the Graphic Co. of Rotterdam.[64] The *Vigilance Record*, published numerous reports on arrests, seizures, and trials related to obscene photographs, postcards, mutoscopes, and cinematographs. The paper especially monitored the global traffic of new visual obscenity, clearly worried about its impact in the colonies. Sigel cites an article from the *Vigilance Record* that describes Louis Hendlemen's trial for selling obscene postcards in September 1911 to Zulus in South Africa and reflects on the harm obscene postcards could have on the empire. What apparently made his crime especially heinous for the white judiciary was that he sold these photographs to the natives. The judgement read:

> You have committed a grave breach of the law. What makes it still worse is this: you sold and showed these most filthy photos to the natives. What the effect on their minds will be I do not know. For you, a white man, to make a living out of the sale of things like this stamps you as a person of no character. I feel bound to make these remarks because I think it is the duty of every white man to endeavour, so far as lies in his power, to instill in the minds of the natives a respect for white men and white women. If you show and sell to natives this sort of thing, how can you expect the natives to show proper respect towards us?[65]

The judge was worried about the colonial repercussions of a graphic realism being shipped abroad, afraid that these postcards would undermine white colonial superiority and power.

My book ends just at the beginning of a major transition in the history of obscenity from print to photographic media. While the print trade in obscenity readily exploited photographic technologies, it did not prevent the remediation of obscenity into a predominately visual form that grew in dominance and market mobility through the twentieth century. I may only catch the beginning of the visual turn in obscenity, but I see this media shift as indicative of the volatility and adaptability of this cultural form since its formation with the explosion of print media at the start of the nineteenth century. The fact that the current London address of the British Board of Film Censors (BBFC), 3

Soho Square, is the same as a late 1890s book shop that distributed the imprints of the Erotika Biblion Society is a wonderfully ironic instance of how forms and notions of obscenity have been trafficked over the years.

As obscenity traversed media, markets, and borders in the nineteenth century, it also took on its distinctive affective qualities for which it is still known today. Secreted in the backroom parlour, the bedroom, the secret library, under the floorboards, and in the attic, its circulation hindered and forbidden, the consumption of obscenity became furtive for the first time in the nineteenth century. A report from the *Times* on 26 September 1851 described an incident where 'the greater part of the most objectionable books and pictures were taken from a private room at the back of the shop, and not from the shop itself.'[66] On 13 January 1875, another report described the seizure of Henry Judge's hidden stock of 100 books and 200 photographs: 'Sergeant Kerley and Detective Marshall found, on searching the second floor room, that a false flooring had been placed over a portion of the room, and beneath this was hidden a quantity of indecent books.'[67] On 6 May 1882, *Town Talk* explained that the trade was 'transacted in the secrecy and privacy of the little black parlours of the shifty places [. . .] or in the rooms above'.[68] Frederick Hankey apparently hid obscene books in an embassy bag in order to smuggle them from Paris to London.[69] Chief Inspector Drew of Scotland Yard, speaking as a witness to the Joint Select Committee on Lotteries and Indecent Advertisements, described how he discovered one publisher, known as De Villers, hidden in a secret room in the roof crouching among his rows of obscene books.[70] Joseph Conrad's opening description of a seedy Soho bookshop in *The Secret Agent* (1907) neatly encapsulates this kind of association between obscenity, cramped exchange, and furtive behaviour:

> The shop was a square box of a place, with the front glazed in small panes. In the daytime the door remained closed; in the evening it stood discreetly ajar. The window contained photographs of more or less undressed dancing girls [. . .]. And the two gas jets inside the panes were always turned low, either for economy's sake or for the sake of the customers. These customers were either very young men, who hung about the window for a time before slipping in suddenly; or men of a more mature age, but looking generally as if they were not in funds.[71]

The phenomenology of obscenity, in other words, was related to the ways it began to be trafficked in the nineteenth century. Its exchange in cramped streets, its illicit mailings via the post, its movements across borders stowed away in embassy bags, informed the corporeal experience of obscenity. Trafficked in these ways, obscenity became associated with blushing, laughter, foreplay, masturbation, sexual fantasy, and (it was feared) graver sexual misconduct.

If regulatory authorities disciplined the putative phenomenological immoderation of obscenity, particularly as experienced in the great metropolis, obscene publications themselves often self-referentially explored the corporeal experience of reading and seeing obscenity. These publications illustrate the pleasures of the consumption, exchange, and circulation of obscenity, offering a counterpoint to regulatory alarm over its affect on susceptible bodies and minds. In a serialised story from *The Pearl* (1879–81), for instance, a boy offers his illustrated copy of *Fanny Hill*, secreted away in a dressing case, to a friend. As he hands the book over, he says, 'Here it is my boy, only I hope it won't excite you too much; you can look it over by yourself.'[72] *Fanny Hill* was also a favourite for Walter, the pseudonymous author of *My Secret Life*. An exchange between Walter and a female friend not only indicates the extent to which he relies on the book to seduce women, but also reveals a connoisseur's interest in the print traffic in *Fanny Hill*:

> 'Do you like reading?' 'Yes.' 'Pictures?' 'Yes.' 'I've a curious book here.' 'What is it?' I took the book out, *The Adventures of Fanny Hill*. 'Who was she?' 'A gay lady, – it tells how she was seduced, how she had lots of lovers, was caught in bed with men, – would you like to read it?' 'I should.' 'We will read it together, – but look at the pictures', – this the fourth or fifth time in my life I have tried this manoeuvre with women.

> I opened the book at a picture of a plump, leering, lecherous-looking woman squatting, and pissing on the floor, and holding a dark-red, black-haired, thick-lipped cunt open with her fingers. All sorts of little baudy sketches were round the margin of the picture. The early editions of *Fanny Hill* had that frontispiece.

> She was flabbergasted, silent. Then she burst out laughing, stopped and said, 'What a nasty book, – such books ought to be burnt.' [. . .] She looked on silently. I heard her breathing hard. I turned over picture after picture. Suddenly she knocked the book out of my hand to the other side of the room. 'I won't see such things', said she. 'Won't you look at it by yourself?' 'If you leave it here I'll burn it.' 'No, you won't, you'll take it to bed with you.'[73]

As Walter guides and describes his friend's visceral reaction to the book – an emotional upsurge of silence, laughter, heavy breathing, and outrage – he describes what was by then the culturally prescribed affect of obscenity: the unique cultural phenomenology of an excitable commodity produced by its associations with its 'extensive traffic' through the metropolis, across empire and beyond, and with the help of every imaginable technology and gadget through the course of the nineteenth century and into the present day.

2
Harems and London's Underground Print Culture

As I take up the subject of the close connections among obscenity, global exoticism, and print traffic in the nineteenth century, I turn first to one of the earliest and favourite themes in the underground trade in obscenity at the time: the oriental harem. Its emergence was an accident of circumstance, set in motion by new technologies of mechanical reproduction, an expanding popular print culture, and increased travel to the Orient. Lord Byron's *Don Juan* (1819–24) figured significantly in the early fixation with this seemingly inviolable space.[1] As the poem was increasingly associated with a politicised and libertarian popular print culture in London, the publication and immediate pirating of its highly erotic harem cantos quickly led to legal debates over obscenity and copyright at a time when both concepts were being redefined. By the end of the 1820s, partly owing to *Don Juan*'s alignment with London's clandestine print communities and orientalism, the harem became a stock commodity for a growing trade in obscenity. Many of the same radical publishers who had pirated *Don Juan* for the common reader subsequently produced obscene harem novels for the private consumption of leisured and affluent gentleman. These novels fed the occidental fascination with the harem, representing it as a microcosm of empire where sexual conquest was commensurate with imperial conquest. This chapter examines how the illicit trafficking in Byron's orientalist poetry initially fuelled populist insurgency over issues of readership, obscenity, and copyright and eventually led to the underground commodification of the harem later in the century by entrepreneurs of obscenity seeking profit. As it was trafficked through various print markets, the harem eventually became one of the most bankable and reproducible *topoi* in nineteenth-century obscenity, a prime example of how the trade thrived on new print technologies and global fantasmatic networks.

1 The unruly copies of Byron's *Don Juan*: harems, popular print culture, and the age of mechanical reproduction

The harem began to emerge as the favourite phantasm for obscenity somewhere between the 1810s and 1820s. These were years when new technologies of print sped up production and democratised publishing and lively debates erupted over the traffic in print.[2] Alarm over the social fallout of a print-centred mass culture galvanised a period of government censorship against publishers, authors, and booksellers, who either grew timorous in the face of prosecution or developed strategies of evasion. Censorship against anti-government publications had followed the volatile post-war years, but climaxed in 1819 with the passing of the prohibitive Six Acts that had targeted seditious and blasphemous libel in the wake of the Peterloo riots.[3] Iain McCalman provides the best picture of London's popular print communities in the 1820s. He argues that post-war radical pressmen gradually shifted to obscenity in face of a trade crisis in the 1820s.[4] He focuses on how obscenity was appropriated by radical politics, but what is more interesting for my purposes is the way in which obscenity grew as a concept and trade from within these fractious and transitional underground print communities in London.

A popular print from 1826 focuses comically, but also nervously, on London's rapidly expanding print-centred popular culture (Figure 3). The image suggests a literate community; all are enlarging their minds and partaking in leisure activities. Posters and placards abound, advertising books and libraries for all and sundry; both a priest and a bricklayer carry octavo-size books; and a boy in the left-hand corner looks at the various authors, including the infamous and often scandalous Lord Byron and Thomas Moore, advertised on the outside of a Breakfast and Reading Room. The image ridicules the so-called 'march of mind', the educational, cultural, and aesthetic advancement and putative corruption of the masses with the circulation of print. Lord Byron (1788–1824), one of the targets of this caricature, was a fulcrum for colliding communities within London's print culture of the 1820s. While he was among the literary elite of Romantic print culture, his combination of blasphemy, political sedition, and hedonistic morality also made him a great favourite among underground publishers with radical allegiances and unconventional morality. They published cheap piracies and spurious imitations of *Don Juan* in particular. These copies multiplied and extended the irreverence, libertinism, and endless erotic energy of the poem, in a sense becoming the mechanism of libertine excess that Roland Barthes associates with the immense and illimitable Sadian eros.[5] Increasingly aligned with an underground radical, libertarian, and obscene press, Byron animated debates about the proliferation of popular print and the mass consumption of cheap copies of *Don Juan*. While

Figure 3 [H. Heath], [*March of Mind*], [1826?]. By permission of the British Museum, London

the mainstream press described its fears about the vulgar masses reading Byron's poetry, underground publishers produced cheap piracies, which even represented the working classes consuming his works. The pirating of his later scandalous harem cantos only escalated the debates and ultimately led to legal deliberation over the poem's copyright. The court had to decide whether or not an obscene work merited protection. The publication history of *Don Juan* shows how obscenity began to operate and gather meaning in relation to reprographic media, popular consumption, and orientalism.

From the moment of publication, Byron's *Don Juan* was received with outrage. As Andrew Elfenbein explains, 'Although his poetry was controversial, a set of typical reactions can be traced: initial enthusiasm for *Childe Harold* and the Turkish Tales, puzzlement at *Manfred* [. . .], and scandalized anger at *Cain* and *Don Juan*.'[6] Hugh J. Luke attributes this outrage to the material conditions of its publication and its popularity among radical presses. What he fails to notice in his otherwise excellent discussion is how its entangled publication in various print communities ignited debates about copyright infringement, the containment of print, and working-class readership that contributed to imputations of immorality and early notions about obscenity.[7]

John Murray initially published the first two cantos in a sumptuous quarto edition for a guinea and a half, attaching the name of neither author nor publisher.[8] Noting that quartos of this price were destined for a 'prestigious clientele', Luke describes how these manoeuvres were attempts to evade prosecution by the Society for the Suppression of Vice (SSV).[9] Yet, Murray's overpriced and unacknowledged edition of *Don Juan* simply announced his temerity, provoking its piracy by radical publishers and thus increasing fear and excoriation of the poem in Tory periodicals and anti-radical pamphlets. These first two cantos, which describe Juan's love affair with Donna Julia, received the severest censure and thus secured the poem's marketability as one of the most scandalous works of the period well before the appearance of the harem cantos. Luke observes that roughly 18 piracies of *Don Juan* were produced before 1832 and suggests that these numbers indicate 'a wide sale to the newly emerging English common reader'. He also describes how these piracies by known radicals 'crystallize[d] the hatred and fear of Byron' among his critics.[10] Many of the publishers of these piracies, including William Benbow, John Duncombe, and William Dugdale,[11] also became key figures in the emergent trade in obscenity. About a month after the first two cantos of *Don Juan* appeared, when the piracies were already circulating, the poem was widely vilified in reviews by the leading periodicals. *Blackwood's Edinburgh Magazine* denounced 'the moral strain of the whole poem' as 'pitched to the lowest key'; the *British Critic* charged it with having the 'spirit of infidelity and libertinism'; and the *Gentleman's Magazine* attacked its 'shameless indecency'.[12] The poem was also reputedly removed from library shelves because of its immorality.[13]

Much of the criticism against the poem's immorality revealed anxiety about readership. Byron's scandal-ridden private life and libertine poetry made him a favourite in popular print. The extent to which the working classes had access to his underground publications is uncertain. Nonetheless, the worry was that *Don Juan* was 'slumming'. William Hone, a radical bookseller-publisher who struggled for the freedom of the press and was charged in 1817 for blasphemous libel, likely generated such fears.[14] He was one of the first to propose that Byron's poetry was common property. In addition to issuing *Don John; or, Don Juan Unmasked* in 1819, which was a scathing exposé of Murray's involvement in the publication of the poem, he also circulated in the same year a specious *Don Juan, Canto the Third*.[15] Byron heard about such 'impostors' and colourfully said 'the devil take the impudence of some black-guard bookseller'.[16] This false third canto is a fascinating, pre-Mayhewian portrait of London's street literature and culture. In bringing Byron's hero, Juan, back to London, the canto recreates him as a hero who spreads his message to the masses. The canto describes Juan's attempts to circulate his anti-government tract, 'Devilled Biscuit'. While Juan dismisses posting his tract 'in the window glass' like some 'common Grub Street ballads', he also exposes the elitism of bourgeois reading practices.[17] He juxtaposes the luxuries of private studies, gaslight, and domestic literacy against muddy streets, cramped thoroughfares, and pathetic (though earnest) literacy:

> 'Tis very well, said he, shut up in a study,
> By Gas Light to be conning learned lore,
> Or reading papers to our dearest Judy,
> While she our breakfast from a teapot pour;
> But horrible indeed, when streets are muddy,
> To queer a mob that paper spelling o'er,
> With visages no doubt for wise and grave meant,
> And have to elbow them, or quit the pavement.

(Don Juan, Canto the Third 15)

After much deliberation, Juan eventually sings his tract from a doorstep to the mob. Like a radical agitator, he is indicted with treason for 'pour[ing] [his] venom thro' [the] lower ranks' (49). The poem finishes with Juan sleeping peacefully in prison awaiting trial, his fate unknown. Luke briefly suggests that Hone turns Juan into a 'radical publisher'.[18] In fact, he turns him into a radical agitator who circumvents illiteracy and scorns profit in order to circulate his radical message. Whether the working classes read Hone's spurious canto is unknown since no price or circulation records survive; the price of his pamphlets ranged from six pence to one shilling, generally too expensive for private consumption, but perhaps not shared.[19] This portrait of a trans-itional underground print community that includes even the illiterate may have been a populist fantasy rather than reality.

An article written for the *Quarterly Review* in 1822, possibly written by Robert Southey, reveals that anxieties grew with the 'multiplication of copies' of *Don Juan* among working-class readers.[20] The essay focuses these anxieties by responding to the piracies and imitations of the poem that emerged with rumours about its lack of copyright. In his discussion of the curious common law introduced by Lord Chief Justice Eyre – that 'there can be no property in what is publicly injurious' – the critic from the *Quarterly Review* argues that copyright law has failed the rightful proprietors as well as the public good because it enables impropriety to become common property. He suggests that piracies help distribute the poem to a class of reader susceptible to its 'indecencies':

[I]f it had been the subject of copyright, [Don Juan] would have been confined by its price to a class of readers with whom its faults might have been somewhat compensated by its merits; with whom the ridicule, which it endeavours to throw upon virtue, might have been partially balanced by that with which it covers vice, particularly the vice to which the class of readers to whom we are alluding are most subject – that which pleads romantic sensibility, or ungovernable passions; to readers, in short, who would have turned with disgust from its indecencies, and remembered only its poetry and its wit. But no sooner was it whispered that there was no property in 'Don Juan' than ten presses were at work, some publishing it with obscene engravings, others in weekly numbers, and all in a shape that brought it within the reach of purchasers on whom its poison would operate without mitigation – who would search its pages for images to pamper a depraved imagination, and for a sanction for the insensibility to the sufferings of others, which is often one of the most unhappy results of their own, and would treasure up all its evil, without comprehending what it contains of good. 'Don Juan' in quarto and on hot-pressed paper would have been almost innocent – in a whity-brown duodecimo it was one of the worst of the mischievous publications that have made the press a snare.

This essay provides one of the earliest and fullest descriptions of a trans-itional underground print community whose business was shifting to obscenity. It describes a new class of reader that reads phenomenologically by 'search[ing]' for images that will titillate 'ungovernable passion'. It also suggests a new breed of publisher, a man 'without any character, seldom any fortune', who with 'nothing to lose, seeks to gain by a robbery'.[21] The article not only demonstrates how the material culture around *Don Juan* – its size, press, appearance, retailer, publisher, and reader – helped brand it indecent, but also reveals how such conditions powerfully influenced the creation of a cultural form like obscenity. Luke suggests that 'the appearance of *Don Juan* in those shops that specialised in Thomas Paine [...] would have radically altered the context of the work for the critical reviews.'[22] While he is right, he overlooks that its appearance in such shops, which would advertise its lack of copyright and degraded readership, also helped brand it obscene. What emerges in the early critical response to *Don Juan*, then, is a nervousness about its uncontrolled reproduction by dubious publishers who pilfer literary property and putatively pander to the dangerous desires of working-class readers.

Radical publishers continued to copy and pirate *Don Juan*. By 1822, these publishers were asserting that the poem was 'common property'. William Hodgson, a radical agitator, insisted in his Preface to his 1822 pirate copy of the poem that 'this work [...] seems [...] a sort of common property amongst the booksellers: for we have had editions of all sorts and sizes.'[23] William Benbow, another radical publisher of the post-war period who also experimented with obscenity, argued that the cultural phenomenon of Byron belonged to the people. In 1822, he issued a six-penny monthly periodical entitled the *Rambler's Magazine* that was a miscellaneous collection of stories, reviews, news, and 'crim. con' trials. Twice prosecuted for obscene libel by the SSV, the magazine was more libertine than obscene and more entrepreneurial than political.[24] However, Benbow's populism, elsewhere subdued in this magazine, emerges in his treatment of Byron. A July 1822 issue, for instance, reviews and condemns John Watkins's *Memoirs of the Life and Writings of the Right Honourable Lord Byron* (1822), which had sold for 14 shillings, a price that precluded working-class readership. The article criticises the work for profiting from Byron's infamy, 'the principle incidents of [whose] life are known to every mechanic who reads the "Tap-tub Paper" in a public-house'. It argues that it aims to 'take advantage of that curiosity which had been excited in the public mind', but disguises its motives with its size and price: 'Though this work is printed in a large octavo volume, at a high price, it comes as completely under the description of a catch-penny publication as any thing that issues from the press of Pitts or catnach of Seven Dials.'[25] With these references to Jonathan Pitts, a ballad sheet publisher, and James Catnach, another radical pressman based in Seven Dials,[26] the magazine accuses the bourgeois press of thieving material, repackaging it as respectable, and effectively excluding the working-class reader. Specifically, the magazine suggests that literary property should be at the disposal of readers rather than publishers and authors. More generally, it implies that the bourgeois press is equally opportunistic when it comes to exploiting Byron's infamy and the print medium.

Because of the already widespread perception of the 'immorality' of *Don Juan*, Murray became increasingly cautious, though he continued to publish

Cantos 3–5 in 1821, where Juan towards the end begins his adventures in the harem. Byron did not revisit the poem again until 1823 after signing on the radical publisher John Hunt.[27] He returned to the poem with Canto 6 and an orgy of detail about the Turkish harem, already an established *topos* in the West remediated in various forms of literary, musical, and visual splendour.[28] The later harem cantos in *Don Juan* excited the greatest excitement and censure; the condemnation of the poem's immorality in the bourgeois press escalated into charges of 'indecency' and 'obscenity' as the criticism began to focus almost exclusively on the harem. This controversy eventually led to judicial interest in controlling what people read.

Byron's 1809–11 oriental tour had deepened his interest in the region. As early as 1813, Byron advised Thomas Moore: 'Stick to the East; [. . .] the public are orientalizing.'[29] Yet, while Moore became wealthy from commodifying the East, reputedly having earned 3000 guineas for *Lalla Rookh*,[30] Byron became scandalous for his prolonged literary visits to the harem. Harems appeared regularly in Byron's orientalist poetry. In Canto 2 of *Childe Harold's Pilgrimage* (1812), the hero briefly glimpses the 'Haram's silent tower' from afar, describing the women in it as submissive prisoners 'tam'd to 'their 'cage' (2.61). In one of his Turkish Tales, the long poem *The Corsair* (1814), the harem is the site of female rebellion and violence: Gulnare murders the Pacha in order to liberate the imprisoned hero whom she loves. In Byron's play *Sardanapalus* (1821), the King succumbs to the 'lascivious tinklings' of the harem, becoming an 'effeminate' and incapable ruler.[31]

It is in *Don Juan*, however, that the harem itself is foregrounded. Juan's journey to the harem begins in Canto 4 when his lover's father sends him into slavery. The Sultan's wife falls in love with him and purchases him at a Constantinople slave market to 'serve a sultana's sensual phantasy' (5.126). She subsequently conceals him in the harem, forcing him to dress as a woman in order to avoid discovery. Ultimately, after he rejects her advances, he must flee the harem in order to escape death. The harem cantos in *Don Juan* reveal a fascination with non-normative sexuality. Juan's description of the slave market proleptically dwells on the multiplicity of women about to be enslaved in the harem, but also suggests the despot's polygamous appetite for sexual variety through national and racial difference:

> But to the narrative: the vessel bound
>   With slaves to sell off in the capital,
> After the usual process, might be found
>   At anchor under the seraglio wall;
>   Were landed in the market, one and all,
> And there with Georgians, Russians, and Circassians,
>   Bought up for different purposes and passions.

(Don Juan, 4.113)

The poem is also fascinated with the harem's 'motley crew' (5.13) whose physical eccentricities allude to the site's sexual perversity: Baba, the 'black neutral personage', or 'third sex' (5.26), who threatens Juan with castration (5.71) and the 'two little dwarfs' (5. 87), 'ugly imps', whose 'colour was not black, nor white, nor gray' (5.87). Also pausing to compare Turkish and European women in order to condemn them both, the poem denounces the first for sexual voracity, the second for frigidity:

> The Turks do well to shut – at least, sometimes –
>   The women up – because in sad reality,
> Their chastity in these unhappy climes
>   Is not a thing of that astringent quality,
> Which in the north prevents precocious crimes,
>   And makes our snow less pure than our morality;
> The sun, which yearly melts the polar ice,
> Has quite the contrary effect on vice.
>
> (*Don Juan*, 5.157)

In Canto 6, when Juan describes his adventures in the harem disguised as a woman (Juanna), he suggests the place's erotic licence and perversion. When 'ogling all their charms from breasts to backs' (6.29), Juan finds himself among a multitude of harem women fighting over who will share his bed. Dudu, the victor, lies with him only to wake up in a fright (6.52). Presumably she discovers he is a man; yet her discovery suggests oriental sapphism. *Don Juan's* harem cantos typify the European eroticisation of this exotic space as the site of limitless sexual possibility.

A number of critics have commented on the gender and sexual ambiguity of the cross-dressing episode in *Don Juan*, though they have not addressed how the harem enables such social transvestisms. Susan J. Wolfson argues that Juan, disguised in female attire, experiences gender instability.[32] Charles Donelan focuses less on the feminisation of Juan than on his 'polysexuality'. 'In the harem episode', he writes, 'we encounter both male fantasy at its most anonymous and pervasive form and gender identity at its most fluid.'[33] Alan Richardson is the first to comment on Juan's cultural cross-dressing, observing that he cross-dresses not only as a woman, but also as a Turkish woman. Richardson concludes that Juan's adventure 'can be read as expressing not so much the fantasy of unlimited sexual access as the desire to materially experience sexual [and cultural] difference', but he does not comment on how the harem setting makes Juan's gender, sexual, and national identity susceptible.[34] Ruth Yeazell has recently provided a survey of European representations of the harem, showing its widespread importance in the European imagination.[35] While overturning pervasive criticism that the harem merely excited fantasies about unlimited male sexual power, she suggests that the harem also functioned as a signifier for erotic licence.[36] Her understanding of the harem bears importantly on Byron's poem. His harem enables the mobility of desires and cultural identities and cultivates a fantasy of trespass rather than of conquest. This spirit of libertinism and irreverence may explain why the poem was so readily pirated and copied for popular consumption and taken up by male and female readers alike.[37]

Byron's harem cantos bore crucially on the poem's reception, not because he was inventing the harem, but because he was invoking a trope already tainted by scandal and given over to populist fantasy. Although the harem was respectable insofar as it was regularly reproduced in legitimate and mainstream media environments, its representation always had the potential to become obscene. Behind every inquiry into harem life – whether avowed or not – there lurked a persistent curiosity about its sexual practices. Part of the fascination of the harem was its inviolability: it was a restricted space where only the oriental despot, his concubines, and his black eunuchs were allowed entry. With its assortment of eunuchs, slaves, and odalisques as well as hookahs, hashish, and perfumes, the harem evoked endless sexual fantasies in the West that revolved around violent incarceration and limitless sensuality. Thus, critics railed against Byron even before the harem cantos simply for his notorious association with the East. In 1819, for example, an article entitled a 'Critique on Modern Poets' from the *New Monthly Magazine* argued

> Lord Byron [. . .] makes love like a sensualist, or a bandit; [. . .] he never remarks or commends one single moral or mental quality in the object of his passion; he appreciates her with all the callous and calculating brutality of a slave-merchant (in the miserable countries in which he wastes his existence) by her locks that sweep to the ground, or her naked feet that outshine the marble; he is a Mahomet (vacillating between lust and ferocity) who would grasp the bright locks of his Irene, and strike off her head before his Bashaws *pour un coup de theatre*[38]

In 1819, Byron also felt that he could defend *Don Juan* in a letter to a friend by deflecting attention onto the moral impropriety of Moore's oriental poem. 'After all what stuff this outcry is', he writes, '– Lalla Rookh and Little – are more dangerous than my burlesque poem can be.'[39] To say something was 'Mahomet' or oriental had become, well before Byron, a figure for indecency. Rowlandson's underground prints reveal the emergence of an obscene understanding of the harem. Sometime in the first two decades of the nineteenth century, he reproduced the European impression of the unfettered indulgence of the Orient in two sexually explicit coloured prints. In the *Harem*, the despot sits in ithyphallic anticipation as he surveys a multiplicity of naked, available, and depilated women (Figure 4). Rowlandson's other

Figure 4   Thomas Rowlandson, *The Harem* [after 1812]. By permission of the British Museum, London

caricature, the *Pasha* (Figure 5), depicts another dark, overendowed despot amid a bevy of white, sexually available women. Rowlandson's two prints participate in the widespread cultural simulations of the Orient, its private spaces, and libidinous sexuality.[40]

Radical pressmen also drew upon the harem, further setting the stage for the pirating and attempted disciplining of Byron's harem cantos. By 1820, William Benbow was exploiting the associations between sexual corruption and the oriental harem for political satire, producing what McCalman calls 'obscene populism'. Like Hone, he was another radical bookseller-publisher of the post-war period. Obscenity never became his trade, but he exploited it to press forth his radical politics. Benbow would have been familiar with the radical tradition of invoking cultural assumptions about oriental debauchery for political satire. In 1820, when George IV divorced Queen Caroline on grounds of adultery, obscene satires supporting the Queen were immensely popular among underground publishers who issued penny ballads, transcripts from the trial, and satirical pamphlets.[41] Obscene pamphlets such as *The Khan of Karistan* (1822) exploited the idea of the harem in order to satirise the sexual misconduct of King George IV.[42] In 1820, Benbow also published Orientalist 'pro-Queen smut',[43] most notably Kouli Khan and *Sultan Sham and his Seven Wives*, which sold anywhere from six pence to a shilling.[44]

Figure 5   Thomas Rowlandson, *The Pasha* [after 1812]. By permission of the British Museum, London

Kouli Khan is a simple poem that recounts the King's debauchery.[45] It develops an allegory that figures the King as an oriental despot and includes crude illustrations that depict him as a Turkish despot both in and out of bed. The satire's rhyming couplets, copious illustrations, and large print suggest that it was intended for elementary readers or oral recitation in a public house. The poem demonstrates how the common reader would have been familiar with the sexual suggestiveness of the harem and its function as satirical allegory.

Benbow's *Sultan Sham* similarly invokes the harem as a shorthand allegory for sexual corruption. It depicts the King as a Sultan with a 'haram' and multiple wives.[46] The House of Lords who aim to dissolve the marriage become the 'Pachas, Deys and Beys' (20). The pamphlet seems to have sold well because Benbow promoted it widely. A large hand-coloured frontispiece introduces the pamphlet and crudely depicts George IV as a lascivious Sultan among his harem women. The sharp eye will find at least three hidden penises in the drawing – the stiff sword between the monarch's legs, the drooping hat, and the drooping robe carried by the token eunuch (Figure 6). A print from 1820 by the Soho artist J. L. Marks also advertised *Sultan Sham* (Figure 7).[47]

Figure 6 J. L. Marks, *Sultan Sham and His Seven Wives*. London: Benbow, 1820. By permission of the British Museum, London

36

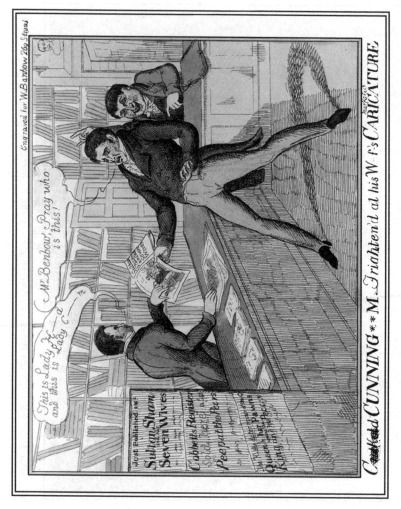

Figure 7 J. L. Marks, *Cuckold Cunning**m Frighten'd at his W – f's Caricature*. London: Benbow, 1820. By permission of the British Museum, London

The illustration is not only a fascinating portrait of Benbow's business, but is also a sophisticated and irreverent depiction of the class politics of readership and consumption. It depicts a well-dressed Benbow in his shop on the Strand showing *Sultan Sham* to a distinguished customer. The shop looks respectable and prosperous, with numerous volumes lining the shelves. As bound books were notoriously expensive, the illustration suggests at least a middle-class clientele. Yet, a poster on the left advertises William Cobbett's *The Register* as well as Benbow's latest political satires – including *Sultan Sham*. On the desk that separates Benbow and his customer, lay copies of pamphlets like those advertised in the poster. They are probably inexpensive, point-of-sale items that indicate another facet of the business and different class of reader. The customer holds one of these illustrated pamphlets. The writing in the pamphlet indicates that it is *Sultan Sham*, though the original pamphlet had only a frontispiece for illustration. The customer, identified as Cuckold Cunnig**m, is shocked by Benbow's explication of the image: one of the women in the Sultan's harem is his wife. A far less distinguished, cartoonish man in the background makes the sign of a cuckold behind the customer; the large shadow of a cuckold's horns behind the customer, and the jeering laughter of the animated bust in the far-right corner only further confirm his cuckoldry. While Benbow is almost indistinguishable in appearance from his customer, he proudly displays and explains his populist tracts. The illustration, like the pamphlet, exposes bourgeois embarrassment. The customer is likely intended to represent the husband of Lady Conyngham, who was the King's mistress before the Marchioness of Hertford replaced her. The pamphlet itself, which was relatively inexpensive, was probably consumed by the common reader who would laugh at the idea of the lascivious monarch in his harem. This illustration encourages viewers to laugh at a gentleman who learns that his cuckoldry is the subject of a cheap tract that is widely copied and disseminated through popular print. A self-conscious examination of the politics of popular print and its consumers, this illustration reveals how harems were reproduced for radical politics. This use of the harem not only suggests a predisposition to read Byron's harem in terms of radical (if not obscene) protest, but also foreshadows the later appropriation of Byron's harem cantos for populist reform. Although Benbow does not invoke Byron's harem for radical satire, he circulated ideas about the harem with the same spirit of burlesque that helped influence an important legal struggle over who had the right to copy Byron's harem.

As the myth of the dissolute harem was pervasive in most print communities, and Byron's poem was already notorious for its radical sympathies and ithyphallicism,[48] it is not surprising that the moral indignation over *Don Juan* escalated with the appearance of Canto 6. In 1821, Byron had left Juan trapped in the harem at the end of Canto 5, his narrator promising to take only 'a few short naps' (5.159). While hampered by censure, but reluctant to bow to 'cant', Byron left his readers wondering about Juan's adventures in the harem for a full two years, with tremendous effect. For a reviewer for an 1823 issue of the *Gentleman's Magazine*, it was the harem that made the sixth canto 'thoroughly scandalously licentious and obscene, and fit only for the shelves of the brothel'. The reviewer explains, 'it describes Juan's abode in the Harem, where he is treated as a female, and forms an attachment that irritates the jealousy of the Sultana.' Because of the harem scenes, the poem becomes fit reading only for lower-class haunts such as the brothel. In the same year, *Blackwood's Edinburgh Magazine* also singled out the sixth canto for its 'unredeemed and unrelieved sensuality and indecency'.[49]

The controversy over *Don Juan's* immorality, the poem's circulation in popular media through cheap piracy and imitation, and the addition of Canto 6 culminated finally in a legal struggle over the 'property' of Byron's harem. Copyright had been protected by statutory law since the Statute of Anne in 1709. It typically gave copyright to the bookseller or publisher for a 14-year term for new works. As Catherine Seville shows, legislation, legal arguments, and debates over copyright in the eighteenth and nineteenth centuries turned upon competing ideas about who should have property in the copy: the publisher, the author, or the reader. While copyright law and practice favoured the publisher in the eighteenth century, it favoured the author in the nineteenth century. Nineteenth-century copyright law, such as the Copyright Acts of 1814 and 1842, gave increasing rights to the author, incorporating the author's lifespan into the copyright term. In the 1830s, radicals petitioned against the new copyright acts arguing that it inhibited the diffusion of knowledge by protecting a trade where book prices were high: by the first half of the nineteenth century, an octavo sold anywhere between 12–14 shillings and a quarto for up to two guineas, well out of the reach of the common reader.[50] Among those publishers active in the underground print culture of the 1820s, it was William Dugdale who first introduced Byron's harems to the populist struggle for copyright. Like Benbow, he was a radical publisher who began to experiment with populist obscenity. It also later became his profession. As early as 1823, however, when Dugdale was still just experimenting with obscenity, he made legal and cultural history by overriding copyright law with questions about obscenity and oriental exoticism.

In August 1823, Byron had obtained an injunction against Dugdale preventing him from publishing pirate editions of Cantos 6–8 of *Don Juan*.[51] In a court of equity, Dugdale argued for the dissolution of the injunction on the grounds that it did not merit copyright protection. Such proceedings were nothing new, but instead escalated in the nineteenth century with the expanded circulation of print. The previous month, Murray had been granted an injunction against Dugdale for 'invading the copyright' of Byron's *Beppo* (1817).[52] A year previously, however, Murray failed to gain an injunction against Benbow for pirating *Cain* because it was deemed too blasphemous for the protection of the Court. After the motion failed, a conversation ensued between Murray's counsel and the judge where they thought it best to *disown* the poem:

Mr Shadwell: I am almost afraid, my Lord, after what your lordship has said, to claim property in this book.
The Lord Chancellor: I know I have no wish to claim a property in it, I assure you.[53]

A year later, when Dugdale argued for the dissolution of the injunction against his publication of Cantos 6–8 of *Don Juan*, he based his argument on its putative obscenity. Submitting an ingenious argument, supported by previous case law,[54] he reasoned that these new cantos were too obscene for copyright protection. Moreover, he shrewdly inverted middle-class anxiety about *Don Juan*'s immorality reaching the masses by suggesting that these cantos would corrupt middle-class readers. As the *Times* reported, Dugdale argued that the poem's 'tendency was immoral in the highest sense of the word, most calculated to taint the mind of the public, licentious, in every way dangerous, and most destructive to the morals of the community at large'. In his allusion to bourgeois reading practices, he also indicated that the cantos contained 'scenes as no father of a family would permit to be read, or for an instant to be listened to'.[55]

Dugdale proceeded to provide the history of *Don Juan*'s publication in order to expose and denounce the publishers' clever, but ethically appalling, entrepreneurial practices. By suggesting that Murray, the first publisher, was well aware of the immorality of *Don Juan*, he argued that profit overcame morals in his bid to get 'first in the market':

The defendant then proceeded to observe, that the work called *Don Juan* first appeared before the public about three years ago, and so convinced was the publisher of its immoral tendency, that he shrunk from avowing himself to be the author of the book. There appeared no publisher's name to the first two cantos; and although Mr. Murray was known to be the publisher, and he sold them publicly in his shop, he had never to this day avowed himself as the publisher. The same observation would apply with equal strength to the three cantos subsequently published. [. . .] The very manner of their appearance [Dugdale] conceived to be a very powerful argument in his favour. They were published in three separate editions, one at nine shillings, another at seven shillings, and a third at the low price of one shilling; and it was announced in the advertisement printed in the public papers, that 'a cheap edition at one shilling to counteract piracy' would be published. The publishers themselves, therefore, assumed most indisputably, that they were conscious that the work did not deserve protection in a court of law or equity. They were anxious to appear themselves first in the market to prevent, if they could, any person from pirating the work.[56]

Dugdale did not defend his own complicity in publishing an immoral book because he was not in a criminal court on trial for obscene libel.[57] In fact, he had to prove that the poem was obscene in order to show it was not subject to copyright. He therefore illustrated the immorality behind so-called legitimate publishing practices in order to prove that Byron's cantos should be common property and readily reproducible. This argument was no doubt motivated by Dugdale's pecuniary needs: publishers threatened his business by undercutting his price. What was underlying this argument, however, was also populist resentment against the double standard in publishing, where obscenity laws were unevenly applied.

Dugdale's argument consequently turned on his proof of obscenity. Significantly, he chose Canto 6 as his primary evidence. The *Times* reported Dugdale's discussion of the offending passage in court:

> In the three cantos which [Dudgale] now held in his hand, the hero (*Don Juan*) was conducted through the most licentious scenes, and their immorality became still more calculated to injure the morals of the public, for their being written in such a warm poetic style. In the first canto the hero having been dressed in female attire, was admitted into the interior of the Grand Sultan's harem, and in the middle of the canto he was introduced among the ladies, with whom he took up his quarters for the night. One of those ladies, who was called his sleeping Venus (laughter), took him to her bed, imagining him to be a female, and in the middle of the night, this sleeping Venus starts up and alarms the rest of the females. This lady, to whom the name of <u>Dudie</u> [sic] was given, then communicated her dream in very equivocal language to the surrounding females. It was impossible to select particular passages to show the immoral tendency of this description, but he believed it to be one of the warmest poems in the English language.[58]

The harem, the exotic property of the East, thus became the site of a British legal argument about literary property and propriety contested by competing print communities. By attempting to disperse copyright, Dugdale hoped to make Byron's harem common property open to infinite exchange and circulation, in a sense replaying the events in Byron's harem where social categories become malleable. In the end, the motion for injunction was denied: Dugdale won the right to publish Byron's three cantos. This case reveals a curious stalemate in English law, where copyright law and obscenity law cancelled one another out. The laughter in the court also suggests that obscenity sometimes escaped sombre moralising.

The *Times* response to these proceedings, in a leading article published on 12 August, offers a comic footnote.[59] The article expresses moral outrage, but it does not focus on the ungoverned circulation of Byron's harems among the masses, as one might expect. It is less concerned about copyright than it is with the extension of the poem's spirit of burlesque:

Nay, it is not sufficient for Mr. Dugdale to entertain the gravest of Courts, by selecting every offensive passage from the work he has printed; but the Judge in equity is modestly desired to take the work home with him, that he may discover, on a deliberate perusal, its general tendency [. . .]. Think of the Lord Chancellor throwing by all the rest of his papers, postponing all the important questions of real property that have been lying 20 years before him, while he pores over the luscious pictures of *Don Juan*.

The article imagines the Judge bringing *Don Juan* home and poring over it. Dugdale, it suggests, makes a mockery of the court by forcing readership (and potentially corruption) on the great and undermining questions of 'real property'. It demonstrates the extent to which Dugdale's rhetorical finesse transforms the desire to own and read the poem into a desire to disown it. He has made the reading of the poem shameful. Perhaps unintentionally, he also helps introduce shame into the act of reading morally dubious books, a phenomenological affect that will shape the covert operations of London's obscene print culture and characterise its consumption.

'While Byron may have been associated with repetition and reproducibility', Elfenbein observes, 'work stemming from his took unexpected directions.' Elfenbein chiefly concentrates on bourgeois instances of Byromania in the nineteenth century: Byron on the stage, Byron among the Chartists, Byron in the tourist industry, Byron in the classroom, and Byron among the Victorians.[60] While Byron's harem continued to be a source of contention over issues of readership and copyright, the emerging trade in obscenity soon regarded it as a commercial venture subject to endless copy and resurrection by new media.

After Dugdale's legal proceedings, conservative critics continued to focus on Byron's propensity for oriental debauchery. As the logic loosely developed over the years, Byron's poem was obscene because it perpetuated popular orientalist fantasies to the masses, and in the wrong people's hands, the harem compromised the morality of the nation. In 1824, a pamphlet appeared, reputedly authored by the Reverend George Burgess, entitled *Cato to Lord Byron on the Immoral and Dangerous Tendency of His Writings*. It castigates him for importing oriental passion in the form of the harem, a 'cast of subject' that pervades the 'libidinous mass' of all his poetry.[61] Like the reviewer for the *New Monthly Magazine*, he accuses Byron of having the soul of a despot: 'the Haram's love and the Musulman's lust, I fear, alone declarative of the nature of your affection towards any woman' (41). He also describes the poem's women as infused with 'the soul of the seraglio' (45) and 'compacted of elements that make up the paradise of Mahomet' (45). The writer concludes that Byron's oriental erotics compromises English morality:

But only let the poetry of Lord Byron become the staple commodity of the realm, and its prophane and libidinous sentiments sway the national taste, – and neither religion, nor law, nor constitution; neither dignity in war, nor reputation in woman, shall ever more give lustre to this devoted land, not shall the British Empire be, as heretofore, a terror to the kingdoms around nor by the power of her arms, but, by the prevalence of her corruption, a scorn, and a proverb, and a contaminating nuisance.

(Burgess, *Cato to Lord Byron*, 126)

Particularly concerned about how *Don Juan* 'spread[s] that infamy in every direction' (128) as it 'run[s] its wild career' (128), the writer creates and reflects the fear that orientalist fantasies, already thoroughly exploited by the radical pressmen, will lead to further political agitation and national degradation. C. C. Colton, in another pamphlet on the 'tendencies' of *Don Juan* from 1825, sums up this concern about the general accessibility of Byron's poem. As he writes, 'But alas! the poison is general, the antidote particular; the ribaldry and the obscenity will be understood by the *many*; the profundity and sublimity will be duly appreciated, *only by the few*.'[62] This ever-replicating poison, which he does not specify, was in many circles already associated with the harem.

While conservative critics continued to vilify *Don Juan's* orientalism, a new breed of publishers began to imitate it. In 1823, the same year that Dugdale debated the property of Byron's harem in court, James Griffin, bookseller, publisher, and radical sympathiser,[63] published an imitation of *Don Juan*, entitled *The British Don Juan*. The spin-off, purportedly authored by Henry Coates, describes the sexual indulgences of a man speciously reputed to be Lady Montagu's son. While observing a restlessness in humans that 'impels us to seek pleasure in variety, and happiness in something unpossessed', the book recounts the hero's travels in the Orient, particularly in Constantinople. In following the culture's custom, he marries numerous times, 'never without a seraglio, filled with the beauties of Georgia, Circassia, and Greece' until he finally finds himself impotent.[64] This book is exploitative rather than populist: it sold its amalgam of *Don Juan* and Lady Montagu's *Turkish Embassy Letters* (1763) for five shillings, not egregiously expensive, but well beyond what working-class readers could afford.

Byron's *Don Juan* was also connected to another underground publication, *Memoirs of Harriette Wilson* (1825), a prostitute's tell-all story over which there was a sensational libel trial in 1825. As controversy grew over the book's libellous claims, the popular press printed numerous pamphlets and images with its eponymous heroine, her rich suitors, and her amorous exploits as their theme, including a satirical print, *The Libel Publisher Cut Up*, that lampoons the prosecution of a publisher named J. J. Stockdale for libel (Figure 8). This print in particular shows that the book's proliferation, as much as its libellous content, was on trial: copies of the *Memoirs* and its spin-offs clutter the right-hand corner of the image where there is even a reference (likely specious) to its 50,000 copies.[65] Curiously, the artist of the

Figure 8 Don Juan [Isaac Robert Cruikshank], *The Libel Publisher Cut Up*. London: J. Fairburn, 1825. By permission of the British Museum, London

print, Isaac Robert Cruikshank, drew under the name Don Juan, a gesture that not only signals the importance of Byron's poem, but also the irreverent culture of the copy that characterised London's popular print culture.

The infamous Dugdale also profited from Byron's harem. While Lisa Sigel argues that he maintained his political commitments throughout his life, he also capitalised on obscenity.[66] He later dominated the trade from 1827 to the 1860s. It was his publishing activities in Holywell Street that contributed to the street's notoriety as the centre of London's underground trade. In 1828, he published *The Private Life of Lord Byron* , authored by Jack Mitford. This biography, a spurious 'piece of soft pornography' according to Elfenbein,[67] begins on a populist note as the narrator observes that 'everything connected with the life and character of so illustrious a bard as the late Lord Byron is public property'. Yet, it devolves into Byron's sexual exploits at home and abroad, noting that 'in the Ottoman dominions, [. . .] you may have more wives and concubines'.[68] The price of the book was not documented, but an octavo-size book generally excluded the working classes. Dugdale, much later in his career, again exploited Byron's harem for London's obscene book trade, but to a different end. In 1866, he published *Don Leon*, a long poem that he sold for ten shillings and six pence.[69] While purporting to be part of a suppressed journal destroyed by Moore, the poem defends sodomitical pleasures in the Turkish harem. When the hero's lover asks him to describe 'strange and jealous men / In secret harems who their consorts pen', he does not respond with a tale of heterosexual orgy, but rather the disappointment of the undesired harem woman:

> She sits immured, or else well-guarded stirs
> But, when the hour is on the noontide tick,
> Her Aga slowly quits the selamlik;
> The harem opens to his lord testoor;
> Humbly she greets his entrance at the door,
> [. . .]
> Perhaps, if still her cheeks their bloom possess,
> He lets her sit – vouchsafes a cold caress,
> Or when the day is sultry, bids her chase
> The gnates away, that buzz about his face.
> But ah! The worst remains behind to tell – [. . .]
> Spurned from his couch, or with neglect dismist
> Another lip than her's, a boys,[sic] is kissed,
> To him with ithyphallic gifts he kneels.[70]

From the time of Byron's separation from his wife, rumours circulated that he was a sodomite. By 1866, Byron's ambiguous sexuality and association with the Orient were bankable for publishers dealing in obscenity. Although he became respectable, as Elfenbein points out, he always had 'the potential to become scandalous'.[71]

I wonder if the widespread controversy over the property and propriety of Byron's harem that erupted in the 1820s, and continued underground well through the nineteenth century, partly contributed to the dispute between two representative figures from separate literary worlds over a certain shop in Leicester Square. By 1824, Benbow was identified as a publisher of obscenity, as well as blasphemy and sedition, through his championing of Byron as a figurehead for the working class and for his print shop. After moving from the Strand in 1822, he set up shop in Castle Street, Leicester Square, naming his new premises Byron's Head. In a letter to the *Courier* in 1824, Southey made this shop infamous in one of his several attacks on Byron:

> It might have been thought that Lord Byron had attained the last degree of disgrace when his head was set up for a sign at one of those preparatory schools for the brothel and the gallows; where obscenity, sedition and blasphemy are retailed in drams for the vulgar.[72]

The passage bases its invective against Byron on his appearance in a print shop that panders to the 'vulgar' consumer. Benbow quickly responded to Southey's charges against his shop, particularly his accusations of obscenity. As he wrote in his pamphlet *A Scourge for the Laureate* (1825), 'The charge the Doctor makes against me of sending forth *Obscenity* [. . .] alludes to my publishing 'Don Juan'. I am no print, caricature, or novel publisher, so he can hint at – nothing else.'[73] Benbow alludes to the increasing traffic in obscenity and identifies its business as primarily illustration and fiction. He thus presents himself as on the fringe of the trade, aware of its business and its practices, but also removed. Yet he does not deny that *Don Juan* is obscene. He remains unapologetic of his pirate edition of the poem, which he sold in cheap instalments from 1822–4. Byron thus became the wry figurehead over which print communities collided in the 1820s as they disputed the circulation of a doubtful poem 'without property'.

2 Harem novels: the *Lustful Turk* to *Moslem Erotism*

By the middle of the 1820s, the business in political sedition appears to have waned as Britain began to restabilise politically. In his examination of underground catalogues, graphic prints, and court records, McCalman demonstrates that radical pressmen such as George Cannon, William Benbow, John Benjamin Brookes, Edward and John Duncombe, and William and John Dugdale who had used Byron as the hallmark of populist insurgency shifted to obscenity in face of a trade crisis, often operating out of the same shops in Soho, Covent Garden, and the Strand that would remain the nucleus of the trade for the remainder of the century.[74] By the 1830s, a trade exclusively devoted to producing obscene publications was thriving, drawing specific readers and viewers, venues and genres, and modes of consumption and exchange. Authorship was generally moot as publications were anonymous or pseudonymous. Despite the practice of false imprints, publishers grew more important, reaping the profits, but also bearing the risk of libel. More saliently, the business began to move away from its origins as a street trade in ephemera to a more established trade in the obscene novel or bound magazine, demonstrating the strategic use of print media in face of a trade crisis. By the late 1820s, publishers were turning to the portable medium of the novel, which ranged between one and five guineas. The introduction of the novel into private, domestic spaces sparked a greater intimacy between the person and the book: reading could take place in the library, in the sitting room, and even in the bedroom. Underground novels did not have any radical pretensions, despite the libertarian pedigree of many of their publishers. In an open letter printed in the 1825 issue of his radical underground periodical *The Republican*, Robert Carlile witnessed the changes in London's transitional print community, insisting that 'these books and prints called obscene are got up chiefly for the use and gratification of the aristocracy' rather than the working classes.[75] A caricature from 1826 entitled *Four Specimens of the Reading Public,* published by the radical publisher John Fairburn,[76] would seem to confirm Carlile's accusations (Figure 9). While the 'Political Dustman' reads Cobbett's radical weekly, *The Register*, 'Sir Larry Luscious' reads the *Memoirs of Harriette Wilson* , the prostitute's memoirs. In this cartoon, the debauched male aristocrat is the new, imagined reader of the obscene novel, one prepared to pay for it, bring it home, and pore over it 'lusciously' (not so unlike the woman seeking the five-volume romance). Women likely had access to such underground novels, but men were both their targeted and imagined readers.

In large part owing to the trafficking of Byron's poem among the radical publishers of the 1820s, the imaginary harem soon occupied an important place in these obscene novels. The notoriety surrounding Byron's life and poetry contributed to the fascination with the harem world of slavery, corsairs, and rebellions. Most major publishers of obscenity produced works that focused on the harem, and some of these same publishers even continued to produce Byron imitations and spin-offs, including Dugdale with his edition of *Don Leon*. In all these novels, the harem houses women from all over the world – Caucasian, Asian, and African – and thus functions as a sexual microcosm of empire. The incarceration of harem women becomes a global allegory for the power dynamic between Europe and the Ottoman World – both geographical and spatial entities that were drastically changing in the nineteenth century. While the Ottoman Empire had been declining since the eighteenth century, slowly withdrawing from Europe as it continued to lose more territory to nationalist uprisings, Europe was growing as a geopolitical, economic, and imperial entity.[77] For the wealthy

Figure 9 Anonymous, *Four Specimens of the Reading Public*. London: J. Fairburn, 7 Aug. 1826. By permission of the British Museum, London

male reader ensconced in his private study or bedroom, these harem novels were portable fantasies of personal empire.

John Benjamin Brookes, once a radical publisher, published approximately a dozen obscene books,[78] including the first series of harem classics: *The Lustful Turk* (1828), *The Seducing Cardinal's Amours* (1830), and most likely *Scenes in the Seraglio* (*c.*1820–30).[79] Sold originally for about two guineas, these early illustrated harem novels focused on the oriental despot, offering especially violent male fantasies about his perverse sexual mastery over a panoply of enslaved women, human curiosities, and oriental luxuries. In these works, the oriental despot functions as a surrogate for the English male reader: through him, the reader can master and enjoy the pleasures of the Ottoman Empire, but still remain psychologically aloof when the despot and his harem must inevitably fall to European power and tenure.

Except perhaps for *Scenes in the Seraglio,* which no longer survives and about which there is virtually no information, *The Lustful Turk* is the earliest of these harem novels. Recent discussions of the Ottoman harem, such as those by Billie Melman and Inderpal Grewal, focus on the representation of women, but its men were an even greater source of fascination in early harem obscenity like *The Lustful Turk* . Byron's exploration of male experiences in the harem was particularly influential. Steven Marcus draws attention to the novel's debt to Byron, describing its male protagonist as 'a Byronic figure'.[80] Byron's greatest intrusion with Juan in the harem explores a vulnerable European masculinity at risk of discovery and castration. *The Lustful Turk* , by contrast, explores the dynamics of male despotism and female enslavement, evoking the mood and themes of licentious gothic novels like *The Monk*.[81] Through a series of letters that nominally allows for multiple viewpoints, this book recounts the violent rape of Italian, Greek, French, and English women in Ottoman harems. The principal narrative is that of Emily Barlow, an English girl who describes how an English renegade pirate abducts her and her servant, Eliza Gibbs, as they sail to India. The pirate sells them to the Dey of Algiers, who enslaves and rapes Emily. Eliza, sent to the Bey of Tunis, endures a similar fate. The secondary narrative, which occupies the latter part of the novel, involves Silvia Carey, Emily's disapproving English friend who has received letters from Emily that describe her willing surrender to the embraces of the lustful Turk. The Dey, having intercepted Silvia's letters, enlists Italian monks to abduct her from Toulon. Silvia, forced to endure the humiliations of a slave market, also eventually inhabits his harem.

Despite the presence of the first-person point of view of harem women like Emily, the book is unquestionably misogynous in its portrayal of these women as voluntary participants in their seduction. Instances of sexual violence against women proliferate to such an extent that almost every sexual activity is tinged with it. The book recounts the brutal rape of one virgin after another and variously describes sexual intercourse as an 'assault' or a 'martyrdom'.[82] Blood, knives, sacrifice, and whips are the language and instruments of sex in this novel. The Dey, who has a penchant for virgins, deliberately initiates them on 'white damask cloth' (53) which he preserves 'reeking with the blood of [. . .] virginity' as a reminder of his conquest (55). Emily, the captive Englishwoman, describes her sexual initiation by the Dey in terms of 'impalement' and 'the cutting of a knife' (32). She also compares sex to being sacrificed: 'I was on the altar', she writes, 'and butcher-like, [the Dey] was determined to complete the sacrifice [. . .] tearing and cutting me to pieces' (31). *The Lustful Turk* also shows us that women who resist the sexual advances of the Turks, like Emily's maidservant Eliza, are brutally beaten. When Eliza resists the Bey of Tunis by scratching his face, he retaliates by binding and flogging her into submission (88). Even women's pleasure is depicted in terms of pain. Female orgasm is almost indistinguishable from sexual torture as Emily describes how she 'lay gasping, gorged, crammed to suffocation with rapture' (43) after one of her more pleasurable trysts with the Dey. The novel ostensibly condemns this violence by referring to the despots as 'barbarous' (17) and 'cruel' (17); however, the recurrence of sexual violence throughout indicates that it intends to titillate.

The deployment of female perspective only thinly disguises an erotics that indulges vicariously in the imagined brutal and perverse sexuality of the despot in his harem. Sigel observes that the novel focuses on how women are 'acted upon'.[83] The novel invites the reader to fantasise about inhabiting this role of rich and rapacious oriental despot whose empire is total, though it may also invite alternative fantasies of female victimisation that could have cross-gender appeal.[84] The title page of one edition of the book promises to describe 'all of the salacious Tastes of the Turks' and indeed it does.[85] The Dey of Algiers, the Turk who captures Emily as well as other European women for his harem, is chiefly identified in terms of his lubricity. The Dey's genitalia substitute synecdochally for him. His penis, in a state of ithyphallic permanency, is 'very long and thick' (23), a 'terrible engine' (31), a 'pillar of ivory' (31), a 'wonderful instrument of nature – the terror of virgins, but delight of women' (39), 'Nature's grand master-piece' (42); his testicles, meanwhile, are 'ivory globes' (111) and 'pendant jewels' (158). Marcus succinctly explains, 'the penis becomes the man' (213). The novel also dwells on the Dey's sexual perversity. The Dey uses sexual aids to hold his erection (36), employs eunuchs (33), and indulges in sodomy (61). The design of the harem itself suggests his profligacy. As Emily describes her rape, for instance, she observes that his bed is surrounded by mirrors:

> The Dey seized my hand and gently drew me towards the bed, which was in one of the corners of the room, made of large velvet cushions in the most magnificent style, after the Eastern fashion; the two sides of the wall which formed the angle in which the bed was placed were entirely covered with looking glass, as was the ceiling above.
>
> (*The Lustful Turk* , 28)

The mirrors allow the reader to luxuriate in the difference of the 'powerful Turk' (34), imagine his empire of women magnified by mirrors, and see his virility confirmed and extended indefinitely. When the Dey reveals that 'under the altar of Venus is another grotto' (61), the novel not only repeats the widespread association between Arabs and sodomy (see the next chapter), but also discloses its central preoccupation with an all-consuming and uninhibited male sexuality that is granted unlimited licence outside of England. The novel emphasises the exotic nature of the geography and sexuality by describing how the Dey reminds Emily, whom he later renames Zulima, 'you are not in England now' (62). *The Lustful Turk* invites the male reader to experience the despot's harem not as someone else's, but his own – precarious though it may be.

While *The Lustful Turk* imagines the violent mastery of the oriental despot, it ultimately confiscates his sexual empire. Imagining the foreign despot's rule over European female captives may be sexually titillating, but is also threatening. There are suggestions that the integrity of European women becomes compromised from exposure to the Deys and Beys of North Africa: they are seduced by these men, titivated in foreign attire (68), and even given foreign names (162). The fetishisation of women's whiteness throughout the book – with its focus on their 'lily thighs' (91), 'alabaster cheeks' (91) 'snowy purity' (109), and 'milk-white neck' (140) – suggests both the desire for, and anxious insistence upon, whiteness. The harem is thus both the locus of the novel's libidinal investments, but also of its racial and national anxieties. It eventually responds to these anxieties by punishing the despots, dismantling their harems, and restoring English sexual customs. Relatively early in the narrative, Eliza nearly fatally wounds the Bey of Tunis by stabbing him (56), but the Dey of Algiers suffers an even worse fate. A Greek harem slave rebels against the Dey as he attempts to sodomise her; she castrates him with a knife. The Dey, realising that the services of his female slaves are now nugatory, releases them. Emily, pregnant with the Dey's child, is overcome by shock and conveniently miscarries. The novel thus concludes with Emily and Silvia safely at home in Britain, the first planning to marry and the other happily wed to an Englishman. The threat of miscegenation averted, the geographical shift back to Britain, and the return to British marital laws and sexual practices all function to mitigate the Ottoman threat. In the end, the only reminders of Ottoman male sexuality are the Dey's genitals: pickled and preserved in glass vases housed in an English girl's boarding-school. They are exotic enough to arouse the girls' 'little mouse traps' (160), as the novel euphemistically suggests, but also sufficiently controlled. The relocation of harem property to the English girl's boarding-school was no idiosyncrasy: while the SSV warned about schools' vulnerability to purveyors of obscenity, obscene books like *The Venus School Mistress* (c.1810) avidly represented its fomenting sexuality.[86]

With its evocation of Barbary corsairs and Christian slavery, *The Lustful Turk* is the most Byronic of the harem novels, but it is also the most directly engaged with the politics of empire. The novel even specifies the time in which the events it describes take place: from 18 June 1814 to 8 May 1816. These were important years in the repositioning of European and Ottoman power. Byron's poetry made famous the misdeeds of corsairs while the *Times* regularly reported attacks on British ships that interrupted European trade and led to the enslavement of Christian subjects.[87] In 1815, at the Congress of Vienna, Europeans came together to make peace and cooperate on foreign policy: for one, they agreed to abolish piracy and slavery.[88] This mission led to the near destruction of the Algerian corsair fleet by an Anglo-Dutch flotilla led by Lord Exmouth in 1816 and the liberation of almost 1200 Christian slaves. As one Dey was murdered after another in Algiers during the period, the English often described the city as the site of murder and mayhem. After the murder of Omar Pacha, the Dey of Algiers, for instance, the *Times* article on 17 October 1817 argued that European policy should be 'to exterminate a horde of savages in whom the spirit of war and vengeance against Christendom is so utterly incapable of restraint';[89] a few days later, on 20 October, the *Times* insisted that 'piracy was the trade of these bloody and rapacious ruffians; and Christian slaves were their profit'.[90] Rebellions and foreign incursions during this period both dramatised and presaged the changing imperial relations between the Ottoman and European worlds. By 1838, *Fraser's Magazine* could describe the 'political decay and moral degradation' of the Ottoman Empire, repeating the old Gibbon view that 'Asiatic luxury' caused the downfall of empire: 'For not only has Turkey foreign enemies, and suspicious protection to guard against from without, but perfidious friends and rebellious subjects to contend against from within.[91]

While *The Lustful Turk* is not a historical narrative, political relations between Europe and Ottoman-controlled North Africa during the early nineteenth century influenced the novel's treatment of the harem. The problem of Christian slavery, to which the novel alludes when Silvia mentions the missionaries on their way to Algiers 'for the redemption of slaves' (99), becomes fodder for fantasy about the sexual enslavement of white women, or as the original title page announces, the 'infamous traffic in young girls'.[92] There is no evidence, however, that white women were regularly stolen from European territories to populate Ottoman harems, though the presence of Caucasian Christian women in the harem, such as the 'fair Circassian', would nonetheless remain an abiding preoccupation for European artists drawn to the idea of white slavery and the racialised aesthetic of the harem.[93] The original title page of *The Lustful Turk* also suggests that its story ends with 'the reduction of Algiers by Lord Exmouth'. In fact, the novel never describes this event. Instead, castration signals the Dey's reduction. His defeat by a Greek woman alludes to the successful Greek revolution against Ottoman rule (1823–31) that eventually forced the Ottoman Empire further out of Europe. It appears, then, that the erotics of

Ottoman Empire which the novel explores through the despot cannot be sustained: European, specifically British, supremacy is asserted in the end with the Dey's violent castration.

The Seducing Cardinal's Amours is similar to *The Lustful Turk* in its depiction of the Ottoman harem. Set in the sixteenth century, it exposes the sexual hypocrisy of the clergy that *The Lustful Turk* also touches upon in its portrayal of slave-trafficking monks. Matthew Lewis's anti-Catholic travesty of the 'lustful', 'licentious', 'amorous' monk, Ambrosio, in *The Monk* was certainly the inspiration, particularly because of its notorious reputation as a naughty book. *The Seducing Cardinal's Amours* recounts the story of Isabella Peto, an Italian woman who is seduced by a Cardinal and then captured by the Bey of Adrianople in Turkey. Although the novel shifts narrative registers, from third- to first-person points of view, it focuses on the brutal rule of the Bey. Isabella, for instance, having heard 'the alarming stories' of 'the cruel behaviour of the Turks to their female slaves for the most trifling misconduct', prepares 'to resign herself without a murmur to his wishes'.[94] While less engaged with contemporary events than *The Lustful Turk*, this novel also imagines sexual empire in terms of the shift in European and Ottoman power relations. At the beginning, the Bey's harem boasts 'slaves of all nations' (39). The Bey's favourite slave, the French Atalide, describes the multiple nationalities collected in his harem, encouraging fantasies about Ottoman Empire. She writes in a letter to the Bey, 'The Persian woman weaves his likeness in tapestry; the Italian composes songs; the young English girl, pensive and melancholy, conceals what she does and only says she thinks on you' (44). By the end, however, the Bey's harem is destroyed. Falling under the suspicion of the Sultan, he is strangled, 'his property [. . .] confiscated, and his slaves and other property sold' (76). The sexual empire of the Ottoman despot is once again the subject of untenable fantasy.

In the end, it is the violence that defines these early examples of harem obscenity that delight in the sadistic enslavement of women, the cult of virginity, and the final subjugation of the Ottoman despot. Some critics have found these novels politically innocent. Edward Said, not surprisingly, insists that *The Lustful Turk* participates in the European 'battery of desires, repressions, investments, and projections' in the Orient, though he does not historicise his claims.[95] However, Yeazell negates the violence and imperial ideology to suggest that *The Lustful Turk* is 'pleasantly sadistic' and even 'jokey'.[96] Most recently, Sigel suggests that both *The Lustful Turk* and *The Seducing Cardinal's Amours* are libertine fantasies that imagine the harem as 'a garden of delight' and site of 'primitive desire' for sexually constrained Western readers.[97] While she notes how the despot must be disciplined in the end, I think these novels imagine violent domination rather than libertine pleasure in sexual difference. This violence derives from the tension caused by changing empires as well as a cruel fascination with the Ottoman world of slavery, corsairs, and rebellions that Byron had romanticised.

These early harem novels were successful, likely because of the harem's mainstream popularity. They were subject to regular reprint and circulation through the nineteenth century. Another edition of *The Lustful Turk* appeared in 1829 for four guineas; Dugdale reprinted it twice in the 1860s for three guineas;[98] Lazenby reprinted it again around 1885 for five guineas;[99] and Charles Carrington sold it for £1.10s at the end of the century.[100] *The Lustful Turk* would become the most celebrated work of nineteenth-century obscenity after *My Secret Life*. *Scenes in the Seraglio* was also reprinted by Dugdale in the late 1850s[101] while *The Seducing Cardinal's Amours* reappeared in Carrington's miscellany collection *The Cabinet of Venus* in 1896.[102] These were the first obscene harem novels that prompted the emergence of others, but they were never superseded by their successors. Their circulation history suggests that they continued to be marketable throughout the nineteenth century even while new harem fantasies surfaced. Here, I agree with Yeazell when she observes that 'this Eastern *imperium* continued its hold on the imagination of Europe'.[103]

By the turn-of-the century, two full-length obscene novels emerged that confidently asserted Western mastery in the harem. These novels signalled the shift – albeit never an absolute one[104] – from the harem obscenity at the beginning of the century. Fantasies of the old Ottoman *imperium* continued to circulate, but it was the colonial harem that increasingly came into focus. In these two novels, the harem is fully visible, not inviolable, and symbolically conquered, not subjugating. Although their readership is still predominantly male, they feature male and female protagonists; Europeans of both genders now enter the harem of their own volition. While these novels underwrite imperial and colonial ideology, they are less overtly preoccupied with violence than their precursors.

A Night in a Moorish Harem, first published around 1896, plainly demonstrates how later harem obscenity shifts its focus from the sadistic Ottoman despot to the roguish English imperialist.[105] First published in Paris, it was sold to English and later American audiences by mail-order catalogue for typically one pound or five dollars.[106] Like earlier harem obscenity, this novel was expensive, but in light of inflation was more accessible to a broader socio-economic group. Putatively authored by the hero of the story, Lord George Herbert, it recounts the shipwreck of his gunboat off the coast of Morocco and secret entry into the harem of Abdullah, the Pasha of the district. He remains in the harem for one night only, but manages to have intercourse with all the women before leaving the next morning. An early catalogue distributed by Carrington, *Publications of the Erotica Biblion Society* (1900), advertised the book by emphasising the international nature of the harem: 'Each lascivious lady is of a different nationality and they in turn gratify the lusty rake with the narrative of the most remarkable event of their lives'.[107] There are nine women – including a Spaniard, Greek, Moor, Italian,

Circassian, Portuguese, Persian, Arabian, and French – each representing 'the most lovely example of a different nationality'.[108] Although piracy was nugatory by the end of the century and Ottoman slavery had been officially abolished by 1885,[109] the hero attributes the presence of these women of varying nationalities to 'wars and shipwrecks and piracy [that] enable the Moorish pashas to choose their darlings from all the flags that float the Mediterranean'.[110] The Ottoman despot is absent in this novel, the virile Englishman occupying his role by invitation rather than violence. The allusion to the gunboat at the beginning situates this fantasy impressionistically within a hostile military environment, whose tension would have possibly been augmented by an awareness that European powers were flexing their imperial muscles over Morocco in the late nineteenth century.[111] Although this fantasy of sexual licence implicitly rests on the ideology of imperialism, it is a flippant production about a sexual frolic to do with European male prowess in the colonial harem.

Moslem Erotism, or Adventures of an American Woman in Constantinople is another example of late harem obscenity. The publication history of this work is inveigling, but Mendes guesses that it was published around 1906.[112] Carrington advertised it in his *Catalogue of Rare and Curious English Books* (*c.*1900), along with *A Night in a Moorish Harem*, for one pound.[113] While he may not have been the original publisher, he retailed it for his English readers who, apparently, still welcomed fictional harem fantasy. The story includes spelling customs and monetary references that suggest it was American authored. Although I have seen only one reference to it in an English catalogue, it may have been distributed to American readers in the same manner as *A Night in a Moorish Harem*. This circulation pattern, along with the drop in price, would suggest the expansion of the harem fantasy across class and national boundaries. It begins with a short, fictional account of a harem to which is attached extracts from Sir Richard Burton's translation of the Arab sex manual, *The Perfumed Garden*. The fictional story imagines a friendly incursion into the harem and even suggests a positive male fantasy that emerged with the sexually liberated New Woman in *fin-de-siècle* literature. The novel follows the adventures of an American woman who willingly prostitutes herself in a Constantinople harem. While her husband leaves her briefly to replenish their funds, she 'lease[s]' (7) herself to a Turk for 500 dollars plus amenities until her husband returns, meanwhile enjoying her sexual escapades with 'a big black Nubian' slave trader (7), 'a black dwarf' (11), 'a turbaned Turk' (14), and a eunuch (17). When her husband finally returns, he joins the interracial and multicultural orgy in the 'erotic elysium' (9). The harem fantasy ends on this note with the cries of female orgasm. What is striking about this story is that it is one of the first to imagine female erotic licence in the harem: she is not harem property, but rather owns her own body and controls access to it. While the fantasy savours this unusual addition to the harem ('American girls are rarities in the harems' [7]), its erotics rest on volition rather than violence. The violence typically associated with the harem is registered only in the descriptions of her unusually frenetic and robust lovemaking:

> Tongue and cock, with maddened energy drew first from me wild squirms and amorous yells; and then a flood of dew, licked ravenously by the Eunuch, while my intestines were deluged by my master's sperm.
>
> (*Moslem Erotism* , 19)

In this fantasy, the harem is no longer at the sole disposal of the Ottoman despot, but easily accessible by Westerners, male and female alike, who explore sexual desire that was generally off limits.

From the controversy over the circulation of Byron's harem cantos to the later trafficking of obscene harem novels, the harem became one of the most enduring subjects of British obscenity. The continuous exchange, circulation, and remediation of the harem in London's print communities not only suggest the intersections among obscenity, media technologies, and exoticism, but also reveal the trade's prescient use of new media for girdling the globe.

3
Sir Richard Burton, the *Arabian Nights*, and Arab Sex Manuals

The prominence of the harem in European popular culture and the appearance of a genre of obscene novel that specialised in the harem *imperium* likely contributed to the emergence of an underground print traffic in translations of Eastern literature. This publishing phenomenon, which spanned 30 years, is my next focus of investigation. Translations, especially of ribald texts in Latin and French, were already the mainstay of Britain's trade in obscenity. In the 1870s, however, obscene translations of Indian and Arab texts emerged at the instigation of Sir Richard Burton (1821–1890). Burton was renowned during his time as a traveller, explorer, orientalist, anthropologist, writer, linguist, and translator. Although a committed imperialist,[1] he also evinced a particular fascination with the Arab language and peoples. He is still remembered for his covert pilgrimage to Mecca disguised as a Moslem, a disguise he refined by having himself circumcised. He is best remembered, however, for his scandalous translation of the *Arabian Nights* (1885–8), the work for which he nevertheless received his knighthood.[2] This was just one of many translations that he published through the Kama Shastra Society, the underground press with false headquarters in Cosmopoli and Benares that he founded with F. F. Arbuthnot and Richard Monckton Milnes along the lines of the Oriental Translation Fund,[3] but with the primary purpose of publishing erotic and semi-erotic Indian and Arab texts. Besides his translation of *The Thousand Nights and a Night* (1885–6) as well as *The Supplemental Nights* (1886–8), the Kama Shastra Society published *The Kama Sutra* (1883), *The Ananga Ranga* (1885), *The Perfumed Garden of the Sheik Nefzaoui* (1886), *The Beharistan* (1887), and *The Gulistan* (1888).[4] Despite Britain's greater colonial and cultural contact with India, the translations of the Arab texts elicited the most discussion, reproduction, and imitation.[5] After the success and controversy of the *Arabian Nights*, translations of a similar nature followed. Burton reworked his earlier translation of the Arab sex manual, *The Perfumed Garden*, producing the incendiary manuscript, *The Scented Garden* (1890). After his death in 1890, he was the cultural cynosure for later, open translations of Arab sex manuals, such as *Marriage – Love and*

Woman Amongst the Arabs (1896) and *The Old Man Young Again* (1898–9), both of which imitated Burton's style and exalted his knowledge of the Arab world.

These underground translations were distinct from the obscene harem novels that we have just examined because they posed as science and scholarship: they claimed to be exact literal renditions and included voluminous English commentary in the form of annotation, excursus, and index. They fell within what Lisa Sigel identifies as the empiricist movement in Britain's obscene print culture.[6] Critics from Steven Marcus to Peter Mendes have neglected this kind of obscenity in favour of more recognisable twentieth-century forms such as illustrated novels and serials like *The Lustful Turk* and *The Pearl*.[7] However, it was one of the more visible and widely controversial forms of obscenity in the later nineteenth century because it was produced and consumed by the intellectual, economic, and political elites. Empiricist obscenity emerged out of privileged intellectual societies such as The Royal Geographic Society, The Royal Asiatic Society, The Athenaeum Club, and The Anthropological Society.[8] Burton, a member of all of these societies and founder of the last, was well acquainted with many important writers and collectors of obscenity directly or tangentially associated with these societies, including Richard Monckton Milnes, Frederick Hankey, Algernon Swinburne, and Henry Spencer Ashbee.[9] As Sigel observes, 'These men's collective biography demonstrates the ways that position and relative wealth allowed them the opportunity to think about sexual matters, buy artefacts of their choice, see the world or as much of it as they chose, and write about what they saw and wanted to see.'[10] With these intellectual societies as their cultural adhesive, certain affluent Englishmen began to produce privately printed works on exotic sexualities under the protective rubric of scholarship.

Despite their claims for scholarship and semantic equivalence, these translations of Arab texts were creative productions that disclosed more about contemporary British sexual preoccupations than they did about Arab sexuality. This chapter shows how their trafficking drove three crucial discourses related to British sexuality. I discuss how Burton's *Arabian Nights* incited the *first* public literary debates about 'pornography' in England, ultimately introducing the term into literary criticism, popular culture, and legislation. I also show how Burton's *Arabian Nights*, as well as his translations of *The Perfumed Garden* and *The Scented Garden*, contributed to early theories of homosexuality. Finally, I focus on how the later translations of Arab sex manuals, *Marriage* and *The Old Man*, still drew from Burton's work to promote the collection of British obscenity. While Burton's biography[11] and orientalism[12] are familiar and well-explored territory, his significance to the history of British obscenity and sexuality has only begun to be investigated by critics like Sigel. However, unlike Sigel, who forcefully argues that Burton's works 'snugly fit the imperial and empiricist agenda' by 'absorb[ing] and finally govern[ing] the sexuality of the colonized',[13] I argue in this chapter that the discourses that emerged around these translations were underscored by an overwhelming and pervasive preoccupation with the idea of British sexual inadequacy. Over close to three decades, Burton's translations and their imitations tested, challenged, and trafficked this self-perception through discussions of pornography, homosexuality, and erotic book collection.

1 'Esoteric pornography': Sir Richard Burton's translation of the *Arabian Nights*

When Burton published his translation of the *Arabian Nights* in 1885, it outraged the British literary community. This collection of Arabic tales (*Alf Laylah Wa Laylah*), which had been circulating in the West since the eighteenth century, had long been familiar and cherished. The romantic and adventuresome stories told night after night by Queen Scheherazade to her husband had already captivated the imagination of Johnson, Coleridge, and the Brontës.[14] Antoine Galland first introduced the Arabic text to Europeans with his adapted French translation of *Les Mille et Une Nuits* (1704–17). After Galland's translation, many eighteenth-century editions followed, both in French and English. In the nineteenth century, three important English editions preceded Burton's: Edward Lane's bowdlerised drawing-room translation (1839–41), Thomas Dalziel's illustrated edition (1863–5), and John Payne's complete and scholarly translation (1882–4). Lane's was a popular edition, but Payne's was a private edition restricted to 500 copies for subscribers. Burton, who had been working on his translation of the *Arabian Nights* for 30 years,[15] decided to profit from Payne's remaining subscribers. From 1885–6, he privately printed through the Kama Shastra Society 1000 copies of his own ten-volume translation entitled *The Book of the Thousand Nights and One Night* and sold the set to subscribers for a prohibitive ten guineas.[16] From 1886–7, he printed an additional six volumes under the title *Supplemental Nights*. Like Payne's translation, Burton's was a 'plain and literal one', yet shockingly different from all previous English translations. The language was lurid and coarse and the style estranging with its Spenserian archaism and awkward literalism. Long familiar tales from the nursery and schoolroom, like that of the Baghdad Porter, now included awful scenes of sexual violence.[17] It was in his footnotes, however, that Burton's translation especially set itself apart from other translations. These footnotes, accompanied by a full scholarly apparatus (Foreword, Terminal Essay, Appendix, and Index), offered, in the words of Mahsin Jassim Ali, a 'panorama of Eastern Life' that incorporated strange anthropological observations on Arab sexual practices such as bestiality, sodomy, eunuchism, clitoridectomy, and miscegenation.[18] His note on Arab women's lust for black men is an infamous example of the commentary he appended to the text:

> Debauched women prefer Negroes on account of the size of their parts. I measured one man in Somali-land who, when quiescent, numbered nearly six inches. This is a characteristic of the Negro race and of African animals; [. . .] whereas the pure Arab, man and beast, is below the average of Europe; one of the best proofs by and by, that the Egyptian is not an Asiatic, but a Negro partially whitewashed. [. . .] In my time no honest hindi Moslem would take his womenfolk to Zanzibar on account of the huge attractions and enormous temptations there are thereby offered to them.[19]

Although the *Arabian Nights* already possessed exotic and sexual appeal in Britain before Burton's translation,[20] his translation emphasised its Arab origin and sexual content. With its focus on the sordid sexuality of the Arabs, Burton's translation was estranging to the British reader who was used to chastened tales of tender British orientalism. In effect, he defamiliarised the Arab text that had been virtually adopted by British culture as its own.[21] His translation violently disrupted the British cultural presentation of the *Arabian Nights* – to such an extent that it was branded 'pornographic'.

Dane Kennedy importantly situates Burton's controversial translation within discussions about contemporary morality and describes the competing uses of orientalism within debates about the translation: where Burton drew on orientalism to criticise British prudery, his detractors also drew on orientalism to voice their objections.[22] However, what is most striking about the circulation history of this translation was the enduring debate it propelled about 'pornography'. 'Pornography' did not enter English vocabulary until 1850 in order to denote sexually explicit literature and art (OED). As Walter Kendrick observes, such works were more generally referred to as 'erotic', 'curious', or 'forbidden'.[23] The term began to enter the language of international moral campaigns in the early 1880s. At a presidential address for a National League Federation conference at Neuchatel in November 1882, Emile de Laveleye cautiously introduced the term as a French import:

> There exists in what are called civilized countries, an inundation of immorality which is frightful; – it might almost be called a species of contagious *satyriasis*, – which infects alike our books, our journals, engravings, photographs, etc., and extends from our fine art exhibits down to our allumette boxes. And the rising tide of *pornography*, if I may venture to use the word, threatens family life itself, the very foundations of society.[24]

In Britain, however, the *first* public literary debate about 'pornography' emerged over Burton's translation of the *Arabian Nights*. Burton, his readers, and his later editors and publishers debated the pornography of the *Arabian Nights* over such diverse issues as intention, accessibility, inconsistency, comparative sexuality, and the Eastern Question. What underpinned this debate about the putative pornography of the *Arabian Nights* was a struggle over its cultural presentation. The British demonstrated nationalist jealousy over the *Arabian Nights*; one reviewer, for instance, derided Galland's French edition for its 'indecency' and tendency to show 'an Oriental [. . .] in the fashionable French hat, gloves, and boots of the last century'.[25] Burton's translation similarly threatened to alter the *Arabian Nights*, changing it from what many British remembered from the nursery and the schoolroom as a storybook of oriental adventure into an Arab erotic almanac fit only for 'the grand old barbarian' (*Supplemental Nights*, 6.451). The appearance of Burton's *Arabian Nights*, was followed by a nationalist debate over its cultural presentation that rendered the issue of pornography its discursive battlefield. C. Knipp suggests that 'Burton's edition is certainly fascinating as a personal document',[26] but it is more important as a British cultural document. The English commentary that visually engulfs the translated text reveals the extent to which these translations were not faithful reproductions of the original Arab text. Neither the translators nor the culture within which they wrote were invisible. Nineteenth-century translation theory assumed that a good translation would achieve semantic equivalence with the original text. In 'The Task of the Translator', however, Walter Benjamin questions the notion of the fidelity of reproduction to suggest that the translator is an artist who recreates the original as a work that echoes it, but also changes it.[27] Burton's translation demonstrates how his transformation of the Arab text elicited an emergent, if unsteady, debate about pornography agitated by British nationalism, British sexual prudery, and prurient interest in Arab sexuality.

Burton anticipated and, to some extent, incited the public controversy over his translation. As Kennedy writes, his 'was a declaration of war against the proponents of purity'.[28] He knew the potential legal repercussions of printing and advertising it – the only Kama Shastra text not masked behind anonymity and secrecy. He was keenly aware of the Obscene Publications Act of 1857, its threat having already led to the miscarriage of his earlier work, *The Kama Shastra*. Yet he was also eager to shock the public and boast of his work's difference from previous translations. As he wrote to Payne from his consular post in Trieste, 'I don't live in England and don't care a damn for the Public Opinion.'[29] Therefore, in the 24,000 to 30,000 advertising circulars posted, he compromised by both suggesting and downplaying the sexual exoticism of his translation. One circular boasted that readers would find 'in the notes a repertoire of those Arabian manners and customs, Beliefs and Practices, which are not discussed in popular works' (*Supplemental Nights*, 6.391). However, Isabel Burton, who acted as 'wife, and mother, and comrade, and secretary, and aide-de-camp, and agent to him' and who was also well informed about the legal repercussions of printing an obscene book,[30] likely encouraged her husband to subdue his intrepid blustering in subsequent circulars. A later, more cautious, circular was included with the first volume 'earnestly requesting that the book might not be exposed for sale in public places or permitted to fall into the hands of any save curious students of Moslem manners' (6.395). On 15 August 1885, Burton also wrote to *The Academy* to emphasise the limited accessibility of his translation:

> One of my principal objects in making the work so expensive [. . .] is to keep it from the general public. For this reason I have no publisher. The translation is printed by myself for the use of select personal friends; and nothing could be more repugnant to my feelings than the idea of a book of the kind being placed in a publisher's hands, and sold over the counter.[31]

These advertisements demonstrate that intention and access were key determinants in assessing obscenity at this point. By indicating that the work would remain in the hands of a 'select' few, they reiterate the persistent class bias that underscored ideas about obscenity. They also indicate – whether they down-play or suggest the exoticism of the translation – that Burton's *Arabian Nights* was like none other in its intimate portrait of Arab culture.

As he was aware of the British cultural investment in the *Arabian Nights*, Burton's Foreword to the first volume anticipated the public outcry. Even before the controversy over his translation, he constructed a defence of the work's *turpiloquium* (the term pornography did not enter the discussion on obscenity until the reviewers introduced it) to pre-empt the nationalist uproar over his transformation of the surrogate British classic. Burton begins his Foreword by defending the sexual content of his work on the grounds of cultural difference, suggesting that Arabs are more straightforward than the British and juxtaposing Arab sexual honesty with European sexual hypocrisy:

> Subtle corruption and covert licentiousness are utterly absent; we find more real 'vice' in many a short French roman, say La Dame aux Camelias; and in not a few English novels of our day than in the thousands of pages of the Arab. Hence we have nothing of that most immodest modern modesty which sees covert implication where nothing is implied and 'improper' allusion when propriety is not outraged; nor do we meet with the nineteenth-century refinement; innocence of the word not of the thought; morality of the tongue not of the heart, and the sincere homage paid to virtue in guise of perfect hypocrisy.
>
> (Burton, *Arabian Nights*, 1.xvii)

He not only justifies his translation by emphasising the sexual differences between British and Arab cultures and by adjoining the customary jingoist calumny against greater French sexual corruption,[32] but also by challenging assumptions about British sexual innocence and decorum. While noting that British sexual prudery is a 'nineteenth-century refinement', Burton also recalls the coarser passages in Shakespeare, Sterne, and Swift (1.xvi) to draw attention to Britain's historically capricious definition of obscenity and to suggest that British and Arab sexual customs were not always so incommensurate. He relies on cultural difference to defend the sexual content of his work and, at the same time, disparage the nineteenth-century British national character as hypocritically prude.

Yet, while Burton's Foreword aggressively defies British sexual custom, he tempers his criticism by demonstrating what his translation offers the British reader. He justifies his focus on the unusual sexual practices of the Arabs by insisting that he aims to instruct the British. He emphasises the potential educational value of his translation for the British scholar and gentleman. His Foreword repeatedly refers to the student at which he aims his work. 'The student who adds Lane's notes to mine', he promises, 'will know as much of the Moslem East and more than any Europeans who have spent half their lives in Orient lands' (*Arabian Nights*, 1.xix). He thus defends his work in terms of its anthropological and orientalist value. He indicates that his edition has provided him with the 'long-sought opportunity of noticing practices and customs which interest all mankind' that 'Respectability' and 'Propriety' would not allow him to explore through his failed Anthropological Society (1.xviii). He even draws attention to the index to his anthropological notes appended to each volume 'for facility of reference' (1.xix). By implying that his commentary surpasses the importance of the text itself, he deftly ensures that his scholarly apparatus accommodates the British orientalist and anthropologist – meanwhile guiding every prurient reader to his most lascivious notes.

Burton's Foreword also defends the sexual content of his translation in terms of British gain by disclosing how it might benefit British imperialist venture in the East. More specifically, he defends his translation as a political answer to the Eastern Question – the nineteenth-century debate about Britain's most advantageous political and cultural relationship with the decaying Ottoman Empire in the face of Russian and French imperial advancement in its receding territories. He stresses the political exigency of dispelling England's 'ignorance concerning the Eastern races with whom she is continually in contact' (*Arabian Nights*, 1.xxiv). He argues that England should concentrate less on India and more on its nearer neighbours:

> This book is indeed a legacy which I bequeath to my fellow countrymen in their hour of need. Over devotion to Hindu and especially to Sanskrit literature, has led them astray from those (so-called) 'Semitic' studies, which are the more requisite for us as they teach us to deal successfully with a race more powerful than any pagans – the Moslems.
>
> (*Arabian Nights*, 1.xxiii)[33]

He also believes that Britain's past political failures resulted from its ignorance about the East, revealed in the Afghan Wars (1839–42; 1878–80) when Britain attempted to extend its imperial rule in India to Afghanistan, and in the bloody aftermath of the 1882 occupation of Egypt. In advancing an imperialist argument, he explains that Britain would govern best through superior knowledge:

> Hence, when suddenly compelled to assume the reins of government in Moslem lands, as Afghanistan in times past and Egypt at present, she fails after a fashion which scandalizes her few (very few) friends; and her crass ignorance concerning the Oriental peoples which should most interest her, exposes her to the contempt of Europe as well as of the eastern world.
> (*Arabian Nights*, 1.xxiii)

How his notes on topics such as castration (5.46n) or condoms (7.190n) might serve Britain's' imperial interests he never elucidates, but implies that sexual knowledge about the Arabs could potentially advance Britain's imperial cause. Even as he transforms the *Arabian Nights* to include sexual exoticism, he justifies his disruption of the cultural presentation of the text in terms of British gain. While his defence aggressively derides British sexual custom, it also outlines how his translation might benefit Britain's imperialist venture in the East.[34]

Burton's Foreword justifies his intent to 'produce a full, complete, unvarnished, uncastrated copy of the great original' (*Arabian Nights*, 1.ix). He defends the sexual exoticism of his translation as a corrective to British sexual insipidness and regards it as a resource for British scholarship and imperialism. In so doing, he adopts the rhetoric of the 'new empiricist pornographers' (Sigel's term) and confirms Ronald Hyam's thesis that the operations of empire offered a 'large escape clause' for soldiers, traders, and missionaries from British sexual morality.[35] At the end of his Foreword, he signs his defence from the Athenaeum Club, the exclusive English gentleman scholar's club on Pall Mall in London that was established in 1824 as an association of distinguished writers, scientists, and artists. Burton's reference to his association with the Club lends his translation cultural authority: he relies on his association with the British intellectual elite to present his exotic and estranging translation as scholarly rigorous, quintessentially English, and worthy of any wealthy collector's library. While he relies on this association to present his translation as respectable, he also points to the symbolic home of the upscale, scholarly works of dubious moral footing that were very different from works like *The Lustful Turk* .[36]

When Burton began receiving reviews for the first volume of *Arabian Nights*, he quickly realised that he would 'play the part' between 'the pornologist and the anti-pornologist' (*Supplemental Nights*, 6.401). What ensued in the daily and periodical press was a virulent public debate about whether or not the work was pornographic.[37] This attack was motivated by the feeling that the depictions of a debased, Arab sexuality made the work particularly offensive. The *Pall Mall Gazette*, an evening newspaper aimed at members of gentlemen's clubs, was at the centre of the controversy with its vitriolic condemnation of Burton's new translation. One of the first reviews by the *Standard* on 12 September 1885 was positive: it concludes that the work contained 'nothing intentionally demoralizing'. The *Pall Mall Gazette*, however, was quick to attack the *Standard* review and censure Burton's translation as pornographic. In an article entitled 'Pantagruelism or Pornography' from 14 September, John Morley (under the pseudonym Sigma) repudiates Burton's claim that his work aims to instruct the student of anthropology and orientalism. In denying the work's scholarship, he asks: 'Students! Students of what? Does any one need to be told that the vast majority of them are simply students of what I shall call [. . .] pornography?' He strives to show that the translation is worse than the extravagantly rude humour of Pantagruel, a character from Rabelais, by searching for a new, even more upsetting term. According to Morley, 'The book would never secure 1,000 subscribers at the large price put upon it, were it not for its actual reputation and its prospective value as one of the grossest [. . .] books in the English language.' He also casts doubt on whether the student will ever see the so-called tome as it has already appeared 'in the window of a second-hand bookseller in a questionable backstreet'. On 24 September, the paper continued to attack Burton's pretence of scholarship by claiming that it could not print a section of it for fear of police seizure. It also equates the translation with street pornography, dismissing its scholarly pretensions. It refers to it as 'the garbage of the brothel' and 'the favourite literature of the stews of Leicester-square', and also, in a shorthand way to explain its pornography, draws attention to its foreign publication by the 'Kamashastra Society of Benares'. On 29 September, Morley also wrote a follow-up article, 'The Ethics of Dirt', to argue that his focus on Arab sexuality makes his translation particularly offensive:

> I am not prepared to formulate a complete 'Ethics of Dirt', but it seems to me clear that there is, for us, a vast difference between the obscenity of our own classics and that of the Mahommedan East, or, to put it generally, between European and Asian obscenity. In the garden of western literature there are many foul quagmires which must be faced by the explorer; but we have a legitimate – nay, an imperative – interest in wading through them. Is there any reason why we should laboriously import the gigantic muck heaps of other races, place them *très curieux*, and charge a high price for the privilege of wallowing in them? I think not.

Morley denounces Burton's translation because it imports Arab sexual perversion to the West. In referring to the translation as 'Captain Burton's Oriental

muck heap', he suggests that its 'esoteric pornography' lies in its defamiliarising exploration and importation of foreign sexuality that disguises itself
under 'the mask of scholarship and culture which enables it to insinuate itself
into the columns of such journals as the *Standard* and appear on the 'unsullied British breakfast table'. Kennedy draws attention to Morley's focus on
oriental debauchery; what is more striking, however, is the fear of contamin-
ation. According to Morley, Burton's *Arabian Nights* was an insidious threat
to the British moral and national character. It threatened the 'unsullied'
sanctity of British domesticity, and British prudery was apparently worth
defending.[38]

Over the next couple of months, subsequent criticism on the *Arabian
Nights* responded to the *Pall Mall Gazette* attack by debating the pornography
of the translation. This debate developed into a stand-off between Burton
and the editor of the *Pall Mall Gazette*, William T. Stead. Stead was a social
reformer and purity campaigner who had just recently become notorious for
the investigative report 'Maiden Tribute of Modern Babylon' on child prostitution in London.[39] Reviewers supported either Burton or Stead, debating
the pornography of the new *Arabian Nights* in relation to its inclusion of
Arab sexual practices. On 29 September 1885, the *Bat* responded to the *Pall
Mall Gazette* by attacking the newspaper and defending Burton's translation:

> Journalists, who had no objection to pandering to the worst tastes of
> humanity at a penny a copy are suddenly inspired by much righteous
> indignation at a privately printed work which costs a guinea a volume,
> and in which the manners, the customs, and the language of the East are
> boldly represented as they were and as they are.

Although he stresses the limited accessibility of Burton's translation as a safeguard to public morals (a precaution that Stead's cheap penny newspaper
could not boast), the reviewer defends his uncensored focus on Arab life.
While acknowledging that Burton shifts the translation from what Galland
and Lane had presented to the West as 'the playbook of generations, the
delight of the nursery and the school-room for nearly two hundred years',
he praises it for offering the 'truth' about the Arabs as no translation had
done before. The reviewer also suggests that 'the blatant buffoons who
have described Captain Burton's work as pornographic only show their own
ignorance of the literature of the East and of pornography.' To describe the
Arabian Nights as pornographic because of its Eastern origins is the mark of
literary and cultural ignorance. Nor, he adds, does its focus on Arab sexuality make it comparable to London street pornography: 'The misguided
lunatic who invests in it in the hope of getting hold of a good thing in
the Holywell Street sense of the term will find indeed that the fool and his
money are soon parted.' On 12 October, the *Echo* contributed to the Burton-
Stead debate by condemning Burton's 'morally filthy book'. In arguing that

Burton had 'out-Heroded Mr. Stead, and cannot plead Mr. Stead's justification or excuse', the review categorically pronounces that his translation
is unfit for British audiences: 'What might have been acceptable to Asiatic
populations ages ago is absolutely unfit for Christian populations of the
nineteenth century.' In a column called 'Acid Drops', the radical paper the
Freethinker prolonged the debate further. On 25 October, it describes Stead as
'getting more pious and Persniffian everyday' for traducing 'Captain Burton,
a gentleman and a scholar whose boots Mr. Stead is not fit to black'. This
reviewer defends Burton's translation by lauding his character, which had
been condemned by Stead supporters. He strategically presents Burton as a
scholar and gentleman – the kind one might find in the Athenaeum Club –
to off-set competing representations of him as non-English.[40] While the
Saturday Review, for instance, draws attention to Burton's covert pilgrimage
to Mecca disguised as a 'True Believer', this reviewer represents him as an
upstanding English gentleman fit to translate a British classic.[41]

In 1886, when the Stead controversy was not so topical, reviewers no
longer framed their response in relation to his newspaper. The perception that Burton's *Arabian Nights* was, as the *Whitehall Review* suggested, a
'monument of labour and scholarship and of research' grew alongside the
competing impression of its pornography.[42] Attitudes about its pornography,
however, were still intimately linked to its focus on Arab sexuality. On 2
January, the *Saturday Review* suggested that the translation was pornographic
because it would tarnish and possibly weaken Britains's international reputation. He rejects Burton's suggestion that the British could learn from Arab
sexual honesty and, instead, lauds English prudery:

> Abroad we English have the character of being the most prudish of
> nations; we are celebrated as having Bowdlerized for our babies and suck-
> lings even the immortal William Shakespeare; but we shall infallibly lose
> this our character should the Kama-Shastra Society flourish.

An even more vitriolic review of Burton's translation appeared in the
Edinburgh Review. Written by Lane's nephew, Stanley Lane-Poole, the article
compares the various translations of *Arabian Nights*. He not only criticises the
archaising translation as 'unreadable', but also denounces its 'varied collection of abominations' as an 'ocean of filth'. In his argument that Burton
is simply 'the chronicler only of their [Arab's] most degraded vices', he
famously concludes that 'Galland [is] for the nursery, Lane for the library,
Payne for the study, and Burton for the sewers.' Lane-Poole also appears
to criticise the anti-democratic nature of the book's production, revealing
a latent hostility toward the cultural and legal permissiveness towards rich
men's peccadilloes. For him, the fact that Burton had the wealth and social
connections to print a translation that would be encased in 'private libraries
or secret cabinets in public libraries'[43] did not excuse his defilation of a British

classic with 'such an appalling collection of degrading customs and statistics of vice' from 'Orient lands'. While Burton drew on his connections with The Athenaeum Club to legitimise his translation, Lane-Poole denounced this kind of social elitism for its importation of oriental debauchery into Britain. Both of these reviewers are protective of the international perception of the British character, apparently worried that pornographic works would seriously compromise it.[44]

Such thinking eventually led Laveleye to write his 1888 piece on 'How Bad Books May Destroy States' for the *Vigilance Record.* In writing about the 'publication of pornographic literature', he argues that 'it is both legitimate and necessary to oppose the circulation of writings which may attack public morality, for nations who respect women and who are pure in their sentiments and feelings grow and prosper; whereas those in which immorality reigns, on the contrary, decline and fall.'[45] This thinking shows the emergent association between nationalism and moral respectability in the nineteenth century, which George Mosse argues reached its height in Europe during the two world wars.[46] Such thinking also shows how the cultural concept of pornography developed with the nationalist sentiment that grew with empire and print traffic.

Although shadowed by the Society for the Suppression of Vice (SSV) during the printing of the *Arabian Nights*,[47] Burton responded to the debate by appending an erudite and scholarly Terminal Essay at the end of the tenth volume of the *Arabian Nights* that became notorious for its sections on 'Pornography' and 'Pederasty'. While he uses his Foreword simultaneously to deny and defend the putative immorality of his edition, he uses his Terminal Essay on 'Pornography' to respond to negative criticism by defining British pornography. His essay on 'Pornography' is brief and embryonic, but notable for being the first British attempt to theorise pornography. In suggesting that the *Arabian Nights* was deemed pornographic because of its explicit renderings of Arab sexual practices such as sodomy, he defends his translation by challenging the implicit association between pornography and Arab sexuality. As he develops the arguments from his Foreword, he suggests that the Arabs are candid where the British are suggestive about sexual matters. He claims the 'suggestive' is more 'seductive' than the 'raw word' and, therefore, exercises a more insidious influence on morality (10.203): 'Theirs is a coarseness of language, not of idea; they are indecent, not depraved; and the pure and perfect naturalness of their nudity seems almost to purify it' (10.203). He maintains that the British, with their suggestiveness, are more immoral than the Arabs with their candour. By use of cross-cultural comparison, then, he defines pornography as British prudery rather than Arab sexual honesty. Burton also rethinks the British bias against sodomy as necessarily pornographic. In addressing the so-called prevalence of sodomy (what he calls 'le vice contre nature') in the *Arabian Nights*, he explains that it 'is one of absolute obscenity utterly repugnant to British readers, even the least prudish' (10.204). Yet he attempts to purge sodomy of its pornographic associations by dealing with it with Arab frankness: 'I proceed to discuss the matter serieusement, honnetement, historiquement; to show it in decent nudity not in suggestive fig-leaf or feuille de vigne' (10.205). Ironically, as he insists on the 'decency' of Arab frankness, he himself displays British circumlocution by resorting to the French, an inconsistency that demonstrates the degree to which the British disavowed sodomy by expunging it from its vocabulary and transferring it to the French. Because he understands that what underlay the debate about the pornography of his *Arabian Nights* was its focus on Arab sexuality, Burton challenges assumptions about British prudery and Arab perversion to justify the sexual exoticism of his translation as morally sound and nationally important in its sexual frankness.

Burton not only responded to his detractors by offering a definition of pornography that redirected opprobrium away from Arab candour to British prudery, but also by contesting their accusations as unfounded and arbitrary. Because he still harboured a grudge against Stead for initiating the public censorship of his earlier translation, he attacked him in later volumes. He exposes the hypocrisy and inconsistency of the *Pall Mall Gazette* which 'mourn[s] over the "Pornography" of the Nights', while overlooking the immorality of many classical texts. 'Why does not this inconsistent puritan', Burton asks, 'purge the Old Testament of its allusions to human ordure and the pudenda; to carnal copulation and impudent whoredom, to adultery and fornication, to onanism, sodomy, and bestiality?' (*Arabian Nights*, 10.254).[48] With characteristic audacity, Burton also included a section entitled 'Reviewers Reviewed' in his final volume of *Supplemental Nights* in which he reproduces the debate, rearticulates his former defence, and calumniates most of his critical reviewers. In particular, he maligns the *Pall Mall Gazette* as 'The Sexual Journal' and 'The Sexual Gazette', because it 'deliberately pimps and panders to this latest sense and state of aphrodisiac excitement' (*Supplemental Nights*, 6.404). As is his wont, he displaces the charge of pornography elsewhere. He describes Stead's portrayal of London as the centre of child prostitution as nothing less than a national scandal that subjects Britain to the ridicule of the French, 'who hold virtue in England to be mostly Tartuffery', and of the Germans, 'who dearly love to use us and roundly abuse us' (6.394). Burton thus justifies his translation, by suggesting that Stead's newspaper is unfit to judge whether or not his *Arabian Nights* compromises the British national sexual character. The debate's true concern was the presentation of British sexual identity.

After the public furore over Burton's *Arabian Nights*, later nineteenth-century editors and publishers of the translation attempted to regain control over its cultural presentation for more sensitive markets. In so doing, they too contributed to the late nineteenth-century popular perception and arbitration of pornography. A struggle over how to present later editions of the *Arabian Nights* arose among Isabel Burton, Burton, and his publisher Leonard

Smithers. While Isabel Burton, who replaced Stead as Britain's moral figure-head in this debate, aimed to make the text familiar again to a general British readership, Burton and Smithers preferred to preserve, and even accentuate, its sexual exoticism. This later dispute over the handling of the sexually explicit passages of the *Arabian Nights* becomes conspicuously gendered. Isabel Burton's active role in her husband's literary affairs gendered the discourse of pornography as the various editors attempted to regulate the cultural presentation of Burton's translation.

Isabel Burton's six-volume edition of her husband's *Arabian Nights* was the first attempt to recuperate Burton's translation from the imputation of pornography. In 1886, the reputable English press Waterlow & Sons published *Lady Burton's Edition of her Husband's Arabian Nights*. Her edition was ostensibly the 'family' version of the translation.[49] Her title page indicates that she chastened the translation for British 'household reading', and her dedication to 'The Women of England' demonstrates that she offered her edition to British women especially. In her Preface, she guarantees 'no mother shall regret her girl's reading this Arabian Nights' (1.vi). In order to fulfil this promise, she excised 215 out of the original 3215 pages (1.vii), including Burton's defence of *turpiquilum* in his Foreword (except the passage when he reassures his readers that 'the general tone of The Nights is exceptionally high and pure'), all sexually explicit commentary (such as his note quoted earlier about debauched women), and, finally, the two final essays on 'Pornography' and 'Pederasty'.

She never condemned the translation as pornographic (in her 1893 biography of her husband she endorses his translation as 'good for the Government' and a benefit to the 'Orientalist'[50]), but nonetheless edited the book for a household readership by regulating its morals. As reviewers from the *Academy* insisted, Isabel Burton consequently restored the *Arabian Nights* to its old familiar self. 'Under Lady Burton's auspices', writes Amelia B. Edwards, '*The Book of the Thousand Nights and a Night* becomes once again the dear old "Arabian Nights" of our youth' fit 'to be read by the fireside on a winter's night'. On 31 December 1887, another reviewer for the *Academy* describes it as the perfect gift book: 'It would not be easy to imagine a more charming Christmas present for young people at this "boxing" time of year, than Lady Burton's dainty and delightful series.'[51] In the hands of Isabel Burton, Burton's scandalous translation becomes a Victorian gift book, no longer a book to be kept under lock and key, but now suitable for general exchange and circulation. The two photographs that accompany the first and second volumes visually encapsulate the achieve-ment of her edition: the first photograph of Isabel Burton figured as a fine Victorian lady is off-set by the second photograph of Richard Burton dressed in Arab frock and tarboosh. She exerts her feminine moral influ-ence over her husband's translation, yet still preserves its oriental character. She never objected to its exoticism, only its sexual content. After excising the obscene passages, she reintroduces the *Arabian Nights* into the British drawing room.

As the female editor of a questionable book, however, Isabel Burton also felt she must justify her own exposure to it. She publicly claimed that her husband 'forbade' her to read the translation until 'he blotted out with ink the worst words'.[52] Yet, as Fawn Brodie discusses, the Burtons together fabricated the story that she never viewed the unexpurgated edition of the translation. Brodie's examination of volumes of the *Arabian Nights*, now housed at the Royal Anthropological Institute in London, shows that Isabel Burton not only read the original translation, but also made copious marginal comments beside the passages she deemed obscene.[53] Other women also read the original translation. It was transcribed by Victoria Maylor, a Catholic friend who read every errant word of the *Arabian Nights*, and later *The Perfumed Garden* (*Supplemental Nights*, 6.91–2). There was a split between public expectation and private practice regarding women's exposure to purportedly obscene material. Public decorum may have demanded that women refrain from reading questionable works, but they could indulge privately without opprobrium. Upper-class women could access family libraries with relative privacy without the scrutiny of booksellers or passersby on questionable streets. Women could and did indeed read Burton's translation of the *Arabian Nights*. However, as Isabel Burton attempted to reintroduce the *Arabian Nights* into the British drawing room, she still confronted the obstacle of her gender. Although she assumed an active role in the arbitration of pornography, she resorted to subterfuge to belie her exposure to questionable material. Her actions demonstrate the difficulties and complexities she faced as a woman who hoped to position her husband's translation as a British classic, but regulate its morals and maintain her respectability.

Although Burton endorsed his wife's edition of his *Arabian Nights* and helped spread the deception of her limited access to it, his satisfaction with its commercial failure (it sold only 457 copies over two years[54]) suggests that he resented her attempt to sanitise his translation. As he wrote, 'The public would have none of it; even innocent girlhood tossed aside the chaste volumes in utter contempt, and would not condescend to aught save the thing, the whole thing, and nothing but the thing, unexpurgated and uncastrated' (*Supplemental Nights*, 6.452). The language in which he expresses his contempt for his wife's bowdlerisation – as if to suggest that she unmans him with her censorship – is conspicuously gendered and sexualised. On other occasions, he also imagines his censor as a female with whom he engages in pitched sexual contest. Before the publication of the *Arabian Nights*, Burton often spoke of his censor as Mrs Grundy, the character from Thomas Morton's novel *Speed the Plough* (1798) who had become a popular stereotype for extreme moral rigidity in the nineteenth century.[55] On a number of occasions, Burton wrote to Payne with barefaced sexism to disparage the efforts of the ubiquitous Mrs Grundy. As he writes in one letter to Payne,

'I know her to be an arrant whore and tell her so and don't care a damn for her.'[56] In another letter, he adds that she 'may howl on her big bum to her heart's content'.[57] While imagining his wife as a kind of incarnation of Mrs Grundy, he threatened to defy her in the same way. Partly in jest, he made plans to publish 'The Black Book of the Arabian Nights', a volume that would comprise all the most offensive material from the translation that his wife had excised. In a manuscript preface to this volume, Burton writes that 'a "bowdlerised" book loses half its influence and bears the same relationship to its prototype as a castrato to a male masculant'.[58] What Burton's gendered language shows, as Mark Turner has argued, was a contemporary movement among male writers like Anthony Trollope and George Moore to masculinise literature and invest it with male libido in the face of a feminised morality.[59] Thus, as Burton disputed with his wife over the cultural presentation of the *Arabian Nights*, he demonstrated that his desire to preserve the 'barbarian' character of his translation was intimately bound up with a sense of manhood threatened by a feminised figure who represented the prudery of the nation.

Isabel Burton and Smithers also fought over the cultural representation and later circulation of the *Arabian Nights*. When Isabel Burton became Burton's literary executor after his death in 1890, she dealt with dubious publishers and booksellers attempting to capitalise on Burton's notoriety.[60] One such publisher was Smithers. James Nelson's recent study has uncovered a wealth of information about Smithers's clandestine publishing activities and his epistolary relationship to the Burtons. While best known for publishing Aubrey Beardsley, Oscar Wilde, and *The Savoy* (1896), his early publishing career revolved around the Burtons. He began corresponding with Burton after the publication of the *Arabian Nights*, to which he had subscribed. Soon, they began collaborating on upscale, scholarly, and unexpurgated translations of classical authors.[61] Smithers himself was a frequent translator of erotic works that were published with his partner and printer Harry Sidney Nichols under the guise and protection of the Erotika Biblion Society of Athens.[62] For Smithers, Burton's death confounded his publishing agenda, not only because their translations were still incomplete, but also because he found himself having to complete them with a widow whose programme was anathema to his own. In their respective roles as 'pornographer' and Catholic moralist, they were possibly the strangest bedfellows of the century. As they corresponded over a four-year period, Isabel Burton and Smithers wrangled over the sexual content and objectionable language of unexpurgated translations like *The Priapeia* (1890) and *The Carmina of Catullus* (1894), to which Burton had contributed.[63] Despite the very real danger of the Obscene Publications Act, Isabel Burton nonetheless participated in the production of these underground publications by Smithers and Nichols.[64] Her participation in the production of these clandestine translations demonstrates, as Mary Lovell's biography shows, that she was not as prudish as history has made her out to be.

The most important dispute between Smithers and Isabel Burton, however, was over the *Arabian Nights*. Smithers had already translated two imitations of the *Arabian Nights* from the French: *The Thousand and One Quarters of an Hour* (1893) and *The Transmigrations of the Mandarin Fuam-Hoam* (1894).[65] He also translated *Oriental Stories* (1893) and published it privately under the guise of the Erotika Biblion Society. This book, an English translation of *La Fleur Lascive Orientale* (1882), features an indiscriminate collection of racy oriental tales that intended to be 'a Supplement to the Editions of "The Book of the Thousand Nights and a Night"' and included a number of stories that appeared in the *Arabian Nights*.[66] Obsessed with the tales, Smithers was also eager to republish Burton's unexpurgated *Arabian Nights*. Lovell reveals that he bought the rights to the *Arabian Nights* for £3000 in 1894 in order to publish what would become the 12-volume Standard Library Edition (1894–7).[67] It was not a clandestine production, but was published by Nichols under a more respectable name than the Erotika Biblion Society – H. S. Nichols & Co. In their frustration with Isabel Burton's censorship of the other translations, Smithers and Nichols gendered the controversy by insisting that they were 'not going to have the thing [the edition of *Nights*] petticoated'.[68] To her astonishment, they deliberately ignored her revisions. They restored four-fifths of the passages that her edition excised, only omitting the rest because of Burton's promise to his initial 1000 subscribers not to publish another complete set (*Supplemental Nights*, 6.391). While Smithers claims in his Editor's Note that he omits words and passages of 'extreme grossness', he allows Burton 'greater latitude of expression' and releases it 'from the burdensome restriction of being kept under lock and key'.[69] He also restored the two final essays on 'Pederasty' and 'Pornography'. Smithers, it seems, won this struggle over the representation of *Arabian Nights*.[70] While preserving Burton's translation almost intact, yet also adapting it for wider circulation, he maintains the sexual exoticism of the translation while accommodating British legal and moral expectation – Isabel Burton excepted. As a reviewer for the *Athenaeum* writes in 1895, 'If Burton had adopted the present redaction for his original issue, a great deal of hostile criticism would have been averted.' Yet, because of the 'inherent coarseness of the Arabic', the same reviewer still cautions that any literal rendering of the *Arabian Nights* must remain under 'lock and key' in Britain.[71]

For more than a decade, the field of cultural traffic that grew around Burton's translation provoked discussion on British pornography that implicated both legitimate and illegitimate print communities. A generalised conception of a new category of obscenity – 'pornography' – emerged as Burton, his reviewers, and his editors struggled over the cultural presentation of the *Arabian Nights*. Strikingly, these debates about its pornography arose over the sexual exoticism of his translation. The focus on Arab sexuality provided an excuse to discuss sexual issues pressing to the British, but was also the reason for the translation's censorship. These debates about the sexual exoticism of the translation, ultimately underscored both a national and gendered investment in the idea of British prudery. Whether the orientalism of Burton's translation was exploited or condemned by readers, the debates illustrated a concern about the representation and perception of British sexual identity – a concern that would increasingly dwell on England's sexual shortfalls in the national and imperial context.

2 'A race of born pederasts': 'Pederasty', *The Perfumed Garden*, and *The Scented Garden*

The traffic in Arab works continued. After the success and notoriety of his *Arabian Nights*, Burton attempted other unexpurgated translations of Arabic works. More specifically, he turned to Arab erotic literature: *The Perfumed Garden* (1886), a sex manual that he later retranslated as *The Scented Garden* (1890). After apparently having exhausted his interest in Indian sexuality with his earlier translations of the *Ananga Ranga* (1883) and the *Kama Sutra* (1885), he appropriated Arabic erotica to explore foreign sexual behaviour. Unlike the *Arabian Nights*, however, his later publications were wholly clandestine. The debate over the 'pornography' of his *Arabian Nights* forced his subsequent translations back underground. No circulars were distributed to advertise these later translations. Once again, Burton was reliant on the subterfuge of the Kama Shastra Society of Benares and the safeguards of limited circulation and private subscription as the debate over the *Arabian Nights* had confirmed these later works as obscene.

Burton's translation of Arab sex manuals focused on a topic that he began to explore in the *Arabian Nights* – male pederasty. At this time, pederasty referred to sexual relations between men and did not strictly denote intergenerational sex (OED). Burton's interest in sodomitical practices endured throughout his life. In 1845, in the employ of the Indian Army, he was commissioned by Sir Charles Napier to investigate rumours about Indian male brothels in Karachi. While in disguise, Burton discovered the practices of sodomy, pederasty, and transvestism. Critics wondered how he obtained this information, and the report, as Frank McLynn argues, damaged his reputation and his advancement in the army.[72] Yet, Burton returned to the subject again in his Terminal Essay on 'Pederasty' in the *Arabian Nights*, his translation of classical pederastic poems in *The Priapeia* and *The Carmina of Catullus*, and his notes to *The Perfumed Garden* and reputedly to *The Scented Garden*. This interest has led some biographers, including Brodie and McLynn, to conclude that he was a repressed homosexual or bisexual.[73] More saliently, however, his interest created and responded to cultural interest in male sodomy and homosexual identity in Britain during the 1880s.

Contemporary scholars have largely neglected Burton's participation in early discourses on homosexuality. Jeffrey Weeks identifies John Addington

Symonds, Havelock Ellis, and Edward Carpenter[74] as the pioneering British thinkers who theorised about homosexuality before the term came into use at the end of the century. But, he overlooks Burton's intellectual contribution except to allude briefly to his Terminal Essay on 'Pederasty'.[75] Even Matt Cook's more recent study of the culture of homosexuality in London at end of the century does not give much attention to Burton in its discussion of erotic anthropology.[76] However, in 'Pederasty', *The Perfumed Garden*, and apparently in *The Scented Garden*, Burton contributed to British discourse on homosexuality by searching for sodomitical practices among the Arabs and relying on assumptions about Arab sexuality. The translation of these sex manuals was an attempt to explain and theorise homosexuality, and eventually instigated a search for what remained largely inexpressible. This textual search turned into a pilgrimage abroad for what was missing in British sexual discourse and practice.

Burton's interest in pederasty, first clearly articulated in his essay in the *Arabian Nights*, was responsive to an emerging cultural awareness in Britain that preceded the zenith of Oscar Wilde in the 1890s. At the beginning of the 1880s, underground publishers, theorists, and legislators began to approach the subject of male homosexual activity in different ways. If the Foucaul-dian thesis is true, that the sodomite evolved from an aberration to a species in the 1870s, then the 1880s, at least in Britain, set about constructing and debating this species.[77] In Britain's obscene print culture, for instance, narratives about male sodomy and male relationships were being featured more prominently. Sodomy was certainly not an unusual occurrence in British obscenity. John Cleland's *Fanny Hill* (1748–9) contains the infamous, and later expurgated, scene where Fanny watches through a peephole two men committing sodomy.[78] In nineteenth-century obscenity, acts of male sodomy also proliferate in *The Romance of Lust* (1873–6) and *My Secret Life* (*c*.1880). However, these works portray sodomy as a deviant or aberrant act within an ethos of heterosexuality.[79] Yet, by the early 1880s, fiction published by William Lazenby, began to feature sodomy. Stories preoccupied with sodomitical acts were serialised in his periodicals *The Pearl* (1878–81) and *The Cremorne* (1882),[80] but his *Sins of the Cities of the Plains, or The Recollections of a Mary-Ann* (1881) is arguably the first British work of fiction on homosexual identities and communities.[81] It contains the fictionalised recollections of Jack Saul, who was an actual male prostitute in London and who later was deposed during the 1889–1890 Cleveland Street homosexual scandal.[82] *Sins of the Cities* describes male streetwalkers in Leicester Square, Regent Street, and the Haymarket (1.7–8), the prevalence of sodomy in 'crowded homes', schools, and army (1.87), secret clubs and brothels (1.81, 1.89–90), Saul's adventures with the male transvestite couple Boulton and Park (1.96ff),[83] and the menace of blackmail (2.58). Throughout, the book also describes anal sex in unabashed detail: 'Slap my arse; bugger me; shove your prick into me as I fuck her, and you shall be well paid!' (1.76). As the book describes different male sexual relationships, from casual encounters in the street to devoted couplings, it contributes to the formation of homosexual identity, as Cook has argued in his reading of the novel.[84]

The book is also significant for the three essays that it appends at the end of the second volume: 'The Same Old Story: Arses Preferred to Cunts', 'A Short Essay on Sodomy', and 'Tribadism'. Anecdotal rather than explanatory, these essays comment on the practice of sodomy and tribadism through time and place. While the essays have comparatively little to reveal about tribadism, described as 'dogging the heels of sodomy' (2.118), they focus on the practice of sodomy in other cultures: they discuss the prevalence of sodomy in Rome, suggest 'the offence is common in France' (2.109), and refer to the medical theories on sodomy by the nineteenth-century French doctor Ambrose Tardieu (*Sins of the Cities*, 2.110–11).[85] It is likely that Burton was familiar with *Sins of the Cities*.[86] As Mendes shows, many of the works published by Lazenby emerged from the Burton-Monckton Milnes coterie, and Lazenby also did business with the obscene publisher and bookseller Edward Avery, who in turn collaborated with Burton's publishers Smithers and Nichols.[87] More importantly, however, the essays on sodomy appended to *Sins of the Cities* may have influenced Burton's own Terminal Essay on 'Pederasty'. C. Knipp suggests that Burton borrowed the idea of the Terminal Essay from Payne, but he may also have been influenced by the essays at the end of *Sins of the Cities*.[88] The tendency in these essays to search for evidence of sodomy in cultures historically and geographically distant is similar to Burton's own method of discussing the subject.

Alongside the emergence of illicit fiction on male homosexual relations, theories about male homosexual relations circulated in Britain and likely influenced Burton's essay on 'Pederasty'. Symonds was one of the earliest British cultural theorists on male love. In 1883, he privately printed ten copies of a pamphlet on Greek pederasty, *A Problem in Greek Ethics* (later republished as part of Ellis's *Sexual Inversion* [1897]). In his pamphlet, he described the practice of pederasty among the ancient Greeks. Through historical and cross-cultural comparison, he defended what he here calls the 'vice' (and later identifies as the 'passion' and 'inverted sexual instinct' in *A Problem in Modern Ethics*).[89] It is this same method – what Symonds later identifies as the 'historical, anthropological approach'[90] – that Burton would adopt with his translations. This cultural justification of sodomy and homosexuality was distinct from the competing medical and psychological discourses on the subject that prevailed over the next few decades in Europe. Symonds's and Burton's similar approach to the subject may be explained by their contact through The Athenaeum Club and their epistolary relationship.[91] On 3 October 1885, Symonds wrote to the *Academy* to defend the first volume of Burton's *Arabian Nights* against charges of pornography and castigated English hypocrisy about the literature it deems offensive.[92] Soon after, on 24 October, he wrote Burton to introduce himself and draw attention to his letter to the *Academy*.[93] Because the tenth volume of the *Arabian Nights* that contains Burton's essay on 'Pederasty' was not issued until early January 1887, Symonds's contact may have influenced Burton's thinking on pederasty. There is no evidence that Burton read his pamphlet on Greek homosexuality prior to 1890 when he was sent a copy; however, Symonds interest in homosexuality was relatively well known by the 1880s. According to Hyde, Swinburne referred to him as 'Soddington Symonds'. Phyllis Grosskurth's biography of Symonds also shows that Edmond Gosse and Henry James exchanged letters in which they speculated about Symonds's innermost 'discomfort'.[94]

While homosexuality became the subject of obscenity and theory in the 1880s, it also became the subject of legal discourse. In 1885, the Labouchère Amendment of the Criminal Law Amendments Act modified English law against sexual relations between men.[95] The Amendment was named after Henry Labouchère, the MP who introduced the clause into the Bill. English law against sodomy was already relaxed in 1861, when the Offences Against the Person Act removed the death penalty and instead made sodomy punishable by ten years to life imprisonment. The Labouchère Amendment relaxed the law even further by reducing the offence to a 'misdemeanour' that was punishable for up to two years with hard labour. However, the Labouchère Amendment was different from previous law, as Weeks has pointed out, because it criminalised all homosexual activity, both public and private.[96] On 1 March 1890, the *Times* reported the Parliamentary debates on the Cleveland Street Scandal (which involved telegraph boys and prominent peers such as Lord Arthur Somerset). During this debate, Labouchère explained that he proposed his amendment in 1885 because 'Mr. Stead sent him a report with reference to the practice of the offence, giving particulars and evidence which went to show the extent of its prevalence.'[97] Stead, whose newspaper the *Pall Mall Gazette* initiated the public furore over the 'pornography' of the *Arabian Nights*, once again adopted the role of British sexual crusader. Because of the lack of earlier documentary evidence, F. B. Smith rejects as spurious Labouchère's claim that Stead's report instigated his support of the Bill.[98] However, in Burton's section 'Reviewers Reviewed' appended to the sixth volume of his *Supplementary Nights* which appeared in 1888, he reveals that Stead suppressed his intended article 'denouncing London as the headquarters of a certain sin named from Sodom' because of the public furore over his 'Modern Babylon' revelations (*Supplementary Nights*, 6. 400–1). Burton's note provides the early documentary support that Smith felt was lacking from Labouchère's 1890 statement.[99] More importantly, Burton shows that he possessed an insider's knowledge about contemporary issues relating to male same-sex relations. If nothing else, connections among Labouchère, Stead, Burton, Symonds, and Lazenby reveal a loose network of men preoccupied with male same-sex practices, demonstrating the growing cultural awareness about homosexuality from which Burton's essay on 'Pederasty' appeared.

Burton contributed to the contemporary discourse on homosexuality by searching and translating Arab texts for evidence of the practice. His essay on 'Pederasty' devotes 50 pages to the subject although there are only four homosexual episodes in the *Arabian Nights*. The essay's relationship to the translation is parasitical: it relies on it as a host to nourish its ideas, but meanwhile compromises the integrity of the translation. Yet, this parasitical relationship is revealing because it demonstrates the extent to which Burton depended on assumptions about Arab sexuality to elucidate his theory of pederasty. From the early nineteenth century, the English believed that Arabs were notorious sodomites. As the author of *The Phoenix of Sodom* (1813) argued,

> The Arabs, indeed, make very light of the offence, especially when committed with a beast; the Mahometans, also, are much addicted to the crime (at least by the testimony by some travellers).[100]

Burton's essay does not situate the practice strictly among the Arabs, but offers a cross-cultural and diachronic history of its origins. It introduces a theory of the 'Sotadic Zone of Vice', after the Greek poet Sotades who wrote about male desire. In this essay, he suggests that pederasty is geographically rather than racially determined. According to Burton, those countries that fall within this zone are more susceptible to the 'vice'. The Sotadic Zone includes the Mediterranean countries, the Middle and Far East, and the South Seas and the New World, but does not include the North or the South ('Pederasty', 10.207). While beginning with the Greeks, he extends his historical survey of pederasty to the Romans, the Moors, Egyptians, Turks, and so forth. Outside the Sotadic Zone, he argues that the 'vice' is subject to 'periodical outbreaks', but not 'endemic' in cities like London, Berlin, and Paris (10.247). Although his essay putatively explores pederasty as it has historically manifested itself in the 'Sotadic Zone', the assumption that the Arabs and Persians are the most inveterate sodomites underpins his thinking. As Burton explains, Egypt is 'that classical region of all abominations' (10.224) and Syria and Palestine are 'another ancient focus of abominations' (10.225), while the Turks are 'a race of born pederasts' (10.232); and 'the corruption is now bred in the bone' among Persians (10.233). Moreover, he suggests that pederasty originated initially in the Middle East. Although he begins with a discussion of the practice among the ancient Greeks, he suggests that they adopted it from the Egyptians and Persians as they 'invented nothing, but were great improvers of what other races invented' (10.211).

Burton's essay reveals a wealth of learning about pederasty, garnered from his readings of Herodotus, Suetonius, Tardieu, and Walt Whitman, that not only demonstrates how his contemporaries may have spoken and learned about a forbidden sexuality, but also legitimises pederasty by describing its rich history. Yet his historically founded theory of pederasty ultimately depends on its relation to Arab sexuality insofar as it is appended to the translation of the *Arabian Nights* and assumes that the Arab peoples proliferated pederasty through cultural and imperial influence. Meanwhile, the essay distances the practice of pederasty from the major European centres by suggesting that it is 'sporadic' ('Pederasty', 10.246). In effect, Burton's essay explores a sexual practice irrelevant to the Arabic text to which it is attached, but denies its own investment in the subject by displacing the sexual deviance onto the Arabs. As Kennedy briefly observes, the essay 'allowed his readers to maintain some psychic distance from pederasty by presenting it as an oriental phenomenon'.[101] This rhetorical displacement of pederasty from the English onto the Arab generally characterises Burton's method of appropriating Arab texts through translation in order to discuss sexual issues that preoccupied the English toward the end of the century.

Burton's essay on 'Pederasty' contributes to the nineteenth-century discourse on homosexuality by uncovering its cultural history. However, the history he constructs is suspect. Knipp, casting doubt on 'the authenticity of the strange and supposedly first-hand observations of eastern sexual practices', observes that the essay is 'an interesting piece of Victorian pornography' that probably reflects 'Burton's own fantasies and extrapolations'.[102] In other words, his essay is as much of a survey as a fantasy: it turns to Arab sexuality not only to study the history of pederasty, but also to indulge in homosexual fantasy. Although the descriptions of homosexual signals in the Roman public baths ('Pederasty', 10.219) or Chinese benwa balls are explanatory (10.238), the accounts of Arab pederasty are anecdotal compositions given to fantasising. As McLynn suggests, sadomasochism and fantasies of homosexual rape seem to pervade Burton's following account of the Persian harem:[103]

A favourite Persian punishment for strangers caught in the Harem or Gynaeceum is to strip and throw them and expose them to the embraces of the grooms and Negro slaves. I once asked a Shrirazi how penetration was possible if the patient resisted with all the force of the sphincter muscle: he smiled and said. 'Ah, we Persians know a trick to get over that; we apply a sharpened tent-peg to the crupper-bone (os coccyges) and knock till he opens.'

('Pederasty', 10.235)

The suggestive language ('strip', 'throw', and 'expose') and the appearance of the Negro slave evokes the Victorian harem fantasy, but transformed by homosexual desire. The essay continues its discussion of Arab pederasty by alluding to the European men victimised by it, such as the missionary who was raped by the Persian Prince-governor and the 'European youngsters' in the Bombay Marine sodomised by an Arab after having been plied with liquor (10.235). As a whole, the description of Arab pederasty revolves around the violent sexual subjugation of European men by Arab men. Whether or not the historicity of Burton's account of Arab pederasty can be confirmed, the section reveals a preoccupation with homosexual rape that intimates an underlying British fantasy around the sexual perversion of the Arab male and relative sexual vulnerability of the European male. The essay appropri- ates an Arab text and exploits Arab sexuality not only to explore forbidden sexual topics in Britain, but also to construct fantasies around a comprom- ised European male sexuality. It inverts the harem fantasy that typically imagines Arab men as effeminate sodomites and European men as virile and masterful. His Orient allows for a 'giving up' of sexual control that contra- dicts Edward Said's suggestion that the Orient was always depicted as exploit- atively rapacious.[104] Although Burton adopted an aggressively masculine erotics to combat a feminised Grundyism, he also fantasised about a vuler- able and violated masculine sexuality that could be experienced among the Arabs. This masochistic male fantasy, as we shall see, recurs among later travellers to Arab countries, particularly Aleister Crowley and T. E. Lawrence.

Soon after his Terminal Essay on 'Pederasty', to which there was no immediate contemporary response, Burton translated another Arab text into English in order to explore homosexual practices. Robson and Kerslake, publishers and booksellers in London who dealt in underground obscenity, brought to Burton's attention the French translation of *The Perfumed Garden of the Sheik Nefzaoui or, The Arab Art of Love*.[105] In 1886, Burton privately printed two editions of this sixteenth-century Arabic sex manual from Algiers or Tunis. Burton's English translation was not from the Arabic original, but rather from Isidore Liseux's 1886 revised edition of the 1876 illus- trated French Autograph Edition *Le Jardin Parfumé*, which in turn was a new edition of an 1850 French translation by a staff officer of the French army in Algeria.[106] These French editions were clandestine productions, privately printed in small numbers (35 copies of the 1876 edition and 220 copies of 1886 edition). *The Perfumed Garden* is a manual on heterosexual sex and, therefore, far more sexually explicit than the *Arabian Nights*. McLynn argues that this is Burton's most 'pornographic' publication. As he writes, it reveals 'the usual Islamic suspicion of women, the same sort of morbid fear of female lustfulness that is found in the *Arabian Nights*, and the work is "phallocratic" in the true sense.' While McLynn's ahistorical argument about Islamic sexism is problematic, he is right to conclude that the book is a misogynous, 'men only' production.[107] The manual preoccupies itself with disciplining male sexuality by cautioning men about the dangers of heterosexual coitus and instilling apprehensiveness about female sexuality. It teaches that vaginal fluid is potentially noxious to the penis,[108] insists that coitus with old women acts as a 'fatal poison' (*The Perfumed Garden*, 107), and also alerts the reader about female lustfulness and treachery (114; 174), even narrating a story about a woman's bestial passion for an ass (182). However, the importance of Burton's translation of *The Perfumed Garden* to the history of nineteenth-century British obscenity lies in its annotative discussion of anal sex. In *The Perfumed Garden*, as in the *Arabian Nights*, the focus on this subject in the critical apparatus seems disproportionate to its presence in the original work. Burton's decision to concentrate on anal sex in a dominantly heterosexual Arab sex manual, but not in the Indian sex manuals, suggests his assumption that Arabs were born pederasts. In these translations, Burton resumed his discussion of homosexuality as part of an imperialist struggle among the English and the French translators over the presentation and interpretation of Arab erotica and sexuality.

In Burton's editions of *The Perfumed Garden*, he acts as an English observer as he translates and reproduces the conversation between the two French editions of the text on the subject of anal sex. Along with his own introductory note and annotations, Burton preserves the prefatory material and notes of both the 1850 and 1876 French editions in his English translation. First of all, he includes the Foreword to the 1850 edition by the French Army Staff Officer that begins the conversation about anal sex. In this Foreword, the French Officer laments its omission from the text:

> It is only to be regretted that this work, so complete in many respects, is defective in so far as it makes no mention of a custom too common with the Arabs not to deserve particular attention. I speak of the taste so universal with the old Greeks and Romans namely, the preference they give to the boy before a woman, and even to treat the latter as a boy.
>
> (Foreword, *The Perfumed Garden*, viii)

Because he presupposes the Arab male's preference for boys, the translator is surprised not to discover it in the text. He is also disappointed not to unearth discussions of tribadism, bestiality, cunnilingus, or fellatio. Unable to accept that these omissions are arbitrary, he suggests that they conceal Arab shame (xiv). In truth, he reveals more about French perceptions of sexual deviance than Arab. At the end of Burton's translation of *The Perfumed Garden* is the Appendix of the 1876 French Autograph Edition that claims to have discovered a final twenty-first chapter on tribadism and pederasty in another Arabic manuscript that contains the material that the first translator felt was omitted (251). Like the previous edition, this one also suggests that it is Arab 'bashfulness' (251) that forces the author to reserve this chapter until the end without any previous allusion:

> See! An Arab, who practises in secret paederasty, affects in public rigid and austere matters, while he discusses without restraint in his conversation everything that concerns the natural coitus.
>
> (Appendix, *The Perfumed Garden*, 252)

Yet, despite the apparent discovery of this astounding twenty-first chapter, the translators do not unveil 'the treasures concealed in the twenty-first chapter' because of space constraints (252). That they admit to having discovered a cache of Arabian sexual teachings, but refrain from printing it is highly suspect. Despite later claims, no one has yet to locate the kind of chapter that they describe, a fact that suggests that in the quest of the underground French publishers to locate 'secret paederasty' in Arabic texts they resorted to fabricating a new publishing history.[109] Ultimately, the French publishers bequeathed the treasures of the twenty-first chapter to posterity, instigating the search for the complete, unadulterated text of *The Perfumed Garden.* 'To the Arabophile who would wish to produce a better translation the way is left open; and in perfecting the work he is free to uncover the unknown beauties of the twenty-first chapter to his admiring contemporaries' (256). Burton took up this challenge – not in *The Perfumed Garden,* where he simply retranslates Liseux's edition, but in his later version *The Scented Garden.* He embarked on a quest that took him to the French Algiers and Tunis in order to produce an English translation that would contain the missing twenty-first chapter.

Between 1888 and 1890, Burton was also collaborating with Smithers on translations of classical pederastic poetry, *The Priapeia* and *The Carmina of Catullus*. Yet, while he engaged in the more dominant Victorian discourse on homosexuality that revolved around classical works, he was primarily interested in discovering its practice in Arab texts. According to Wright, he became preoccupied with the missing twenty-first chapter of *The Perfumed Garden,* reputed to be 500 pages of Arabic.[110] Lovell shows that he wrote to Liseux in 1887 in hope of discovering the translator of the autograph edition – the one who first referred to the missing chapter. Unable to find information in Europe, he then travelled to Algiers and Tunis in 1889 in order to locate the original manuscript and in anticipation of plundering its sodomitical passages. He visited the Algiers Bibliothèque Musée as well as bazaars and bookshops in both cities, but never located the chapter.[111] He compensated for its absence by supplying the references to sodomy from other sources in a later version of the work that he planned to call *The Scented Garden.* Unlike his lightly annotated first translation, this one was to be a direct translation of the Algiers manuscript with full scholarly apparatus; it was similar to the *Arabian Nights* in character, even sharing the same subscribers. His translation of *The Scented Garden,* had it survived, would have consisted of 882 pages of text and footnotes, 100-page preface, 200-page treatise on homosexuality, and another 100 pages of excursus for a total of 1282 pages.[112] The treatise on what he called 'the third sex' was apparently a direct translation of the German sexological works of Numa Numantius (Karl Ulrichs), an important early theorist of congenital homosexuality introduced to him by Symonds.[113] Burton's pilgrimage for the missing chapter reveals a profound belief in Arab knowledge about homosexuality, but it also demonstrates how nineteenth-century publishers of obscenity indiscriminately exploited and reinvented Arab sexuality in order to discuss this emergent interest.

Burton seized *The Scented Garden* from the Arabs in order to discuss sodomy, but he also confiscated the text from the French who had first discovered and translated it. Thus, his translation could be best described as an act of double appropriation. His discussion of anal sex not only revolves around assumptions about Arab sexuality, but also around British competition with the French over knowledge and control of this sexuality. While this textual struggle over the 'best translation' between Burton and the French has mundane, economic motives, it is also a textual extension of the rivalry between Britain and France over political influence and power in North Africa and the Mediterranean in the 1880s. While France occupied Algeria since 1830, control of Tunisia vacillated between the French and the British until 1881 when France finally made it a protectorate as a strategic response to Britain's occupation of Cyprus in the late 1870s. The imperial contest between Britain and France coupled with Burton's longstanding contempt for French rule in Northern Africa[114] suggest that his trip to the sites of French imperial rule for the complete manuscript of *The Scented Garden* not only incorporated a desire to stimulate British discourse on homosexuality, but also to wrest this discourse from the French. Burton's translation of Liseux's *The Perfumed Garden* began with a conversation between two French translators. This conversation subsequently instigated his trip to Northern Africa, and resulted in his translation of *The Scented Garden*. The history of this text's redaction shows how the English translation appropriated the Arabic text from the French, but also reveals the imperial politics that subtly underlay this struggle to control the orientalist discourse of homosexuality.

Burton's essay on 'Pederasty' and his later translations of Arab sex manuals galvanised British discourse on homosexuality for the next two decades. Because of the especially sensitive subject matter, however, it did not provoke the same furore that emerged over the first few volumes of the *Arabian Nights*. The varied cultural reactions included programmes to destroy and suppress Burton's work, underground attempts to reproduce it, and efforts to cite and imitate it.

The effort to censor and destroy Burton's translations of Arab erotica began almost as soon as he died in 1890. After his death, his cultural scripters and biographers attempted to expunge his interest in male same-sex desire from the historical chronicle. As her husband's executor, Isabel Burton censored and burned much of his unpublished material on pederasty. She forced Smithers to abandon the more elaborate second edition of *The Priapeia*, which he had first published in 1888, but had later begun revising with Burton's collaboration. The manuscript of the abandoned edition of *The Priapeia*, promised 'long excursions into pederasty of either sex, bestiality, masturbation, the cunnilingus',[115] but Isabel Burton deemed it unacceptable and forced Smithers to have a tamer version privately published in Cosmopoli in 1890 without acknowledgement of Burton's contribution. As for *The Carmina of Catullus*, to which Burton's name is appended, Isabel Burton refused to show Smithers the original manuscript and instead provided him with her heavily edited version. Correspondence between the two shows wrangling over the use of 'pedicate' instead of 'sodomize'.[116] In his Introduction to the translation, Smithers suggests that the lacunae in the text were her attempts at censorship.[117]

Isabel Burton found *The Scented Garden* particularly offensive and burnt the nearly completed manuscript. In a melodramatic letter to the *Morning Post* on 19 January 1891, she publicly confessed to burning the manuscript:

> My husband has been collecting for 14 years information and materials on a certain subject. [. . .] He then gave himself up entirely to the writing of this book, which was called *The Scented Garden*, a translation from the Arabic. It treated of a certain passion. Do not let anyone suppose that Richard Burton ever wrote a thing from the impure point of view [. . .] I remained for three days in a state of perfect torture as to what I ought to do about it [. . .] I said to myself 'out of 2,000 men, 14 will probably read it in the spirit of science in which it was written; the other 1,485 will read it for filth's sake, and pass it to their friends, and the harm done will be incalculable' [. . .] It would, by degrees, descend amongst the populace of Holywell Street.[118]

As she reveals that the work was primarily concerned with a 'certain passion', she admits to having destroyed the manuscript in order to protect the public and safeguard her husband's name from possible moral turpitude. She undermines her earlier comments about the book's address to the orientalist scholar by suggesting here that its real appeal is to publishers and consumers of obscenity. Yet, she was ultimately motivated by personal reasons to destroy the manuscript. First, as both Brodie and McLynn observe, she was anxious about what her husband's preoccupation suggested about his own sexuality.[119] She reveals this unease in a letter to Smithers: 'I wish you would counsel me on one point. Why did he wish the subject of unnatural crime to be so aired and expounded? He had such an unbounded contempt for the Vice and its Votaries.'[120] Her other reason for burning the manuscript developed from a need to emphasise her role in his literary career. She regarded herself as Burton's literary collaborator in her post as accountant and publicist. His interest in same-sex desire and practices, however, disrupted the fiction of their literary domesticity. By eradicating this interest to which she could not respectably subscribe, she could reintroduce herself as his literary partner and emphasise her participation in his career as a man of letters. At the end of her biography, after she discusses his last days working on *The Scented Garden*, she describes how his attention shifts away from his pet subject to their partnership. As he was engaged on the last page of his manuscript, she makes sure to cite him abandoning his interest in the 'passion' in favour of a literary project that includes her: 'To-morrow I shall have finished this, and I promise you that I will never write another book on this subject. I will take to our biography.'[121]

It is ironic, of course, that Isabel Burton's letter to the *Morning Post* had the opposite effect than she intended: she created controversy over the burning and elicited interest in the subject of *The Scented Garden*. After her confession, letters to the *Morning Post* denounced her act of destruction. She also regularly received anonymous and obscene letters harassing her on the subject.[122] Georgina Stisted, Burton's niece, was one of the many to repudiate Isabel Burton's actions. The controversy over the burning did not entirely focus on her desecration of his manuscript, but rather on the way in which her public confession damaged his reputation. Stisted especially shared Isabel Burton's desire to suppress the homosexual content of Burton's writing, but felt that such censorship should have been exercised privately. As Stisted writes in her biography, Isabel Burton advertised Burton's interest in a forbidden sexuality 'when she should have veiled it in absolute silence'.[123] In their different ways, whether censorship or silence, both women wanted to suppress evidence of Burton's interest in the unspeakable crime in order to protect him from future calumny. Despite their attempts to suppress the matter, they unwittingly made Burton into one of the homosexual insignias of the late nineteenth century.

Isabel Burton's concern about *The Scented Garden* falling into the hands of Holywell was figuratively, if not literally, justified. As we have already seen, underground publishers of obscenity, like Smithers, immediately moved to capitalise on Burton's notoriety after his death. They were especially interested in his translations of Arab works that focused on male same-sex desire. Lovell's biography shows how a struggle ensued over *The Scented Garden* between Isabel Burton and a group of opportunistic, amateur publishers after Burton's death. While Smithers offered her £3000 for the manuscript, another bid was made for £6000. Even after news of the burning was circulated, a story circulated that the manuscript remained intact. Isabel Burton also discovered a packet of letters that revealed a scam among Burton's friends to publish a new version of *The Scented Garden* as Burton's work. Isabel Burton, realising that this work would probably reach the 'Great Uneducated' rather than the scholar, had her solicitors monitor the shops of pornographic booksellers. Those involved in this scheme intended to print 2000 copies of a fully illustrated edition based on the old 1886 version of *The*

Perfumed Garden Peter Jones, one of the men involved in this scheme, wrote a letter to Smithers that intimated his intent to exploit Burton's interest in homosexuality:

> Of course it would not be an impossible task to bring it out. Its style was that of the *Nights* and that can be imitated, and the notes are the same. What might prove even more interesting can be a preface with the story of the conversion two hours after death, and many other interesting details . . . .

In an illustration of his overarching interest in the homosexual content of Burton's work, Jones even followed Burton's footsteps by visiting Tunis and Algiers in search of the missing chapter.[124] Jones and his co-schemers thus followed Burton's programme of appropriating Arab erotica with the belief that homosexual practices defined Arab sexuality. Even though this sham translation of *The Scented Garden* was never released, its fomenters adopted and perpetuated Burton's orientalist discourse of homosexuality.

Burton's influence on British homosexual discourse spread and was not limited to *The Scented Garden*. In Symonds's second study of homosexuality, *A Problem in Modern Ethics* (1891), he surveys modern European thought on the subject, citing Burton's essay on 'Pederasty' as one of his authorities. He argues against Burton that homosexuality is social rather than climatic, but also emphasises that Burton's knowledge of inversion was incomplete because it 'was principally confined to Oriental nations'.[125] In a letter to Havelock Ellis in 1892, Symonds again acknowledges Burton as one of the day's primary theorists on homosexuality only to disparage his ignorance:

> The ignorance of men like Casper-Liman, Tardieu, Carlier, Taxil, Moreau, Tarnowsky, Krafft-Ebing, Richard Burton is incalculable, and is only equalled to their presumption. They not only do not know ancient Greece, but they do not know their own cousins and club-mates.[126]

Yet others still continued to be influenced by Burton's study of homosexuality through cultural and textual reference to the Arabs. Carpenter, best known for his treatise *The Intermediate Sex* (1908), also viewed Burton as an authority on the subject of homosexuality and adopted his strategy of justifying homosexuality through cross-cultural comparison. In his *Intermediate Types among Primitive Folk* (1914), he regularly cites Burton's essay on 'Pederasty'[127] and approaches the study of 'sexual inversion' by examining its presence in ancient Greek *and* Arab cultures. In 1910, Aleister Crowley translated and had privately published the Persian text *The Scented Garden of Abdullah*. Crowley indicates that his interest in these pederastic love poems began with his assumption that it was the 'sacred and secret' book that Burton's wife burnt.[128] Moreover, his inclusion of an introductory essay

'On Pederasty' (apparently authored by Rev. P. D. Carey) borrows its title from Burton's essay and even links him to contemporaneous theorists of homosexuality, such as Richard von Krafft-Ebing, Ellis, and Ulrichs (23). While vigorously defending the practice of anal sex, the essayist writes, 'I tell thee, man, that the first kiss of man to man is more than the most elaborately manipulated orgasm that the most accomplished and most passionate courtesan can devise' (27). He also makes a biological argument for sexual preference by suggesting that a sodomite is 'born, not made' (30). In the late nineteenth and early twentieth century, then, Burton's essay and translations stimulated British discourse about homosexuality around Arab sexuality while also providing a way of speaking about the subject by displacing the practice onto another culture and concealing its study under the guise of orientalism and anthropology.

Burton's influence on British homosexual discourse through his translations of Arab texts and commentary on Arab sexuality not only inspired their print traffic, but also influenced nineteenth-century sex traffic. In noting that 'the Orient was a place where one could look for sexual experience unobtainable in Europe', Said lists a series of writers and travellers who partook of this quest, particularly Gustave Flaubert.[129] Burton, however, motivated a particular homosexual quest to North Africa. His search in Algiers and Tunis for the missing chapter on sodomy, repeated by Jones, contributed to the international coterie of wealthy homosexuals who travelled to North Africa. Burton's underground translations served as sexual guidebooks, not only migrating and transforming the Arab text to accommodate the English armchair sexual adventurer, but even inciting migration among wealthier readers to the presumed source of sexual deviance and fulfilment as well as the birthplace of European homosexual identity.

Under French colonial administration, Algiers and the surrounding areas became a popular winter resort for affluent and convalescent Europeans. It was easily accessible by steamer, featured all the amenities of home (telegraph lines, British newspapers, clubs, churches), and offered exotic appeal. Numerous guidebooks published toward the end of the century encouraged and directed such travel. George W. Harris's *'The' Practical Guide to Algiers* (1890) even inserts an epistolary preface by Isabel Burton endorsing the guidebook, an inclusion that shows the influence of the Burton's over late nineteenth-century English travel.[130] Burton was likely indirectly behind the infamous encounter between Oscar Wilde and André Gide in Algiers in 1895. In *Si le Grain ne Meurt* (1920), Gide recounts his homosexual exploits in Algiers and Tunis, along with those of Wilde and Lord Alfred Douglas.[131] In Blidah, not far from Algiers, Gide and Wilde met by happenstance at the Grand Hôtel d'Orient; a few days later, they also met in Algiers. As Gide recounts, he disclosed his homosexuality for the first time to Wilde in Algiers. In revealing how Wilde regularly used guides to lead him to Arab boys for sex, he describes how on this occasion Wilde arranged for two

Arab boys to return to their rooms. Gide boasts how he subsequently had sex with a young musician named Mohammed five times in the night. As Jonathan Dollimore explains, 'Gide's experience in Africa is one of the most significant modern narratives of homosexual liberation' for he feels free to express his desire.[132] For Gide, his trip abroad to Algiers entails more than the availability of the Arab boys or the permissiveness of colonial culture: it is preoccupied with the freedom of sexual expression and alternative identity. Burton's assumptions about the prevalence of sodomy among the Arabs influenced this winter migration of European homosexuals to Algeria that culminated in this significant meeting between Wilde and Gide. Such homosexual migrations also continued well into the early twentieth century. In 1909, Aleister Crowley, profoundly influenced by Burton, visited Algeria in order to perform sex magic that involved homosexual rituals, which he described as 'consuming every particle of [his] personality'. Crowley did not visit the Orient for its sexual opportunities, but to shatter and reinvent his sexual identity. As Alex Owen writes, 'if there was a subtext for Crowley's North African adventure, [. . .] it was the life and work of [. . .] Burton.'[133] I would stress, however, that this relationship was textual, not subtextual: the product of a dynamic, if underground, obscene print culture. As Kaja Silverman has discussed, T. E. Lawrence's homosexual exploits in the Middle East were also influenced by the cultural association between homosexuality and Arabia that was theorised by his predecessor, Burton. Like Burton's rape fantasies and Crowley's masochistic sex magic, Lawrence sought homosexual abjection in the Arab countries where he travelled.[134]

In North Africa, travellers discovered what was missing and underground in British sexual life and discourse. The circulation history of Burton's translations of Arab sex manuals fulfilled a sexual longing in British culture by displacing it onto Arab culture, but constructed theoretical models and experiential practices to accommodate a deviant, reviled, and undeveloped sexuality. Said may be right to conclude that the European study of the Orient is irretrievably self-reflexive,[135] but, in terms of the Burton phenomenon, such study is less impressive for its demonstration of European superiority than for its expression of Englishmen's sexual longing and shortfall.

3 Collecting British obscenity: *Marriage – Love and Woman Amongst the Arabs* and *The Old Man Young Again*

So far I have suggested that Burton's *Arabian Nights* and his two versions of *The Perfumed Garden* were cultural magnets for early discussions on pornography and homosexuality. Another discourse also developed around the circulation of Burton's translations of Arab literature. A small group of readers and publishers promoted the collection of Burton's translations and their legacy of sequels. In so doing, they attempted desperately to compensate for what was perceived as a dilapidated British sexuality and a denigrated erotic literary tradition. Like the earlier discourses on pornography and homosexuality, however, this one also relied on Arab works for its expression.

Later publishers of Burton's translations marketed his books in sumptuous, limited editions as rare collectors' items. After Burton's death, Smithers vied for the publication of the Library Edition of the *Arabian Nights* in order to replace Bernard Quaritch as London's chief antiquarian bookseller and publisher. According to Nelson, one of Smithers's contemporaries explained that the publisher's main ambition 'to push Quaritch from his throne in the Antiquarian Book World' as specialist in oriental literature and as Burton's sometime publisher.[136] Quaritch, a prosperous bookseller and publisher in the mid-nineteenth century who dominated the rare books trade in Europe until the 1880s, also trafficked Burton's translations abroad. A memo from 13 September 1897 from Madras customs reports the confiscation of Quaritch's editions which had been imported by Messrs Higginsbotham & Co., a firm of booksellers and publishers in Madras:

> The Madras customs authorities have confiscated, on the ground that they are obscene, three books (the Kama Sutra, The Perfumed Garden, & Ananga Ranga) which were being imported by Messrs. Higginsbotham & Co. The latter appealed, but the Board of Revenue and the Madras Govt. supported the Collector's decision. In support of their contention that the works were unobjectionable Messrs. H. produced a letter from Mr. Quaritch (who had supplied them) stating that they are freely circulated in his country. The Govt. of Madras now send the papers home, thinking that the S. of S. may wish to lay the matter before the Home Office.

Messrs Higginsbotham responded to this seizure by writing a letter to the Collector of Sea Customs, defending these books on the grounds of their aesthetic value and specialty market:

> We have been importing these high class Aesthetic works at various intervals [...] but the Aesthetic books you have denounced as 'Obscene' are not intended for the ordinary reader, and much less for the multitude. They are special works of a scientific character, written for scientific and learned men, and whose price is far above the means of the general reader, and yet useful to specialists in such subjects as Physiology, Anatomy, and other medical topics. We may mention that these books have always been procured to special order, for use of the native Nobility and the Rajahs in this Presidency, and not for sale, which fact will serve as a guarantee that there was nothing objectionable in the supply of such books to persons of rank and position in the country.

The British Home Office may not have accepted the argument that these translations had aesthetic value, but it did not believe that they were worth prosecuting at home or abroad on account of their limited circulation. But, a letter from the Home Office on 18 October 1897 left the matter up to the Indian government:

> The Metropolitan Police, so far as is known, have not interfered with the sale of the books you forwarded, on the ground – not that they are anything but obscene – but that judging from the price charged and the general price of them they are not likely to have a wide sale, nor consequently to do much harm, especially as it is not probable that they will fall into the hands of young people. This policy has been approved by the Secretary of State in other similar cases.
>
> It is not known whether other Police forces have interfered, but if it is true that these books 'circulate freely' in England it is probable that it is true only because the circulation is small. I do not think that the fact – if it is a fact – that the books have not been suppressed as obscene in England, need in any way embarrass the Indian Government in dealing with them. There is no doubt that their obscenity would be recognised by English courts if the occasion arose.[137]

The idea that these translations were special, collector's items was so persuasive that it not only squashed serious judicial intervention, but it also circulated to print communities in the colonies.

The Grolier Society similarly issued sumptuous editions of Burton's works. In the numerous prospectuses for an illustrated edition of Burton's *Arabian Nights*, the Grolier Society made unashamed appeals to the book collector by describing it as a 'masterpiece which must appeal in the strongest manner to all who possess libraries or care for books'. For an enormous amount, 120 guineas, the publishers even offered the gourmand bibliophile a limited Edition de Grand Luxe of the *Arabian Nights* that was bound 'in white vellum, with red inlay, heavily tooled in gold' and came in 'a casket in polished mahogany, with handsome mouldings of darker shade' with 'plate-glass doors [. . .] overlaid with brass lattice work, hung on brass hinges, with two locks and key of Oriental design'. Apparently its bid for respectability was successful, probably because it made sure to omit the essay on 'Pederasty' from its edition. Although it came under the scrutiny of the British Home Office, it was not deemed a threat. As a memo from 19 February 1904 read: 'This is an old story: similar circulars were issued at least a year ago, so it looks as if the Grolier Society's Edition of Burton has not been a striking success. At all events it is scarcely a book to institute criminal proceedings about.'[138]

In the late 1890s, lavish translations of Arab works began to appear that were heavily influenced by Burton. Charles Carrington published two

Arab sex manuals 'Englished' for 'the first time' by an 'English Bohemian': *Marriage – Love and Woman Amongst the Arabs* (1896) and *The Old Man Young Again* (1898–9).[139] The two translations were inspired by Burton, who mentioned them in the *Arabian Nights* as erotic works distributed in pamphlet form in the East (10.200–1). While Carrington published obscenity from Paris, where he opened a bookshop in 1895 and also ran a mail-order business, he published English-language obscenity for wealthy British clientele. In his early career, as Mendes's research shows, he also had contact with others in the trade, working as a travelling agent for Avery in the late 1880s in London and also conducting business with Smithers.[140] Carrington, whose private subscription catalogues show that he specialised in the obscenity of empire, may have even been exposed to Burton's translations of Arab erotica through his contact with Smithers and his semi-erotic imitations of the *Arabian Nights* and *Oriental Stories*. Unlike Burton's translations, Carrington's translations do not presuppose their importance, but instead anxiously defend it. He justifies their worth by marketing them as status symbols for British gentlemen, by linking them to Burton, and by placing them within a history of British obscenity.

One way in which Carrington promoted the collection of his books was to market them as status symbols. He suggests the cultural cachet of his obscene publications in his catalogues and prospectuses by advertising them not only as 'curious' and 'voluptuous', but also 'rare'. In his *Catalogue of Rare Curious and Voluptuous Reading* (1896), he endorses his book, *Marriage*, not only as a 'supplement' to Burton's *Arabian Nights*, but also as a supplement to a book 'now so scarce and dear'.[141] His catalogues also emphasise the quality of the publications. In *Privately Printed Books*, a catalogue preserved in a bound volume called *Prospectuses*, Carrington suggests that his publications compete with the finest Arts and Crafts presses of the late nineteenth century: 'These works are equal in scholarship and typography to the finest productions of The Kelmscott Press, or the books issued by the Kama Sutra, or Villon, Societies.'[142] Carrington also increases the prestige of his publications by insisting on the exclusivity of his clients. Addressing 'Bibliophiles' as well as 'Scholars', he stipulates in an advertisement at the back of *Marriage* that 'Only a limited number will be issued and not sold to any, except Responsible People.'[143] For the prestige of owning such a book, Carrington also demanded a steep price. The price for *Marriage* in 1896 was four guineas, but reduced to one guinea around 1904. The price for *Old Man*, about which there remains less information, was listed at £4.55 s.[144]

The other way in which Carrington promoted his translations of Arab sex manuals was to establish their connection to Burton. Carrington's use of Burton to promote his translations signals his own participation within a larger movement among smaller British presses to publish *livres d'artistes*, but his publishing activity was a more thoroughly underground operation that attempted to control a niche market in the translations of Arab erotica. In

1902, for example, Carrington promoted *Marriage* and *Old Man* in *Forbidden Books*, an annotated listing of obscene works he had published that addresses the book collector looking for the rare item or the *edition de luxe*. Carrington endorses *Marriage* by drawing attention to its inclusion of Burton's Terminal Essay 'from the tenth volume of the original edition of his now famous and rare translation of "The Arabian Nights" '.[145] He underscores the rare and notorious excerpt from Burton's *Arabian Nights* and thus legitimises his publication on the grounds of its rarity and connection to Burton.

Like Carrington's advertisements, the translations of *Marriage* and *Old Man* also establish their connection to Burton. *Marriage*, the first work translated by the 'English Bohemian', is an anecdotal sex manual in praise of women and heterosexual copulation that is sandwiched between English explanatory notes, quotations, and essays on topics such as 'The Woman Riding' (181) and 'Oriental Rabelaisianism' (199). English excursus visually surrounds and dominates the Arab text, suggesting that it supersedes it in importance. A casual glance through the translation reveals its *modus operandi* to constitute and legitimise itself through its relation to Burton. The obsequious dedication to Burton and Payne on the title page immediately draws attention to the relationship between the Burton and Carrington translations:

> Dedicated to the memories of two of the Greatest Arabic Scholars and Linguists that England has ranked among her Sons in the Nineteenth-Century R.F.B. and E.H.P. The 'hem of whose garment' The Unworthy Translator would have been happy to touch.

The translation also borrows Burton's epigraphs to the *Arabian Nights*, quoting from Rabelais, *The Decameron*, and the Arab proverb 'To the pure all things pure'. In his Foreword, the translator also further aligns himself with Burton by suggesting that his own translation might become 'as famous as the *Perfumed Garden*' (*Marriage*, xlviii). References and extracts from Burton's *Arabian Nights* and *The Perfumed Garden* also pervade the text. His Terminal Essay on 'Pederasty' is even extracted in full under the heading 'A Bypath of Human Passion' (203). In addition to direct references to Burton, there are numerous stylistic and thematic borrowings. The prefatory notes, footnotes, and final excursus are all indebted to Burton's scholarly apparatus. The comments in his Foreword on Arab sexual frankness and British reticence recall Burton's perspective on the sexual difference of the Orient and Occident (vii). The translator's reference to Stead's 'Maiden Tribute' (x) is also a nod back to Burton's struggles with British purity movements (already a decade old by the time of his translation). Like Burton, moreover, the translator addresses British sexual hypocrisy and shortfall:

> Yet, precisely the people, who wade sedulously through the filthy columns of garbage that adorn the great English Dailies – the latest spicy

divorce suit, seduction and paternity case, revelations of the erotic tendencies of massage, or an affair of rape on girl or child, – are the first to
condemn a book issued in a limited edition to a selected circle of private
subscribers.

(*Marriage*, vii)

In obsessively imitating and referencing Burton, the translator of *Marriage*
unequivocally presents his work as the literary descendent of Burton's
obscene translations of Arab literature.

Like *Marriage, The Old Man Young Again* also attempts to establish itself
as Burton's successor. The translator quickly dismisses a previous French
translation as invalid because it 'was evidently issued for the purposes of
exciting the passions'.[146] Instead of following the French example, he models
his translation after Burton's. Stylistically, the translator imitates Burton
by once again including the kind of scholarly apparatus Burton uses in
his translations. His notes in this two-volume translation, however, are far
more opportunistic than Burton's. The first volume contains an 87-page
Foreword that includes bizarre sections on subjects like the 'Genital Dyno-
meter', an abridgement of the first part of the Arabic text on aphrodisiacs, followed by an excursus with essays on 'The Romance of the Genital
Powers', 'Aphrodisiacs, their History, Nature and Use', and 'How to Tame
Wild Coyntes'. The second volume contains the latter part of the Arab text,
The Secrets of Woman, and discusses women's sexual beauty and various
sexual postures before finishing with a series of erotic stories meant to
'arouse the passions' (120). Both volumes, with their excess of commentary,
demonstrate how the translation subordinates the Arab text to the English
commentary.

The Foreword, more specifically, reveals this tendency to ignore the Arab
text. It overlooks the history of the Arab text in order to focus on Burton, the
inspiration and guide behind his translation. Adopting Burton's justifying
rhetoric, the translator designates his intended audience as 'the student and
anthropologist' (*Old Man*, 3) and explains that the present work is not 'a
compendium of mere sensual imaginings, but rather, as Burton himself has
said, "an intelligent study of the art and mystery of satisfying the physical
woman at a certain stage and period of man's life"' (24). As in *Marriage*,
the translator repeats Burton's views on British sexual hypocrisy, noting
that the Arabs 'have none of that false, stupid, and sometimes infamous,
mock-modesty which, every now and again, renders England the laughing-
stock of the world' (25). He also joins Burton's struggle against the Obscene
Publications Act. As the Foreword alludes to the obscenity charges levelled
against Henry Vizetelly in 1888 and a bookseller who sold a copy of Havelock
Ellis's *The Psychology of Sex* in 1898 (5, 25),[147] the translator identifies himself
with Burton as men willing to defy 'the present benighted state of English
law' (5). The translator thus cultivates an ethos of indignant opposition

to British obscenity laws that aligns him with Burton and consequently confirms the value of the English translation.

The driving force behind the presentation of the Carrington translations as status symbols modelled after Burton's translations was the need to create a history of British obscenity. The publisher and translator together largely dismiss the authorship and history of the Arab texts in order to emphasise the British origins of the texts and ensconce them in the bookshelves of wealthy British collectors. The repeated references to underground British publications in the commentary on the Arab texts further suggests a desire to construct a history of British obscenity. In *Marriage*, for instance, allusions to Burton's translations predominate, but the translator also draws from other authorities to give his work empirical weight and situate it within an even larger British tradition. In so doing, the translation records a rich history of British obscenity even while it outlines England's sexual short-comings. In addition to referencing classical writers of erotica like Ovid and Catullus (*Old Man*, 9n) or harem pundits like Montesquieu (xxix), the translator also cites underground British productions: John Davenport's *An Apology for Mohammed and the Koran* (xxff) and *Curiositates Eroticae Physiologiae* (121), Burton's *The Priapeia* and *The Ananga Ranga* (181), and Ashbee's *Index Librorum Prohibitorum* (182n).[148] In effect, the translation compiles a bibliography that functions as a reference and resource guide to British obscenity – an ironic peculiarity considering that British readers are consuming Arab instructional sex manuals. The Arab sex manual becomes the footnote to the translator's commentary. Even its subscribers had diffi-culty accepting its authenticity as an Arabic text and believed it to be a British fabrication (6).

As the translator of *Old Man* aligns himself with Burton's in a sexual crusade against British sexual reticence, he also constructs a history of British sexual writing. As in *Marriage*, he establishes this history by citing various obscene and sexological works, including *The Battles of Venus* (1.14), *The Lustful Turk* (1.20), William Acton's *The Functions and Disorders of the Reproductive Organs* (1.27), and later *Randiana* (2.69n) and *Untrodden Fields of Anthropology* (2.65n).[149] The translator draws from these works to comment authoritatively on Arab sexuality and contradict assumptions about British sexual prudery. While quoting from Burton, the translator admits that Britain, sexually speaking, has a deplorable international repu-tation to the extent that 'it is said abroad that the English have the finest women in Europe and least know how to use them' (1.25); however, his translation appears to assert British sexual dominion through its ostenta-tious display of British obscenity within the Arab text. *Old Man* appro-priates the Arab text in order to highlight British sexual knowledge and obscenity. The translation thus creates an awkward tension between a parasitic reliance on Arab texts to construct a history of British obscenity around Burton and an imperious negation of the Arab sex manuals upon which the construction and definition of such a British history relies.

This making of a history in both *Marriage* and *Old Man* is not simply a marketing ploy to promote their collection by the British erotophile, but is also a defence of the vigour of Britain's sexual writing and national sexual character amid nervousness about their shortfalls. From Ashbee onward, there was a sense among publishers and collectors of continental obscenity that British prudery had derogated from the nation's sexual writing. As Ashbee argued,

> That English erotic literature should never have had its bibliographer is not difficult to understand. First and foremost the English nation possesses an ultra-squeamishness and hyper-prudery peculiar to itself, sufficient alone to deter any author of position and talent from taking in hand so tabooed a subject; and secondly, English books of that class have generally been written with so little talent, delicacy, or art. [...] The greatest name of which England can boast is John Cleland, and he is, after all, but a star of very inferior magnitude.[150]

With his obsessively detailed bibliographies, Ashbee engendered a new masculine personality in Britain's obscene print culture: the collector and bibliographer who could vie with the great French bibliographers of erotica like Jules Gay who published *Bibliographie des Ouvrages Relatifs à l'Amour* (1861).[151] In 1885, William Laird Clowes imitated Ashbee by compiling his own bibliography of obscenity with an equally lavish Latin title: *Bibliotheca Arcana Seu Catalogus Librorum Penetralium.* He too condemned British prudery for destroying the 'records' and 'monuments' of British sexual expression:

> While therefore, we rightly consign these works to the secret cabinets of our public or private museums or libraries and to the prudent care of collectors, we have to guard against the mock asceticism which would ignorantly wage truceless war against the records and monuments of national characters, passions, or depravities, as if these records were merely vulgar obscenities and unmitigated evils.[152]

As G. Legman notices, Carrington's *Forbidden Books*, where he advertises *Marriage* and *Old Man*, is not unlike Ashbee's and Lawes's bibliographic efforts to promote the collection of British obscenity.[153] Yet, through the figure of Burton, he discovers a way to construct a history of British obscenity and off-set feelings of national sexual inadequacy – albeit via the Arab text.

With his translations of Arab writings, Burton participated in discourses on pornography, homosexuality, and collection. What began with Burton's translation of the *Arabian Nights* developed into fractious cultural discourses that appropriated Arab works and the figure of Burton to explore British sexuality and confront its perceived prudery. British prudery was not a modern reconstruction of Victorian sexuality, but was rather a national self-characterisation and sometimes a hidden sexual worry explored and perpetuated through the underground traffic in Eastern sex manuals.

4
The English Vice and Transatlantic Slavery

The East was not the only exotic peregrination in Britain's clandestine print trade in the nineteenth century. The trade in obscene publications also travelled across the Atlantic Ocean for its themes and eventually its audience, following the image of the flogged slave woman. As with the erotic fixations on the oriental harems and Eastern sex manuals, the preoccupation with the history of transatlantic slavery was caught up in larger circuits of desires and different print communities. From the late eighteenth century to the mid-nineteenth century, the flogged slave woman was a ubiquitous rhetorical and visual image in Britain largely introduced by transatlantic abolitionism. The image appeared in parliamentary debates, abolitionist pamphlets and newspapers, visual arts, and slave narratives. The flogged slave man did not have the same abolitionist appeal,[1] but the image of the flogged slave woman was repeatedly reproduced for public consumption, provoking Christian compassion, abolitionist zeal, and, disturbingly, prurience. The image underwent a series of literary and visual repetitions and transformations influenced by the British libidinal investment in the whip – what Ian Gibson has called 'the English Vice'.[2] This chapter explores four historical versions of the image of the flogged slave woman which was trafficked in diverse print communities over the course of the nineteenth century and shows how a preoccupation with flagellation influenced its reception and in turn produced an underground industry that made explicit the denied sexual desires associated with it. I look at the early emergence and reception of the image among British abolitionists, its appropriation by a publisher of obscenity in the 1880s, its later appropriation by another illicit publishing ring in the 1890s, and finally its apparent disappearance by the early twentieth century. The transformations this image underwent were, to say the least, unexpected. It crossed historical periods and print communities as well as nationalities and desires. Britain's underground trade in slavery obscenity was the product of the widespread circulation of fantasies about the racialised sexual violence of slave cultures generated in mainstream, and often socially conscious, print communities of the nineteenth century.

1 The prurient gaze: the flogged slave woman among British abolitionists

Let me begin by contextualising the emergence of the image of the flogged slave woman. In the early nineteenth century, British politics and culture were preoccupied with transatlantic slavery and its ethos of violence. Statutory law abolished the slave trade in 1807 and colonial slavery by 1833. In the 1830s and 1840s, transatlantic abolitionist movements flourished, especially under the initiative of Quakers, Nonconformists, and evangelicals. In the early 1850s, Harriet Beecher Stowe's American anti-slavery novel *Uncle Tom's Cabin* enjoyed enormous commercial and popular success in Britain, both benefiting from and nourishing the British appetite for real-life American slave narratives.[3] As Audrey Fisch observes, the public spectacle of fugitive slaves, like Frederick Douglass, who would describe their personal experiences under slavery and provide proof of its atrocities by displaying their scars, was also popular among mid-Victorian audiences.[4] The British were politically neutral, but rapt observers of the American Civil War, which finally ended in 1865. At the end of the century, the British were still concerned about the persistence of slavery around the world: in parts of South America, the Ottoman Empire, and, as David Livingstone discovered, Africa. Between 1880 and 1920, roughly 124 works were published in Britain on the subject of slavery (STC).

Over the century, competing interests mottled the British perspective on slavery in the Americas. Christian humanitarianism underlay abolition campaigns. Rivalling economic investments in the East and West Indies also determined many people's stance on abolition in British colonies. Later, during the American Civil War, the British reliance on cheap cotton led many to denounce abolition as economically disruptive. However, for many, as Richard Fulton argues, the persistence of slavery in America consolidated a British sense of national superiority for having abolished it first.[5] While humanitarian and economic investments underlay public interest in transatlantic slavery, so too, in some instances, did British sexual curiosity. Karen Halttunen has shown that the humanitarian impulse made fashionable by the eighteenth-century cult of sensibility was often aroused by a 'pornography of pain'. As she argues, sentimental portraits of suffering and tortured animals, women, and slaves satisfied a sadistic spectatorship that helped shape the new erotics of cruelty in the late eighteenth-century.[6] Information about the graphic violence and corrupt sexuality of the slave system produced sympathy and disgust among many, but for some it also elicited sexual arousal and fantasy. This history developed around the circulation of images of the flogged slave woman, first introduced in abolitionist print communities.

To understand this history, one must recognise that the British sexual preoccupation with the whip indelibly underwrites it. Gibson famously described this widespread cultural investment in flagellation in *The English Vice*. In the nineteenth century, flagellation was widespread in the English home, school, army, and prison. By mid-century, with the passing of the Whipping Act of 1862[7] and escalating debate about corporal punishment, flagellation was increasingly rejected as a form of punishment. Nonetheless, corporal punishment informed Victorian men's early experiences. For many, as Lucy Bending argues in *The Representation of Bodily Pain*, it was regarded as the privilege of public-school education, where beatings tested and formed the gentleman.[8]

Historically, the association between whipping and sexual pleasure probably emerged through the combined stimulation to the genital area and public exposure of genitals and buttocks. This form of sexual pleasure undeniably emerged within all-male communities and was profoundly homoerotic, but it also explored other sexual desires and was subject to outside influence. However, theories about nineteenth-century British flagellation obscenity have inaccurately tended to homogenise it. Following Freud, Steven Marcus suggests that despite the variety of flagellation fantasies, all present 'the same unvarying idea' – that of the boy being beaten by the phallic mother who is a surrogate for the father. He argues that the fantasy blurs sexual identities as a 'last-ditch compromise with and defence against homosexuality'.[9] For Marcus, flagellation obscenity represents one of the earliest – albeit unconscious – forms of homosexual literature. Gibson concurs and argues that the fantasy represses and displaces homosexual desire.[10] While these psychoanalytic readings are important for disclosing the layers of the flagellation fantasy – in which manifest content sometimes disguises latent meaning – they ignore its historical specificities and mutations by always reading the fantasy as a homosexual one.

Flagellation literature was already in vogue in the eighteenth century as Edmund Curll was charged with obscene libel in 1727 for publishing Johann Heinrich Meibomius's *Treatise on the Use of Flogging in Venereal Affairs* . Flagellation also appeared in obscene writing as a perversion to provide *piquance* to the sexual act. Flagellation is briefly featured in John Cleland's *Fanny Hill* (1749), for instance, to demonstrate an aberrant desire.[11] Julie Peakman notes the growth of flagellation obscenity in the late eighteenth century, citing such works as *The Birchen Bouquet* (1770), *Exhibition of Female Flagellants* (1777), and *Venus Schoolmistress* (c.1808–10).[12] By the early nineteenth century, flagellation obscenity developed into a separate genre that catered to the British sexual proclivity exclusively and accumulated its own set of conventions. By the 1830s, as Iain McCalman shows, George Cannon specialised in elite, high-end flagellation obscenity, reprinting eighteenth-century works especially. Much of this literature survives and even more is recorded in Henry Spencer Ashbee's late nineteenth-century bibliography of erotica. In his bibliography, he includes a treatise on flagellation that cites obscene works on the subject. He also comments on the relationship between whipping and sexual excitement. 'It cannot be denied', he writes, 'that to some constitutions flagellation is a powerful aphrodisiac, an active inciter of sexual enjoyment.'[13]

Besides a concentration on the shape of the buttocks, flagellation obscenity focuses on the binding of the victim, his cries for mercy and writhings, the reddening and bleeding of his buttocks, the quality of the birch, and finally the reaction of the spectators.[14] While the most frequent flagellation scenario involved a strict schoolmistress (a Mrs Birch or Miss Switchem) beating a boy, there were numerous varieties: a schoolmistress beating a girl, a man beating a boy or a girl, a wife beating her husband to titillate his flagging sexuality, a girl seeking revenge on her schoolmistress, and so forth. Toward the end of the century, once flagellation was an established genre of obscenity, its sexual deviance seems to have diminished with its ubiquity. It therefore incorporated more contemporary forms of sexual deviance into the flagellation narrative such as sodomy, tribadism, transvestism, and interracial sex.[15]

Recent and controversial scholarship has shown that the British sexualised images of the flogged female slave in early abolitionist discourse and imagery because of their predisposition to flagellation and sexual violence. Mary Favret, in her essay entitled 'Flogging: The Anti-Slavery Movement Writes Pornography', argues that Romantic abolitionist rhetoric in parliamentary debates and pamphlets demonstrates a prurient fascination with the flogging of black female slaves that 'imported the difference of race into' the already existent flagellation fantasy. She suggests that descriptions of slave flogging nourished the British 'sexual investment in the whip': 'What abolitionist tactics contributed to the literature of flagellant erotica was an explicitly racialised sexuality, where black women, substituting for the usual blushing white boy, were displayed as erotic objects for the punitive desires of (usually) white men.' Although she overgeneralises about the sexual relationships found in flagellation obscenity, Favret argues provocatively that the abolitionist focus on the flogged, naked body of the slave woman was the safest and most politically effective fantasy for gentlemen to entertain: it 'prompt[ed] the men of England to recognize their power – and desire – to act', but did not unman them by encouraging an over-identification with the image of the flogged black woman.[16] One wonders, of course, what appeal such a fantasy would have had to the many British women involved in British abolition movements. Between 1839 and 1869, there were approximately 100 auxiliaries of the British and Foreign Anti-Slavery Society of London: one-third of these were female societies.[17] Favret argues that women viewers filtered the pornographic gaze. But, is it not possible that women, despite their probable gender identification with the victimised woman, were also aroused by the image's suggestion of sexual dissipation? That women sexualised the image of the flogged slave woman with their gaze is also a real possibility.

Marcus Wood's *Blind Memory*, extends Favret's thesis to the visual arts. In his discussion of British visual representations of flogging from early abolitionist movements against the slave trade to later movements to end slavery, he argues that such depictions were regularly 'contaminated by pornography'. He also makes an important point: flagellation obscenity did not flourish *until* the height of abolition.[18] The image of slave flogging 'contaminated' flagellation obscenity as much as it 'contaminated' the abolitionist image. In his discussion of sexualised representations of the flogged slave woman, Wood focuses on a copper engraving entitled 'The Flagellation of a Female Samboe Girl' by William Blake that accompanied John Stedman's *Narrative of a Five Year's Expedition Against the Revolted Negroes of Surinam* (1796).[19] He discusses how this engraving, which displays a slave woman who has been stripped and flogged, invites an erotic viewing (Plate 1):

> Staring front on at an almost naked and physically magnificent young woman, who is pushed right up against the viewer, it is hard not to become compromised. Blake seems to be inviting us to enjoy the sexual frisson elicited by such suffering beauty. [. . .] [His] image teeters on the verge of pornography in order to confront us with our own corruptibility.

Wood, like Favret, suggests that Blake demonstrates sympathy for the slave, but inflames the passions in order to elicit political action – what one might identify as an abolitionist strategy of political arousal.[20]

Wood tends to oversimplify the sexual fantasies that emerged around the image of the flogged female slave as an aggressively heterosexual one that centres on a white man's sexual domination over a black slave woman. He discusses an engraving from an 1805 version of Stedman's *Narrative*[21] that visualises the same whipping scene as depicted in Blake's engraving, but he ignores the complexities of the fantasy it suggests (Figure 10). As he notices, this image curiously whitewashes the flogged slave woman, but it also depicts the white men gazing at the half-naked black overseers. The image demonstrates how race is manipulated to construct fantasies about abased white women, but also reveals the homoerotic desire that so often underwrites British flagellation.

From the beginning, then, the image of the flogged slave woman in abolitionist print communities roused sadistic flagellation fantasies about whipping white women, fantasies that were superimposed on the homoerotics of flagellation. The fantasies that emerged around this image were layered, complex, and often incoherent, revealing the competing and confluent influences of British flagellation and transatlantic slavery in the early history of Britain's production of obscenity. The discussion of the relationship between the consumption of violent flagellation and the anti-slavery campaign can also be extended to the slave narrative. Slave narratives,

'The Barbarous Cruelty inflicted on a Negro. —— at Surinam.'

Figure 10 Anonymous, 'The Barbarous Cruelty Inflicted on a Negro', *Curious Adventures of Captain Stedman, During an Expedition to Surinam*. London: Thomas Tegg [c.1805]. By permission of the British Library, London

a later abolitionist enterprise and regular transatlantic feature in the British literary market especially after the 1830s, repeatedly displayed the image of the flogged slave woman as they focused on the atrocities and sexual violence of slavery with varying degrees of explicitness. There was a tendency among some nineteenth-century British readers to view slave narratives as racy transatlantic products. Twenty American slave narratives appeared in British editions by mid-century, many of which appeared in the most respectable of middle-class institutions, Mudie's Circulating Library.[22]

Slave narratives focused on the sexual violence of the slave system. For instance, *The History of Mary Prince: A West Indian Slave* , published in London in 1831, alluded to the sexual violence of her white master:

> He had an ugly fashion of stripping himself quite naked, and ordering me to wash him in a tub of water. This was worse to me than all the licks. Sometimes when he called to me to wash him I would not come, my eyes were so full of shame. He would then come to beat me.[23]

The Narrative of the Life of Frederick Douglass, An American Slave, Written by Himself, which appeared both in America and Britain in 1845, also alluded to sexual violence within the slave system. In graphic terms, Douglass describes how his master flogs his Aunt Hester in order to display his sexual power:

> He was a cruel man, hardened by a long life of slaveholding. He would at times seem to take great pleasure in whipping a slave. I have often been awakened at the dawn of day by the most heart-rending shrieks of an own aunt of mine, whom he used to tie up to a joist, and whip upon her naked back till she was literally covered with blood. No words, no tears, no prayers, from his gory victim, seemed to move his iron heart from its bloody purpose. The louder she screamed, the harder he whipped; and where the blood ran fastest, there he whipped longest. He would whip her to make her scream, and whip her to make her hush; and not until overcome by fatigue, would he cease to swing the blood-clotted cowskin. [. . .]

> This occurrence took place soon after I went to live with my old master, and under the following circumstances. Aunt Hester went out one night, – where or for what I do not know, – and happened to be absent when my master desired her presence. [. . .] Why master was so careful of her, may be safely left to conjecture. She was a woman of noble form, and of graceful proportions, having very few equals, and fewer superiors, in personal appearance, among the colored or white women of our neighborhood.[24]

While Douglass vividly details the violence – the method, the weapon, the screaming, and the blood – he is more circumspect about describing its sexual horrors. Instead he sexualises his aunt's body to imply her master's lust. Yet, the nineteenth-century reader, who was accustomed to coded sexuality, would not have been left guessing about Douglass's meaning. *The Narrative of William W. Brown, a Fugitive Slave, Written by Himself* (1847), first published in England in 1849, was another slave narrative that focused on sexual violence. Like many narratives, it painstakingly describes the instruments of torture. As Brown writes, 'the handle was about three feet long, with the butt-end filled with lead, and the lash six or seven feet in length, made of cowhide with platted wire on the end of it.' More suggestively than either Prince or Douglass, Brown also hints at the master's sexual abuse of slave women. In a scene reminiscent of the flogging of Aunt Hester in Douglass's narrative, Brown describes how his master beats the servant girl, Patsey, because she disobeys his sexual command:

> Mr. Colburn tied her up one evening, and whipped her until several of the boarders came out and begged him to desist. The reason of whipping her was this. She was engaged to be married to a man belonging to Major William Christy [. . .]. Mr. Colburn had forbid her to see John Christy. The reason of this was said to be the regard which he himself had for Patsey.[25]

Slave narratives featured gross acts of violence and allusions to sexuality that far surpassed other nineteenth-century genres. They were more shocking than the most daring sensation novel, but circulated freely.

Contemporary British reviews of slave narratives emphasised their violence. As Fisch notes, emphasis on violence was typical in the reviews of slave narratives. A review of Douglass's narrative from 1846 in *Chambers's Edinburgh Journal* exemplifies this interest in violence with its lengthy quotations of descriptions of flogging in the narrative.[26] Fisch argues that some journals, such as the *Anti-Slavery Advocate*, found the violence educative insofar as it revealed the cruelty of the slave system and America itself.[27] However, she also concentrates on the *Athenaeum* reviews, the middle-class journal which felt that slave narratives degraded the literary marketplace with their gratuitous depictions of violence. A review from 31 March 1855 denounced John Brown's *Slave Life in Georgia* for its 'stereotyped accounts of horrors' and 'sickening amplifications on the effect of the bull-whip and the cobbling-ladle': 'The severities of masters, incarcerations, escapes, captures, floggings, and excessive task-work, occur in one as in another, and we scarcely see how the public is to be instructed by repetitions of accounts so piteous and so harrowing.'[28] Similarly, a later review from 4 April 1857 accused the white author of the fictionalised biography *Autobiography of a Female Slave* of 'high-flown sentimentality, mixed up with ghastly and minute details of the floggings and brutalities to which slaves are represented as exposed'.[29]

Nineteenth-century reviewers and critics also commented on the corrupt sexuality depicted in slave narratives. Slave narratives provided salacious reading that resulted from the widespread verbal and visual spectacle of the flogged slave woman already introduced by abolitionists and fuelled by the erotics of flagellation. Even before the popularisation of the slave narrative in England in the 1840s, this image was sexually encoded for readers, listeners, and viewers. The *Anti-Slavery Advocate* repeatedly mentioned incidents of sexual abuse within slavery. In March 1857, for instance, it included an interview with a slave woman entitled 'A Talk with a Slave Woman' that describes the 'criminal intercourse' between a white master and a slave woman:

> Some is weak and willin', poor things; but the most on 'em is forced to it. There was Elizy. I know how Massa Tom came in, and I heard him a beatin' her; she screamed and cried, but nobody couldn't help it; And afterwards, when the pretty little thing was born, and the missus saw it, she was ready to kill it.[30]

This article would have provoked sexual readings of the jealous mistress and loitering master, characters with which any reader of slave narratives would have been very familiar. In so doing, it tutored readers on how to infer sexuality from suggestive scenes.

If Favret and Wood have concentrated on the early nineteenth-century fascination with the image of the flogged slave woman, I am interested in its field of cultural traffic through the remainder of the nineteenth century. How was the image repeated and transformed? As this image was trafficked, it accumulated the 'half-life' of former fantasies. The image of the flogged slave woman titillated British curiosity about racialised sexual violence and incited prurient viewing. Later nineteenth-century obscenity, I will show, *confirms* an underlying British sexual response to flogging and the emergence of racialised flagellation fantasies. What was understated in abolitionist print culture found full expression in the nation's underground literature – albeit not until the 1880s.

2 Slavery obscenity in the 1880s: William Lazenby's *The Pearl* and *The Cremorne*

The sexualised representations of the flogged slave woman in abolitionist print communities allowed later publishers of obscenity to appropriate the image. In the 1880s, obscene stories created and reflected fantasies about the sexual excesses within slavery. William Lazenby introduced this genre of obscene writing. He was widely known in London as a prolific publisher of flagellant obscenity.[31] He published old favourites such as *The Birchen Bouquet* (c.1830, 1881) and original works including *The Quintessence of Birch Discipline* (1883) and *The Romance of Chastisement* (1883).[32] In the 1880s, however, he began to add race and slavery to embellish what had become an exhausted genre. Between 1879–81, he was the publisher, editor, and sometime author of *The Pearl*. It remains one of the best-known productions of Victorian obscenity after *My Secret Life* (*c*.1888–94) and *The Lustful Turk* (1828).[33] The magazine features serialised stories, anecdotes, poems, and chromolithographs that are sexually explicit and liberally embellished with flagellation. One of its serialised stories includes a narrative on the flogging and libidinous excesses of a slave plantation in Santa Cruz[34] told by a West Indian schoolgirl to her British school friend. Ashbee, who felt the work featured stories as 'cruel and crapulous' as those in Marquis de Sade's *Justine*, indicates that it had a private issue of 150 copies. In being marketed exclusively to a wealthy British male clientele, the set appears to have been sold anywhere between £18 and £25.[35] In 1882, Lazenby produced a sequel to *The Pearl*, titled *The Cremorne; A Magazine of Wit, Facetiae, Parody, Graphic Tales of Love, etc*. The title alludes to the Cremorne Gardens on the embankment in Chelsea, which became notorious after dusk when prostitutes replaced picnickers.[36] Like *The Pearl*, it was also published privately with a small issue of 300. Each number initially sold for a guinea.[37] It was also falsely dated back to 1851 in order to confound legislators and vigilante moralists. Similar to *The Pearl* in style and content, it also contains a story about slavery, one that accentuates and parodies the most gruesome aspects of sexual violence and flogging described in slave narratives.

It is within the new historical context of the 1880s that Lazenby's tales appear: at this time, abolition in the Americas had been achieved, flagellation obscenity was creatively exhausted, new sexual preoccupations were emerging, and increased imperial encounters were altering cultural fantasies about racialised sexuality. These new contexts led to unexpected results. Lazenby's stories about slavery in the Americas suggest new and developing British sexual fantasies that relate to changing desires, literary tastes, and imperial encounters.

The Pearl serialised the first obscene tale about slavery in the Americas between 1880 and 1881, demonstrating the industry's emergent interest in its history as an imaginative resource. This story, entitled *My Grandmother's Tale: or May's Account of her Introduction of the Art of Love,* describes a variety of sexual activities in explicit detail: lesbian gambols among schoolgirls, sex between upper and serving classes, threesomes, sodomy, voyeurism, and paternal incest. The story adds to this sexual panoply with its attention to the sexual licence and violence within slavery. Yet, even before 'Kate's Narrative', the embedded story that recounts a schoolgirl's life on a West-Indian slave plantation, there is an earlier reference to racialised sexuality. The tutor Mr T seduces the two schoolgirls with a series of obscene illustrations involving a white girl and a black man:

> In the first he [the Negro] is sitting on a chair, playing the banjo, his trousers open, and his great black tool sticking out. She has her eyes fixed

on it, while she holds up her dress, and points to a most voluptuous cunt between a pair of widely extended fat thighs, as much as to say 'Look here, Sambo, here is a place that will soon take the stiffness out of your prick.'

(The Pearl, 2.153–4)

Other vignettes follow that similarly draw on widespread Victorian stereo-types about black men as monstrously virile and yet laughable at the same time. The African American minstrel figure with his banjo seems to have offset the threat of his putative sexual endowments. These pictures, which are described, but not shown, introduce the theme of racialised sexuality and suggest the Victorian preoccupation with miscegenation. However, these pictures supplement rather than complement the story's primary interest in the white man's sexual power over the black slave woman. They suggest an alternative kind of racialised sexual union that both enhances and destabil-ises the fantasy that follows in 'Kate's Narrative'. In fact, the pictures focus on a theme that will emerge in later slavery obscenity.

'Kate's Narrative', which is allotted separate and significant space within *My Grandmother's Tale*, develops the fantasy of white male sexual dominion over black slave women by rewriting scenes from abolitionist reports and slave narratives. In one of its first incidents, it appropriates the image of the flogged slave woman, explicitly sexualising the brutal flogging of a black slave girl by an overseer of ambiguous colour acting under the authority of the white plantation owner. As Jim (the white overseer's son who is later haphazardly renamed Joe by the slipshod writer) recounts to Kate, 'You know Jim who has the cat, and flogs the slaves when they misbehave. Well, when the women are sent he flogs their backs, but when the girls are sent he flogs their bottoms' *(The Pearl*, 3.12). Young Jim further describes the sexual nature of the violence as he illustrates how rape follows the beating: 'He opened his pantaloons, and out started Oh! Such a big one, it would have frightened you, as he pushed it against her bottom' (3.12). 'She liked it beyond anything', the boy insists as he negates her sexual victimisation, 'I knew it by the way she stuck out her bottom' (3.13). After Jim's description of the flogging, he and Kate attempt intercourse, having been aroused by the flogging.

After this flogging incident, the narrative continues to depict white male sexual access to black slave women, while demonstrating cultural knowledge about the open secret of slavery. Jim recounts to Kate how he surreptitiously watched his father cavorting with several slave women, regular night-time visitors who 'like to come to him for they get plenty of rum, and are sure of a half-holiday next day' (3.13). They discover Jim 'peeping' on them and subsequently invite him into the room where he is sexually initiated. As before, Jim's act of telling arouses the youngsters who now succeed at having intercourse. Jim proceeds to stress the sexual difference of the black women by negatively comparing their genitalia to Kate's 'soft round white lips' (3.14). Kate further explores the crossing of the colour line with her descriptions of her father's sexual access to the 'almost white' (3.15) slaves he retains in the house, especially one woman named Nina. Kate eventually has Nina freed and travels to England with her in order to attend school. 'Kate's Narrative' thus travels to England, where its tales of white male sexual power over slave women titillate the British schoolgirls, whose response undoubtedly enhanced the erotic effect of the description of West Indian slave life for the story's presumed white male British readers. This story even invokes the slave narrative with its first-person account of slavery, escape, and travel, pilfering from it for a curious British audience (3.13–15).

A curious illustration accompanies the scene where Jim finds himself among his father's slave women. The illustration depicts the ithyphallic father and boy surrounded by four naked slaves. There are two versions of this illustration that accompany different editions of *The Pearl* that correspond to the textual erotics in different ways (Plates 2 and 3). The first illustration comes from the first edition of the magazine, which Patrick Kearney discovered in Gerard Nordmann's collection in Geneva; the second illustration accompanies a later reprint of *The Pearl* from around 1890. Mendes suggests that the reprint added hand-coloured lithographs based on the originals.[38] While the theme and composition of the illustrations are virtually the same, the difference lies in the visual imagery: specifically the colouration and characterisation of the female slaves. Although more sexually graphic in its explicit portrayal of genitalia and pubic hair, the second illustration portrays a far less bacchanalian scene. The women are composed, with their tidy hair, neat smiles, and decorous jewellery. The illustration also does not emphasise their race, surprising in light of the narrative focus on their sexual difference and availability. If the illustration were not attached to the narrative, one would have difficulty identifying these women as black, let alone West Indian slaves. While the second illustration suppresses the slave women's blackness and sexuality, the first illustration emphasises both. The women are dark brown in colour, their skin starkly contrasting with the pale skin of the men. Their untidy hair and wide grins as well as their protuberant breasts and bottoms at once suggest their degeneracy and sexual libidinousness: these are the women who would prostitute themselves for rum. The bold, hurried lines of the drawing convey a sense of activity not found in the wooden *tableaux vivants* of the second illustration, while the warmer tones suggest the hot, exotic setting of the tropics. Both drawings depict white male sexual licence over black female slaves, but the second illustration supplements the text with alternative sexual possibilities. It may be depicting the desirability and sexual vulnerability of mulattoes that the narrative suggests with its introduction of Nina, or it may be invoking the idea of white women's slavery that later slave obscenity would explore. Because little is known about the illustrations that accompanied the magazine, I can only speculate about the significance of the two versions. What was the relationship between illustrator and text: did the illustrator have direct access, or did the publisher simply provide a description or a drawing? Without being able to answer these questions, one must focus on effect rather than intent. Put simply, the visual message is not parallel to the textual one. The second illustration, which possibly dates ten years after the first, suggests another fantasy related to slavery and racialised sexuality, allowing undeveloped preoccupations to supplement the primary textual fantasy about white male sexual power over black female slaves. Wood, in his analysis of the Stedman engravings, discovers a tendency to whitewash the slave woman in early nineteenth-century visual depictions of flogging. The second illustration from 'Kate's Narrative' may invoke this early visual trend; it also foreshadows the slave fantasy's turn-of-the-century transformations. As with the pictures described at the beginning of *My Grandmother's Tale*, these ones reveal the rich archaeology and layered fantasies of slavery obscenity that revolved around colour and race.

The Pearl instigated further sexualised readings of American slavery with its libidinal investment in racialised sexuality and the flogged female slave. Just a few years later, Lazenby returned to the same fantasy in *The Cremorne*, emphasising its sexual violence by obsessively returning to the image of the flogged slave woman. *The Cremorne* includes a story entitled *The Secret Life of Linda Brent, a Curious History of Slave Life* that is a parody of Harriet Jacobs's American slave narrative, *Incidents in the Life of a Slave Girl* (1861). In brief, Jacobs's story, told by the pseudonymous Linda Brent, dramatises her sexual harassment by her master, Dr Flint, as well as her attempt to frustrate his efforts by having an extramarital affair with a white man, Mr Sands, with whom she has two illegitimate children. Jacobs's narrative was not as well recognised in England as those of Frederick Douglass or John Brown. It did not appear, for instance, in Mudie's Circulating Library catalogues. Yet, even though her book did not have the exposure of some of the earlier slave narratives, two British editions of the narrative appeared in 1862 as *The Deeper Wrong*, published by the abolitionist London publisher, W. Tweedie.[39]

There is little doubt that Jacobs's narrative was appealing to publishers of obscenity because of its sexual content: it is the most explicit of the slave narratives on the subject of sexual abuse. The American slave narrative had already been branded as unnecessarily violent and degraded. Jacobs's narrative was largely praised and most reviewers only obliquely alluded to its focus on women's sexual exploitation. The *Athenaeum*, however, roundly denounced it in a review from 19 April 1862 because of its sexual content:

> Every fault which an abolitionist novel can have is present in this repulsive tale, which is equally deficient in truth, decency and dramatic interest. 'I am well aware', says L. Maria Child, in her Preface, 'that many

will accuse me of indecorum for presenting these pages to the public; for the experiences of this intelligent and much-injured woman belong to a class which some call delicate subjects, and others indelicate. This peculiar phase of slavery has generally been kept veiled; but the public ought to be made acquainted with its monstrous features, and I willingly take the responsibility of presenting them with the veil withdrawn. I do this for the sake of my sisters in bondage, who are suffering wrongs so foul, that our ears are too delicate to listen to them.' Having given this frank intimation of the coming disclosures, L. Maria Child 'withdraws the veil'. Those only who have an appetite for what is cruel, and a taste for what is unclean, will part on good terms with the strong-minded woman who edits a slave-girl's disgusting revelations.[40]

The review, which questions the narrative's veracity, disparages Child's indecency, and denounces the unspecified slave girl's depravity, demonstrates beyond a doubt that British readers were aware of women's sexual vulnerability within slavery and reveals the interpretive capacities of nineteenth-century British readers to infer sexuality. It also displays self-conscious concern about the indecency of such readings of slave narratives.

Jean Fagan Yellin, the critic who in 1981 established the authenticity of Jacobs's narrative and subsequently revived interest in it, observes that her slave narrative is the only one 'that takes as its subject the sexual exploitation of female slaves – thus centring on sexual oppression as well as oppression of race and condition'.[41] In addition to telling Jacobs's story, her narrative relentlessly exposes the great open secret of slavery – namely, black women's sexual victimisation by white slave owners:

No pen can give an adequate description of the all-pervading corruption produced by slavery. The slave girl is reared in an atmosphere of licentiousness and fear. The lash and the foul talk of her master and her sons are her teachers.

(*Incidents*, 51)

Although Jacobs is generally more explicit about the sexual violence carried out in slavery than her contemporaries, she is often oblique about her own sexuality. Recent critics have observed how her narrative obfuscates, omits, and conceals her sexuality, displacing the plain facts of the abuse and 'sexual nonconformity' with elaborate discursivity.[42] Karen Sánchez-Eppler examines how the narrator writes her sexuality to titillate her white women readers, but also to conceal her sexual transgression by shifting focus from her sexual vulnerability to her motherhood. Deborah Garfield discusses how Jacobs switches between the roles of speaker and listener in order to underplay her agency in the telling of her indecorous story. Finally,

P. Gabrielle Foreman comments on the narrator's strategic use of 'under-tell' when disclosing information. She observes that Jacobs's undertellings moderate a subject matter that may have been deemed obscene:

> Jacobs's confession [of her sexual liaison with Mr. Sands], in contrast, with its emphasis on a rapacious master, could easily collapse for her readers into the arousal of imagined sadistic pornography. Yet Jacobs carefully contains her writing, refusing to describe Linda's more private moments with Mr. Sands, and so distinguishes the more acceptable titillation and resolution of confession and absolution from the pornographic excitement that would be labeled unacceptably illicit in Victorian America.[43]

Perhaps it was this combination of unusual explicitness and restraint in Jacobs's narrative that titillated the British publisher, familiar with sexualised readings of slavery and, like other Victorian readers, adept at decoding sexual scenes.

Lazenby's *The Secret Life of Linda Brent* is a fragmentary parody of Jacobs's slave narrative that covers only the first years of her life, but manages to rewrite the sexual violence described in Jacobs's narrative as sadistic obscenity. It distorts slave women's sexual victimisation as grossly carnal and rejects Jacobs's anxious professions of virtue by overtly sexualising her: she watches a slave and a white overseer copulating (35), masturbates (43), and engages in sexual 'games' with another mulatto woman (44). *The Secret Life* dwells particularly on the sexual violence that accompanies white men's sexual access to black women in slave society. The parody lifts the flogging scene from 'Kate's Narrative', repeats it four times, and in so doing reveals sadistic fascination with the sexual torture of female slaves. In its descriptions of flogging, the parody overwrites the British flagellation fantasy with a racialised flogging fantasy. However, *The Secret Life* does not follow the fantasy structure that it sets up, but is instead diverted by another sexual impulse. What begins as a fantasy about white male brutal sexual power over slave women becomes a homoerotic fantasy that includes graphic descriptions of sodomy and male same-sex desire. The parody appropriates the image of the flogged slave woman, by now thoroughly contaminated by sexualised readings and repetitions, as a disguise for its true preoccupation with homoerotic desire.

The first flogging scene in *The Secret Life* features Jacobs's grandmother. It functions primarily to undermine the importance of the grandmother in Jacobs's slave narrative who is the matriarch of the slave community. A freed slave who owns her own house near Dr Flint's, she is at once community leader, moral keystone, and symbol of freedom. Jacobs's narrative only briefly alludes to her grandmother's history as a young slave and never intimates sexual abuse or impropriety; as Foreman observes, her private life is not subject to scrutiny. What she discloses is that 'she was a little girl when she was captured and sold to the keeper of a large hotel' and fared 'hard [. . .] during childhood' (12). The parody, however, denies the influence the grandmother holds in the slave narrative as a seasoned older woman who has survived slavery. It imagines her as a young slave girl – Martha, rather than Aunt Martha – still vulnerable to sexual abuse by her 'rascally master, the hotel keeper' (4). In ridiculing Jacobs's language of sensibility as well as women's role in the abolitionist movement, the parody imagines Linda's grandmother confessing to 'a sympathising anti-slavery lady' about how 'her modesty was overcome' (4). The fantasy thus unfolds. In the parody, Martha describes how her master, Jackley, detains her for a wealthy and lecherous Colonel who is a guest at his hotel. As she is confined in one of the rooms, the Colonel spanks and birches her while her master watches with 'quiet but intense enjoyment' (8). The beating is frankly sexualised: in the manner of British flagellation obscenity, its instrument is the birch and its focus is the nude buttocks rather than the back where the slave was usually whipped. Yet, the fantasy also relies on the *frisson* of difference for its erotic effect. The Colonel eroticises and racialises the woman, revealing the erotics of colour, by describing her 'beautifully-polished skin – the slight olive tint of which looked far more voluptuous than the white skin of an Britishwoman's' (10). With this slippage, the parody reminds us of its British audience and reveals how its erotics depends on racial difference and transatlantic displacement for its effects.

Up until this point, *The Secret Life* is a heterosexual fantasy that viciously repudiates the feminist and abolitionist appeal of Jacobs's slave narrative for the victimised slave girl. However, as soon as the parody constructs this heterosexual fantasy, it transforms it. What begins as the beating and rape of a black slave girl shifts into a sexual exchange between the two white men where the black girl is never even penetrated. Jackley, pleading the excuse that he must preserve Martha's maidenhead in order to sell it later at a good price (15), sodomises the Colonel. Meanwhile, the Colonel performs cunnilingus on Martha, who has her first orgasm. This Sedgwickian triangle demonstrates white male homoerotic desire expressed through the spectacle of the brutalised black woman. Martha is both the pretext and the victim of this homoerotic exchange, her blackness and femininity at once arousing the white men and providing the excuse for their homoeroticism.

A second flogging scene immediately follows the first and also reveals underlying homoerotic desire. Immediately after the assault on Martha, the Colonel cautions her with a story about how he had another intractable female slave, a mulatto named Cherry, disciplined. While giving her up to an overseer, a 'great black big fellow' (16), he describes how he watched while she was flogged and sexually tortured:

Well, he put his great big prick into her; he hugged her close to his black hairy breast, and kissed her pretty little lips with his great thick black ones. More than that, he put his great stiff prick into her pretty little bottom hole, and pushed it in until she was all torn and bleeding, and because she objected to this, and screamed, he flogged her until the skin and flesh of her bottom was all hanging in strips, and her blood ran down into her shoes; and when she screamed he thrust the handle of his whip into her cunt. So that little Cherry was quite subdued, and was laid up for months.

(*The Secret Life*, 16)

On the one hand, this passage is a heterosexual fantasy about male sexual power over the black woman. On the other hand, it is also a homoerotic fantasy from which the Colonel derives sexual pleasure from watching the black man and knowing that he enacts his sexual will. The Colonel directs his gaze primarily at the imposing physicality and blackness of the overseer. He lingers over the overseer's 'great big prick', 'black hairy breast', and 'great thick black' lips' (16). The black woman, his sexual victim, seems less significant than this racialised spectacle of the virile and brutish black man. The kinds of sexual acts described also reveal the parody's deviation from the typically heterosexual flagellation and flogging fantasies. In addition to heightening the black woman's pain and humiliation, these acts parody heterosexual coitus and make it redundant. This passage, then, allows for homoerotic desire to cross the colour line, but in so doing, also exploits the colour line in such a way that the Colonel is able to discuss deviant sexuality from a racial remove. In other words, although the Colonel relishes the homoerotics of this flogging scene, he displaces the act of sodomy from white male sexuality onto black male sexuality and depicts sodomy in terms of a brutal male black sexuality that is willing to penetrate any orifice, however unusually. Indeed, this entire passage could be read as an anxious and corrective fantasy in response to the first flogging fantasy where the two white men engage in anal sex. The Colonel's story of the black overseer indulges in the spectacle of manliness and the performance of sexual deviance, but removes white male sexuality from an act perpetrated by a black man on a black woman.

The third flogging scene also constructs a heterosexual fantasy only to distort it. It draws from an incident in Jacobs's slave narrative where Dr Flint punishes the cook by confining her for a day away from her nursing baby, and conflates it with another incident on the same page where Dr Flint ties one of his male slaves up to the joist and flogs him for accusing him of fathering his wife's child (*The Secret Life*, 23). In the parody, Dr Flint binds and flogs the cook who is the mother of his child. He switches from the British birch, used in the previous flogging scenes, to the American cowhide, a detail that demonstrates knowledge about American technologies of slave torture. The cook for 'shame' asks to be flogged on the back rather than the bottom, so revealing the sexual impulse behind the flogging. As with the other flogging fantasies, this one features a display of white male racial and heterosexual power only to interrupt it with the introduction of anal penetration. After flogging the cook, Dr Flint penetrates her anally with a broom (43). As before, anal penetration takes the place of penile-vaginal coitus, diverting the course of the heterosexual rape fantasy. Also, as before, the parody distances the white man from sodomy by making sure that Dr Flint's penis does not perform the act, but instead he uses another object.

In these last three flogging scenes, then, *The Secret Life* repeats the image of the flogged slave woman to transform it, becoming otherwise preoccupied with white male sexual deviance, homoerotic desire, and sodomy. The reasons underlying the appropriation of this image also explain its transformation. By the 1880s, first of all, flagellation obscenity had become tired and seems to have depended on the inclusion of racial difference or anal sex for its revival. During the period, Lazenby's works on flagellation were increasingly turning to depictions of deviant sexual activities. His serialised stories from *The Pearl*, including *Miss Coote's Confession*, *Lady Pokingham*, and *Sub-Umbra*, each contains reference to flagellation as well as male or female homosexuality. The image of the flogged slave woman functioned as a diversion to introduce male same-sex desire. The discussion of a criminalised sexual act like sodomy would have been less anxious at a geographical and historical remove. The addition of racial and cultural difference to the British flagellation fantasy via the image of the flogged slave woman disassociated the fantasy from the British. It thus enabled the inclusion of British homoerotic fantasies about sodomy – already a powerful, but latent, component of the flagellation fantasy – while blaming such acts on the degeneracy of the American plantation owner and the American system of slavery.

The Secret Life also includes a fourth flogging scene, but it is unlike the others. It explores other forms of sexual violence within slavery. More specifically, it examines the idea that Jacobs emphasises in her narrative: 'Cruelty is contagious in uncivilized communities' (47). The parody describes how the regular crossing of the colour line corrupts other members of the plantation household. It borrows a scene from Jacobs's narrative where Mrs Flint forces her to remove her new shoes ('whose creaking grated harshly on her refined nerves'[19]), and orders her to run errands barefoot in the snow. The parody recasts this punishment as flogging and describes how Mrs Flint beats Linda with her new shoes: 'she drew my petticoats over my head, exposing my naked bottom to her own gaze, and – worse – the gaze of the precocious little rascal Nicholas' (67). Linda becomes the object not only of Nicholas's erotic gaze, but also Mrs Flint's. This scene reveals a shrewd reading of Jacobs's description of Mrs Flint's predatory sexual jealously: 'Sometimes I woke up, and found her bending over me. At other times she whispered in my ear, as though it was her husband speaking to me, and listened to hear what I would answer' (34). Recent critics, like Sánchez-Eppler, have suggested that this scene is one of the most graphically sexual in the narrative: once Mrs Flint enters the bedroom, she 'occupies precisely the position of erotic dominance repeatedly denied the doctor'.[44] By having Mrs Flint flog Linda, a punishment that has been repeatedly sexualised, the parody possibly draws on the intimations of other forms of sexual abuse in Jacobs's narrative. Up until this fourth flogging scene, *The Secret Life* is a profoundly homoerotic piece that uses the image of the flogged slave woman simultaneously to arouse, displace, and deny this British male homoeroticism. In the final scene, however, it notices another power relationship within slavery, namely that between the slave woman and the jealous mistress. This final scene demonstrates the astute – albeit vicious – reading of the various forms of sexual abuse described in Jacobs's narrative. It also reveals the historical imbrications of its sexual fantasy: the parody resurrects sexualised reading of the flogged slave woman, recontextualises the image as homoerotic fantasy, and introduces other fantasies circulating around the sexualised and racialised violence within slavery.[45]

An illustration that accompanies *The Secret Life* adds to its historical complexity. This illustration (Plate 4) suggests alternative fantasies surrounding the image of the flogged slave woman. It depicts the first flogging scene where Jackley and the Colonel beat Linda's grandmother, but whitewashes the grandmother. Nothing in the illustration suggests that the flagellation is racialised and perpetrated in the antebellum South. Moreover, there is no suggestion of homoerotic desire. Anal sex and homoerotic desire are frequently described in nineteenth-century obscenity, but were apparently deemed too transgressive for visual depiction. In effect, the illustration shows a typical British flagellation scene, non-distinguishable from the illustrations in Lazenby's ordinary flagellation obscenity. The illustration seems to revert to the British flagellation fantasy upon which the flogging fantasy is built, omitting reference to racial difference and sodomy and recalling visual iconography that would have been familiar and innocuous to readers of obscenity. The illustration offsets the racial and sexual brutality that it describes and, in so doing, neutralises the most transgressive and objectionable elements of the parody. More importantly, with the whitewashing of the grandmother, it both recalls early visual iconography around slave flogging and foreshadows future appropriations of flogging and slave narratives where white women as slave victims becomes the dominant fantasy.

3 Slavery obscenity at the turn-of-the-century: *Dolly Morton* to *White Women Slaves*

The underground fascination with slavery in the Americas diminished after Lazenby's imprisonment in 1886. After a decade, however, slavery once again became topical in clandestine print traffic. The re-engagement with this particular phase in history extended from the 1890s to 1910s, driven by a loose consortium of British, French, and American publishers, agents,

1 William Blake, 'Flagellation of a Female Samboe Slave', John Stedman, *Narrative, of a Five Year's Expedition Against the Revolted Negroes of Surinam, in Guiana, on the Wild Coast of South America: From the Year 1772, to 1777*. London: n.p., 1796. By permission of Simon Fraser University Special Collections, Burnaby

2 Anonymous lithograph from *My Grandmother's Tale, The Pearl. A Journal of Facetia Voluptuous Reading*. Unknown, reproduced from Patrick Kearney, *A History of Erotic Literature*. London: Macmillan, 1982. By permission of Pan Macmillan

3 Anonymous lithograph from *My Grandmother's Tale*, *The Pearl. A Journal of Facetia Voluptuous Reading*. Vols 2–3. London: Printed for the Society of Vice [Augustin Brancart?], 1879–81 [1890]. By permission of the British Library, London

4 Anonymous lithograph from *The Secret Life of Linda Brent, a Curious History of Slave Life, The Cremorne; A Magazine of Wit, Facetiae, Graphic Tales of Love, etc.* London: Privately Printed [Lazenby?], 1851 [1882]. By permission of the British Library, London

5 British Telecom Prostitute Cards, *c*.2000–02. London

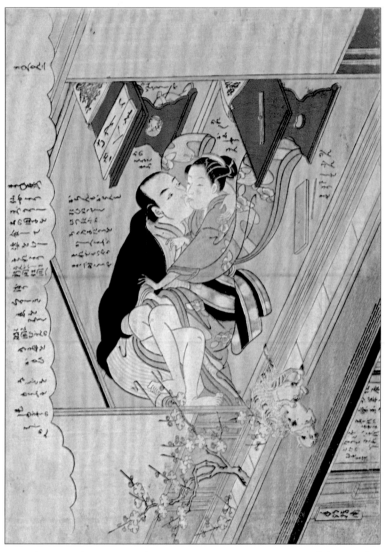

6 Sazuki Harunobu, *Lovers with Rutting Cats*, 1765. By permission of the British Museum, London

7 Japanese Pillow Book, early nineteenth century. By permission of the Kinsey Institute for Research in Sex, Gender, and Reproduction, Bloomington, Indiana

8 Anonymous photographic postcard of Salome, *c.*1910. By permission of the Museum of New Zealand Te Papa Tongarewa

and interests. The image of the flogged victim retained its fascination, but underwent further transformation. Fantasies around this image, preserving elements from flagellation literature and slave narratives, now shifted their focus from the flogged black woman to the white woman.

This new development in slavery obscenity was accompanied by a heightened awareness about its historical and national origins. Lazenby's productions addressed British gentlemen exclusively and dehistoricised slavery to explore homoerotics through racial and sexual domination. However, later slavery obscenity addressed men of various national backgrounds and detailed the historical circumstances of slavery in the Americas. The publishers of later slavery obscenity, such as Charles Carrington and Select Bibliothèque, marketed the titillating image of the flogged white female slave variously for different national audiences. These publishers based decisions about censorship, open or clandestine publication, and cultural ownership upon national sensibilities, proclivities, and legalities.

It was the indomitable Carrington who first returned to the subject of slavery in the Americas. While immersed in the bohemian literary culture of Paris, he also became the most prominent publisher of British and French obscenity in the late nineteenth century. By the end of the nineteenth century, as Mendes observes, Carrington 'produced a vast amount of "scientific", "oriental" and flagellatory semi-erotic books openly, and in addition controlled most of the clandestine trade in pornography for the British-speaking market.'[46] The British Home Office had him under surveillance, and he was the bane of Scotland Yard until 1907 when he was deported from France, though he returned in 1912.[47] During his career, he demonstrated keen global entrepreneurialism, creating and responding to a market for racialised erotics. He focused on oriental harems, Eastern sex manuals, American slavery, and later, even war-torn Africa.[48] His increased focus on the Americas corresponded to the expansion of the American traffic in obscenity. The American trade in obscenity developed later than that in Europe, emerging when the Irish immigrant, William Haynes, began to publish 'improper' books in the mid-nineteenth century. Anthony Comstock, a founder of the New York Society for the Suppression of Vice (SSV) helped secure federal obscenity legislation in America. After the law's passage in 1873, he claimed to have seized '200,000 pictures and photographs; 100,000 books; 5,000 packs of playing cards; and numerous contraceptive devices and allegedly aphrodisiac medicines'.[49] Carrington slowly developed this transatlantic trade. After a private interview with St George Best, Gershon Legman discovered how this man acted as Carrington's American agent after the turn of the century. Legman writes that 'it was Best's job to smuggle Carrington's pornographica into America, through Cuba and Mexico, and deliver them safely to paying customers and fashionable booksellers in the United States.'[50]

Carrington did not immediately turn to fantasies about flogging and the white female slave, but revealed an early interest in race relations and slavery in the Americas. As direct evidence of Carrington's familiarity with Lazenby's interest in slavery, he reprinted two of his publications that touch on slavery and race relations in the Americas: *My Grandmother's Tale* (as *May's Account* [1904]) and *The Adventures of Lady Harpur* (*c.*1906). The first is a reprint from *The Pearl*, the latter a reprint of *Queenie* (1885).[51] Again directed at wealthy, mail-order clients, *The Adventures of Lady Harpur* sold for three guineas. Like Lazenby's stories from *The Pearl* and *The Cremorne*, this novel is fascinated with the libidinal possibilities of the slave plantation and the mythic immensity of the black man's penis; however, unlike Lazenby's other works, it does not focus on the floggings and cruelties concomitant with slavery. This story of father-daughter incest, intergenerational sex, and rape, uses West-Indian slavery as its backdrop primarily to explore the sexual intermingling of black and white bodies. Although there are occasional references to the history and geography of West Indian and American slavery, the story is mostly concerned with coloured corporeality. Queenie, the heroine of the story, expresses the preoccupation that runs through the story: 'Although the colour did not much matter, provided that they were equally strong and active, she preferred being fucked by a white man; but that some of the blacks, and especially Sambo, had most enormous tools.'[52]

Before his Lazenby reprints, Carrington demonstrated his interest in race relations in the Americas in other ways. In the 1890s and early 1900s, from his base in Paris, Carrington published a series of original, English-language works with American settings: *The Memoirs of Madge Buford or, a modern Fanny Hill* (1892), *A Town-Bull, or The Elysian Fields* (1893), *Sue Suckitt; Maid and Wife* (1893), *Maidenhead Stories* (1894), *Dolly Morton* (1899), and later *The Story of Seven Maidens: Slavery in West India* (1907).[53] Mendes posits that Best, Carrington's later American agent, may have authored some of these works.[54] He bases his theory about Best's authorship on his discovery that he was publishing stories in an Anglo-American magazine in Paris in the 1890s. Yet, it is difficult to determine whether Britons or Americans authored these works. By comparing typographical features, Mendes convincingly traces all these books back to Carrington, but they feature different original places of publication: *Madge Buford, A Town-Bull,* and *Sue Suckitt,* New Orleans; *Maidenhead Stories,* New York; *Dolly Morton ,* Paris; and *Seven Maidens,* Cambridge. Clandestine catalogues, however, indicate that these works were initially directed to a British market.[55] For the most part, the content is no more revealing about their national origins. *Dolly Morton ,* with its male British narrator, was most likely authored by an Englishman; however, the other books blend American and British references.[56] Authorship aside, what is important about the publication history of these books is that they demonstrate European interest in American sexualities. Moreover, while American sexuality seems to have been a source of interest for a certain class of French and British reader, a certain class of American reader also seems to have been equally interested in European depictions of their sexuality – though not until later when these publications reached America through recirculation and reprint.

Except for *Maidenhead Stories*, all of these novels focus on racialised sexualities in the Americas. The last in the series, *Dolly Morton*, is by far the most noteworthy and deserves closer attention. The earlier books, however, establish and develop Carrington's interest in the topic. *A Town-Bull* focuses on the sexual escapades of a virile American man who eventually finds himself as the forefather of a Southern commune (his Elysium), whose offspring display a 'fine scale of color, from purest white to a rich chocolate brown'.[57] The implicit and likely unconscious logic of this story is that indiscriminate sexuality brings the harmonious mixing of races. *Sue Suckitt* explores male same-sex desire by introducing the black man as a well-endowed sodomist. The frenetic sexual combat between a black and white man leaves little doubt as to where desire is located in this novel:

Like gladiators they faced each other, standing each lance in rest [. . .] and with a lustful yell they closed, writhed in each other's arms like athletes in a wrestling match, then jutting out their bellies, each seized out his own prick and handling it like a foil in fencing, rubbed them together, titled at each other, stabbed each other, until the cream like gore began to shoot, when, rolling on the floor heads and heals, their salacious mouths sucked frantically each other's sperming spigots [. . .][58]

Unlike Jacobs's parody, this novel does not separate the white man from sodomy, but explores his participation with interest. *Madge Buford*, putatively authored by D'Arcy St John, also focuses on racialised sexuality in America. In this novel, the black male slave is sexually deviant and degraded – he commits bestiality with a female dog and fellates a male dog.[59] *Seven Maidens* concentrates on female flagellation in Cuba. These novels reveal a range of attitudes toward black American sexuality, from playful to debasing, but as group, they are significant because they demonstrate Carrington's publishing interests and suggest the commercial viability of black American sexuality to underground European and, later, American book markets.

Of Carrington's publications with an American setting, *Dolly Morton* is the most significant in terms of reproduction, influence, and literary quality. Oscar Wilde was reputedly familiar with the novel. Charles Reginald Dawes, moreover, places it 'as being amongst the very few good erotic works of its period', lauding its historical realism 'even *Uncle Tom's Cabin* leaves a lot out that is to be found in *Dolly Morton'*.[60] There is little doubt as to what details the novel adds. *Dolly Morton*, like the stories from *The Pearl* and especially *The Cremorne*, reproduces fantasies about the flogged slave woman by overwriting flagellation and slave narratives. However, the white woman now assumes the role of the flogged female slave.

Like earlier slavery obscenity, *Dolly Morton* turns to the physical and sexual violence inflicted upon women for its erotic effects. It represents itself as a first-hand account of the American slave system before the Civil War that focuses particularly on the physical and sexual violence inflicted upon slave women. The novel opens in New York in 1866, describing an Englishman's sexual encounter with a prostitute, Dolly. Following their encounter, this man records verbatim Dolly's narrative about her life in the South. Before the Civil War and after hearing about the execution of the white abolitionist rebel John Brown, she moves to Virginia with an abolitionist Quaker woman, Miss Dean, in order to run an underground railway for escaped slaves. The Southerners, however, discover their duplicity and viciously punish them with a whipping. Randolph, one of the Virginian plantation owners, offers to help Dolly if she becomes his mistress. She yields in order to avoid further punishment. The rest of her story documents her sexual victimisation as well as that of the female slaves on his plantation. With the onset of the Civil War and the Battle of Fair Oaks in Richmond, Randolph finally loses his hold on and interest in Dolly, eventually allowing her to leave for the North where she establishes a house of prostitution in New York and meets the original narrator, the Englishman.

Dolly Morton reveals the same mixed origins that are the trademark of Lazenby's slavery obscenity. The novel's subtitle, which appears in Carrington's original 1899 edition, immediately announces the combined influence of flogging and flagellation: 'An account of the Whippings, Rapes, and Violences that Preceded the Civil War in America With Curious Anthropological Observations on the Radical Diversities in the Conformation of the Female Bottom and the Way Different Women endure Chastisement.' A novel preoccupied with the whip, it continually reproduces the image of the whipped woman by drawing on flagellation and flogging conventions. Here, in a typical scene, Dolly is stripped and whipped by a Lynch mob for her involvement in the running of an underground railway:

'Now, as to the punishment of the gal. I propose to give her a dozen strokes, but not to draw blood.' [...]

'You bet I'll lay them on smart, and you'll see how she'll move. I know how to handle a hick'ry switch, and I'll rule a dozen lines across her bottom that'll make it look like the American flag, striped red and white. And when I've done with her I guess she'll be sore behind, but you'll see that I won't draw a drop of blood. Yes, gentlemen, I tell you again that I know how to whip. I was an overseer in Georgia for five years.' [...]

All the time the man was holding forth, I lay shame stricken at my nakedness and shivering in awful suspense, the flesh of my bottom creeping and the scalding tears trickling down my red cheeks. The man raised the switch and flourished it over me [...].

I winced and squirmed every time the horrid switch fell sharply on my quivering flesh. I shrieked, and screamed and I swung my hips from side to side, arching my loins at one moment and then flattening myself down on the ladder, while between my shrieks, I begged and prayed the man to stop whipping me. [. . .]

'There boys, look at her bottom. You see how regularly the white skin is striped with long red weals; but there is not a drop of blood. That's what I call a prettily whipped bottom. But the gal ain't got a bit of grit in her. Any nigger wench would have taken double the number of strokes without making half the noise.'[61]

This passage borrows conventions from flagellation and flogging, blending them in what is now a familiar fashion: the American overseer, for example, wields the British switch and hickory. What is different, of course, about this fantasy is that it imagines the white woman as slave. Dolly, after all, is unquestionably white: 'Her skin was as white as milk and without a blemish' (*Dolly Morton*, 9). While the above passage eroticises her whiteness, dwelling on the red weals that contrast with the white skin of her bottom, it implicitly compares her to a black slave woman. Like a black slave woman, she is tied and beaten by an overseer. This overseer further suggests the parallel between Dolly and the female slave by comparing their responses to a beating. If this passage only draws an implicit comparison between Dolly and slave woman, another makes the comparison more explicit. Randolph decides to whip Dolly one last time before he leaves her, and he promises, 'I am going to whip you as if you were a naughty slave girl' (26). In a few words, he sums up the erotics of this novel. The repeated scenes of whipping, inflicted on women of all colours, demonstrate that gender rather than race finally becomes the preoccupying concern in the whipping fantasy – recalling the whitewashing of the slave woman at the beginning of its history. As Randolph bluntly states to Dolly, 'you will soon find that many other men besides me are fond of spanking a woman till she squeals' (267).

However, American slavery still remains the pretext of the fantasy. In many ways, *Dolly Morton* is influenced by the structure and themes of a woman's slave narrative as it recounts Dolly's story of prostitution in the South and her 'escape' to the North. In effect, the novel is a white woman's slave narrative, one that draws on the history of slavery to document a white woman's sexual victimisation. The novel literalises the sexual abuse implied in American slave narratives such as Jacobs's by making *it* the circumstance of bondage, rather than race. While it is not an outright parody of the slave narrative such as Lazenby's parody of Jacobs, it exploits the slave narrative in order to titillate its predominately male readers with scenes of sexual violence. A later imitation of Carrington's publications confirms this notion that he is borrowing from the slave narrative in *Dolly Morton*. *Woman and her Slave: A Realistic Narrative of a Slave who experienced His Mistress' Love and*

Lash, a novel of unknown date, origin, and pagination, appropriates the slave narrative.[62] This novel is not explicitly obscene and does not preoccupy itself with whipping: its suggestive title functions to establish the book's connection with Carrington, but does not fulfil its promise. Instead, the book describes a male slave of mixed race who has a sexual relationship with his white mistress. It appropriates the slave narrative in order to explore another possible sexual dynamic within the slave system. It callously overturns the political protest that is so crucial to the genre by transforming it into an interracial love story, where the lovers read *Othello* to one another to disclose their feelings, but where he learns to despise his blackness as 'unfitted for freedom'. While the fantasy is altogether different from that which emerges in *Dolly Morton*, it comments on Carrington's salacious interest in slavery and the slave narrative. It reflects back on *Dolly Morton*, revealing how this book depends on historical contexts and genres in order to fantasise about a white woman being beaten.

This image of 'the white female slave' may respond to what Cecily Devereux has discussed as the rhetorical association between prostitution and white slavery by the end of the nineteenth century. As early as 17 January 1880, *Town Talk* developed the connection between the slave trade and female prostitution in an article on the 'British and Foreign Traffic in Girls'.[63] By 1912, London hosted an International Conference on Obscene Publications and the White Slave Trade. However, the French and British editions of *Dolly Morton* did not elaborate this relationship between slavery and the sexual trafficking of white women. Instead, they focused on the whiteness of the flogged woman *only* to displace the fantasy elsewhere. In demonstrating a heightened awareness about the novel's historical and national origins, these editions were engaged in nationalist struggles to disown the fantasy. While Carrington's British versions of the novel marketed it as American history, his French versions described it as an expression of the English vice.

Dolly Morton was first published in Britain openly, rather than clandestinely. Sold to affluent clientele for three guineas, it appeared amid a recrudescence of flagellation literature for which Carrington was known. An early 1896 advertisement for the novel marketed the book to the 'Historian, and Students of Medical Jurisprudence', the 'Anthropologist', and the 'Student of Flagellation'.[64] Carrington's later Preface, however, focuses on the novel as history. By amassing historical detail around the novel, it reveals detailed knowledge about abolitionist history, referring to Wilbur H. Siebert's study *The Underground Railroad from Slavery to Freedom* (1898) and the 'romantic narratives' of Frederick Douglass and John Brown.[65] While, on the one hand, the Preface suggests that the novel is a sympathetic historical account of abolitionist history, on the other hand, he uses this history to exploit the image of the flogged woman:

> Women who were caught in this business were ruthlessly stripped and
> whipped – their persons exposed to the lustful eyes of lascivious men

and, on many of them, other violences of a far more intimate nature were perpetrated. These ardent Southern men were, after all men in a sexual sense also, and few men, we ween can witness the chastisement and skin-warming of pious lovely, white women, without feeling promptings of a passionate nature.

(Preface, *Dolly Morton,* ix)

He manipulates history, imagining a scenario for which, to my knowledge, there is no recorded fact, to suggest the legitimacy of a dubious work. In so doing, he displaces the prurient preoccupation with the image of the flogged woman – now transformed into a white woman – to the annals of American history. As he sets up this history, however, he shamelessly endorses the novel's prurient gaze:

Again we see beautiful women and delicately nurtured, stripped bare under a Southern sun; we hear their cries and pleadings for mercy as, one by one, their robes and petticoats are torn off or tucked up, their drawers unfastened and rolled down; our eyes are shocked and, by an inevitable natural impulse, delighted at the sight of the white, well-developed hemispheres laid bare and blushing to our gaze, only to receive the cruel lash.

(Preface, *Dolly Morton*, ix–x)

In using personal and possessive pronouns such as 'we' and 'our', he also implicates the reader in this erotic viewing. All subsequent British reprints of his novel were printed clandestinely, a fact that suggests that his historicising Preface was not altogether convincing.[66]

While British editions reimagined history to disown the fantasy, French editions did the same by marketing it as British. Carrington openly published a French translation of the novel in 1901 as *En Virginie.*[67] As Donald Thomas notes, Carrington's publishing activities were relatively unregulated in France because he expurgated French editions of British works.[68] Except for the expurgation of explicit sexual acts, however, this edition remains intact and retains the descriptions of violent flagellation, including the description of Dolly's flogging. His French edition, moreover, includes a preface by Jean de Villiot, a pseudonym frequently used by Carrington, that denounces British hypocrisy by juxtaposing strange British proclivities against its legendary prudery.[69] Aggravated by the National Vigilance Association's (NVA) denunciation of French literature as immoral, Villiot responds to the British tirade by disparaging British sexuality as an extreme of vice and virtue and reproducing the idea of the sexually hypocritical Victorians:

Là, règne cette dangereuse maxime qu'une austérité rigoureuse est la seule sauvegarde de la vertu. Le mot le plus innocent effraye; le geste le plus naturel devient un attentat. Les sentiments, ainsi réprimés, ou s'étouffent ou éclatent d'une manière terrible. Tout pour le vice ou tout pour la vertu, point de milieu; les caractères se complaisant dans l'extrême, et l'on voit naître des pruderies outrées et des monstres de licence [. . .][70]

Later, in his 'Bibliographie des Principaux Ouvrages Parus sur la Flagellation' that appears at the end of the book, Villiot specifically links flagellation to the British: 'C'est incontestablement l'Angleterre qui tient la tête en cette matière.'[71] In addition to perpetuating the national and sexual rivalry in this French edition of Dolly Morton, Carrington continued to do so in a French series on flagellation entitled 'La flagellation à travers le monde'. This series focused largely on British flagellation and identified the act as British. He produced such titles as *Le fouet à Londres* (1904) and *Etude sur la flagellation [. . .] avec un exposé documentaire de la flagellation dans les écoles anglaises et des prisons militaries* (1899),[72] thus selling the series as a spectacle of British vice to a French market steeped in de Sade.

Other publishers besides Carrington also imagined the white woman slave. In the first decade of the twentieth century, Select Bibliothèque privately printed first in French and then in English a series of underground obscene books on American slavery putatively authored by Don Brennus Aléra, a composite pseudonym much like Jean de Villiot. The British editions appeared in 1910: *White Women Slaves* , *Barbaric Fêtes*, *Under the Yoke*, and *In Louisiana*.[73] Works such as *White Women Slaves* finally encapsulate my argument. In this book a white Louisiana lover says to his fiancé, 'I want you as a slave, but I will not have you for a wife [. . .]. I shall be obliged to chastise that fine skin, just as much as the coarse black skin of an intractable negress.'[74] As the only books in the series translated into English, they demonstrate the peculiar appeal of the subject matter to the British and Americans. An advertisement at the back of *White Women Slaves* reveals that these books also had an American audience: they were priced at 16 shillings or four dollars. A few editions have also made their way to the Kinsey Institute for research in Sex, Gender, and Reproduction. The subjugated white woman, one of the implicit fantasies surrounding the image of the flogged slave woman, finally finds literal expression at the turn of the century, but is now trafficked among British, French, and American publishers and readers, provoking nationalist debates and questions about history, imaginative property, and censorship.

4 Whipping in the twentieth century: the fugitive image

By the 1920s, the image of the flogged slave woman seems to have disappeared. I speculate, however, that the image has not disappeared in the twentieth century, but has been dehistoricised with its global trafficking. When it does reappear, it generally reappears *outside* the context of the historical slave system. I want to suggest that whipping fantasies are ineradicably linked to the history of slavery. Regardless of the sexual relationships they imagine, whipping fantasies are predicated on a transatlantic image that emerged in the late eighteenth century.

At the beginning of the twentieth century, while fantasies about the white slave woman were still circulating in British underground publications, the image of the flogged female slave was transformed into the figurative trope of master and slave. This trope had long been circulating in England – appropriated by various reform movements – but, as far as I know, it was not introduced into obscenity until the turn of the century. Carrington himself introduced the trope through his publications. In 1901, he published an underground flagellation novel entitled *Suburban Souls: The Erotic Psychology of a Man and a Maid* that describes sexual domination in terms of the master/slave relationship. Later, in 1905, he also published *The Mistress and the Slave: A Masochist Realistic Love Story* that reverses gender roles, but still relies on the figures of master and slave to explore the erotics of domination.[75] This transformation of the image of the flogged female slave at the beginning of the twentieth century marks its figuration at the same time as its most intense globalisation. The efflorescence of sales catalogues, obscene publications, and regulatory actions by the early twentieth century demonstrates that the international trade in obscenity experienced unprecedented growth in the West at this time. However, although widely recirculated, the image became fugitive.

Every twentieth-century whipping fantasy or practice in the West not only relies on this image, but also traffics it. In other words, the image of the flogged slave woman has never disappeared. *Histoire d'O*, written by Dominique Aury for Olympia Press in 1958 under the pseudonym Pauline Réage, demonstrates the insidious influence of the image. If the following passage from the novel were placed out of context, one might almost attribute it to a slave narrative: it not only invokes the hierarchies of slavery, but also borrows its instruments and language of torture:

> You are here to serve your masters. [. . .] The whip will be used only between dusk and dawn. But besides the whipping you receive from whoever may want to whip you, you will also be flogged in the evening, as punishment for any infractions of the rules committed during the day [. . .]. Actually both this flogging and the chain – which when attached to the ring of your collar keeps you more or less closely confined to your bed several hours a day – are intended less to make you suffer, scream, or shed tears than to make you feel, *through* this suffering, that you are not free but fettered [. . .][76]

Similarly, the illustrated advertisements (Plate 5) found in any British Telecom phone booth in London today play on a wry British self-consciousness about the rich historical tradition of the English Vice. Prostitute cards such as 'Strict Victorian Punishment Taken', 'Genuine Victorian

Punishment', and 'Victorian Punishment' reverse the gender roles of the typical Victorian flagellation fantasy, but also invoke pornographic nostalgia for the public boy's school. While the advertisements situate beating within a British erotic tradition and do not offer any explicit references to slavery, I suggest that they are influenced by the history of slavery. Had it not been for transatlantic abolitionism, this image may not have been so enduring.

Twentieth-century theorists of whipping fantasies have overlooked their historical origins within the context of slavery. In 'A Child is Being Beaten' (1919), Freud notices how Harriet Beecher Stowe's *Uncle Tom's Cabin* stimulated erotic beating fantasies among his patients. As he recognises one of the most influential novels on the Western cultural imagination in the nineteenth century, however, he dismisses it and explains how the beating fantasy originates in early childhood.[77] Similarly, in *Erotism: Death and Sensuality*, Georges Bataille uses the Hegelian master/slave dialectic to describe the erotics of domination in relation to the taut tension between life and death, but overlooks how the history of slavery directly informed G. W. F. Hegel's psychological paradigm of self-consciousness.[78] More recently, Lynda Hart has turned to Butlerian theories of performativity and subversion in order to defend lesbian sado-masochism (s/m) as libratory. While acknowledging the use of symbols associated with historical atrocities in s/m role-playing, especially fascist ones, Hart defends such role-playing by suggesting it destabilises static representations of power.[79] Yet, whipping fantasies are profoundly influenced by a transatlantic cultural exchange that began at the end of the eighteenth century when nineteenth-century abolitionist print communities disseminated the image of the flogged female slave in Britain and across Europe. Marquis de Sade's *Justine* (1791) and Leopold von Sacher-Masoch's *Venus in Furs* (1870) – both influential on British flagellation literature, fantasies, and theoretical vocabularies – were also influenced by slavery.[80] Research into overlapping abolitionist and obscene print communities in Britain recontextualises the so-called English vice and its continued global trafficking within the history of slavery.

5
Japanese Erotic Prints and Late Nineteenth-Century Obscenity

Toward the end of the nineteenth century, Japan caught Europe's attention. While many scholars have explored the European cultural and commercial traffic in all things Japanese, there has been no sustained discussion of the sexually radical and often clandestine print traffic that grew from this widespread fixation. This latter-day interest in Japanese eroticism and sexual mores can be explained by the fact that the country only emerged from its political and economic seclusion in 1854 when it negotiated a treaty with America and began to form trade agreements with European nations. This renewed contact between Japan and the West not only generated consumer and creative frenzy in Britain and France, producing doubtful classics such as Gilbert and Sullivan's Japanese-inspired comic opera *The Mikado* (1885), but also provided a new sexual geography for the West to explore. Japanese prints were particularly popular.[1] Japan entered the West's commercial and phantasmatic circuits of desire when erotic versions of these prints began to surface by the middle of the century. This chapter examines how the traffic in these erotic prints influenced the British artist Aubrey Beardsley, who adapted their media aesthetics for his racy and frequently censored line drawings, especially those for Oscar Wilde's play *Salome* (1894).[2] Linda Gertner Zatlin has undertaken a significant study of Beardsley's relationship to Japanese art and eroticism,[3] but has not examined the extent to which his remediations of Japanese prints contributed to renewed debates about obscenity in late-Victorian popular culture and formed strong connections to underground print communities. What has also remained unnoticed is that by the turn of the century, the traffic in these erotic prints led to semi-clandestine sociological studies of Japanese prostitution as well as obscene underground novels on the same subject. These publications included reproductions of Japanese prints and occasionally even incorporated them thematically. Japan was perhaps too geographically distant for widespread erotic investment, and Japanese prints perhaps struck too many as an outmoded visual medium in the era of the photograph and early film. Nonetheless, this chapter shows how the sparse unconventional lines offered by Japanese erotic prints influenced underground obscenity and helped shape cultural and aesthetic understandings about it during a transitional period before the trade turned almost entirely to photographic media.

1 The traffic in Japanese erotic prints

These woodblock prints (known in Japan as *ukiyo-e* 'pictures of the Floating World') were as distinct for their ornamentation, elaborate costuming, grotesque homunculi, and sexual themes as they were for their delicate linearity, flatness, asymmetry, vertical format, and minimalism. It is uncertain exactly how these Japanese prints that influenced master painters, radical artists, and clandestine publishers alike found their way to Europe and America. Evidence of their circulation lies in contemporary accounts and surviving prints, but their route West is a matter for speculation. Dutch merchants, who sustained commerce with Japan during its political isolation, helped introduce Japanese prints to Europe before the nineteenth century, but the latter half of the nineteenth century saw the most significant European traffic. James Laver, writing about James Whistler and his circle, describes their unexpected discovery in Paris in the 1850s. In 1856, Félix Bracquemond, an artist acquaintance of Whistler's, entered a printer's shop where he noticed a small book with a limp red cover that had come as packing in a parcel of porcelain sent from Japan. Upon discovering woodcuts inside the book, he was apparently 'fascinated by the vigour of the little figures and the beautiful arrangement of each print'.[4] Laver guesses that Bracquemond introduced this album to Whistler. Japanese prints and *objets d'art* were soon sold at Madame de Soye's La Porte Chinoise, a shop that was opened in 1858 and was frequented by avant-garde artists and writers like Bracquemond, Baudelaire, the Goncourt Brothers, Whistler, Degas, and Zola. The Goncourt Bothers, French literati and publishers were instrumental in extending this enthusiasm for Japanese prints, eventually publishing two works on famous Japanese print masters, *Outamaro* (1891) and *Hokousai* (1896).[5]

Whistler is often credited with spreading this interest in Japanese prints among British artists. Many of his paintings show their influence. His *Caprice in Purple and Gold* (1864) not only reveals Japanese costume, accessory, and furniture, but also incorporates prints, probably Andô Hiroshige landscapes. He also became famous for his Japanese-inspired interior design of F. R. Leyland's dining room, which he renamed The Peacock Room for the peacocks he had painted in gold against a deep-blue background. According to Holbrook Jackson, Whistler reportedly introduced the Pre-Raphaelite painter and poet Dante Gabriel Rossetti to his collection of Japanese woodcut books and coloured prints. Beardsley's letters show that he was also familiar with Whistler's work. While he often mocked Whistler and others who influenced him, he reputedly dissolved into tears when his truculent mentor finally praised his illustrations.[6] However, the 1862 International Exhibition in South Kensington, London, which Frank Whitford explains included a Japanese section with Sir Rutherford Alcock's collection of prints, attracted the wider culture industry.[7] Once the exhibit was over, a London businessman, Arthur Liberty, purchased the Japanese collection and by 1875 formed Liberty's, a London shop on Regent's Street that specialised in oriental fashion, decoration, and art. This exhibit inspired the painter John Leighton's essay 'On Japanese Art'(1863) where he reveals that Japanese 'printing excites our wonder'.[8] From the 1860s to the mid-1890s, the enthusiasm for the Japanese print grew, becoming increasingly familiar to middle-class consumers and modern artists.

Erotic Japanese prints circulated alongside the standard varieties, though not as openly. Known as *shunga* ('spring pictures'), they appeared as painted scrolls, loose prints, or printed albums. They show explicit sexual acts and tumescent genitalia in domestic urban settings. Depictions of so-called European perversions, such as homosexuality, bestiality, and voyeurism, are also not uncommon in *shunga*. Suzuki Harunobu's print, *Lovers with Rutting Cats* (1765), is a classic example of *shunga*, though not a particularly explicit one (Plate 6). As lovers copulate over calligraphy, a homunculus ardently watches and two cats emulate the humans. It is the combination of sexual delicacy and vulgarity that fascinates. Timon Screech's *Sex and the Floating World: Erotic Images in Japan 1700-1820* discusses how in Japan such images were intended chiefly for masturbation for garrisoned men in cities like Edo, Modern Tokyo.[9]

There is evidence that albums of erotic prints, known as pillow books, made their way to America in the nineteenth century. The Kinsey Institute for Research in Sex, Gender, and Reproduction owns over half-a-dozen pillow books that date from the nineteenth and early twentieth centuries. Their provenance is unknown, but American servicemen likely brought them to the country. Some of these albums are pocket-sized and easily portable while others are larger and more unwieldy. One of the more unwieldy albums at the Kinsey Institute, which may date from the early nineteenth century, contains eleven large coloured prints and is bound with wooden boards. The prints in this album are sexually explicit, though non-violent, and often show mutual pleasuring (Plate 7).[10]

European encounters with *shunga* have also been documented. Screech's research has uncovered that as early as 1615, 'certaine lasciuious bookes and pictures' found their way to London.[11] By the late nineteenth century, when Japanese prints circulated in Europe more freely, a number of artists owned and collected *shunga*. According to Laver, Emile Zola was 'so far bitten by the craze for Japanese prints that he had the staircase of his house hung with some of the less reticent examples – the "furious fornication" which excited the interest of Mr. George Moore when he went to pay the novelist his first visit'.[12] The Goncourt Brothers not only described the circulation of *shunga*, but also suggested the Japanese government's attempts to suppress this traffic because of derisive foreigners:

La conversation va au Japon, aux images obscènes qu'il m'affirme ne plus venir en Europe, parce que, au moment où le pays a été ouvert aux étrangers, ils ont acheté ces images avec des moqueries et des mépris publics pour la salaudérie des Japonais, et que le gouvernement a été blessé, a fait rechercher ces images, et les a fait brûler.[13]

John Singer Sargent was also an avid collector of erotic prints and his set still remains the most significant in London. The British Museum holds a collection of *shunga* bequested by Gerald Kelly in 1972 and rumoured to have been reluctantly brought in by his wife. A letter accompanying the bequest states that the prints originally belonged to Sargent. The Victoria and Albert Museum also has an important collection of *shunga*, providing further evidence of the circulation of these prints and their appeal to artists excited by exotic sexual imagery and a minimalist aesthetic.

But, one of the most fascinating enthusiasts of Japanese erotic prints was Beardsley. Anecdotal evidence reveals his delight in their technique and obscenity. His contemporaries described how he exhibited these prints on his walls, partly for inspiration and partly for provocation. As Alfred Julius Meier-Graefe writes:

At Beardsley's house one used to see the finest and most explicitly erotic Japanese prints in London. They hung in plain frames against delicately coloured backgrounds, the wildest phantasies of Utamaro, and were by no means decent, though when seen from a distance, delicate, proper, and harmless enough. There are but few collectors of these things, as they cannot be exhibited, so they were comparatively cheap ten years ago, and among them the best preserved prints are to be found.[14]

William Rothenstein offers another description of Beardsley's prints, noting how even his female relatives were not shielded from their display:

The walls of his room were distempered a violent orange, the doors and skirtings were painted black; a strange taste, I thought; but his taste was all for the bizarre and exotic. Later it became somewhat chastened. I had picked up a Japanese book in Paris, with pictures so outrageous that its possession was an embarrassment. It pleased Beardsley, however, so I gave it to him. The next time I went to see him, he had taken out the most indecent prints from the book and hung them around his bedroom. Seeing he lived with his mother and sister, I was rather taken aback.[15]

Beardsley's letters further describe how he circulated these prints among his friends and fellow artists. He acknowledged receipt of Rothenstein's beautiful 'Book of Love' and left 'a set of erotic Japanese prints' for his later publisher, the inimitable Leonard Smithers, to peruse.[16]

Their provenance a mystery, erotic Japanese prints circulated in a number of communities, coming into contact with sailors and artists attracted to the strange and exotic graphic print medium that came from so far away. They quickly became a new source of obscenity for the West, attracting, as they circulated, the attention of men like Beardsley interested in their media eroticism and underground publishers fascinated with the mythology of geishas.

2 Aubrey Beardsley's libidinal line: *Japonisme, Art Nouveau*, and obscenity

Beardsley's illustrations from 1893–5 show the influence of these Japanese prints, particularly their curvilinear style. During these years, he borrowed Japanese techniques and aesthetics, an artistic fad that was known in the period as *japonisme*. His relationship with Japanese prints was important both in terms of its impact on his early art and its impression on viewers. He was engrossed by the possibilities offered by this exotic print medium, delighting in its freedom from European graphic conventions, its urbanity, its sexual frankness, and its offensiveness. Yet, if Beardsley discovered a new erotics of medium, his detractors saw a crime of medium. His illustrations produced feelings of desire and disgust that became enmeshed in *fin-de-siècle* aesthetic debates about *art nouveau, japonisme*, and obscenity.

To understand the appeal of Japanese aesthetics for Beardsley, it is important to realise that he wanted to radicalise art. His preferred graphic medium was the fine-art book, but he sought to reinvent the medium with his illustrations. Arthur Symons, possibly the most insightful and sympathetic of Beardsley's early commentators, described how the union of Beardsley and Bodley Head publisher John Lane in the early 1890s, when Beardsley was experimenting with Japanese technique and aesthetics, marked a period of innovation and modernity in the art of the book. Years after his friendship with Beardsley, he wrote:

> Fresh moods, indeed, began to show in his art the moment he began to work with John Lane. Lane was already half established as appointed publisher to the clique of writers who represented, in the public mind as in their own, the new aesthetic attitude, which was emphasised by the novel aspect of their books. Strangeness was valued for its own sake by those who held, with Poe and Bacon, that it was an attribute of all excellence. The combination of Lane and Beardsley was soon fruitful.[17]

Wilde's trial and conviction for gross indecency in 1895 abruptly broke the relationship between Lane and Beardsley because of the artist's presumed association with Wilde. The years before their break, however, were characterised by technological innovation in book illustration and design. While William Morris's Kelmscott Press looked towards the printing techniques and medievalism of the past, Lane and his circle embraced new aesthetics and media technologies, identifying themselves with the French *art nouveau* scene. As Symons observes, 'It is enough to point out that the Kelmscott borders were laboriously cut on wood at the very moment that Beardsley was welcoming the mechanically cut zinc block.'[18] Beardsley's distinctive black and white illustrations were reproduced by means of photomechanical line-block process, one of the latest printing techniques lauded by and advertised in new art journals like *The Studio*. This method involved the transfer of an image by means of a photographic negative onto a light-sensitive block that was then engraved. While some praised photo engraving, which allowed for greater intimacy between the artist and his work, others denounced it as best suited for 'slight sketches' rather than 'highly-finished subjects'.[19] However, it suited Beardsley's style, perfectly reproducing his curvilinear line.

Beardsley did not write about his philosophy of art, but his interview in 1894 for an article entitled 'The New Master of Art' for *To-day* is revealing. For one, it reveals his thorough knowledge of the new transfer process and the line block:

> I should say that the first thing is to have a good drawing. People talk a great deal of cant about 'processes'; as a matter of fact, the actual printing of the thing is of far more importance than the making of the block. Get hold of a good printer, and almost anyone can make the process block, remembering always, of course, that the drawing must be clear and good.

In this same interview, he also describes his peculiar linear style:

> I represent things as I see them – outlined faintly in thin streaks (just like me). I take no notice of shadows, they do not interest me; therefore, I feel no desire to indicate them. I am afraid that people appear differently to me than they do to others; to me they are mostly grotesque, and I represent them as I see them.

Beardsley's emphasis on the line and the grotesque immediately conjures Japanese prints. But, when the interviewer asked about his inspiration, Beardsley strangely denied the Japanese influence. As he insisted, 'Certainly no Japanese painter, though my work is said to recall the methods of the East, for as a matter of fact I knew nothing of this style of art till quite lately, beyond, of course, the fans and vases which one's eye meets everywhere.'[20] The interview revealed his intimate relationship to his graphic medium, from the printed book, to the mechanical process, to the line, all of which he desired under his artistic control and vision. But, it also showed his strange denial of the Japanese influence. His illustrations from this period and interests in Japanese prints, erotic and otherwise, immediately raise questions about this self-stylisation. The simple explanation is that he mocked his influences, for the influence of Japanese prints on his work in this period is undeniable and integral to his modernising project.

Zatlin suggests that *japonisme* pervades all of his work, but she may be underrating his other influences. Beardsley's Japanese effects arguably have their origins in an English aesthetic tradition: the flat quality of his line drawings is that of the Pre-Raphaelites and the fussy ornamentalism that of William Morris. Meier-Graefe adds that Beardsley 'could be Baroque, Empire, Pre-Raphaelite, Japanese, and [...] sometimes all of those together in the same picture'.[21] Meier-Graefe could also have mentioned Hellenistic art: Whitford reveals that Beardsley studied the often very libidinous Red and Black Attic Vases at the British Museum.[22] In other words, the Japanese influence on Beardsley's prints in the early 1890s is mixed with a number of other aesthetic traditions, English and otherwise. According to Jack Stewart, 'the aesthetic and decadent movements of the 1890s are marked [...] by increasing symbiosis of the arts: forms and themes mutate and migrate, as one medium fertilizes another.'[23] Despite his denials of Japanese influence, Beardsley adapted the Japanese print to the line block in this spirit of cross-fertilization, mixing the two print media and a pastiche of aesthetic precedents to create a new art form. His illustrations for Wilde's play *Salome* best represent his Japanese phase, though there are many other examples.[24] With his new mixed medium, he explored the stylised freedom and obscenity of his flat curvilinear line. In the process, he explored an erotics of medium that challenged the sexual, aesthetic, and cultural proprieties of the day.

Wilde wrote *Salome* first in French between late 1891 and early 1892. It is a highly abstract rewriting of the biblical story of Salome and King Herod, which imagines Herod's perverse desire for Salome and Salome's forbidden desire for the prophet, John the Baptist (Iokanaan). Much to Wilde's disgust, the Examiner of Plays for the Lord Chamberlain, Edward T. Smyth Pigott, refused to license its performance in England in 1892 on the grounds of religious irreverence. Despite the controversy, the French version of the play was published in France with illustrations by Félcien Rops in 1893, and the English version was published in England by Lane with illustrations by Beardsley in February 1894. Beardsley's Japanesque drawing *J'ai Baisé Ta Bouche Iokanaan, J'ai Baisé Ta Bouche*, which was published in the first issue of *The Studio* in April 1893 and inspired by Wilde's play, had attracted the attention of both Lane and Wilde, so much so that they chose him to illustrate the English version (Figure 11). The English *Salome* had a significant first-edition run, 750 copies in violet canvas (which Wilde hated) and 125 in Japanese vellum, but the richly illustrated quarto was clearly marketed to the

FROM A DRAWING IN ILLUSTRATION OF MR. OSCAR WILDE'S "SALOME"
BY AUBREY BEARDSLEY

Figure 11 Aubrey Beardsley, *J'ai Baisé ta Bouche Iokanaan. The Studio* 1 (April 1863)

art industry rather than the common reader. Much to Wilde's consternation, Lane also aggressively publicised the play's controversy in order to increase sales.[25]

Beardsley's ten full-page illustrations for Lane's edition of *Salome* had, as Stanley Weintraub observes, 'more erotic details than had ever been seen before in a book openly published and distributed in England'.[26] Genitals are nearly self-propagating, and sexual symbols need little undressing. Even so, some of his original drawings were suppressed or altered because of their sexual content, only appearing in later editions of the play. Beardsley alluded to these pre-publication expurgations in his letters. In September 1893, he wrote to Rothenstein that 'the *Salomé* drawings have created a veritable fronde, with George Moore at the head of frondeurs.' In November 1893, he wrote to Wilde's long-time companion Robbie Ross: 'I have withdrawn three of the illustrations and supplied their place with three new ones (simply beautiful and quite irrelevant).'[27] Brian Reade discusses these expurgations: a fig-leaf was added to the youth's penis in *Enter Herodias*, and the original *The Toilet of Salome I* was rejected because of the seated masturbating youth (Figures 12 and 13).[28]

Most of the commentary on Beardsley's illustrations for *Salome* has focused on the relationship between his illustrations and Wilde's play. While some critics argue that the illustrations are extraneous, or even irreverent, others argue that they are collaborative.[29] Beardsley's admission that some of his illustrations were 'irrelevant'[30] and Wilde's putative comment that 'dear Aubrey's designs are like the naughty scribbles a precocious schoolboy makes on the margins of his copybooks'[31] have helped fuel this critical debate. Rothenstein's comment about the competing orientalism between text and illustration is perhaps the most revealing: apparently 'Wilde admired, though he didn't really like, Beardsley's *Salome* illustrations; he thought them too Japanese, as indeed they were. His play was Byzantine.'[32] In my view, Beardsley was following his own aesthetic and erotic agenda that was separate from Wilde's.

Beardsley's illustrations for *Salome* aimed both to shock, titillate, and even offend with their defamiliarising effects and rebellion against aesthetic proprieties. They immediately attract attention with their startling deviation from European graphic conventions. As Chris Snodgrass notes, they depict a 'groundless earth', 'floating figures', and a 'reckless lack of perspective'.[33] Matthew Sturgis explains further:

> The relationship between form and content was deliberately upset. Characters floated without moorings, dominated by their fabulous clothes or by the decorative devices that – without reference to sense or probability – swirled about them. Their figures were drawn out (beyond even the elongations of Burne-Jones) and smoothed down to a disconcerting androgyny. These oddly sexless bodies were then given faces that spoke of untold depravity.[34]

Beardsley's illustrations upset conventional visual coherence (as well as semiotic coherence): *The Stomach Dance* and *A Platonic Lament* with their split diagonal and vertical perspectives, *The Woman in the Moon* with its vast empty white space, and *The Eyes of Herod* and *The Peacock Skirt* with their mania of meaningless ornament, filament, and pointilist detail (Figures 14–18). The unconventional look of these illustrations is that of the Japanese print. The repetition of exotic motifs also underlines this aesthetic: the Japanesque signature piece, the Whistlerian butterflies and peacocks, the costumes, postures, tassels, and furniture, and the hideous grotesques. These strange illustrations are visual surrogates for nameless perversion, which the naked bodies, suggestive shapes, and lurid faces repeatedly suggest is obscene.

While Beardsley aimed to offend with his graphic anomalies, he also showed pleasure and stylised abandon in exploring the mixed medium he had created. His sparse, curvilinear line, influenced by the Japanese masters and used in most of his *Salome* drawings, best conveys his hedonistic delight with the aesthetic and, in turn, sexual promise of his transcultural remediation. For his frontispiece, *The Woman in the Moon* , this line is free, though not yet libertine (cf. Figure 16). It blurs the distinction between bodies and clothes, suggesting the performance and indeterminacy of gender and sexual identities. *The Peacock Skirt*, though a busier drawing, introduces a hectic, emancipated line in the form of escaping peacock feathers (cf. Figure 18). The line also becomes obsessed with the folds of the woman's Japanese garment on the right. These folds, because of their position and vulval shape, immediately suggest the female pubis. The hand awkwardly positioned inside one of these folds is not the first or only hint of masturbation. *The Stomach Dance* shows a similar sexual fixation with the folds of a garment (cf. Figure 14). It is difficult to determine the garment of the female figure on the right, but the sweeping vulval creases between her thighs accentuate her pubis. At the bottom left of the illustration, a grotesque handles a lyre, but the crude positioning of his fingers, the suggestive opening at the bottom of the instrument, and the multiplying phalli in his garment exemplify Beardsley in what Snodgrass has called his 'pornographic coding'.[35] In the original *The Toilet of Salome I* , Beardsley's line is totally uninhibited: outlined hands disappear between thighs, a wanton hand strums a lyre, elbows double for fatigued breasts, and the pierrot's outfit sprouts two giant pert breasts (cf. Figure 13). In the bowdlerised version of the same drawing, *The Toilet of Salome II*, the pierrot's elbow doubles for a hanging breast (Figure 19). The pierrot in the final *cul-de-lampe*, entitled *The Burial of Salome*, similarly has a garment of breasts (Figure 20). This illustration, however, is far more sinister as the speared puff on the coffin symbolises the satyr's necrophilic rape of the naked Salome. It is shocking, in fact, that this illustration was not censored along with the others. After a while, one searches for concealed male and female organs in all of the illustrations, participating in and extending Beardsley's linear *jouissance* and excess. Beardsley finally realised the pure expression of this linear style two years later when he designed the cover for

Figure 12 Aubrey Beardsley, *Enter Herodias*, uncensored version for Oscar Wilde, *Salome*. London: John Lane, 1894. By permission of the Victoria and Albert Museum, London

Figure 13 Aubrey Beardsley, *The Toilet of Salome* I, original version for Oscar Wilde, *Salome*. London: John Lane, 1894. By permission of the Victoria and Albert Museum, London

Figure 14 Aubrey Beardsley, *The Stomach Dance* for Oscar Wilde, *Salome*. London: John Lane, 1894. By permission of Harvard University Art Museums, Cambridge, Massachusetts

Figure 15 Aubrey Beardsley, *A Platonic Lament* for Oscar Wilde, *Salome*, London: John Lane, 1894. By permission of the Victoria and Albert Museum, London

Figure 16 Aubrey Beardsley, *The Woman in the Moon* for Oscar Wilde, *Salome*. London: John Lane, 1894. By permission of Harvard University Art Museums, Cambridge, Massachusetts

Figure 17 Aubrey Beardsley, *The Eyes of Herod* for Oscar Wilde, *Salome*. London: John Lane, 1894. By permission of Harvard University Art Museums, Cambridge, Massachusetts

Figure 18 Aubrey Beardsley, *The Peacock Skirt* for Oscar Wilde, *Salome*. London: John Lane, 1894. By permission of Harvard University Art Museums, Cambridge, Massachusetts

Figure 19 Aubrey Beardsley, *The Toilet of Salome* II, altered version for Oscar Wilde, *Salome*. London: John Lane, 1894. By permission of the Victoria and Albert Museum, London

Figure 20   Aubrey Beardsley, *The Burial of Salome* for Oscar Wilde, *Salome*. London: John Lane, 1894. By permission of Harvard University Art Museums, Cambridge, Massachusetts

Ernest Dowson's *Verses* (1896), a 'near to nothing' design (as Reade observes) of a few vulval lines stamped in gold (Figure 21).[36]

Critics have speculated about the social implications of Beardsley's experimental aesthetics. Derek Stanford believed that Beardsley's poor health governed his 'erotic universe': 'his obsession with the erotic was largely the sick man's obsession with health, and, later, the dying man's obsession with life.'[37] Richard Ellmann, Chris Snodgrass, Richard Dellamora, and Lorraine Janzen Kooistra have more recently argued that Beardsley's highly sexualised pictures challenge normative gender and sexual categories. Zatlin has also suggested that Beardsley upsets Victorian patriarchy and xenophobia, possibly owing to the influence of Japanese *shunga*. As she writes, 'Beardsley learned a great deal from *shunga* about the portrayal of sexuality. *Shunga* would have taught Beardsley that sexuality could be suggested, rather than leeringly presented, and the prints may have assisted the artist in subverting Victorian perceptions of women.'[38] Zatlin generalises about the patriarchal violence of Western pornography in order to defend *shunga*, but she is one

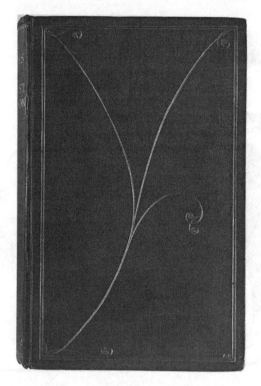

Figure 21   Aubrey Beardsley, Cover for Ernest Dowson's *Verses*. London: Leonard Smithers, 1894. By permission of the Victoria and Albert Museum, London

of the only critics to consider the influence of Japanese erotic imagery and prints on Beardsley's art. I agree that Beardsley's aesthetics are suffused with sexual rebellion, but his illustrations for *Salome* also show the enormous pleasure he derived from the mobility of his Japanese-inspired line that could cross identities, desires, cultures, proprieties, and print media.

If Beardsley explored the erotics of his mixed print medium, his viewers debated its crimes. With his shocking, but titillating illustrations for *Salome*, he introduced a dialectic of desire and disgust that dominated the reception of his illustrations and produced a discourse of obscenity. Jonathan Dollimore theorises about such a dialectic, writing that the 'active incitement of disgust can be an effective strategy of critical critique and political opposition: a confronting of culture with its constitutive repressions, a provocative violation of cultural boundaries and bodily properties'. He also adds that 'sexual disgust is also a prime motor of censorship.'[39] The British reception of Beardsley's Japanesque drawings for *Salome* (and to a lesser extent its immediate successor, *The Yellow Book*) reproduced this oscillation between desire and disgust. Critics did not concentrate exclusively on content, but mostly on media aesthetics (style, pattern, form, line). Some critics praised the modernity and minimalism of his linear designs and others negatively associated them with French *art nouveau,* exoticism, and obscenity. The latter response is especially interesting because it denied the English aesthetic influence on Beardsley's art in order to galvanise a cultural debate about his exotic, miscegenated style. The most fascinating responses to Beardsley's designs, however, were the visual parodies in *Punch; or the London Charivari,* the illustrated periodical whose social conservativism had been established for decades. While these parodies mimicked Beardsley's style to exaggerate its putative crimes, they also showed pleasure in the interface. In other words, the division between desire and disgust began to break down, the crimes of medium blending into the erotics of medium with the persuasions of Beardsley's stylised libidinal line of miscellaneous origins.

In April 1893, Joseph Pennell introduced 'A New Illustrator' to art aficionados. It was this article on Beardsley in the first volume of *The Studio* that attracted the attention of Lane and Wilde with its reproduction of his drawings, including *J'ai Baisé Ta Bouche* (cf. Figure 11). Pennell focuses on Beardsley's 'mechanical engraving'[40] and 'Japanesque' designs, publicising both his technological innovations and exotic tendencies. He insists, nonetheless, that 'most interesting of all is his use of the single line, with which he weaves his drawings into an harmonious whole, joining extremes and reconciling what might be oppositions – leading, but not forcing, you properly to regard the concentration of his motive.'[41]

In that same month, however, D. Tinto from the *London Figaro* wrote a response to Pennell's article, announcing his refusal to worship Beardsley's *art nouveau.* His hostility focuses on the photomechanically reproduced print:

> The drawings are flat blasphemies against art. Burne Jones I admire, and the oddities of Japanese draughtsmen I can appreciate, but when a man mixes up impotent imitations of Burne Jones at his very worst with pseudo-Japanese effects, and serves up the whole with a sauce of lilies and peacock feathers, I think it is only charitable to think that the author of all this rococo business has a twist in his intellects.[42]

For this reviewer, Beardsley's two-dimensional linearity is offensive: its flatness somehow explains its blasphemy. This attack against the audacious flatness of Beardsley's designs also signals profound hostility against the mixing of styles and the influence of Japanese prints, known for their vertical perspective, but lack of chiaroscuro.

The appearance of *Salome* in February 1894 fuelled this antagonism against Beardsley's art. As Beardsley himself acknowledged in his interview for *To-day,* 'My illustrations of Mr. Oscar Wilde's *Salome* were what have created most sensation and brought down most wrath.'[43] Despite Beardsley's many defenders, a discourse of disgust quickly emerged. The *Times* review of *Salome* from 8 March 1894 initiated an early, but virulent attack against Beardsley's illustrations:

> As for the illustrations by Mr. Aubrey Beardsley, we hardly know what to say of them. They are fantastic, grotesque, unintelligible for the most part, and, so far as they are intelligible, repulsive. They would seem to represent the manners of Judea as conceived by Mr. Oscar Wilde portrayed in the style of Japanese grotesque as conceived by a French decadent. The whole thing must be a joke, and it seems to us a very poor joke.[44]

The review suggests that the illustrations flaunted a Japanese exoticism that was linked with French decadence. As Jane Haville Desmarais shows, the British mainstream conservative press was 'hostile to international influence in the visual arts'.[45] Instead of showing delight with this mixed medium, the reviewer finds it 'repulsive'. He also reveals a deep wariness about the purpose of the illustrations that stems their unusual form: he finds them 'unintelligible', but worries that they are parodic, possibly subversive.

The *Saturday Review* published an article on 'Salome' on 24 March 1894 that echoed the *Times* review and encapsulated popular anxieties about Beardsley's *art nouveau* style. Like the *Times*, it denounced its mixed French and Japanese effects. As the reviewer wrote, 'Illustration by means of derisive parody of Félicien Rops, embroidered onto Japanese themes, is a new form of literary torture; and no one can question that the author of *Salome* is on the rack.'[46] Rops was a Belgian illustrator with connections to the French *literati*, including Baudelaire and the Goncourt Brothers, who became associated with continental decadence and known for his sexually violent and blasphemous images of mutilated women. As Beardsley's letters reveal, he was familiar with the artist, who had illustrated the French version of Wilde's *Salome*, but their styles were dissimilar.[47] Nonetheless, his admixture of continental and Asian influences also lets the reviewer brand his illustrations as derivative:

> They suggest the imitation of Rops too closely, and sometimes, as in the marvellously decorative design called 'The Peacock Skirt', they borrow, without sufficient and indeed without any adaptation, the ritual of Japanese ornament. Mr. Beardsley must assimilate a style; it is not enough for him to reproduce at will variations on eccentric existing styles which please his temperament. We fancy that, in dealing with *Salome*, he has not cared to do more than indulge his ingenious predilection for the paradoxical and the fantastic.

This reviewer, like the one for the *Times*, finds Beardsley's medium defamiliarising: he can only restate platitudes that his illustrations are 'paradoxical' and 'fantastical'. He ultimately reveals hostility, though not quite sexual disgust, toward Beardsley's decadence and exoticism. Yet a notable exclusion from his reading of the published *Toilette of Salome II* also intimates an anxious reaction to the sexual temperament of Beardsley's art. Of this illustration, he writes, 'We are allowed to read the backs of Salome's favourite books, and they explain her unseemly attitude toward Iokannan; we find among them *Nana* and *Manon Lescaut* and *The Golden Ass* , not to mention something worse.'[48] The book he omits to mention, of course, is that by the Marquis de Sade – French, sexually explicit, and cruel. The reviewer's assault against Beardsley's crimes of medium overlap with an unspeakable revulsion with his barely veiled allusions to sex and obscenity.

In April, the following month, reviews of *Salome* and *The Yellow Book* continued to circulate and developed this dialectic of desire and disgust over Beardsley's art. Not surprisingly, the second volume of the *Studio* published an article on 'New Publications' that praised Beardsley's illustrations for *Salome*:

> In the new edition of *Salome* we find the irrepressible personality of the artist dominating everything – whether the compositions do or do not illustrate the text – what may be their exact purpose or the meaning of their symbolism, is happily not necessary to consider here. Nor is it expedient to bring conventional criticism to bear upon them, for nothing in ancient or modern art is akin that you could place it side by side for comparison. Audacious and extravagant, with a grim purpose and power of achieving the unexpected – we have almost written the impossible – one takes it for itself, as a piquant maddening potion, not so much a tonic as a stimulant to fancy.

According to this reviewer, the illustrations are shockingly modern and original, especially insofar as form supersedes content and reference to Wilde's play. In the end, he claims that 'all collectors of rare and esoteric literature will rank this book as one of the most remarkable productions of the modern press',[49] perhaps suggesting that this work, like the 'esoteric pornography' of Sir Richard Burton, could contribute to the British erotic tradition of the superb printed book.

Reviews of the same period, however, began to register disgust with Beardsley's art. On 20 April, the *Times* published a scathing review of the first volume of *The Yellow Book*:

> If the New Art is represented by the cover of this wonderful volume, it is scarcely calculated to attract by its intrinsic beauty or merit; possibly, however, it may be intended to attract by its very repulsiveness and insolence [...] . Its note appears to be a combination of English rowdyism with French lubricity.

A week later, on 28 April, the *Academy* also reviewed *The Yellow Book*. Although the reviewer acknowledges 'a certain attractiveness of 'line', he insists 'Beardsley must forget the Japanese'. Beardsley's mixed medium, the review suggests, is corrupted by foreign influence. On 1 June, the *Dial* reiterated this position in its review of *The Yellow Book*. In directing particular attention to its Art editor, the reviewer maintains, 'Now Mr. Beardsley is a very clever young man, and he sometimes displays a real mastery of line, but he misses as frequently as he hits, and he has distinctly missed in the present instance.' Once again, Beardsley's line is described as technically skilful, but egregiously misdirected. Such misdirection, the critics suggest, relates to a mixed foreign aesthetic that is sexually perverse and even downright obscene. By 9 February 1895, the *Pall Mall Gazette*, always on the search for sexual misconduct, could deride Beardsley's moral reputation with a sharp one-liner – 'Mr Beardsley is already the patron saint of the back parlour.'[50]

While Beardsley's art may not have been widely reviewed, his illustrations gained enough distinction and notoriety to be noticed by *Punch; or The London Charivari*. An illustrated magazine of political and social satire, *Punch* had its pulse on Victorian popular culture. It had popularised the Pre-Raphaelites, the Japanese craze, and Aestheticism with its typically conservative response to the arts. It also popularised Beardsley's distinctive style through a series of visual parodies. These parodies mocked his Japanese designs and branded them as deviant and repulsive, yet discovered, perhaps accidentally, vicarious pleasure in reproducing his wanton, riotous lines.

The *Punch* parodies of Beardsley's art appeared predominately between 1894 and 1895. J. Bernard Partridge, who had been drawing for *Punch* since 1891, produced a couple of notable Beardsley parodies, sometimes adding arachnids and death heads to mock his morbid tendencies and other times cross-dressing him to suggest his gender transgressions.[51] However, Edward T. Reed, who first began to draw for *Punch* in 1889,[52] produced brilliant Beardsley parodies that reveal an intimate familiarity with his mixed medium and libidinal line. They did not specifically attack his *Salome* drawings, but they began to appear in early spring 1894, soon after their publication.

Reed's relationship with the artist began with his illustrations for *Punch* 'She-Notes'. These were parodies of Lane's Keynotes series that featured controversial novels about gender and sexual transgression by New Woman writers like George Egerton and Grant Allen. As illustrator and designer for the Keynotes series, Beardsley did the cover art as well as the key design that appeared on the volume's title page, spine, and back cover. The first 'She-Notes' parody appeared on 10 March 1894, making a travesty of Egerton, not so subtly renamed Borgia Smudgiton. Appearing underneath the title is the italicised phrase '*With Japanese Fan de Siècle Illustrations by Mortarthurio Whiskerly*'. The title plays on Beardsley's name, mocks his Japanese and Medieval tastes, and suggests his French decadence. Reed's accompanying illustration extends the derision (Figure 22). A quick glance reveals a caricature of the New Woman, aggressive mien, cigarette, and fishing rod operating as immediate visual markers. A closer look at the musical notes and the signature key at the bottom left reveals that the drawing is also a parody of the Keynote series. The illustration thus appears to be derisive of the books and personalities of the *fin-de-siècle*. A little knowledge of Beardsley's art, however, shows that it is also an incisive parody of it, particularly of his illustrations for *Salome*. The woman's riotous black hair streaked with white evokes his Japanese coiffures. The comic figure at the top of the key impersonates his ubiquitous Japanese grotesques. The foot of the woman's skirt mimics the stylised curve of the 'peacock skirt', while the mask at its base plays on his theatrical motifs throughout. Finally, the blood dripping from the heart recalls the sexual violence of Salome's murder of Iokannan as implied in *The Climax* (Figure 23). Beardsley's libidinal line can also be discovered in the suggestive outline of the woman's outstretched hand. Reed followed up this drawing for the second part of the 'She Notes' parody that appeared on 17 March. Like the first drawing, it copies Beardsley's Japanesque designs by means of ornament, costume, line, and technique (Figure 24).[53] In short, Reed understood the obscenities concealed in Beardsley's drawings and evoked by his unusual medium. Yet, the energy with which Reed reproduces Beardsley's wanton line might also intimate a shared pleasure. As Sturgis notices, Reed's caricatures 'had been slowly displaced by a desire to imitate'.[54]

After the series of Beardsley parodies that appeared in *Punch*, Beardsley's black and white curvilinear art signalled perversion. His stylistic eccentricities were so associated with sexual perversions that they became visual contractions for these putative crimes. 'The Woman Who Wouldn't Do', which was published on 30 March 1895, was the third Keynote parody illustrated by Reed that took full advantage of these parodic echoes and contractions of Beardsley's obscenities. A travesty of Grant Allen's controversial New Woman novel *The Woman Who Did* (1895), the work attacks Allen's overwrought free-love message.[55] Reed's illustration appears to complement the conservative ideology of the *Punch* text by depicting a malevolent woman who dominates the landscape and overshadows the male figure in the background (Figure 25). In our discussion of the reception history of Allen's novel, Vanessa K. Warne and I have observed that this illustration imitates Beardsley's art in order to suggest the gender and sexual perversities of Allen's characters. Warne and I have also noted how the female figure is sexualised:

> Her hair, her loose clothes, and her languishing posture all contribute to this characterization. Her appearance also aligns her with the larger landscape, a setting which emphasizes her sexuality, with its curved slopes and clouds, and a single dark shrub which functions as a vaginal symbol.[56]

Figure 22   E. T. Reed, 'She-Note', *Punch* 10 March 1894

Figure 23 Aubrey Beardsley, *The Climax* for Oscar Wilde, *Salome*. London: John Lane, 1894. By permission of the Victoria and Albert Museum, London

Figure 24   E. T. Reed, 'She-Note', *Punch* 17 March 1894

Beardsley's drawing for the *Pall Mall Magazine*, *The Kiss of Judas* (1893), was Reed's template for the parody (Figure 26). He evokes *The Kiss of Judas* in the woman's reclining posture, outstretched hand, Japanese coiffure, and pointilist accents. The more pronounced *japonisme* of the *Salome* drawings was also likely an influence. Reed reproduces Beardsley's mixed medium with considerable skill, expertly copying his Japanese line and pointilist accents. Once again, Reed also explores the libidinal line, recovering Beardsley's coded obscenities. The woman's awkwardly positioned hand lies next to her pubis, which is accented by two vulval lines and recalled by the peculiar ornamental bush. The bush recalls the giant powder puff in *The Burial of Salome*, which in turn evokes women's pubic hair in many *shunga* prints (cf. Figure 21). Reed thus decodes Beardsley's suggestions of auto-eroticism and female sexuality. By so doing, he exposes Beardsley's crimes of medium, but also participates in the artist's 'pornographic coding' because his subtly obscene lines also evade the censors. He thus reveals not only a pleasure in looking at Beardsley's Japanesque drawings, but also in executing them. Desire overrides disgust through an imitation of Beardsley's style and favourite print medium and transforms Reed's project into an exploration of its erotics.

Figure 25 E. T. Reed, *'The Woman Who Wouldn't Do'*, *Punch* 30 March 1895

Figure 26 Aubrey Beardsley, *The Kiss of Judas, Pall Mall Magazine* July 1893

Reed also produced a full-size parody entitled 'Britannia à la Beardsley' for the *Punch Almanack* of 1895 (Figure 27). As Desmarais observes, its criticism is more national in perspective and illustrates 'how the influence of foreign ideas (French and Japanese in particular) undermine[s] British

Figure 27   E. T. Reed, *Britannia à la Beardsley, Punch's Almanack*, 1895

values'.[57] The female figure represents Boadicea, the historical defender of England against Roman invaders. But the symbols of emasculated national pride that surround her – the delicate lion, the effeminate bull-terrier, the effete Punch figure – suggest her current failings. The French coast looms in the background, indicating the source of the problem. As with his other parodies, however, Reed shows interest in Beardsley's medium even as he uses it to imply decadence, exoticism, and obscenity. The stylised waves in the background, which Beardsley himself never produced in his own illustrations, imitate Hokusai's water landscapes. The rock landscape on the left, accented with pointilist detail, also recalls Japanese prints. The libidinal lines, though not pronounced, emerge in the penile shapes of the tassels – yet another Japanese effect. This illustration, though clearly preoccupied with anxieties about British national and moral sustainability, reveals, but does not acknowledge, the appeal of Beardsley's art, particularly its foreign influences.

After 1895, and the Wilde scandal, the cultural industry around Beardsley contracted. There were, however, eloquent defences of his linear technique after his death. His friend Robbie Ross admired his mastery of form. In 1898, Ross described how 'no one ever carried a simple line to its inevitable end with such sureness and firmness of purpose'.[58] Jackson also suggested the desire of a line carried by exoticism: 'The frozen realities of Japan became torrid reflections of occidental passion expressed in crisp shadows and sweeps of line in black and white, suggesting colours undreamt of even in the rainbow East.'[59] But it was Symons once again who offered the most astute commentary on Beardsley's art. In his essay on Beardsley published in May 1898 for the *Fortnightly Review*, he praises his urbanity, describing his art as 'meant for the street, for people who are walking fast', but he particularly notices his line:

> And after all, the secret of Beardsley is there: in the line itself rather than anything, intellectually realised, which the line is intended to express. With Beardsley everything was a question of form: his interest in his work began when the paper was before him and the pen in his hand. [...] And the design might seem to have no relation with the title of its subject, and indeed, might have none: its relation was of line to line within the limits of its own border, and to nothing else in the world.

After arguing that Beardsley took 'freely all that the Japanese could give him, that release from the bondage of what we call real things', he concludes that this exotic influence allowed for 'new possibilities for an art': 'conceived as pure line, conducted through mere pattern, which, after many hesitations, has resolved finally upon a great compromise, that compromise which the greatest artists have made, between the mind's outline and the outline of visible things'.[60] Symons thus recuperated Beardsley's line. It is problematic, particularly in terms of Beardsley's erotic legacy, that Symons empties his art of sexual expression through his moral aesthetisation of his medium as 'pure line'. But he captures the libertine spirit of Beardsley's line that more recent critics have ignored. Zatlin has observed that his 'delicacy of line' was 'useful in subverting censorship',[61] while Elliott Gilbert has described it as 'tortuous'.[62] It was also the exotic character of the line that created the controversy and excitement about its perverse twists and folds.

With his Japanese-inspired illustrations, Beardsley abstracted the obscene, causing offence, but also drawing reluctant enthusiasts. Allison Pease argues that Beardsley avoided aligning himself with obscenity by privileging aesthetics over sensuous pleasure. In suggesting that he aestheticised his sexualised drawings in order to legitimise it as high art, she argues that 'the deployment of the pornographic [. . .] is almost always accompanied by an ironic distancing that focuses not on the sexual representation itself, but on how that representation is mediated and received.'[63] She suggests that Beardsley amused himself with pornographic tropes, but maintained his status as an artist of repute. However, Pease's argument falters when one considers how Beardsley aligned himself with publishers of obscenity, how he reflected upon the function of obscenity, and how his Salome drawings was readily exploited for the trade in obscenity. He may have asserted the 'high-cultural aesthetic' of his art[64] and most of his work may have evaded the censors, but these factors never excluded the obscene. After his death in 1898, his prints were in fact trafficked in illicit contexts, confirming his close connections with the techniques and phantasms of the obscene and raising questions about his status as an artist or a pornographer.

When alive, Beardsley himself was certainly no stranger to the underground publishing scene in London and Paris. When Lane dropped Beardsley over the Wilde scandal, Smithers became his publisher. Beardsley became the chief artist for Smithers's decadent periodical *The Savoy* (1896), produced cover art for Smithers's catalogues, and famously illustrated Alexander Pope's *The Rape of the Lock* (1896).[65] He was also versed in Smithers's underground operations as his letters show that he read Smithers's *Priapeia.*[66] Smithers was also his underground publisher. His sexually explicit illustrations for Aristophanes's *Lysistrata* (1896) probably explain why Smithers had it privately issued in 100 quarto copies under the imprint of the Erotika Biblion Society. These drawings are notable for their 'priapic freakishness' and 'phallic isolation'.[67] With Smithers, he had also published a highly metaphorical work of obscenity, *The Story of Venus and Tannhäuser* (1897), which includes stylised descriptions of masturbation, bestiality, coprophilia, and pederasty. A shorter, expurgated version had appeared as *Under the Hill* in *The Savoy*, but Smithers had 350 fine copies of this version privately circulated.[68] Because of this association with Smithers, Beardsley gained a reputation for cerebral, but sordid, lechery. His contemporaries noted this. Rothenstein denounced Smithers as a 'bizarre and improbable figure' who, being a disciple of the Marquis de Sade, exercised an 'evil influence' on Beardsley.[69] According to Jackson,

> [Beardsley] was fond of adventuring in strange and forbidden bookish realms of any and every age. The romance, *Under the Hill*, suggests deep knowledge of that literature generally classed under facetia and erotica by the booksellers, and there are passages that which read like romanticised excerpts from the *Psychopathia Sexualis* of Krafft-Ebing.[70]

Not surprisingly, Smithers's son, Jack Smithers, represented the relationship differently and insisted that Beardsley was the corrupting influence:

> When commissioned to do legitimate art for *The Savoy*, Beardsley was not content with this; he persisted in sending to London, or bringing them personally, obscene drawings which from their very nature were unsalable, begging my father to take them and sell them for him. Beautifully executed in such technique and medium as only Beardsley was master of, yet devilish in subject. I have seen some of these, and believe me, they could only have been sold to the utterly depraved. Wishful of further continued work from Beardsley, Smithers accepted them and hid them away, promptly forgetting all about them.[71]

Jack Smithers shows that Beardsley was not immediately associated with legitimate art. That Beardsley himself was not impervious to this indictment is evident in his last letter. In his 'death agony', he wrote to Smithers, 'I implore you to destroy *all* copies of *Lysistrata* and bad drawings. [...] By all that is holy *all* obscene drawings.'[72] He may have felt compunction about his 'bad drawings' at the end of his life, but as an artist he did not uncomplicatedly distance himself from the obscene.

Before the deathbed renunciation, Beardsley had also given thought to the functions of obscenity. His bookplate design for his correspondent Jerome Pollitt suggests the relationship between hand-held books and reading pleasures. It depicts a naked woman reaching out for a bound volume, one of Beardsley's favourite pictorial themes (Figure 28).[73] In *The Story of Venus and Tannhäuser*, Beardsley again reflects on the relationship between obscenity and print media. There is a lengthy description of the 'delightful pictures' on the walls:

> Within the delicate, curved frames lived the corrupt and gracious creatures of Dorat and his school; slim children in masque and domino, smiling horribly, exquisite lechers leaning over the shoulders of smooth doll-like

Figure 28   Aubrey Beardsley, Bookplate Design for Herbert J. Pollitt, n.d. By permission
of Harvard University Art Museums, Cambridge, Massachusetts

ladies, and doing nothing particular, terrible little pierrots posing as
mulierasts, or pointing at something outside the picture, and unearthly
fops and strange women mingling in some rococo room lighted myster-
iously by the flicker of a dying fire that throws huge shadows upon wall
and ceiling. One of the prints showing how the old marquis practised
the five-finger exercise, while in front of him his mistress offered her
warm kisses to a panting poodle, made the chevalier stroke himself a
little.[74]

The print described here could be any number of Beardsley's illustrations,
including those for *Salome*. The passage acknowledges how the print can
wantonly instigate masturbation and even suggests the reader's proper
response to his story. Arguably, he remediates his own illustrations for *Salome*
by describing them in an underground publication and by divorcing them
from the kind of fine art books and magazines where he published much of
his work. He thus imagines and encourages the underground traffic of his
work, revelling in the mutability and mobility of sexual expression.

Beardsley's illustrations for *Salome* were circulated in just such a fashion
in diverse media environments after his death. If the later circulation of
these prints is any indication, Beardsley was regarded as a pornographer, as
much as a skilled artist, for the next 20 years after his death. In *Salome with
the Head of John the Baptist* (*c*.1907), Franz von Bayros, a German illustrator
who specialised in erotica and was influenced by the decadent art of the
1890s, reimagined the Beardsley's *Climax* from *Salome* (Figure 29). Bayros's
illustration, mixing the baroque style of Beardsley's *Rape of the Lock* with his
Japanese line, offers a far more sexually explicit image of a naked Salome
whose breast is being suckled by the decapitated John the Baptist.[75] A half-
tinted early twentieth-century French postcard, which has found its way
to Wellington in the Museum of New Zealand Collection, also reimagines
Beardsley's *The Climax* (Plate 8; cf. Figure 23). A naked Salome sits cross-
legged on a table from which juts John the Baptist's severed head. The hair
ornament, chrysanthemums, fans, and Japanese ladies on the wallpaper all
recreate Beardsley's Japanese effects. While the postcard does not recreate
Beardsley's style or mimic his print medium, it crudely appropriates his
japonisme for obscene purposes.

D. H. Lawrence also used Beardsley's drawings for his own purposes.
Jack Stewart has recently discussed Lawrence's knowledge of the visual arts,
including late nineteenth-century decadence. His first novel, *The White
Peacock* (1911), includes a scene that has characters poring over Beardsley's
drawings for *Salome*. Cyril Beardsall discovers the pictures before showing
them to a female companion:

I came upon reproductions of Aubrey Beardsley's 'Atalanta', and of the
tail-piece to *Salome*, and others. I sat and looked and my soul leaped out
upon the new thing. I was bewildered, wondering, grudging, fascinated.

Figure 29 Franz von Bayros, *Salome with the Head of John the Baptist* (c.1907). By permission of the Kinsey Institute for Research in Sex, Gender and Reproduction, Bloomington, Indiana

I looked a long time, but my mind or my soul, would come to no state of coherence. I was fascinated and overcome, but yet full of stubbornness and resistance.[76]

This passage reveals how reproductions of Beardsley's prints were separated from their original book format, an indication of how their erotics was more dangerous and titillating than Wilde's prose. Cyril's violent reaction to the illustrations also shows that they are coded as obscene. For another character in the novel, Beardsley's libidinal line, borrowed from the Japanese print masters, arouses sexual desire:

I want her more than anything. – And the more I look at these naked lines, the more I want her. It's a sort of fine sharp feeling, like these curved lines. I don't know what I'm saying – but do you think she'd have me? Has she seen these pictures?[77]

Charles Ricketts wrote in 1932 that 'old and backward men of the official type speak of "Salomé", on hearsay, as if it were by De Sade.'[78] The actress Maud Allen took the lead in the 1918 production of Wilde's play in Britain only to be accused of being a member of 'the cult of the clitoris'.[79] Beardsley's illustrations for *Salome*, with their wanton line adapted from the masters of Japanese print, not only tarnished the afterlife of the play and its heroine, but also powerfully associated them both with French decadence, Japanese exoticism, and gentleman's obscenity.

3 Japanese prostitution: *Amorous Adventures of a Japanese Gentleman* to *Yoshiwara: The Nightless City*

At the turn of the century, another cluster of publications emerged out of this erotic investment in Japan and Japanese prints. A number of sociological works on Japanese life were published. They concentrated particularly on Japanese prostitutes and the red-light districts (known as the *Yoshiwara*), which were frequently the subject of Japanese prints. While these sociological studies were openly published, they also revealed anxiety about their subject matter. This reluctance, of course, simply concealed the primary motive behind these works: the unveiling of Japan's sexual curiosities. True to form, underground publishers were savvy readers and did not miss this opportunity for the expansion of their trade. They produced a series of novels that were the obscene counterparts to these so-called sociological studies, sharing the same fascination with the geisha and the art of *shunga*.

One of the first works that dealt with Japanese prostitution was Sir Henry Norman's *The Real Japan*,[80] which was first published in London in 1892 and later published in America where it was favourably reviewed by the *Atlantic Monthly*.[81] Alongside illustrations of geisha girls from 'instantaneous photographs', this work features a chapter with the enticing title, 'The Yoshiwara: An Unwritten Chapter of Japanese Life'. At the start of this chapter, in a note, Norman offers the reader a letter supporting the legitimacy of the work despite its sensitive nature. The latter begins, 'certainly it must go on – it can offend no one whose opinion is worth a bootlace. It is clean and simple, and of course it is interesting.'[82] He then carefully defends his investigation of these districts by suggesting that they control sexual behaviour rather than associate it with moral and social degradation:

This is not the place to express any opinion upon the principles involved; but as I have written so frankly, it is only fair to the Japanese authorities to point out that their peculiar system has absolutely eradicated the appearance of vice in Tokyo; you might walk the streets of this city of a million people for a year without seeing a sign of it – a state of things probably without parallel in the civilized world. Then, too, they have dissociated it from riot and drunkenness and robbery; the streets of the Yoshiwara are as quiet and orderly as Mayfair or Fifth Avenue. And nobody in Japan can fall into temptation unwittingly: he must go in search of it. That these are matters of some value at any rate, the people who are responsible for the police de moeurs and Mabille, for the Strand and the Haymarket, for the purlieus of Sixth Avenue and the hells of Chicago and San Francisco are hardly in a position to deny.[83]

One of the fascinating aspects of this defence is that Norman aligns Tokyo with other world cities, placing Japan's cities on a global scale and revealing the developing interest in Japan's participation in a sex trade that was increasingly seen as global.

Another late nineteenth-century sociological work on Tokyo's Yoshiwara was J. E. Becker's *The Nightless City, or the History of the Yoshiwara Yukwaku* , which was first published anonymously in 1899, putatively in Yokohama. Although it was not reviewed, it appears to have been popular. Becker added his name to subsequent editions, which were published internationally. It also appeared under other titles. The New York American Anthropological Society published it as *The Sexual Life of Japan* (n.d.), and it found its way to France, where it was grossly plagiarised by Dr Tresmin-Trémolières under the new title *La Cité d'Amour au Japon* (1905).[84] Like *The Real Japan*, it was copiously illustrated with drawings, photographs, and coloured reproductions of Japanese prints of courtesans by Utamaro. While these prints appear as authenticating documents, their fine reproduction and abundance imply the continued sexual investment in their exoticism. In fact, the varied images of geishas provide colour to an otherwise stultifying book and likely sold it. Again, as in *The Real Japan*, the author proves defensive about his study, justifying it anxiously in the Prefaces to new editions. In his Preface to the first edition, he rehearses the argument that the Japanese are no more immoral than Westerners:

> To Japanese who may think that the Yoshiwara is a disgrace to Japan I would remark that this empire has by no means a monopoly on vice; and to foreigners who declaim against the 'immorality of the Japanese' I would say frankly – 'Read the *'History of Prostitution'* by Dr. W. W. Sanger of New York, also the *'Maiden Tribute of Modern Babylon'* which appeared in the Pall Mall Gazette fourteen years ago.[85]

In the fourth edition, he claims that his work met with opprobrium, but he refused to be deterred by the 'mawkish sensibility of Mrs. Grundy'.[86]

Despite the anxious moral posturing that pervaded these works on Japanese prostitution, they seem to have functioned more as legitimate receptacles of the myth of Japan as 'The Island of Girls in the Eastern Sea'.[87]

Two obscene novels, published clandestinely, confirm this salacious curiosity in the Yoshiwara. Not surprisingly, Charles Carrington commissioned them. One of his earlier publications, *Suburban Souls* (1901), briefly indulged in the phantasm of the Japanese geisha when a French woman named Lily dresses up as a geisha to titillate her father and lover who have been looking at a photograph of the father's Japanese mistress amidst a collection of obscene pictures.[88] But this scene is brief, overshadowed by the numerous references to underground books of the time. A few years later, however, he published two novels that fixated on the geisha fantasy. The first was *Amourous Adventures of a Japanese Gentleman*, which claimed to have been originally published in Yokohama by the Diamio of Satsuma in 1897, but was probably first published in Paris by Carrington in 1907.[89] The novel, possibly authored by an American, describes the amorous adventures of two American Naval Officers among geisha girls in Japan in all the predictable ways. The Diamio of Satsuma, who plays host to the men, recounts their story, frequently juxtaposing his gallantry against American vulgarity. The narrator includes numerous sycophantic apologies to the reader: 'Reader, I reproduce the man's language as it fell from his lips. Pardon me should its vulgarity fill thy honorable mind with disgust.'[90] In addition to the reaffirmation of national stereotypes, meant to oblige continental anti-Americanism, the novel nourishes the exoticism of the Far East with scenes of orgies and bestiality. It even includes one scene where a Japanese girl has sex with a tiger.[91] There is little information on the circulation history of this book, other than that there was a later reprint and another rare edition with illustrations entitled *Shore Leave* (which is part of Michael Goss's collection in London). The work appears to have been rare, but it signals how underground traders were beginning to exploit the Far East for obscenity.

Yoshiwara: The Nightless City , another underground novel on Japanese prostitution, was purportedly published for the members of the Erotic Society of Japan in Paris by Carrington in 1907. However, a handwritten note on the title page casts doubt on the publication: 'Publ. by Targ in Chi[cago]. Not Carrington.'[92] The work was falsely attributed to Becker, the author of *The Nightless City* . It clearly hoped to draw from the popularity of Becker's study and its barely concealed sexual fixation with the geisha. This novel also reveals the continued fascination with Japanese *shunga*. There are sexually explicit black and white line drawings in the Japanese style throughout the novel, apparently based on the works of the Japanese master, Utamaro (Figure 30). The story, which follows the vicissitudes of a Japanese prostitute known as The Lily, even features a story about Utamaro. About halfway through the novel, The Lily meets him when he is commissioned by the

Figure 30 Anonymous illustrations from *Yoshiwara: The Nightless City*. Paris [Chicago?]: Charles Carrington [Targ?], 1907. By permission of the Kinsey Institute for Research in Sex, Gender, and Reproduction, Bloomington, Indiana

Count of Mito to paint her with a young man in amorous exchange. The Lily is delighted to comply because of his reputation:

> But the name had meant something to The Lily. She had heard of the great artist, Utamaro, during her days at the *geisha* school and she had admired his work consistently, not only because of the artistic quality, but because the subjects and subject matter, in most cases, had pertained to the *Yoshiwara* and its inhabitants.
>
> (*The Nightless City* , 231)

The novel reveals familiarity with the *shunga* masters and demonstrates the extent to which these prints were an exciting print medium not only for artists like Beardsley, but also publishers of obscenity. The novel's attention to the viewing and making of Utamaro's art also shows the fixation with the medium. Utamaro, for instance, describes his images as an aphrodisiac. As he says, 'It seems that this Count must first gaze at such pictures before he is able to have an erection and thus be enabled to make use of the hundred and one concubines he owns. For a year he has been annoying me for the silken scroll' (*The Nightless City* , 236–7). The representation of Utamaro's erotic artistry is also suffused with traditional Japanese imagery. The description of 'his brush poised in the air like a heron about to make a swift dive downward to spear a fish in the flashing rapid of a mountain stream' (236) recalls numerous Japanese prints. The description of Utamaro at work with 'pendant stroke [brought] down to the white expanse of the virgin paper' also eroticises the compressed aesthetic of his 'smoothly flowing black line' (237–8). As the novel fantasises about the sexual promiscuity of women in the Far East, it incorporates the teachings of the underground Utamaro who says 'the crux of Japanese art is suggestion' (238). In effect, this passage that expatiates on Japanese erotic prints and draws its sexual scenarios from their imaginary production could easily be described as novelised *shunga*.

The field of cultural traffic surrounding Japan reached its apogee by the first decade of the twentieth century. By the First World War, artists and consumers no longer had the same mania for Japanese things and customs. *Shunga*, though still admired, also lost their appeal with the advance of photographic media. It is true that there are a few striking photographic imitations of Japanese prints that date from the early twentieth century. One particularly beautiful photograph shows two lovers in an embrace (Figure 31); the soft curved lines of their bodies reminiscent of the posture and mood of *shunga* prints. Another photographic series features two European looking women in Japanese costume presumably posing as women of the *Yoshiwara* (Figure 32). These images show too much realistic detail to suggest the Japanese print; nonetheless, their focus on the toilette of prostitutes recalls many of the *Yoshiwara* prints and perhaps even Beardsley's image of Salome with Japanese coif primping (cf. Figure 19). Photography,

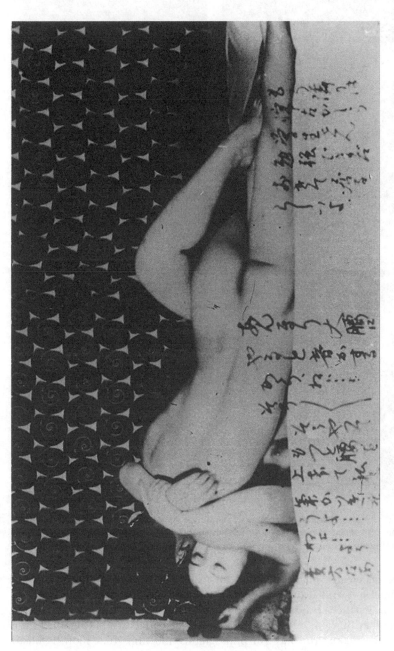

Figure 31 Anonymous photograph of lovers, c.1911–25. By permission of the Kinsey Institute for Research in Sex, Gender, and Reproduction, Bloomington, Indiana

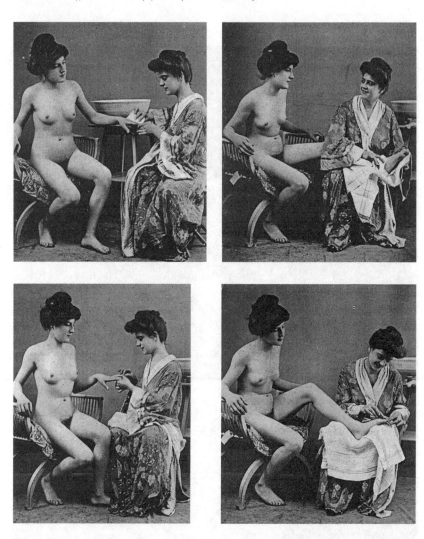

Figure 32 Anonymous photographic sequence of women washing, *c.*1903–5. By permission of the Kinsey Institute for Research in Sex, Gender, and Reproduction, Bloomington, Indiana

however, created a new demand for realism in obscenity that undid the minimal line and sexual subtlety offered by the older medium of Japanese *shunga*. Japanese prints fed the modernist flight from the integrity of the image that thrilled Beardsley and alarmed his detractors, but retained little influence against the wave of photographs and films that soon began to dominate the business of obscenity in the twentieth century.

Coda: The Obscenity of the Real

The rapid internationalisation of printed materials that was reflected both in market penetration and exotic thematics vitally underscored the emergence of obscenity as a new publishing phenomenon in the nineteenth century. This book has shown how the expanding traffic in works on harems, Eastern literature, slavery, and Japanese prints informed larger legal and cultural debates about sexuality, obscenity, pornography, exoticism, and mass print media. But this book also concludes just at the beginning of a major transition in the history of obscenity. While it began as a print crime, it shifted media toward the end of the nineteenth century. In the twentieth and twenty-first centuries, the industry has become much more reliant on photography, film, and eventually digital images easily exchanged via electronic networks.

Even so, obscenity has continued to circulate according to same market logic that saw its formation at the height of Britain's empire. It is still one of the most opportunistic commodities of modernity, navigating diverse media and geographical scales in its continual renewal and resurrection. Nineteenth-century fantasies of sexuality and exoticism have circulated through various mediascapes beyond England, even Europe, to the outskirts of empire, and the centre of colonial and postcolonial confrontation. An English writer muttered in the nineteenth century that 'empire did not improve morals', but many parts of the developing world today decry the spread of Western vices, perpetuating the nineteenth-century discursive association between the obscene and the foreign while turning it on its head.

President Robert Mugabe's remarks at an African Summit in 1998 on 'Towards E-Development: Closing the Digital Gap', are a case in point. At the summit, he identified Internet pornography as a global problem whose eradication was integral to the process of decolonisation:

Through pornography, disinformation, the popularization and internationalization of crime, drug networking and character assassinations of public office holders and governments, the toll-free and regulation-free information highways and the internet threaten the very being and essence of our nations and communities.[1]

Although Mugabe campaigned for access to information technology in the developing world, he also saw a need 'to stem the intrusion of undesirable, nay destructive information and information habits into our societies'.[2] Mugabe's belief that the dispersion of first-world vice in the electronic age posed a threat to African postcolonial identities has often been reflected in the application of Zimbabwe's Censorship and Entertainment Control Act, an archaic Rhodesian law that the judiciary still uses to suppress political dissent and control the media. On 14 March 2002, Trevor Ncube and Iden Wetherell from the daily *Independent* newspaper were charged under this act for publishing a Reuters photograph that showed a group of naked Austrians outside a Viennese department store. Ncube revealed the politics behind these charges: 'At a time when Zimbabweans are facing unprecedented hardships as a result of gross economic mismanagement and corruption, it is significant that the attorney-general, a member of the cabinet, has instructed the police to investigate a newspaper that has been outspoken in its criticism of government for not upholding the rule of law.'[3] In short, he accused the government of suppressing local dissidents by fabricating censorship charges based upon assumptions about the immorality of foreign media, the London-based Reuters Media organisation. Zimbabwe, certainly not alone in taking a postcolonial stance against Western vice, has thus in its recent political history illustrated the extent to which obscenity continues to be understood in relation to its global trafficking.

What I believe distinguishes the traffic in obscenity today from that in the nineteenth-century is, of course, its scale and accessibility, but also more importantly its extreme realism. The shift from print to photographic media that escalated at the end of the nineteenth century gave rise to a new intimacy between obscenity and graphic realism. Obscenity continues to intersect media, markets, and borders, but now must meet the demand for the real, the great – if false – promise of photographs and films. In the nineteenth century, obscenity was associated with gothic genres (as with *The Lustful Turk*), scientific discourses (as with Burton's translations), or aesthetic perversities (as with Beardsley's prints). Granted, at the time, there was increased alarm about the heightened visibility offered by the obscene photograph. The artistic status of the female nude, for instance, came under attack when it was translated from painting to photograph, out of the galleries and onto the streets. An article from the *Vigilance Record* on 'An Indecent Exhibition' from September 1892 reported that George Reid, a London a showman was charged with 'exposing to public view an obscene exhibition of photographs at his shop':

There was a sort of peep-show going on, and the spectators took their turns looking through eight powerful magnifying glasses. There were photographs behind the glasses, illuminated by candles. The majority of the photographs were nude female figures, and some of them which were partly clad, were decidedly indecent.[4]

The sharpened detail and the visual aides provided by the photographic exhibition were apparently the cause of the uneasiness. Yet, while there was an emergent discourse linking visual obscenity with extreme realism in the nineteenth century, it was not yet fully articulated. To take this study of the traffic in obscenity further into the twentieth century, we need to turn our attention to the ways in which obscenity now relies on technologies of visual realism in its global adventures.

Jean Baudrillard has begun to open up this line of inquiry with his idea of the 'obscenity of the real'. While contributing to larger philosophical discourses about the passion for the real in the twentieth century, he argues that this information practice is mobilised by a libidinal desire to see and know. In his view, obscenity is no longer repressed or conjured, but infinitely overexposed, in the age of high capitalism where information and communication circulate indiscriminately. One can no longer distinguish the obscene from the real and the real from the obscene. As he explains,

> Obscenity lies in the fact that there is nothing to see. It is not a sexual obscenity, but the obscenity of the real. The spectator does not lean over out of sexual curiosity, but to check the texture of the skin, the infinite texture of the real. Perhaps our true sexual act consists in this: *in verifying to the point of giddiness the useless objectivity of things* .

Often our erotic and pornographic imagery, this array of breasts, asses, and genitalia has no other meaning but to express the useless objectivity of things. Nudity is but the desperate attempt to emphasise the existence of something. The genitalia is but a special effect.

> Sexuality is but a ritual of transparency. Where once it had to be hidden, sexuality today hides what little remains of reality, and, of course, participates in all of this disembodied passion.[5]

Baudrillard's understanding of 'obscenity of the real' recognises that the search for the real is mostly futile, but reveals our profound investment in the obscene to confirm its existence. Elsewhere, his language shows the extent to which his ideas are steeped in the realist techniques of photographic media: the 'frenzy of the image' that drives obscenity plays out in a series of 'zoom-ins' and 'close-ups'.[6] Baudrillard offers one perspective on the interplay between obscenity and realism, but many questions still need to be posed. How does this relationship between the real and the obscene play out in the global mediascape? How does exoticism come into play?

How do we explain the rise of virtual reality and extreme reality, in the form of pseudo-photographs, teledildonics, and snuff films, in the porn industry? Why is there this doubling of real-life news events and obscenity, as we saw with the Abu Ghraib photographs and their awful evocation of Pier Paolo Pasolini's almost unwatchable film *Salo: Or the 120 Days of Sodom*?[7] These are just a few questions about today's traffic in obscenity that need to be answered.

Notes

Chapter 1 The traffic in obscenity

1 John Ashcroft, Remarks, Federal Prosecutors' Symposium on Obscenity, National Advocacy Center, Columbia, SC (6 June 2002); *Report from the Joint Select Committee on Lotteries and Indecent Advertisements* (London: Vacher & Sons, 1908).

2 Steven Marcus, *The Other Victorians: A Study of Sexuality and Pornography in Mid-Nineteenth-Century England* (New York: Basic, 1964).

3 The earliest legal term for this print crime in Britain was obscenity, and I therefore prefer it to more recent terminology.

4 Michel Foucault, *The Archaeology of Knowledge*, 1969, trans. A. M. Sheridan Smith (London: Routledge, 2001).

5 *Society for the Suppression of Vice* (London: S. Gosnell, 1825), 29.

6 Robert Darnton, *The Forbidden Best-Sellers of Pre-Revolutionary France* (New York: Norton, 1995); Jay David Bolter and Richard Grusin, *Remediation: Understanding New Media* (Cambridge: MIT, 1999); Lisa Gitelman and Geoffrey B. Pingree eds, *New Media, 1740–1914* (Cambridge, MA: MIT 2003); and David Thorburn and Henry Jenkins, eds, *Rethinking Media Change: The Aesthetics of Transition* (Cambridge, MA: MIT Press, 2003).

7 Anthony Giddens, *Runaway World: How Globalization is Reshaping Our Lives* (New York: Routledge, 2002), 1.

8 Jean Baudrillard, *The Ecstasy of Communication*, ed. Sylvère Lotringer, trans. Bernard and Caroline Schutze (Paris: Editions Galilée, 1988), 22, 24.

9 Laurence O'Toole, *Pornocopia: Porn, Sex, Technology and Desire* (London: Serpent's Tale, 1999), 51.

10 Baudrillard, *The Ecstasy*, 24.

11 Edward Said, *Orientalism* (New York: Vintage, 1979), 87.

12 Saree Makdisi, *Romantic Imperialism: Universal Empire and the Culture of Modernity* (Cambridge: Cambridge University Press, 1998), 128.

13 Thomas Pakenham, *The Scramble for Africa, 1876–1912*, 1991 (London: Abacus, 2001), 140, 122.

14 *The Book of the Thousand Nights and a Night*, 10 vols, trans. Sir Richard Burton (London: Printed by the Kama-Shastra Society, 1885–[6]), vol.10, 251.

15 'Is Empire Consistent with Morality?' *Pall Mall Gazette* (19 May 1887) 3.

16 Ronald Hyam, *Empire and Sexuality: The British Experience* (Manchester and New York: Manchester University Press, 1990), 90.

17 Peter Gay, *The Bourgeois Experience: Victoria to Freud*, vol. 1 (Oxford: Oxford University Press, 1984); Michael Mason, *The Making of Victorian Sexual Attitudes* (Oxford: Oxford University Press, 1994).

18 Linda Williams, *Hard Core: Power, Pleasure, and the 'Frenzy of the Visible'*, 1989 (Berkeley: University of California Press, 1999); O'Toole, *Pornocopia*; Frederick S. Lane III, *Obscene Profits: The Entrepreneurs of Pornography in the Cyber Age* (London: Routledge, 2001).

19 Peter Mendes, *Clandestine Erotic Fiction in English 1800–1930: A Bibliographical Study* (Hants: Scholar, 1993); Patrick Kearney, *The Private Case: An Annotated*

Bibliography of the Private Case Erotica Collection in the British (Museum) Library (London: Jay Landesman, 1981).

20   Darnton, *Forbidden Best-Sellers*; Lynn Hunt, ed., *The Invention of Pornography: Obscenity and the Origins of Modernity, 1500–1800*, (New York: Zone, 1993).

21   Iain McCalman, *Radical Underworld: Prophets, Revolutionaries, and Pornographers in London, 1795–1840* (Cambridge: Cambridge University Press, 1988); Lisa Sigel, *Governing Pleasures: Pornography and Social Change in England, 1815–1914* (New Jersey: Rutgers University Press, 2002); Allison Pease, *Modernism, Mass Culture, and the Aesthetics of Obscenity* (Cambridge: Cambridge University Press, 2000); Lynda Nead, *Victorian Babylon: People, Streets and Images in Nineteenth-Century London* (New Haven, CT: Yale University Press, 2000); Bradford Mudge, *The Whore's Story: Women, Pornography, and the British Novel, 1684–1830* (Oxford: Oxford University Press, 2000); and Julie Peakman, *Mighty Lewd Books: The Development of Pornography in Eighteenth-Century England* (Basingstoke: Palgrave Macmillan, 2003). For early scholarship on historical obscenity, see Ivan Bloch, *Sexual Life in England Past and Present*, trans. William H. Forstern (London: Francis Aldor, 1938); Ralph Ginzburg, *An Unhurried View of Erotica* (London: Secker & Warburg, 1959); David Loth, *The Erotic in Literature: A Historical Survey of Pornography as Delightful as it is Indiscreet* (London: Secker & Warburg, 1961); H. Montgomery Hyde, *A History of Pornography* (London: Heinemann, 1964); Wayland Young, *Eros Denied* (London: Weidenfeld & Nicolson, 1965); Gershon Legman, *The Horn Book: Studies in Erotic Folklore and Bibliography* (New York: University Books, 1964); Ronald Pearsall, *The Worm in the Bud: The World of Victorian Sexuality* (London: Weidenfeld & Nicolson, 1969); Eric Trudgill, *Madonnas and Magdalens: The Origins and Development of Victorian Sexual Attitudes* (London: Heinemann, 1976); Fraser Harrison, *The Dark Angel: Aspects of Victorian Sexuality* (London: Sheldon, 1977); and Wendell Stacey Johnson, *Living in Sin: The Victorian Sexual Revolution* (Chicago: Nelson-Hall, 1979). For more recent studies on specific aspects of nineteenth-century obscenity, see Peter Webb's thematic survey of Victorian underground novels in 'Victorian Erotica', *The Sexual Dimension in Literature*, ed. Alan Bold (London: Vision, 1982); Frank A. Hoffman's study of the underworld in Sherlock Holmes's novels in 'The Victorian Sexual Subculture: Some Notes and a Speculation', *The Baker Street Journal*, 35:1 (1985) 19–22; Coral Lansbury's exploration of the connections between medical science, vivisection, and obscenity in *The Old Brown Dog: Women, Workers, and Vivisection in Edwardian England* (Madison: University of Wisconsin Press, 1985); Tracy Davis's discussion of 'The Actress in Victorian Pornography', *Theatre Journal*, 41 (1989) 294–315; William Scheick's suggestion that H. Rider Haggard's *King Solomon's Mines* functioned as 'adolescent pornography' in 'Adolescent Pornography and Imperialism in Haggard's *King Solomon's Mines*', *English Literature in Transition*, 34:1 (1991) 19–30; John Woodrow Presley's tenuous discussion of James Joyce's allusions to *The Pearl* in ' *Finnegans Wake, Lady Pokingham*, and Victorian Erotic Fantasy', *Journal of Popular Culture*, 30:3 (1996) 67–80; Tamar Heller's study of flagellation in 'Flagellating Feminine Desire: Lesbians, Old Maids, and New Women in "Miss Coote's Confession", a Victorian Pornographic Narrative', *Victorian Newsletter*, 92 (1997) 9–15; Michael Gamer's theory of how protean versions of 'gothic' and 'pornographic' came into existence at the same time in 'Genres for the Prosecution: Pornography and the Gothic', *PMLA*, 114 (1999) 1043–54; and, finally, James Nelson's examination of Leonard Smithers's involvement in London's obscene print culture in *Publisher to the*

Decadents. Leonard Smithers in the Careers of Beardsley, Wilde, Dowson (University Park: Pennsylvania State University Press, 2000).

22 McCalman, *Radical Underworld*, 235.

23 Pierre Bourdieu, *The Field of Cultural Production: Essays on Art and Literature*, ed. Randal Johnson (Cambridge: Polity, 1993).

24 Henry Spencer Ashbee [Pisanus Fraxi], *Index Librorum Prohibitorum* (London: Privately Printed, 1877); *Centuria Librorum Absconditorum* (London: Privately Printed, 1879); *Catena Librorum Tacendorum* (London: Privately Printed, 1885).

25 Lord Byron, *The Complete Poetical Works: Lord Byron*, 7 vols, ed. Jerome McGann (Oxford: Clarendon, 1980–93).

26 *The Book of the Thousand Nights and a Night; Supplemental Nights to the Book of The Thousand Nights and a Night*, 6 vols, trans. Richard F. Burton (London: Printed by the Kama Shastra Society for Private Subscribers Only, 1886–8); *The Perfumed Garden of the Sheik Nefzaoui or, The Arab Art of Love* (Cosmopoli: For Private Circulation Only, 1886).

27 Oscar Wilde, *Salome* (London: John Lane, 1894).

28 The history of obscenity has been made possible only by the persistence of collectors and librarians who believe that obscenity has cultural value and is worth preserving and discussing. The British Library houses the largest and most significant collection of European obscenity – the Private Case. It was established as early as 1841 at the British Museum, and collectors and library officials – most notably Henry Spencer Ashbee, E. J. Dingwall, and Charles Reginald Dawes – have enlarged the collection over the years. It is worth noting that Dawes's unpublished manuscript on nineteenth-century obscenity is housed at the British Library and is a particularly rich source of titles; see P. J. Cross, 'The Private Case: A History', *The Library of the British Museum, Retrospective Essays on the Department of Printed Books*, ed. P. R. Harris (London: The British Library, 1991), 203, 209, 214, 219; and Charles Reginald Dawes, *A Study of Erotic Literature in England, Considered with Especial Reference to Social Life* (1943, unpublished). Other major collections of European and American obscenity are housed at The Bibliothèque Nationale in Paris, The Bodleian Library in Oxford, and The Kinsey Institute in Bloomington, Indiana. For more bibliographical information about these collections, see Mendes, *Clandestine Erotic Fiction*; Sigel, *Governing Pleasures*; and Martha Cornog, ed., *Libraries, Erotica, Pornography* (Phoenix: Oryx, 1991). For bibliographies on historical obscenity, see Ashbee's three annotated bibliographies, published clandestinely under the pseudonym Pisanus Fraxi, *Index Librorum Prohibitorum*, *Centuria Librorum Absconditorum*, and *Catena Librorum Tacendorum*. Also see William Laird Clowes's (writing as Speculator Morum), *Bibliotheca Arcana Seu Catalogus Librorum Penetralium Being Brief notices of books that have been secretly printed, prohibited by law, seized, anathematized, burnt or Bowderlised*, By Speculator Morum (London: G. Redway, 1885); [Charles Carrington], *Forbidden Books: Notes and Gossip on Tabooed Literature by an Old Bibliophile* (Paris: For the Author & his Friends, 1902); Rolf. S. Reade [Alfred Rose], *Registrum Librorum Eroticorum*, 2 vols (London: Privately Printed, 1936); Terence J. Deakin, *Catalogi Librorum Eroticorum: A Critical Bibliography of Erotic Bibliographies and Book-Catalogues* (London: Cecil and Amelia Woolf, 1964); Kearney, *The Private Case*; and Mendes, *Clandestine Erotic Fiction*.

29 Mendes, *Clandestine Erotic Fiction*, 3–45.

30 David Foxon, *Libertine Literature in England, 1660–1745* (New York: University Books, 1965); Roger Thompson, *Unfit for Modest Ears: A Study of Pornographic, Obscene, and Bawdy Works Written or Published in England in the Second Half of the*

Seventeenth Century (London: Macmillan, 1979); and Peakman, *Mighty Lewd Books*. Also see John Wilmot Rochester, *Sodom; or, The Quintessence of Debauchery*, 1684, ed. Patrick J. Kearney ([London: P. J. Kearney, 1969]); [Cleland, John], *Memoirs of a Woman of Pleasure* (London: G. Fenton, 1749); and John Wilkes, *An Essay on Woman* (London: Printed for the Author, [1763]).

31 *L'École des Filles, ou la Philosophie des dames*, 1655 (Fribourg: Roger Bon Temps, 1668); Nicolas Chorier, *Algoisiae Sigeae satyra sotadica*, c.1660 (N.p.: n.p., c.1680).

32 Roy Porter and Lesley Hall, *The Facts of Life: The Creation of Sexual Knowledge in Britain, 1650–1950* (New Haven, CT: Yale University Press, 1995). Also see Aristotle's *Master-Piece; or the Secrets of generation*, 1684, (London: Printed by F. L. for J. How and sold by Thomas Howkins, 1690); Nicolas Venette, *Conjugal Love, or The Pleasures of the Marriage Bed* (London: Garland, 1984).

33 George Robertson, *Obscenity: An Account of Censorship Laws and Their Enforcement in England and Wales* (London: Weidenfeld & Nicolson, 1979), 17.

34 Donald Thomas, *A Long Time Burning: The History of Literary Censorship in England* (London: Routledge & Kegan Paul, 1969), 74.

35 Jean Barrin, *Venus in the Cloister; or, The Nun in her Smock* (London: [Edmund Curll], 1725); Johann Heinrich Meibomius, *A Treatise on the Use of Flogging in Venereal Affairs* (London: E. Curll, 1718). For Curll's trial, see *R.* v. *Curl* [sic] (1727) 2 Strange 788, 1 Barnard. B.R. 29; E.R. 849.

36 Thomas, *A Long Time Burning*, 80.

37 Edward J. Bristow, *Vice and Vigilance: Purity Movements in Britain since 1700* (Dublin: Gill & MacMillan, 1977), 38.

38 See one of the early SSV tracts, *Society for the Suppression of Vice*, 5, 9.

39 For early nineteenth-century British statutes related to the regulation of obscenity, see the Vagrancy Acts 5 Geo.4, c.83 and 1 & 2 Vict., c.37; the Metropolitan Police Act 10 & 11 Vict., c.89; the Obscene Publications Act 20 & 21 Vict., c.83. Note that the legal definition of obscenity did not appear until 1868 during the trial of *R* v. *Hicklin* over the publication of *The Confessional Unmasked*, a sexually explicit anti-clerical work. In his judgement, Justice Alexander Cockburn provided a definition of obscenity: those works written 'to deprave and corrupt those whose minds are open to such immoral influences and into whose hands a publication of this sort might fall'. This test would remain the legal definition of obscenity until the revamped Obscene Publications Act of 1959; see *R.* v. *Hicklin* (1868) L.R. 3 Q.B. 360 and 7 & 8 Eliz., c.66.

40 *Hansard's Parliamentary Papers* 144–8 (1857), 145.103.

41 *Hansard's*, 146.1154; Alexandre Dumas fils, *La Dame aux Camélias*, 1848 (Paris: n.p., 1852). The streets around the Strand, such as Holywell and Wych, housed many bookshops that specialised in obscenity in the nineteenth century, but disappeared in 1900 with the construction of Aldwych.

42 For later nineteenth-century British statutes that attempted to regulate obscenity and its distribution networks, see the Customs Consolidation Act of 1876 39 & 40 Vict., c.36; the Post Office (Protection) Act 47 & 48 Vict., c.76; and the Indecent Advertisements Act 52 & 53 Vict., c.18. For critical analyses of nineteenth-century obscenity laws, see Alec Craig, *The Banned Books of England and Other Countries* (London: George Allen & Unwin, 1962); Thomas, *A Long Time Burning*; Robertson, *Obscenity*; M. J. D. Roberts, 'Morals, Art, and the Law: The Passing of the Obscene Publications Act, 1857', *Victorian Studies*, 28 (1985) 609–29; Colin Manchester, 'Lord Campbell's Act: England's First Obscenity Statute', *The Journal of Legal*

History, 9 (1988) 223–41; and David Saunders, 'Victorian Obscenity Law: Negative Censorship or Positive Administration', *Writing and Censorship in Britain*, ed. Paul Hyland and Neil Sammells (London: Routledge, 1992) 154–170.

43   The National Vigilance Association (NVA) archive includes the proceedings from these early twentieth-century conferences against the international traffic in obscenity; see 'Objectionable Literature' Boxes 107 & 108 4/NVA S88.

44   *Society for the Suppression of Vice*, 29, 31, 41, 10. For more extended accounts of the SSV's operations against obscenity, see Thomas, *A Long Time Burning*; Bristow, *Vice and Vigilance*; and M. J. D. Roberts, 'Making Victorian Morals? The Society for the Suppression of Vice and its Critics, 1802–1886', *Historical Studies*, 21:83 (1981) 157–73.

45   Henry Mayhew, *London Labour and London Poor*, 1861, 4 vols, (London: Frank Cass, 1967), vol. 1, 440–1, 240.

46   'Holywell Street Literature', *Town Talk* (6 May 1882) 6.

47   *Times* (6 Sept. 1843) 7. For other articles from the *Times* on women's involvement in the trade, see (21 Sept. 1838) 7, (17 Apr. 1856) 11, (23 Aug., 1872) 9, (26 Aug. 1880) 9. There is also evidence that women were in the courtroom during trials for obscene libel. In one instance the presence of 'several ladies' in the courtroom was the cause for much consternation: the women insisted that it was 'their right as citizens to remain and hear the evidence', but the Alderman refused to read out extracts in the name of 'propriety'; see the *Times* (18 Apr. 1877) 11.

48   For the involvement of Dugdale's family in the trade, see the *Times* (27 Feb. 1850) 7, and (13 Mar. 1851), 8. Sigel offers a detailed synopsis of the familial character of the trade in the early nineteenth century; see Sigel, *Governing Pleasures*, 21.

49   Mendes, *Clandestine Erotic Fiction*, 421.

50   *Times* (7 Aug. 1868) 9.

51   These titles, listed in chronological order, appear in the following articles from the *Times*: (12 July 1822) 3, (28 May 1830) 6, (1 Jan. 1831) 4, (23 Nov. 1839) 7, (20 Feb. 1890) 3, (29 Jan. 1870) 11, (3 Feb. 1871) 9, (6 Apr. 1877) 11, (5 Aug. 1880) 11, (28 Dec. 1877) 10, (9 July 1886) 3. With the exception of *Venus's Album*, these works survive, their circulation perhaps boosted by the publicity of high profile King's and Queen's Bench trials. See *The Rambler's Magazine; or, Annals of Gallantry, Glee, Pleasure, & the Bon Ton*, 2 vols (London: Pub. by J. Mitford, [1827–9]); *The Festival of the Passions; or Voluptuous Miscellany* (Glenfucket [London?]: Abdul Mustapha, [1863]); *The Ferre: An inquisitive, quizzical, satirical and theatrical censor of the age* (London: 1870); *The Confessional Unmasked: showing the depravity of the priesthood* (London: Thomas Johnston, 1851); *Fruits of Philosophy; or, The Private Companion of Young Married People* (London: J. Watson, 1841); *The Wild Boys of London* (London: Farrah, [1873?]); and *Modern Babylon, and other poems* (London: n.p., [1872]).

52   The NVA existed from 1886 to 1953. It advertised its activities and campaigns in the *Vigilance Record* (1887–1932). For an overview of the origins and activities of the NVA, see Bristow, *Vice and Vigilance*, 154–74.

53   NVA Box 108: S88R.I.

54   Beatrice Farwell, *The Cult of Images: Baudelaire and the 19th-Century Media Explosion* (Santa Barbara: UCSB Art Museum, 1977), 8.

55   Jonathan Crary, *Techniques of the Observer: On Vision and Modernity in the Nineteenth Century* (Cambridge, MA: MIT, 1990), 150.

56   Malek Alloula, *The Colonial Harem*, 1981, trans. Myrna Godzich and Wlad Godzich (Minneapolis: University of Minnesota Press, 1986), 29.

57   Hardwicke Knight, 'Early Microphotographs', *History of Photography*, 9:4 (1985) 311.

58   For collections of nineteenth-century photographs and stereographs, see Serge Nazarieff, *Early Erotic Photography* (Berlin: Taschen, 2002) and *The Stereoscopic Nude, 1850–1930* (Berlin: Taschen, 1990). Also see Graham Ovenden and Peter Mendes, *Victorian Erotic Photography* (New York: St Martin's, 1973).

59   For these catalogues, see *Album 7: Catalogues and Prospectuses* (unpublished, 1889–*c*.1908): a collection of underground catalogues and advertisements held at the British Library.

60   Simon Brown, a film historian from the British Film Institute in London, has catalogued many of these early erotic films, both those held at the BFI and elsewhere in Europe. In his discussions about the history of these films with me on two separate occasions, he explained that the provenance of many of these films is unknown, some of them even having made their way from the Warsaw Archives in the mid-1970s.

61   Richard Abel, *The Red Rooster Scare: Making Cinema American, 1900–1910* (Berkeley: University of California Press, 1999), 25.

62   The BFI library holds a collection of Pathés Frères film catalogues from 1896–1914.

63   *Times* (2 Nov. 1871) 3.

64   National Archives, Basutoland DO 119/865; Indecent Publications HO 144/543/A54388; Indecent Publications HO/144/238/A52539B.

65   Quoted in Sigel, *Governing*, 72.

66   *Times* (26 Sept. 1851) 7.

67   *Times* (13 Jan. 1875) 6.

68   *Town Talk* (6 May 1882) 6.

69   James Pope-Hennessy, *Monckton Milnes: The Flight of Youth, 1851–1885* (London: Constable, 1951), 118.

70   *Report from the Joint Select Committee*, 41. A copy of the report is currently located in the NVA archive under 'Objectionable Literature' Box 107 4/NVA/S88/J.

71   Joseph Conrad, *The Secret Agent: A Simple Tale* (London: Methuen, 1907), 1–3.

72   *The Pearl, A Journal of Facetia Voluptuous Reading*, 3 vols (London: Printed for the Society of Vice [Augustin Brancart], 1879–80 [*c*.1890]), 1, 37, 39.

73   *My Secret Life*, ed. Gershon Legman (New York: Grove, 1966), 3.586. For other instances of how obscene publications are put to use in this work, see 1.180–1, 2.199, 2.224–6, 7.1375, 9.1767. The authorship of *My Secret Life* has been long debated in studies of underground Victorian publications. In *Erotomaniac*, Ian Gibson draws upon Legman's earlier suspicions, revealed in his edition of *My Secret Life*, that Ashbee was the author of the memoirs. Gibson develops the argument by providing a number of correspondences between Ashbee's life and the contents of the book. However, I remain undecided about the authorship of *My Secret Life* if only because I wonder why such a connoisseur of obscenity would mention only *Fanny Hill* in 11 volumes. On the authorship of these memoirs, see Ian Gibson, *Erotomaniac: The Secret Life of Henry Spencer Ashbee* (London: Faber & Faber, 2001), and most recently John Patrick Pattinson, 'The Man Who Was Walter', *Victorian Literature and Culture*, 30 (2002) 19–40.

Chapter 2 Harems and London's underground print culture

1 All references to Byron's poetry, including *Don Juan*, are from *The Complete Poetical Works: Lord Byron*, 7 vols, ed. Jerome McGann (Oxford: Clarendon, 1980–93).

2 Advances in print technologies included mechanised paper-making in 1803, the steam-powered press in 1814, and the multiple-cylinder stereotype press in 1827. New print technologies in the early nineteenth century saw the rapid expansion and diversification of a print-centred popular culture that grew in visibility and influence. See Patricia Anderson, *The Printed Image and the Transformation of Popular Culture, 1790–1860* (Oxford: Clarendon, 1991); B.E. Maidment, *Reading Popular Prints, 1790–1870* (Manchester: Manchester University Press, 1996); and Sheila O'Connell, *The Popular Print in England, 1550–1850* (London: British Museum, 1999).

3 See Richard D. Altick, *The English Common Reader: A Social History of the Mass-Reading Public, 1800–1900* (Chicago: University of Chicago Press, 1957), 327; William H. Wickwar, *The Struggle for the Freedom of the Press, 1819–1832* (London: George Allen, 1972), 271. The Six Acts quickly followed the Peterloo Massacre, where magistrates killed and wounded radical protestors in Manchester. The Acts attempted to suppress the spread of radical politics by placing a four-penny stamp duty on most newspapers, making blasphemy and sedition transportable offences, and preventing gatherings of over 50 people. For the Stamp Act, which affected the literary output of radicals, see 59 Geo. 3, c.39.

4 Iain McCalman, *Radical Underworld: Prophets, Revolutionaries, and Pornographers in London, 1795–1840* (Cambridge: Cambridge University Press, 1988), 214.

5 Roland Barthes, *Sade, Fourier, Loyola*, trans. Richard Miller (London: Cape, 1977), 125.

6 Andrew Elfenbein, *Byron and the Victorians* (Cambridge: Cambridge University Press, 1995), 56.

7 Hugh J. Luke, 'The Publishing of Byron's *Don Juan*', *PMLA*, 80 (1965). For discussions on the critical reception of *Don Juan*, also see Samuel C. Chew, *Byron in England: His Fame and After-Fame* (London: John Murray, 1924); Edward Dudley Hume Johnson, '*Don Juan* in England', *ELH*, 11 (1944) 135–53; Robinson Blann, *Throwing the Scabbard Away: Byron's Battle Against the Censors of* Don Juan (New York: Peter Lang, 1991); Elfenbein, *Byron and the Victorians*; and Charles Donelan, *Romanticism and Male Fantasy in Byron's* Don Juan: *A Marketable Vice* (London: Macmillan, 2000).

8 [Lord Byron], *Don Juan: Cantos I, II* (London: N.p. [John Murray], 1819).

9 Luke, 'The Publishing of Byron's *Don Juan*', 200.

10 Luke, 'The Publishing of Byron's *Don Juan*', 203, 209.

11 Pirated editions of *Don Juan* were typically duodecimos with cheap coloured plates. Although the price is not indicated, their size suggests that they were inexpensive, probably no more than a few pennies. Publishers of these pirate copies include William Benbow, Peter Griffin, William Dugdale, John Hodgson, and John Duncombe. See *Don Juan: Cantos I to V* (London: Benbow, 1821); *Don Juan: Cantos VI, VII, VIII* (London: W. Dugdale, 1823); *Don Juan: Cantos XVII–XVIII* (London: Duncombe, [1823]); *Don Juan: In Five Cantos* (London: Peter Griffin, [1823]); *Don Juan: A Poem* (London: W. Benbow, 1822); *Don Juan: A Poem* (London: Hodgson, 1823); *Don Juan: With a Preface by a Clergyman* (London: Hodgson, 1822).

12   Rev. of *Don Juan*, by Lord Byron, *Blackwood's Edinburgh Review* 5 (1819) 513; Rev. of *Don Juan*, by Lord Byron, *British Critic* 12 (Aug. 1819) 197; Rev. of *Don Juan*, by Lord Byron, *Gentleman's Magazine* 89 (1819) 152.

13   Samuel C. Chew, *Byron in England: His Fame and After-Fame* (London: John Murray, 1924), 28n.

14   McCalman, *Radical Underworld*, 143.

15   *Don John: or, Don Juan unmasked* (London: William Hone, 1819); *Don Juan, Canto the Third* (London: William Hone, 1819).

16   Lord Byron, *Byron's Letters and Journals*, 12 vols, ed. Leslie Marchand (London: John Murray, 1979), 6.237.

17   *Don Juan, Canto the Third*, 14. Further page references appear in parentheses.

18   Luke, 'The Publishing of Byron's *Don Juan*', 201n.

19   Most pamphlets from the early 1820s were priced between six pence and one shilling. See *Satirical Songs and Miscellaneous Papers, connected with the Trial of Queen Caroline* (unpublished); *Pamphlets Relating to Q. Caroline* (unpublished); and *English Cartoons & Satirical Prints, 1320–1832* (Cambridge: Chadwyck-Healey, 1978). These are collections of radical pamphlets, prints, and ballads from the early nineteenth century held at the British Library.

20   [Southey, Robert?], 'Art. IV – Cases of Walcot V. Walker', *Quarterly Review*, 27 (1822) 127. See Luke, 'The Publishing of Byron's *Don Juan*', 202.

21   [Southey, Robert?], 'Art. IV – Cases of Walcot V.Walker', 125, 127–8.

22   Luke, 'The Publishing of Byron's *Don Juan*', 203.

23   William Hodgson, *Don Juan. With a Preface by a Clergyman* (London: Hodgson, 1822), vi.

24   In the first prosecution against Benbow for publishing the *Rambler's Magazine*, the jury found him not guilty, but he was found guilty in the second trial. Of particular issue in the second trial was the price of the magazine, which was 'within the reach of servants, of boys, and of girls'. In response, Benbow's solicitor argued that the SSV 'would do more good if they would suppress the vices of the rich'; see the *Times* (12 July 1822) 3, and (25 Feb. 1823) 3. Robert Carlile, Benbow's fellow radical publisher, vehemently condemned the magazine, arguing that there was no place for obscenity in radical reform. As he wrote in the *Republican*, 'At the time I first heard of it, I could not help expressing my disgust at finding such publication sold from the same shop with the works of Thomas Paine; because I knew that it would, above every thing, gratify these Vice suppressing hypocrites, to have an identification of those works in the same shop'; see Robert Carlile, 'The Defeat of the Vice Society', *The Republican* (19 July 1822) 226.

25   *The Rambler's Magazine: or, Fashionable Emporium of Polite Literature* (July 1822) 318–9; also see John Watkins, *Memoirs of the Life and Writings of the Right Honourable Lord Byron* (London: H. Colburn, 1822).

26   McCalman, *Radical Underworld*, 165–6.

27   Lord Byron, *Don Juan: Cantos VI, VII, VIII* (London: J. Hunt, 1823).

28   The oriental harem – whether Turkish, Algerian, or Egyptian – has been one of the most beguiling spaces for the West. From the eighteenth century, European writers have repeatedly reproduced the harem for publication, exchange, and consumption, making it a symbol for the sexual excesses, perversions, and possibilities of an exotic Orient that has included parts of Europe, Africa, and Asia, and has extended from Albania to China. Some of the most celebrated literary forays in the harem include Antoine's Galland, *Les Mille et Une Nuits, contes Arabes*, 1704–17 (Paris: M. Aimé Martin, [1843]); Baron de Montesquieu, *Persian Letters*, trans. John Ozell, 2 vols (London: J. Tonson, 1722); and Lady Mary Wortley

Montagu, *Turkish Embassy Letters*, 1763, ed. Anita Desai (London: Pickering & Chatto, 1993).

29 Marchand, ed., *Byron's Letters*, 3.101.

30 Nigel Leask, *British Romantic Writers and the East* (Cambridge: Cambridge University Press, 1992), 13.

31 Lord Byron, *Three Plays: Sardanapalus; The Two Foscari; Cain*, 1821 (Oxford: Woodstock, 1990), 5, 6.

32 Susan J. Wolfson, '"Their She Condition": Cross-Dressing and the Politics of Gender in *Don Juan*', *ELH*, 54 (1987) 585.

33 Charles Donelan, *Romanticism and Male Fantasy in Byron's* Don Juan: *A Marketable Vice* (Basingstoke: Macmillan, 2000), 95.

34 Alan Richardson, 'Escape from the Seraglio: Cultural Transvestism in *Don Juan*', in Alice Levine and Robert N. Keane, eds, *Rereading Byron: Essays Selected from Hofstra University's Byron Bicentennial Conference* (New York: Garland, 1991),182–3.

35 Ruth Bernard Yeazell, *Harems of the Mind: Passages of Western Art and Literature* (New Haven: Yale University Press, 2000). The harem has attracted its fair share of critical lyricism, of varying analytical rigour. Norman Penzer ostensibly dispenses 'fact[s]' about the imperial harem in Constantinople, overturning the myth of the reprobate Sultan surrounded by naked women, 'heavy perfume, cool fountains, soft music, and over-indulgence in every conceivable kind of vice that the united brains of jealous, sex-starved women could invent for the pleasure of their lord'. His history, however, relies heavily on Sir Richard Burton's fantastic account of Eastern sexuality; see N. M. Penzer, *The Harem*, 1936 (London: Spring, 1965), 13. Malek Alloula, who discusses erotic fantasies surrounding the Algerian harem in French colonial postcards, discusses how this 'sexual phantasm' of 'a lascivious world of idle women that lie adorned as if ready for unending festivities' is a form of 'colonial violence'. As Barbara Harlow writes in her Introduction to Alloula's book, he returns the postcard to the sender, examining it not only as a question, but also as a 'wound'; see Malek Alloula, *The Colonial Harem*, 1981, trans. Myrna Godzich and Wlad Godzich (Minneapolis: University of Minnesota Press, 1986), 5, 34. Rana Kabbani, poignantly aware of the masculinist nature of such fantasies, explores the Western sexual yearning for the harem, but also reproduces this desire with her lingering paratactic prose. She writes that 'Europe was charmed by an Orient that shimmered with possibilities, that promised a sexual space, a voyage away from the self, and escape from the dictates of bourgeois morality.' She later elaborates: 'The European was led into the East by sexuality, by the embodiment of it in a woman or a young boy. He entered an imaginary harem when entering the metaphor of the Orient, weighed down by inexpressible longings'; see Rana Kabbani, *Imperial Fictions: Europe's Myths of Orient*, 1986 (Pandora: London, 1988), 67. Most recently, Yeazell has written a book entirely devoted to the West's cultural reproduction of the harem, what she calls 'harems of the mind'. That she can dedicate an entire project to one 'blank space' peopled by Western imaginings reveals its extraordinary allure.

36 Criticism on the harem has typically suggested that male fantasies of the harem imagine patriarchal dominance whereas female ones focus on feminist sisterhood. In service of this argument, Montesquieu's *Persian Letters* and Montagu's *Turkish Embassy Letters* are often juxtaposed. For example, Joseph Lew suggests that Montesquieu displays classical orientalism, whereas Montagu allows for cross-cultural 'exchange'. Similarly, Inge Boer contrasts Montesquieu and Montagu to argue that the first fantasises about women's incarceration in the harem, while the latter imagines feminist resistance. More generally, Billie Melman argues that women

travellers humanised the harem, while men sexualised it. See Joseph W. Lew, 'Lady Mary's Portable Seraglio', *Eighteenth-Century Studies*, 24 (1991) 433, 450; Inge E. Boer, 'Despotism from Under the Veil: Masculine and Feminine Readings of the Despot and the Harem', *Cultural Critique*, 32 (1995–96) 50, 56; and Billie Melman, *Women's Orients: English Women and the Middle East, 1718–1918: Sexuality, Religion and Work* (Basingstoke: Macmillan, 1992), 61.

37   In his analysis of the reception of Byron's poetry, Elfenbein shows that female readers sexualised Byron and his heroes while male readers experimented with 'erotic possibilities that for the most part were strictly off limits'; see Elfenbein, *Byron and the Victorians*, 70.

38   'Critique on Modern Poets', *The New Monthly Magazine*, 12 (1 Nov. 1819) 372.

39   Marchand, ed., *Byron's Letters*, 6.232.

40   As there is little information about the date or circulation of Rowlandson's erotic prints, it is impossible to discern who would have had access to them. For an extended discussion of these prints and their rejection of elite aesthetics, see Bradford K. Mudge, 'Romanticism, Materialism, and the Origins of Pornography', *Romanticism On the Net*, 23 (2001) 1–23. <http://users.ox.ac.uk/~scat0385/23mudge.html>.

41   McCalman, *Radical Underworld*, 162–77, 204, 214.

42   *The Khan of Kharistan* no longer survives. For information about this work, see [William Laird Clowes], *Bibliotheca Arcana*, 31; and Peter Mendes, *Clandestine Erotic Fiction in English, 1800–1930: A Bibliographic Study* (Hants: Scholar, 1993), 426.

43   McCalman, *Radical Underworld*, 205.

44   Benbow's knowledge of the sexual suggestiveness of the harem may have arisen from his familiarity with the predecessors of his periodical: *The Rambler's Magazine: or, Fashionable Emporium of Polite Literature* (London: Benbow, 1822 [–5]). These predecessors were *The Rambler's Magazine: or, the Annals of Gallantry, Glee, Pleasure, & the Bon Ton*, 7 vols (London: n.p., 1783–90) and *The Bon Ton Magazine; or Microscope of Fashion and Folly*, 5 vols (London: Printed by W. Locke, 1792 [1791–6]). These early bawdy magazines, which were probably not aimed at a working-class readership, were notable for their lurid exoticism. The first *Rambler's Magazine* imagines bringing the harem home: it depicts English actresses as beauties that would suit the 'Master Turk' (2.286) and reproduces Sophie Watson's *Memoirs of the Seraglio of the Bashaw of Merryland* (1768), a pamphlet that describes a harem in England and the (impotent) man who travels the world to people it; see Sophie Watson, *Memoirs of the Seraglio of the Bashaw of Merryland* (London: S. Bladon, 1768). The *Bon Ton Magazine* includes more expository accounts of the harem, like the 'Visit to the Morocco Harem' by the Christian doctor, 'The Eunuch', and 'The Condition of The Female Slave in Arabia'. Henry Spencer Ashbee, the notorious collector of erotica, describes these magazines, but leaves no record of their price or circulation; see Henry Spencer Ashbee [Pisanus Fraxi], *Index Librorum Prohibitorum* (London: Privately Printed, 1877), 327–36. As printing was even more expensive in the eighteenth than the nineteenth century, they probably had a small clientele. After Benbow stopped publishing his magazine, other imitations followed. One of the most interesting sequels was published by Jack Mitford between 1827–9 and sold by Dugdale: *The Rambler's Magazine; or, Annals of Gallantry, Glee, Pleasure, & the Bon Ton*, 2 vols (London: Pub. by J. Mitford, [1827–9]). In 1830, Dugdale was found guilty of displaying this illustrated magazine, which was deemed obscene, in his shop window in Covent Garden; see the *Times* (28 May 1830) 6.

45   *Kouli Khan: or, the Progress of Error* (London: William Benbow, [1820]).

46 *Sultan Sham, and the Seven Wives: An Historical, Romantic, Heroic Poem, in 3 Cantos by Hudibras, the younger,* (London: Printed and Published by W. Benbow, 1820), 37. Further page references appear in parentheses.

47 McCalman, *Radical Underworld,* 166.

48 See, for instance, 'Critique on Modern Poets', *The New Monthly Magazine,* 12 (1 Nov. 1819) 375. This essay elaborated on Byron's erotic poetry: 'The Priapus must be attired in full-dress, drawers of the thinnest silk to make his hideous organism more prominent and obtrusive.'

49 Rev. of *Don Juan,* by Lord Byron. *Gentleman's Magazine,* 93 (1823) 251; Rev. of *Don Juan,* by Lord Byron, *Blackwood's Edinburgh Review,* 14 (1823) 293.

50 Catherine Seville, *Literary Copyright Reform in Early Victorian England: The Framing of the 1842 Copyright Act* (Cambridge: Cambridge University Press, 1999), 8.

51 *Times* (9 Aug. 1823) 2.

52 *Times* (23 July 1823) 3.

53 *Times* (13 Feb. 1822) 3.

54 The *Quarterly Review* listed these cases in an article, probably by Southey, on copyright: they included Walcot v. Walker, Southey v. Sherwood, Murray v. Benbow, and Lawrence v. Smith. See [Robert Southey?], 'Art. IV – Cases of Walcot V. Walker', *Quarterly Review,* 27 (1822) 123–38.

55 *Times* (9 Aug. 1823) 2.

56 *Times* (9 Aug. 1823) 2.

57 In a court of equity, Dugdale could admit with impunity that he had published an obscene libel. He ran the risk of being separately prosecuted for obscenity, but the SSV never pursued the case. For a discussion of the conflict between the civil law of copyright and the criminal law of obscenity, see David Saunders, 'Copyright, Obscenity and Literary History', *ELH,* 57:2 (1990) 434.

58 *Times* (9 Aug. 1823) 2.

59 *Times* (12 Aug. 1823) 2.

60 Elfenbein, *Byron and the Victorians,* 79, 89.

61 [Burgess, George Rev.], *Cato to Lord Byron on the Immorality and Dangerous Tendency of His Writings* (London: W. Wetton, 1824), 14, 42. Further citations appear in parentheses.

62 C. C. Colton, *Remarks on the Talents of Lord Byron, and the Tendencies of* Don Juan (London: Longman, 1825), 2.

63 McCalman, *Radical Underworld,* 155.

64 Henry Coates, *The British Don Juan; Being a Narrative of the Singular Amours, Entertaining Adventures, Remarkable Travels, &c, of the Hon. Edward W. Montagu* (London: James Griffin, 1823), 1, 208.

65 *Memoirs of Harriette Wilson, written by herself,* ed. T. Little, 2nd edn (London: J. J. Stockdale, 1825). There were numerous editions of *Memoirs of Harriett Wilson* published over the years. Some came with suggestive, but never obscene, printed engravings. Stockdale, its first publisher, sold it for half a crown. Robert Blore, who figured in the *Memoirs,* successfully brought a libel suit against Stockdale and won £300 in damages. During the trial itself, whose proceedings Stockdale published in pamphlet form and bound with copies of the book, he quoted Byron as part of his defence: 'Nowhere, was the society of the great so universally corrupt.' The Judge was apparently unmoved by this line of argument and pressed the jury to consider the extensive sale of the book (citing 7000 copies) when making their decision; see *Memoirs,* 24, 57. A later edition of the book, titled *Clara Gazul, or Honi Soit Qui Mal Y Pense* (London: The Author, 1830), also chose an

epigraph from Byron's *Don Juan*: 'If any person should presume to assert / This story is not moral, first, I pray / That they will not cry out before they're hurt.' Byron's association with early nineteenth-century clandestine publications was unmistakable.

66   Lisa Sigel, *Governing Pleasures: Pornography and Social Change in England, 1815–1914* (New Jersey: Rutgers University Press, 2002), 18–23.

67   Elfenbein, *Byron and the Victorians*, 77.

68   Jack Mitford, *The Private Life of Lord Byron; Comprising His Voluptuous Amours, Secret Intrigues* [etc.] (London: Printed by H. Smith [Dugdale], [1828]), 3, 90.

69   *Don Leon; A Poem by the Late Lord Byron*, (London: Printed for the Booksellers [Dugdale], 1866). Ashbee records the conversation he had with a friend about the curious provenance of *Don Leon*. Dugdale acquired the manuscript believing it was truly written by Byron: 'About the year 1860 he brought it to me as a great literary curiosity, and wanted me to advise him as to how he could best approach Lady Byron, from whom he expected to get a large sum to suppress the publication.' See Ashbee, *Centuria Librorum Absconditorum* (London: Privately Printed, 1879), 189, 192. The association between sodomy and blackmail pre-existed later draconian anti-sodomy laws. Included in this same volume of *Don Leon* is an epistle entitled *Leon to Annabella* which suggests that Byron's penchant for sodomy caused his separation from his wife.

70   *Don Leon*, 38, 40–41.

71   Elfenbein, *Byron and the Victorians*, 83, 209.

72   Quoted in William Benbow, *A Scourge for the Laureate* (London: Benbow, n.d. [1825]), iv.

73   Benbow, *A Scourge*, 13–14.

74   McCalman, *Radical Underworld*, 214.

75   Robert Carlile, 'Letter 'To John Herbert Brown' Member of the Society for the Suppression of Vice', *The Republican* (1 July 1825) 822.

76   McCalman, *Radical Underworld*, 164–5.

77   Albert Hourani, *A History of the Arab Peoples* (New York: Warner, 1991), 259. Serbia, Albania, Greece, and Bulgaria were just some of the countries that attempted to seek independence from the Ottomans. While Britain did not follow a policy of imperial expansion in Ottoman territories until the end of the nineteenth century, they were crucial economic and cultural contact zones from the beginning of the century; see Hourani, *History*, 268 and 280.

78   Mendes, *Clandestine Erotic Fiction*, 421.

79   *The Lustful Turk, or Lascivious Scenes in a Harem*, 1828 ([New York]: Canyon, [1967]) and *The Seducing Cardinal's Amours with Isabelle Peto & Others*, 1830 (London: Published as the Act directs, by Madame Le Duck [Lazenby and Avery?]; and to be had by all respectable booksellers, 1830 [c.1886]). *Scenes in the Seraglio* has not survived. Ashbee outlines the plot of the novel: 'This work is similar to *The Lustful Turk*, and could very well have been written by the same author. Adelaide, a young Sicilian beauty, is carried off by the corsair Tiek. [...] Tiek conveys his yet undeflowered victim to Constantinople, and sells her to Achmet, Sultan of Turkey, who treats her with great kindness and delicacy, and at last induces her to submit willingly to his wishes.' See Ashbee, *Catena Librorum Tacendorum* (London: Privately Printed, 1885), 130–7.

80   Steven Marcus, *The Other Victorians: A Study of Sexuality and Pornography in Mid-Nineteenth-Century England* (New York: Basic, 1964), 209.

81   Matthew Gregory Lewis, *The Monk: A Romance* (London: n.p., 1796).

82   *The Lustful Turk*, 32, 35. Further page references appear in parentheses.

83 Sigel, *Governing Pleasures*, 42.

84 In *Bibliotheca Carringtoniensis: Being a Collection of the Descriptive Title Pages of Certain Books Published by Mr. Charles Carrington of Paris* (unpublished), a prospectus for Charles Carrington's 1900 edition of *The Lustful Turk* suggests a female readership, or at least fantasises about it. The editors explain how the work made its way from Europe to America by the hands of a woman: 'We came across the copy of which the preset is a reprint, in a peculiar way. Whilst travelling from Madrid to Seville in a first-class carriage we were struck by the intentness with which a lady about thirty-four years, a seductive brunette with blue eyes, was perusing a small book. She left the train at one of the stations, abandoning the book on her seat, and when we called after her from the carriage window that she had forgotten the little work, she denied that it was hers, although a shame-faced look somewhat belied her words. In any case, we pocketed the book, and, on our return to Chicago, submitted it to several friends, who voted enthusiastically its reproduction.'

85 Ashbee, *Catena Librorum Tacendorum*, 135.

86 George Prichard, in his SSV report before the Police Committee of the House of Commons, described how obscenity was infiltrating the schools. He mentioned, in particular, the prosecution against a man in 1816 for selling obscenity to a girl's school; see *Society for the Suppression of Vice* (London: S. Gosnell, 1825), 31, 38; and *Venus School-Mistress, or, Birchen sports*, *c*.1808–1810 (Paris: Société des Bibliophiles [Carrington?], 1898).

87 The *Times* report on 'Christian Slavery' from 1822, for example, revealed alarm about Ottoman slavery and the complicity of European renegades: 'Vessels bring young Greek girl slaves as presents to the Bardo, and boys, all under 10 years of age, who have been circumcised. What appears most extraordinary is, that this nefarious traffic in Christian blood is not only carried on under the flags of the Holy Alliance, but the two vessels in question were actually escorted from Smyrna to Cape Passaro by an Austrian ship of war'; see 'Christian Slavery', *Times* (22 Nov. 1822) 2.

88 John B. Wolf, *The Barbary Coast: Algiers Under the Turks 1500 to 1830* (New York: Norton, 1979), 331.

89 *Times* (17 Oct. 1817) 2.

90 *Times* (20 Oct. 1817) 3.

91 'A Visit', *Fraser's Magazine* (1838) 679.

92 Ashbee, *Catena Librorum Tacendorum*, 134.

93 See, for example, Jean Lecome de Nouÿ's painting *L'Esclave blanche* (1888).

94 *The Seducing Cardinal's Amours*, 37. Further page references appear in parentheses.

95 Edward Said, *Orientalism*, 1978 (New York: Vintage, 1979), 8.

96 Yeazell, *Harems of the Mind*, 117, 118.

97 Sigel, *Governing Pleasures*, 42.

98 Ashbee, *Catena Librorum Tacendorum*, 135.

99 Mendes, *Clandestine Erotic Fiction*, 132–3.

100 *List of Rare*, cf. *Album 7: Catalogues and Prospectuses* (1889–*c*.1908). Unpublished.

101 Ashbee, *Catena Librorum Tacendorum*,136.

102 Mendes, *Clandestine Erotic Fiction*, 156–7.

103 Yeazell, *Harems of the Mind*, 8.

104 The appeal of the old Ottoman imperium was still powerful in 1896 when Carrington published *Sheaves from an Old Escritoire*. One letter contains a story about sodomy and pedophilia in the Albanian harem of Ali Pacha, whom Byron

celebrated and made famous in Canto 2 of *Childe Harold*; see Mendes, *Clandestine Erotic Fiction*, 268.

105 Lord George Herbert, *A Night in a Moorish Harem*, c.1896 (North Hollywood: Brandon House, 1967).

106 Mendes, *Clandestine Erotic Fiction*, 266.

107 See *Album 7*.

108 Herbert, *A Night in a Moorish Harem*, 20.

109 Melman, *Women's Orients*, 109. The English naval blockade against slave ships significantly curtailed the activities of slave runners in East Africa; see the *Times* (29 May 1889) 8. An article from the *Vigilance Record* in 1902 indicates a fear of white enslavement in Ottoman territory, but this focus on Constantinople is extremely rare in all the NVA literature on the trafficking of prostitutes in Europe; see 'The White Slave Trade in Constantinople', *The Vigilance Record* (1 Apr. 1902) 31.

110 Herbert, *A Night in a Moorish Harem*, 20.

111 Hourani, *A History of the Arab Peoples*, 284.

112 *Moslem Erotism, or Adventures of an American Woman in Constantinople* (N.p.: n.p, n.d [c.1906]). Further page references appear in parentheses. Also see Mendes, *Clandestine Erotic Fiction*, 377.

113 See *Album 7*.

Chapter 3 Sir Richard Burton, the *Arabian Nights*, and Arab sex manuals

1 Burton held positions with the Indian Army and the Foreign Office, during which time he supported English imperial rule in India,the conquest of eastern Africa, and the annexation of Egypt; see Frank McLynn, *Burton: Snow Upon the Desert* (London: John Murray, 1990), 48, 120, 328.

2 McLynn, *Burton*, 74, 329.

3 Thomas Wright, *The Life of Sir Richard Burton*, 2 vols (London: Everett, 1906), 86. The Oriental Translation Fund was established in 1828 as an associate organisation of the Royal Asiatic Society for the advancement of oriental learning; see *Report on the Proceedings of the First General Meeting of the Subscribers to the Oriental Translation Fund* (London: n.p., 1828).

4 *The Book of the Thousand Nights and a Night*, 10 vols, trans. Richard F. Burton (London: Printed by the Kama Shastra Society, 1885–[6]); *Supplemental Nights to the Book of The Thousand Nights and a Night*, 6 vols, trans. Richard F. Burton (London: Printed by the Kama Shastra Society for Private Subscribers Only, 1886–8); *The Kama Sutra of Vatsayana* (Benares: Printed for the Hindoo Kama Shastra Society, For Private Circulation Only, 1883); *Ananga Ranga; (Stage of the Bodiless One) or, The Hindu Art of Love. (Ars Amoris Indica.)*, trans. A. F. F. and B. F. R. (Cosmopoli: Printed for the Kama Shastra Society of London and Benares, and for private circulation only, n.d. [1885]); *The Perfumed Garden of the Sheik Nefzaoui or, The Arab Art of Love* (Cosmopoli: For Private Circulation Only, 1886); *Beharistan (Abode of Spring) By Jami, A Literal Translation from The Persian* (Benares: Printed for the Kama Shastra Society for Private Subscribers Only, 1887); *The Gulistan or Rose Garden of Sa'di, Faithfully Translated Into English* (Benares: Printed by the Kama Shastra Society for Private Subscribers only, 1888). For a list of other proposed translations of Indian works as well as information about the translators, see Wright, *The Life*, 57, 63.

5   Lisa Sigel suggests that 'British pornography centered on India', but there was not as much interest in Indian sexuality as Arab sexuality; see *Governing Pleasures: Pornography and Social Change in England, 1815–1914* (New Jersey: Rutgers University Press, 2002), 121. *The Kama Shastra* was first printed in 1873, but limited to four copies. The Kama Shastra Society reprinted it in 1885 as *The Ananga Ranga*, after first printing *The Kama Sutra* in 1883. Attached to the back of the British Library copy of *The Kama Sutra* are letters dating from 1883 from Arbuthnot, Ashbee, the reviewer J. Knight, and a Paris bookseller. The letters disclose the exchange of the book in London, its sale in bookshops like Bernard Quartich's in Piccadilly, and its migration to the continent. In Paris, a French translation by Isidore Liseux of Arbuthnot and Burton's *The Kama Sutra* appeared in 1885, but no other translations appeared until 1910 with the publication of *Le Livre d'Amour de L'Orient*, which includes both *The Ananga Ranga* and *La Fleur Lascive Orientale*. See Henry Spencer Ashbee [Pisanus Fraxi], *Catena Librorum Tacendorum* (London: Privately Printed, 1885), 282; *Les Kama Sutra de Vatsyayana. Manuel d'Erotologie Hindoue*, trans. Isidore Liseux (Paris: Imprimé à deux cent vingt exemplaire pour Isidore Liseux et ses Amis, 1885); and *Le Livre d'Amour de l'Orient: Ananga-Ranga, La Fleur Lascive Orientale – Le Livre de Volupté* (Paris: Bibliothèque des Curieux, 1910). Obscenity that looked to India includes Edward Sellon's paper 'On Phallic Worship in India' that he presented to the Anthropological Society, Captain Deveureux's *Venus in India* (1889), and a series of privately published works on Indian phallic worship. See Edward Sellon, 'On Phallic Worship in India', *Memoirs Read Before the Anthropological Society of London, 1865–1866* (London: Trubner, 1866); *Phallic Miscellanies* (N.p. [London]: Privately Printed [Hargrave Jennings], 1891); and *Phallic Objects, Monuments, and Remains* (N.p. [London]: Privately Printed [Hargrave Jennings], 1889).

6   Sigel, *Governing*, 76.

7   Steven Marcus, *The Other Victorians: A Study of Sexuality and Pornography in Mid-Nineteenth-Century England* (New York: Basic, 1964); Peter Mendes, *Clandestine Erotic Fiction in English, 1800–1930: A Bibliographical Study* (Hants: Scholar, 1993). Mendes's bibliography on clandestine English fiction excludes sex manuals as well as pseudo-anthropological and scientific texts and thus overlooks their significance in the British print trade in obscenity. Also see *The Lustful Turk: or Lascivious Scenes in a Harem*, 1828 ([New York]: Canyon, [1967]); *The Pearl: A Journal of Facetia Voluptuous Reading*, 3 vols (London: Printed for the Society of Vice [Augustin Brancart], 1879–80 [*c*.1890]).

8   Burton founded the Anthropological Society of London in 1863 and produced the periodical *Anthropologia*. His motive behind the journal 'was to supply travellers with an organ which would rescue their observations from the outer darkness of manuscript and print their curious information on social and sexual matters out of place in the popular book'; see *Arabian Nights*, (1.xviii). Sigel discusses the 'carnal exoticism' of the Society's inner circle, the Cannibal Club, to suggest that it demonstrated a cruel interest in the sexual practices of other cultures. The Cannibal Club, which included Burton, Monckton Milnes, and Hankey, endorsed unofficial ventures in Africa to locate human skin for the express purpose of binding volumes of de Sade; see Sigel, *Governing*, 72–3.

9   Monckton Milnes, Lord Houghton, owned an extensive collection of French and Italian obscenity and was one of Burton's intimate friends. In 1859, he introduced Burton to Hankey, his Paris agent who purchased obscene works for Monckton Milnes and ingeniously undermined the vigilance of British customs. In 1861, he also introduced Burton to the young Swinburne, who, owing to Monckton

Milnes's influence, developed an obsession with the Marquis de Sade and likely contributed *The Whippingham Papers* (London: n.p. [Avery?], 1888 [1887]), a literary compendium on flagellation published clandestinely in 1887. Burton was also well acquainted with Ashbee. For information of these intimacies, see McLynn, *Burton*, 328, 330, James Pope-Hennessy, *Monckton Milnes: The Flight of Youth, 1851–1885* (London: Constable, 1951), 118, 132; and Mendes, *Clandestine Erotic Fiction*, 9.

10   Sigel, *Governing*, 84.

11   There are numerous biographies on Burton. For the most recent and detailed, see Mary Lovell, *A Rage to Live: A Biography of Richard and Isabel Burton* (London: Little, 1998).

12   Edward Said, for instance, discusses Burton's orientalism. He suggests that despite Burton's obvious interest in and knowledge about Arab culture, he elevates himself to a position of supremacy over the Orient. As he writes, 'In that position his [Burton's] individuality perforce encounters, and indeed merges with, the voice of Empire.' Rana Kabbani reiterates Said's perspective on Burton: 'His East was the conventional sexual realm of the Western imagination, a realm that could only be depicted, in his age, by an unconventional man [...], [who] helped only to further confirm the myth of the erotic East.' See Edward Said, *Orientalism* (New York: Vintage, 1979), 196; and Rana Kabbani, *Imperial Fictions: Europe's Myths of Orient* (Pandora: London, 1988), 66.

13   Sigel, *Governing*, 93.

14   For a range of essays on the impact of the *Arabian Nights* on British literature, see Peter Caracciolo, ed., *The Arabian Nights in English Literature: Studies in the Reception of* The Thousand and One Nights *into British Culture* (Basingstoke: Macmillan, 1988).

15   *Arabian Nights*, 1.ix. Further page references appear in parentheses. Both Wright and C. Knipp dispute Burton's account that he spent 30 years translating the *Arabian Nights*. They argue that his translation is heavily indebted to Payne's earlier translation and they also suggest that his lurid annotations and Terminal Essay are alone what make his translation distinct; see Wright, *The Life*, 105; and C. Knipp, 'The *Arabian Nights* in England: Galland's Translation and its Successors', *Journal of Arabic Literature*, 5 (1974), 45.

16   *Supplemental Nights*, 6.390. Further page references appear in parentheses.

17   Burton's version of 'The Porter and the Three Ladies of Baghdad' includes vulgar references to genitalia, female nudity, and flagellation; see *Arabian Nights*, 1.90–7). Even a favourable reviewer for *Bat* in 1885 was shocked by Burton's translation of the tale: 'The conduct of the three fair ladies is decidedly eccentric; their language, to put it mildly, is copious, expressive, and direct in the extreme; their customs, in the phraseology of the burlesque, are very peculiar; and very improper is their behaviour as judged by our occidental standards'; see Rev. of *The Book of a Thousand Nights and a Night*, by Richard Burton, *Bat* (29 Sept. 1885) 876.

18   Mahsin Jassim Ali, *Scheherazade in England: A Study of Nineteenth-Century English Criticism of the* Arabian Nights (Washington: Three Continents, 1981), 115.

19   *Arabian Nights*, 1n6.

20   Before Burton's translation, the *Arabian Nights* had already been the inspiration for a serialised story entitled 'Conjugal Nights' that appeared between 1842 and 1844 in *The Exquisite*. The story, which consists of a series of racy tales recounted by a husband to his wife each night and broken off at a critical point until the following evening, borrows its title, frame, and narrative technique from the

Arabian Nights. It appropriates the text for erotic purposes, recreating these stories as conjugal sex aids. See *The Exquisite: A Collection of Tales, Histories, and Essays* 3 vols ([London]: Printed and Published by H. Smith [Dugdale], n.d. [1842–4]), 2.61.

21 The *Arabian Nights* had long been westernised before Arab scholars reclaimed it. The tremendous popularity of the *Arabian Nights* in the West actually stimulated Arab interest in the text that had been previously derided; see Knipp, 'The Arabian Nights in England', 47.

22 Dane Kennedy, '"Captain Burton's Oriental Muck Heap": *The Book of the Thousand Nights* and the Uses of Orientalism', *Journal of British Studies*, 39 (July 2000) 320, 326.

23 Walter Kendrick, *The Secret Museum: Pornography in Modern Culture* (New York: Viking, 1987), 71.

24 Emile de Laveleye, 'How Bad Books May Destroy States', *The Vigilance Record* (1 June 1888) 59–60.

25 Quoted in Ali, *Scheherazade in England*, 720.

26 Knipp, 'The Arabian Nights in England', 46.

27 Walter Benjamin, 'The Task of the Translator', *Illuminations*, ed. Hannah Arendt, trans. Harry Zohn (New York: Schocken, 1968), 73. Recent critics also acknowledge this disruption between the original and translated text as the product of linguistic, gender, colonial, or historical difference. For a discussion of various semantic disruptions that occur in translations produced in a postcolonial context, see for instance, Douglas Robinson *Translation and Empire: Postcolonial Theories Explained* (Manchester: St Jerome, 1997).

28 Kennedy, '"Captain Burton's Oriental Muck Heap"', 325.

29 Metcalf Burton Collection Box 43 RFB 1426.

30 Isabel Burton, *The Life of Captain Sir Richard F. Burton*, 1893, ed. W. H. Wilkins (London: Duckworth, 1898), 449. During the production of the *Arabian Nights*, Isabel Burton sought counsel about the Obscene Publications Act through the criminal lawyer George Lewis who had worked for the National Vigilance Association; see Lovell, *A Rage to Live*, 685.

31 Sir Richard Burton, 'The Thousand Nights and a Night', *Academy* (15 Aug. 1885) 101.

32 References to the indecency of French literature proliferated in late nineteenth-century popular culture. In 1882, an article on 'Immoral Current Literature' in *Town Talk* insisted that 'a French novel is but a synonym for obscenity'. In 1885, another article entitled 'Indecent French Novels' appeared in the same magazine, claiming that 'this literature is steadily sapping all strength and energy from the French people', and asking 'is it to be allowed to emasculate our hardy manhood?' See 'Immoral Current Literature', *Town Talk* (12 May 1882) 3; and 'Indecent French Novels', *Town Talk* (31 Jan. 1885) 1.

33 In the last volume of the *Arabian Nights*, Burton repeats the same imperialist argument for studying the Arabs: 'In fact, I consider my labours as a legacy bequeathed to my countrymen at a most critical time when England the puissantest of Moslem powers is called upon, without adequate knowledge of the Moslem's inner life, to administer Egypt as well as to rule India.' See *Supplemental Nights*, 6.438–9.

34 Burton's argument that his sexual knowledge of Arab peoples was in the service of British empire still found an audience in the twentieth century. Frank Harris, author of the salacious autobiography *My Life and Loves* (1925–9), believed in Burton's political importance. While comparing him to the German imperialist Bismarck, he argues that Burton would have acquired an empire for England

from the Cape to Cairo if England had given him due regard. He explains more fully in his earlier *Contemporary Portraits* (1915) that Burton's knowledge of Egypt and Sudan would have 'made [him] an ideal ruler of a Mohammedan people.' He described Burton as 'a sensualist of extravagant appetites, learned in every Eastern and savage vice', but this 'pornographic leaning' still made him suited for an Eastern throne; see Frank Harris, *My Life and Loves*, 4 vols (Paris: Obelisk, 1945), 59, and *Contemporary Portraits: First Series* (London: Methuen, 1915), 171, 179–80.

35   Sigel, *Governing*, 76; Ronald Hyam, *Empire and Sexuality: The British Experience* (Manchester and New York: Manchester University Press, 1990), 58.

36   Burton likely donated a set of the *Arabian Nights* to The Athenaeum Club. The Club's Library holds all of the original volumes, except for the first that would provide details about their provenance.

37   See Richard and Isabel Burton's separate accounts of the reviews on his *Arabian Nights*: Sir Richard Burton, *Supplemental Nights*, 6.385–457; and Isabel Burton, *Lady Burton's*, 6.430–8.

38   To follow these reviews, see Rev. of *The Book of a Thousand Nights and One Night*, by Richard Burton, *Standard* (12 Sept. 1885) 5; Sigma [John Morley], 'Pantagruelism or Pornography?' *Pall Mall Gazette* (14 Sept. 1885) 2, 3; 'Occasional Notes', *Pall Mall Gazette* (24 Sept. 1885) 3; Sigma [John Morley], 'The Ethics of Dirt', *Pall Mall Gazette* (29 Sept. 1885) 2; and Kennedy, ' "Captain Burton's Oriental Muck Heap"', 326. Over the month, the *Pall Mall Gazette* also published a number of spurious notices about impending libel action against the book. There is no evidence that Burton was ever prosecuted for his publication of the *Arabian Nights*. Yet, the *Pall Mall Gazette* claimed that 'it was resolved by the authorities to request Captain Burton not to issue the third volume and to prosecute him if he takes no notice of the invitation', and the same paper later announced that the 'Government has at last determined to put down Captain Burton with a strong hand'.

39   Stead was famous for publishing his 1885 report on child prostitution. He was subsequently jailed for three months for 'abducting' a child in order to prove his case. His findings nonetheless forced Parliament to raise the age of sexual consent to 16 in the Criminal Law Amendment Act of 1885.

40   For some, Burton's unconventionality signalled his non-Englishness: his fellow Indian Army officers called him 'The White Nigger'; see McLynn, *Burton*, 34.

41   To follow these reviews, see Rev. of *The Book of a Thousand Nights and a Night*, by Richard Burton, *Bat* (29 Sept. 1885) 876; Rev. of *The Book of a Thousand Nights and One Night*, by Richard Burton, *Echo* (12 Oct. 1885) 2; 'Acid Drops', Rev. of *The Book of a Thousand Nights and One Night*, by Richard Burton, *Freethinker* (25 Oct. 1885) 339; Rev. of *The Book of a Thousand Nights and a Night*, by Richard Burton, *The Saturday Review* (2 Jan. 1886) 27.

42   Quoted in *Lady Burton's*, 431. Further page references appear in parentheses.

43   This mention of secret cabinets in public libraries is likely a reference to the Private Case collection formerly housed at the British Museum and now at the British Library.

44   To follow these reviews, see Rev. of *The Book of a Thousand Nights and a Night*, by Richard Burton, *The Saturday Review* (2 Jan. 1886) 26; [Stanley Lane-Poole], Rev. of *The Book of a Thousand Nights and a Night*, by Richard Burton, *Edinburgh Review*, 164 (1886) 180, 183–5.

45   de Laveleye, 'How Bad Books May Destroy States', 60.

46   George Mosse, *Nationalism and Sexuality: Respectability and Abnormal Sexuality in Modern Europe* (New York: Howard Fertig, 1985), 133.

47   Lovell, *A Rage to Live*, 691. According to Isabel Burton, it was only Benares, the Kama Shastra Society's false place of publication, that saved the Burtons from discovery and prosecution.

48   Burton often turned to the Old Testament to point out inconsistent attitudes about pornography. He puzzled over why the British accepted free translations from this 'ancient Oriental work', but not his own unexpurgated *Arabian Nights*; see *Supplemental Nights* 6.437.

49   Isabel Burton may also have hoped to profit from the financial success of Burton's translation, which made a gross profit of £10,000; see Isabel Burton, *Life* 459.

50   Isabel Burton, *Life*, 458.

51   For these reviews, see Amelia B. Edwards, 'Literature', Rev. of *Lady Burton's Edition of her Husband's 'Arabian Nights'*, by Isabel Burton, *Academy* (11 Dec. 1886) 387; Rev. of *Lady Burton's Edition of her Husband's 'Arabian Nights'*, by Isabel Burton, *Academy* (31 Dec. 1887) 439.

52   Isabel Burton, *Life*, 458. The Burtons fostered this myth elsewhere in their writing; see Sir Richard Burton, *Supplemental Nights*, 6.452 and Isabel Burton, 'Sir Richard Burton's Manuscripts', *The Morning Post* (19 June 1891) 3.

53   Fawn Brodie, *The Devil Drives: A Life of Sir Richard Burton* (London: Erie & Spottiswoode, 1967), 310; also see McLynn, *Burton*, 344. Like Isabel Burton, Georgina Stisted, Burton's niece, also felt compelled to explain that she had never read the original translation at her uncle's 'special request', even though she defended the *Arabian Nights* in her 1896 biography of Burton on the grounds of its limited accessibility to the 'select few' and its difference from 'the latest nauseous case from the Divorce Courts'; see Georgina M. Stisted, *The True Life of Capt. Sir Richard F. Burton* (London: H. S. Nichols, 1896), 403.

54   McLynn, *Burton*, 345.

55   Thomas Morton, *Speed the Plough*, 1798, 3rd edn (Dublin: Burnet, 1800).

56   Quoted in Ali, *Scheherazade in England*, 126.

57   Metcalf Burton Collection Box 43 RFB 1426.

58   Quoted in James Nelson, *Publisher to the Decadents. Leonard Smithers in the Careers of Beardsley, Wilde, Dowson* (University Park: Pennsylvania State University Press, 2000), 37.

59   Mark Turner, *Trollope and the Magazines: Gendered Issues in Mid-Victorian Britain* (Basingstoke: Macmillan – now Palgrave, 1999), 199.

60   Lovell, *A Rage to Live*, 779.

61   Nelson, *Publisher to the Decadents*, 11, 12.

62   Between 1888 and 1894, Smithers and Nichols collaborated on various underground projects. They were involved in the production of a number of clandestine works together, the most important titles including *Gynecocracy. A narrative of adventures and psychological experiences of Julian Robinson, afterwards Viscount Ladywood, under petti-coat rule, written by himself*, 3 vols (London: Privately Printed, 1893), and *Teleny, or the Reverse of Medal: A Physiological Romance of To-day*, 2 vols (Cosmopoli [London]: n.p. [Smithers], 1893). They had connections with other underground publishers such as Edward Avery in London and Carrington in Paris. After 1891, they also opened shops in Soho. Their partnership ended in 1894 when Nichols's interests deviated from the expensive, upscale obscenity that Smithers preferred. Smithers's son, Jack Smithers, drolly recounted in 1939 his experiences with Nichols. While he insists that his father produced only legitimate works, he shows that Nichols's print press 'was nothing more or less than a wholesale factory of pornographic books and photographs' that often resorted to blackmailing its customers. See Nelson, *Publisher to the Decadents*,

43; Malcolm Lawrence, 'Leonard Smithers – The Most Learned Erotomaniac', *American Libraries* (1973), 6; and Jack Smithers, *The Early Life and Vicissitudes of Jack Smithers* (London: Martin Secker, 1939), 82.

63 *Priapeia, or The Sportive Epigrams of divers Poets on Priapus* (Athens [London]: Imprinted by the Erotika Biblion Society For Private Distribution Only [Smithers], 1888 [1889]); *The Carmina of Catullus*, trans. Richard Burton and Leonard Smithers (London: Printed for the Translators, 1894). See the correspondence between Isabel Burton and Smithers in the Metcalf Burton Collection Box 17–23.

64 Not only did the correspondence between Burton and Smithers reveal anxiety about surveillance by the NVA, but also that between Isabel Burton and Smithers. When Isabel Burton wrote to Smithers about *The Priapeia*, she also used a pseudonym, 'Hermaphrodite'; see Lovell, *A Rage to Live*, 766 and Metcalf Burton Collection Box 4 RFB 244. For a discussion of Isabel Burton's correspondence with Smithers before and after her husband's death, see Dane Kennedy and Burke Casari, 'Burton Offerings: Isabel Burton and the "Scented Garden" Manuscript', *Journal of Victorian Culture*, 2:2 (1997) 235, 240.

65 *The Thousand and One Quarters of an Hour*, ed. L. C. Smithers (London: H. S. Nichols, 1893); *The Transmigrations of the Mandarin Fum-Hoam*, ed. L. C. Smithers (London: H. S. Nichols, 1894).

66 Apparently there was a previous English translation of this text: *Oriental Lascivious Tales* (London: Bibliomaniac Society, 1891). It no longer exists. See *Oriental Stories (La Fleur Lascive Orientale)* (Athens: Erotika Biblion Society, for private distribution only, 1893), ix–x. Smithers struggled with the French translator to gain control over this work, a conflict that is enacted in the margins of the English translation of *Oriental Stories*. The combination of French and English commentary included in the English translation at first seems harmonious until one realises the extent to which Smithers obfuscates its French literary heritage by fabricating an English one. For instance, the stories from the *Arabian Nights* are probably extracts from a French translation of the work, particularly since the French translation preceded Payne's and Burton's by a few years. Yet, when Smithers translates these stories into English, he alludes to Burton, suggesting that they derive from him. His translation reveals an effort to assert literary dominion over the French. In so doing, he constructs an erotic literary legacy for the British by appropriating the Arabic texts, obfuscating French involvement, and making Burton the founding author. A similar sort of struggle between French and English translators transpires over *The Perfumed Garden*, a work I discuss later.

67 Lovell, *A Rage to Live*, 775; *The Book of the Thousand Nights and a Night*, trans. Richard F. Burton, ed. Leonard Smithers, 12 vols (London: H. S. Nichols, 1894–[7]).

68 Metcalf Burton Collection Box 4 RFB 242.

69 *The Book of the Thousand Nights and a Night*, trans. Richard F. Burton, ed. Leonard Smithers, 12 vols (London: H. S. Nichols, 1894–[7]), 1.vii–viii.

70 Isabel Burton, however, countered Smithers's betrayal by thwarting future would-be pornographers. She wrote instructions to the executors of her will to burn Burton's unpublished works and send all relevant material to the NVA. In an early letter, Isabel Burton condemns 'that hideous humbug The Society for the Suppression of Vice'. However, faced with antagonistic publishers intent on republishing Burton's works, she eventually sought the aid of one such society; see Lovell, *A Rage to Live*, 685, 783.

71 Rev. of *The Library Edition*, ed. Leonard Smithers, *Athenaeum*, 23 (Feb. 1895) 247.

72 McLynn, *Burton*, 41–5.

73 Brodie, *The Devil Drives*, 105–6; McLynn, *Burton*, 106.

74 Symonds, Ellis, and Carpenter were all early English theorists of homosexuality who rejected pathological or morbid theories in favour of congenital ones. Their major works on homosexuality are, respectively [John Addington Symonds], *A Problem in Greek Ethics* ([N.p.]: Privately Printed for the Author's Use, 1883); Henry Havelock Ellis, *Studies in the Psychology of Sex: Sexual Inversion*, vol. 1 (London: Wilson & Macmillan, 1897); and Edward Carpenter, *The Intermediate Sex: A Study of Some Transitional Types of Men and Women* (London: Swan Sonnenschein, 1908).

75 Jeffrey Weeks, *Coming Out: Homosexual Politics in Britain from the Nineteenth Century to the Present* (London: Quartet, 1990), 47.

76 Matt Cook, *London and the Culture of Homosexuality, 1885–1914* (Cambridge: Cambridge University Press, 2003), 91–4.

77 Michel Foucault, *The History of Sexuality*, vol. 1, trans. Robert Hurley (London: Allen Lane, 1979), 43. Historical evidence weakens Michel Foucault's thesis that homosexual identity did not emerge in Europe until the 1870s. From the Molly Houses in the eighteenth century, homosexual communities have existed and defined themselves collectively and individually through sexual difference. There are two nineteenth-century examples of English works that show awareness of homosexual identity and community. *The Phoenix of Sodom* (1813) is a defence of the owner of a male brothel on Vere Street raided by the police in 1810. In this defence, he reveals the practices of the Vere Street coterie like the mock marriage ceremonies in the 'Chapel' that features 'bride maids' and 'bride men' who then consummate their marriage. It also reveals that these male brothels were widespread in London. *The Yokel's Preceptor* (*c*.1855) describes male prostitutes and identifies these 'poufs' as different on account of their effeminacy, fashionable dress, and walk. See *The Phoenix of Sodom, or the Vere Street Coterie* (N.p.: n.p., 1813), 10, 14; and *Yokel's Preceptor: or, More sprees in London!* (London: H. Smith [Dugdale], n.d [*c*.1855]).

78 [Cleland, John], *Memoirs of a Woman of Pleasure* (London: G. Fenton, 1749). The work is commonly known as *Fanny Hill*.

79 *The Romance of Lust: or Early Experiences* (London: N.p., 1873–6); *My Secret Life*, 11 vols (Amsterdam: Privately Printed, n.d. [*c*.1888–94]). In *The Romance of Lust*, sodomy proliferates, but is neither restricted to men or suggestive of homosexual identity. As Marcus argues, this novel is a classic example of 'pornotopia' that displays every type of sexual act; see *The Other Victorians*, 274. As for *My Secret Life*, Weeks argues that the author experiments with anal sex with a man 'after years of compulsive sex with all manner of women', but 'there is no suggestion that his own basic self-concept was in any way disturbed'; see *Sex, Politics, & Society: The Regulation of Sexuality Since 1800* (London: Longman, 1982), 108.

80 *The Cremorne; A Magazine of Wit, Facetiae, Parody, Graphic Tales of Love, etc.* (London: Privately Printed [Lazenby?], 1851 [1882]). 'The Sub-Umbra' in *The Pearl* is preoccupied with sodomy and sexual relations between men. However, the story conceals its central concern. As a classic example of the Sedwickian triangle, it disrupts the homosexual desire between two boys by introducing a girl into their sex play. Two boys who have intercourse with a girl at the same time, one vaginally and one anally, focus on the sensation of their 'pricks throbbing against each other in a most delicious manner, with only the thin membrane of the anal canal between them', see *The Pearl*, 101.

81 *The Sins of the Cities of the Plain or the Recollections of a Mary-Anne with Short Essays on Sodomy and Tribadism*, 2 vols (London: Privately Printed [Lazenby?], 1881). Further page references appear in parentheses.

82 The Cleveland Street homosexual scandal broke in 1889 when police discovered a male brothel that specialised in telegraph boys and serviced gentlemen. The incident became a public scandal when peers like Lord Arthur Somerset were implicated. For further information about the scandal and the subsequent trials, see Montgomery Hyde, *The Other Love: An Historical and Contemporary Survey of Homosexuality in Britain* (London: Heinemann, 1970); and William A. Cohen, *Sex Scandal: The Private Parts of Victorian Fiction* (Durham: Duke University Press, 1996).

83 Ernest Boulton and Frederick William Park were two male transvestites who were arrested in 1870 and charged with conspiracy to commit sodomy. Their trial, which lasted three days in 1871, aroused immense public interest as doctors discussed the physical evidence and disputed whether or not they had committed sodomy. See Hyde's *The Other Love* and Cohen's *Sex Scandal* for further information.

84 Cook, *London*, 18–22.

85 Ambrose Tardieu, *Etude medicale-legal suer les attentats aux moeurs*, 1857, 7th edn (Paris: n.p., 1878). In this work, Tardieu pathologises sodomy as a disease.

86 The publishing history of *The Sins of the Cities* is uncertain and complex, but involved people with whom Burton had contact. Mendes suggests that James Campbell Reddie – known to Burton – likely wrote the original manuscript first published by Lazenby; see Mendes, *Clandestine Erotic Fiction*, 215. Lazenby then wrote the sequel, *Letters from Laura and Eveline* (London: Privately Printed, 1903).

87 Mendes, *Clandestine Erotic Fiction*, 7, 16.

88 Knipp, 'The Arabian Nights in England', 46. I am indebted to Mark Turner for drawing my attention to the similarities between the terminal essays in *Sins of the Cities* and Burton's Terminal Essay on 'Pederasty'.

89 John Addington Symonds, *A Problem in Modern Ethics: Being an Inquiry into the phenomenon of Sexual Inversion* (London: n.p., 1896), 2–3.

90 Symonds, *A Problem in Modern Ethics*, 78.

91 The Athenaeum Club is an exclusive English gentleman scholar's club on Pall Mall in London that was established in 1824 as an association of distinguished writers, scientists, and artists. Burton, Symonds, and Monckton-Milnes were all members.

92 Symonds, 'The Arabian Nights' Entertainments', *Academy* (3 Oct. 1885) 223.

93 Herbert M. Schueller and Robert L. Peters, eds, *The Letters of John Addington Symonds*, 3 vols (Detroit: Wayne State University Press, 1969), 90.

94 Hyde, *The Other Love*, 101; Phyllis Grosskurth, *John Addington Symonds: A Biography* (Longman: London, 1964), 270.

95 For the Criminal Law Amendments Acts, see 48 and 49 Vic. Cap. 69.

96 Weeks, *Coming Out*, 103.

97 *Times* (1 Mar. 1890) 7.

98 F. B. Smith, 'Labouchère's Amendment of the Criminal Law Amendment Bill', *Historical Studies*, 17 (1976) 172.

99 Louise Jackson notes that there was a 'rent-boy scandal' around 1885; a document related to this scandal may have been the infamous report on sodomy to which Burton and Labouchère refer. See Louise A. Jackson, *Child Abuse in Victorian England* (London: Routledge, 2000). Richard Dellamora, offering another theory for Labouchère's motives, suggests that he promoted the amendment in order to punish the wealthy homosexual dandy who discomfited his own aristocratic masculinity. See *Masculine Desire: The Sexual Politics of Victorian Aestheticism* (Chapel Hill: University of North Carolina Press, 1990), 202.

100 *The Phoenix of Sodom,* 25–6.
101 Kennedy, ' "Captain Burton's Oriental Muck Heap" ', 335.
102 Knipp, 'The Arabian Nights in England', 46.
103 McLynn, *Burton,* 52.
104 Said, *Orientalism,* 188–90.
105 The booksellers and publishers Robson and Kerslake were involved in underground obscenity from *c.*1873–*c.*1900; see Mendes, *Clandestine Erotic Fiction,* 15–16. Isabel Burton mentioned them among other booksellers who might sell a fraudulent version of *The Scented Garden;* see Lovell, *A Rage to Live,* 695, 779 and Metcalf Burton Collection Box 3 RFB 214.
106 Isidore Liseux, *Le Jardin Parfumé du Cheikh Nefzaoui* (Paris: Pour Isidore Liseux et ses Amis, [1886]), vi. See Lovell, *A Rage to Live,* 875n72. The British Library holds a copy of the 1876 autograph edition that Liseux probably used as the basis of his edition. There are handwritten editorial corrections throughout, and the semi-erotic illustrations are scratched out. One illustration showing an Arab man exposing his penis to another man is vehemently destroyed, an act that suggests the editor's discomfort with the subject matter; see Cheikh Nefzaoui, *[The Perfumed Garden],* Traduit de L'Arabe par Monsieur le baron R**, Capitaine d'Etat Major ([Algiers], N.p., 1850 [1876]), 65.
107 McLynn, *Burton,* 334.
108 *The Perfumed Garden,* 70. Further page references appear in parentheses.
109 Charles Carrington published an edition of *The Perfumed Garden* in 1907, now held at the Kinsey Institute. He not only claims that it is based on the Algiers manuscript that Burton was working on at the time of his death, but he also says that it contains the twenty-first chapter. As he writes in the Foreword, 'Now, in the Twenty-First Chapter, that remained untranslated but which, in my translation is given in its entirety, all the questions are subjects are handled very freely.' However, only the first volume seems to have been published, and it does not contain the promised chapter. See *The Perfumed Garden for the Soul's Delectation* (Paris: The Kamashastra Society [Charles Carrington], 1907), 55, 63.
110 Wright, *The Life,* 2. 216.
111 Lovell, *A Rage to Live,* 705, 718, 723.
112 Lovell, *A Rage to Live,* 751.
113 Karl Ulrichs (1825–95), a German theorist of homosexuality in the 1860s, influenced Symonds as well as Burton with his congenital theories about 'Urnings'; see Weeks, *Coming,* 48. On Burton's knowledge of Ulrichs, see Wright, *The Life,* 197; and Schueller and Peters, eds, *The Letters,* 500.
114 Of the French in Algeria, Burton wrote that 'French mismanagement beats ours holler, and their hate and jealousy of us makes their colonies penal settlements to us'; quoted in Wright, *The Life,* 220. Burton preferred Tunis to Morocco because it was not as influenced by French culture; see Lovell, *A Rage to Live,* 722.
115 Quoted in Nelson, *Publisher to the Decadents,* 15.
116 Metcalf Burton Collection Box 20 RFB 1131.
117 *The Carmina of Catullus,* xvii.
118 Isabel Burton, 'Sir Richard Burton's Manuscripts', 3.
119 Brodie, *The Devil Drives,* 328; McLynn, *Burton,* 363.
120 Quoted in Brodie, *The Devil Drives,* 329.
121 Isabel Burton, *The Life,* 529; also see Isabel Burton, 'Sir Richard Burton's Manuscripts', 3.

122 Lovell, *A Rage to Live*, 766.

123 Stisted, *The True Life*, 404–45.

124 Lovell, *A Rage to Live*, 749, 779–80. For Isabel Burton's correspondence on the subject, see Metcalf Burton Collection Boxes 3, 8, 17–23.

125 Symonds, *A Problem in Modern Ethics*, 78.

126 Schueller and Peters, eds, *The Letters*, 694.

127 Edward Carpenter, *Intermediate Types among Primitive Folk: A Study in Social Evolution* (London: George Allen, 1919), cf. 28, 34, 76, 167.

128 *The Scented Garden of Abdullah, the Satirist of Shiraz*, trans. Aleister Crowley (London: Privately Printed, 1910), 4. Further page references appear in parentheses.

129 Said, *Orientalism*, 190.

130 George W. Harris, *'The' Practical Guide to Algiers* (London: George Philip & Son, 1890).

131 André Gide, *Si le Grain ne Meurt*, 1920 (Paris: n.p., 1928).

132 Jonathan Dollimore, *Sexual Dissidence: Augustine to Wilde, Freud to Foucault* (Oxford: Clarendon, 1991), 12.

133 Alex Owen, 'The Sorcerer and His Apprentice: Aleister Crowley and the Magical Exploration of Edwardian Subjectivity', *Journal of British Studies*, 36 (1997) 107, 113.

134 Kaja Silverman, *Male Subjectivity at the Margins* (New York: Routledge, 1992), 300, 332.

135 Said, *Orientalism*, 3.

136 Nelson, *Publisher to the Decadents*, 33. For further information on Quaritch, see Nicolas Barker, 'Bernard Quaritch', *Book Collector: Special Number* (1997) 3–34.

137 For the correspondence on the confiscation of Burton's works in Madras, see the India and Oriental Collection at the British Library, IOR/L/PJ/6/456, File 1865.

138 See National Archives, 'Indecent Publications' HO 45/10299/116126.

139 *Marriage – Love and Woman Amongst the Arabs otherwise entitled The Book of Exposition*, literally translated from Arabic by a English Bohemian (Paris: Charles Carrington, 1896); *The Old Man Young Again or The Age-Rejuvenescence in the Power of Concupiscence* (Paris: Charles Carrington, 1898–9). Carrington published *Marriage* openly, but *Old Man* privately. Yet, he advertised and sold both through his underground sales catalogues. See Mendes, *Clandestine Erotic Fiction*, 34; and *Album 7: Catalogues and Prospectuses* (1889–*c*.1908), unpublished.

140 Mendes, *Clandestine Erotic Fiction*, 33.

141 *Catalogue of Rare Curious and Voluptuous Reading* (N.p.: n.p., 1896), 8.

142 *Prospectuses* (N.p.: n.p., n.d.), 1. For a similar claim, see Carrington's *List of Choice English Books* (Paris: Charles Carrington, n.d.).

143 Marriage, 288. Further page references appear in parentheses.

144 *Album 7*.

145 Charles Carrington], *Forbidden Books: Notes and Gossip on Tabooed Literature by an Old Bibliophile* (Paris: For the Author and his Friends, 1902), 139, 144.

146 *The Old Man Young* Again, 10. Further page references appear in parentheses.

147 In 1888, Henry Vizetelly was charged with obscene libel for publishing Emile Zola's novels, and in 1898 a bookseller was charged with the same for displaying Ellis's work in the store window; see Weeks, *Coming*, 60 and *Times* (11 Aug. 1888) 13, and (1 Nov. 1888) 13.

148 Davenport, John, *An Apology for Mohammed and the Koran* (London: Printed for the Author, 1869); *Curiosites Eroticae Physiologiae: or Tabooed Subjects freely*

treated (London: Privately Printed, 1875); and Henry Spencer Ashbee [Pisanus Fraxi], *Index Librorum Prohibitorum* (London: Privately Printed, 1877). See earlier chapter notes for other works.

149 William Acton, *The Functions and Disorders of the Reproductive Organs* (London: John Churchill, 1857); *Randiana: or Excitable Tales; being the Experiences of an erotic Philosopher* (New York [London]: n.p. [Avery?], 1884); and *Untrodden Fields of Anthropology: Observation on the esoteric manners and customs of semi-civilised peoples*, 2 vols (Paris: Librairie des Bibliophiles, 1896).

150 Henry Spencer Ashbee, *Index Librorum Prohibitorum*, xvii–xviii.

151 Jules Gay, *Bibliographie des principaux ouvrages relatifs a l'amour* (Paris: n.p., 1861).

152 [William Laird Clowes], *Bibliotheca Arcana Seu Catalogus Librorum Penetralium Being Brief notices of books that have been secretly printed, prohibited by law, seized, anathematized, burnt or Bowderlised* (London: G. Redway, 1885), x.

153 G. Legman, *The Horn Book: Studies in Erotic Folklore and Bibliography* (New York: University Books, 1964), 37.

Chapter 4 The English vice and transatlantic slavery

1 While the image of the brutalised slave man circulated in abolitionist pamphlets and slave narratives, it was rarely eroticised. Such images typically emphasise his suffering or resistance. For a discussion of nineteenth-century representations of slave torture, see Marcus Wood, *Blind Memory: Visual Representations of Slavery in England and America, 1780–1865* (Manchester: Manchester University Press, 2000).

2 Ian Gibson, The English Vice: Beating, Sex and Shame in Victorian England and After (London: Duckworth, 1978).

3 Harriet Beecher Stowe, *Uncle Tom's Cabin, or Life among the Lowly* (London: H. G. Bohn, 1852). As Audrey Fisch observes, *Uncle Tom's Cabin* was so popular in Britain that it was imitated. In 1852, the British novel *Uncle Tom in England* appeared which appropriated the novel's abolitionist message for Chartist reform and initiated a discourse of 'white slavery' that rhetorically linked British workers to American slaves. As she argues, 'the novel translates the issues of American slavery into the homegrown English discourse of class'; see Audrey A. Fisch, *American Slaves in Victorian England: Abolitionist Politics and Culture* (Cambridge: Cambridge University Press, 2000), 35.

4 Fisch, *American Slaves in Victorian England*, 70.

5 Richard D. Fulton, ' "Now only the *Times* is on our Side": The London *Times* and America Before the Civil War', *Victorian Review*, 16.1 (1990) 54.

6 Karen Halttunen, 'Humanitarianism and the Pornography of Pain in Anglo-American Culture', *The American Historical Review*, 100.2 (1995) 307–8.

7 For the Whipping Act, see 25 Vict., c.18. In the periodical press, one of the most curious debates surrounding flagellation appeared in *Town Talk*. The magazine published correspondence on flagellation that chiefly debated the 'indecent whipping of girls'. One woman wrote to the editor about how her daughter was birched: she 'was compelled to stand before all the other girls in a most indecent way, with half her clothes off and the other half tucked up over her shoulders while the mistress whipped her with a birch rod till the blood trickled down her legs'; see *Town Talk* (26 July 1879) 3. In 1885, the magazine published a separate one-shilling pamphlet that collected all the flagellation correspondence; it also

promised to sell (by private subscription) another pamphlet that included letters that the magazine had deemed unsuitable for publication. While the magazine claimed to expunge immorality by exposing it, it clearly intended to titillate; see *Town Talk* (4 April 1885). Because of its explicit content, the magazine was continually under the threat of obscene libel charges, and it periodically interrupted publication whenever the editor was convicted.

8 Lucy Bending, *The Representation of Bodily Pain in Late Nineteenth-Century English Culture* (Oxford: Clarendon, 2000), 244.

9 Steven Marcus, *The Other Victorians: A Study of Sexuality and Pornography in Mid-Nineteenth-Century England* (New York: Basic, 1964), 260.

10 Gibson, *The English Vice*, 282.

11 Johann Heinrich Meibomius, *A Treatise on the Use of Flogging in Venereal Affairs* (London: E. Curll, 1718); [Cleland, John], *Memoirs of a Woman of Pleasure* (London: G. Fenton, 1749).

12 Julie Peakman, *Mighty Lewd Books: The Development of Pornography in Eighteenth-Century England* (London: Palgrave Macmillan, 2003), 172; *The Birchen Bouquet: or Curious and Original Anecdotes of Ladies fond of administering the Birch Discipline*, c.1770 (N.p.: Birchington-on-Sea [Avery?], 1881); *The Exhibition of Female Flagellants*, c.1777 (London: Theresa Berkley [Dugdale?], [c.1840]); and *Venus School-Mistress, or, Birchen sports*, c.1808–10 (Paris: Société des Bibliophiles [Carrington?], 1898).

13 Iain McCalman, *Radical Underworld: Prophets, Revolutionaries, and Pornographers in London, 1795–1840* (Cambridge: Cambridge University Press, 1988); Henry Spencer Ashbee, *Centuria Librorum Absconditorum* (London: Privately Printed, 1879), 445. Ashbee also provides information about brothel houses that specialised in flagellation, naming the 'queen of [the] profession' as Mrs Theresa Berkley. After cataloguing her various instruments of torture, he writes that 'at her shop, whosoever went with plenty of money, could be birched, whipped, fustigated, scourged, needle-pricked, half-hung, holly-brushed, furse-brushed, butcher-brushed, stinging-nettled, curry-combed, phlebotomized' (1. xliv).

14 Gibson, *The English Vice*, 265–8.

15 For more recent commentary on flagellation obscenity, see Tamar Heller, 'Flagellating Feminine Desire: Lesbians, Old Maids, and New Women in "Miss Coote's Confession", a Victorian Pornographic Narrative', *Victorian Newsletter*, 92 (1997) 9–15; and Coral Lansbury, *The Old Brown Dog: Women, Workers, and Vivisection in Edwardian England* (Madison: University of Wisconsin Press, 1985). Both Lansbury and Heller discuss its new trends after the 1870s, showing that flagellation obscenity was not homogenous in the nineteenth century, but diverse and responsive to changing views about sexuality and deviance. Although they recognise the history of the genre, they miss that it is irretrievably linked with the history of slavery in the Americas.

16 Mary A. Favret, 'Flogging: The Anti-Slavery Movement Writes Pornography', *Essays and Studies*, 51 (1998) 26, 32, 39.

17 Christine Bolt, *The Anti-Slavery Movement and Reconstruction: A Study in Anglo-American Cooperation, 1833–77* (London: Oxford University Press, 1969), 4.

18 Wood, *Blind Memory*, 260–1; also see McCalman, *Radical Underworld* 215.

19 John Stedman, *Narrative, of a Five Year's Expedition Against the Revolted Negroes of Surinam, in Guiana, on the Wild Coast of South America: From the Year 1772, to 1777*, 2 vols (London: n.p., 1796); Wood, *Blind Memory*, 236–7.

20 Wood's most recent work, *Slavery, Empathy, and Pornography*, expands on these ideas regarding the sexual dynamics of representations of slavery. More specifically, he discusses the emergence of plantation pornography. His only historical example, however, is Stedman's *Narrative*, which was not an underground publication. His definition of pornography is inadequate, generally referring to sexual content rather than a new publishing phenomenon. He also states that 'pornography focused on slave imagery flourished in the eighteenth and nineteenth century', but he does not provide any evidence. See Marcus Wood, *Slavery, Empathy, and Pornography* (Manchester: Manchester University Press, 2003), 89.

21 John Stedman, *Curious Adventures of Captain Stedman, during an expedition to Surinam* (London: Thomas Tegg, [*c*.1805]).

22 Fisch, *American Slaves in Victorian England*, 52.

23 [Mary Prince], *The History of Mary Prince, A West Indian Slave* (London: n.p., 1831), 13.

24 [Frederick Douglass], *Narrative of the Life of Frederick Douglass, an American Slave, Written by Himself* (Dublin: Webb & Chapman, 1845), 5–7.

25 William Wells Brown, *Narrative of William W. Brown, an American slave: Written by himself*, 1847, (London: Charles Gilpin, 1850), 14–15, 24.

26 Rev. of *Narrative of the Life of Frederick Douglass*, by Frederick Douglass, *Chambers's Edinburgh Journal*, 5 (1846) 56–9.

27 Fisch, *American Slaves in Victorian England*, 60.

28 Rev. of *Slave Life in Georgia*, by John Brown, *Athenaeum* (31 Mar. 1855) 378.

29 Rev. of *Autobiography of a Female Slave*, by Anonymous, *Athenaeum* (4 Apr. 1857) 134–5.

30 'A Talk with a Slave Woman', *Anti-Slavery Advocate*, 2.3 (1 Mar. 1857) 102–3. Americans read the slave narratives for many of the same reasons as the British. Charles Nichols discusses the commercial success of slave narratives in America and suggests that their 'sensationalism' and 'thrilling adventures' were partly responsible for their popularity; see Charles Nichols, 'Who Read the Slave Narratives?' *Phylon*, 20:2 (1959) 152. Although Nichols does not address this point, American reviewers were also aware of the sexual abuse within slavery. A reviewer for the *National Anti-Slavery Standard*, describes the 'legalize[d] concubinage' and 'licentiousness' of slavery as described in Harriett Jacobs's slave narrative, about which I shall say more later; quoted in Jean Fagan Yellin, 'Texts and Contexts of Harriet Jacobs', *Incidents in the Life of a Slave Girl: Written by Herself*, *The Slave's Narrative*, ed. Charles T. Davis and Henry Louis Gates Jr. (Oxford: Oxford University Press, 1985) 270. Karen Sánchez-Eppler, moreover, argues that slave narratives actively enlisted sexual responses from their white female readers to provoke a political response by reminding them of their own sexual vulnerability; see Karen Sánchez-Eppler, *Touching Liberty: Abolition, Feminism, and the Politics of the Body* (Berkeley: University of California Press, 1993), 104. While there are no examples of obscene appropriations of slave narratives in American obscenity (most likely because the industry was still fledgling), George Thompson's open publications (which he published under the pseudonym Greenhorn) suggest prurience surrounding slavery and sexual violence. He was one of the most popular and prolific authors of the antebellum era who wrote lurid novels about race, urbanisation, and poverty in such works as *Venus in Boston: A Romance of City Life* (1849). William Haynes published his works and eventually became the father of the America's obscene book trade. See Greenhorn [George Thompson], *Venus in Boston: A Romance of City Life* (New York: n.p. [Haynes],

[1849]); and H. Montgomery Hyde, *A History of Pornography* (London: Heinemann, 1964), 107.

31   William Lazenby dominated the British underground trade in obscenity from around 1873 until 1886, when he was prosecuted and imprisoned in November. He operated his business under various aliases, including Duncan Cameron, Henry Ashford, and Thomas Judd. After 1884, he seems to have collaborated with Edward Avery, who took over control of the trade after Lazenby's imprisonment. See Peter Mendes, *Clandestine Erotic Fiction in English, 1800–1930: A Bibliographical Study* (Hants: Scholar, 1993), 4–7. Also see the *Times* for reports on his prosecutions: (17 July 1871) 13; (16 Sept. 1876) 11; (12 Nov. 1886) 13.

32   *The Birchen Bouquet: or Curious and Original Anecdotes of Ladies fond of administering the Birch Discipline*, c.1770 (N.p.: Birchington-on-Sea [Avery?], 1881); *The Quintessence of Birch Discipline* (London: Privately Printed [Lazenby], 1870 [1883]); and *The Romance of Chastisement or, Revelations of the School and Bedroom* (N.p. [London?]: n.p. [Lazenby?], 1870 [1883]).

33   *The Pearl: A Journal of Facetia Voluptuous Reading*, 3 vols (London: Printed for the Society of Vice [Augustin Brancart], 1879–80 [c.1890]). All references to *The Pearl* are to the c.1890 reprint at the British Library. Page references appear in parentheses. Also see *My Secret Life*, 11 vols (Amsterdam: Privately Printed, n.d. [c.1888–94]); and *The Lustful Turk, or Lascivious Scenes in a Harem*, 1828 ([New York]: Canyon, [1967]).

34   Santa Cruz, the West Indian island to which the story refers, is presumably St Croix, now part of the US Virgin Islands. While the island's colonial rulers shifted through history, there was significant English settlement from as early as 1625.

35   Henry Spencer Ashbee, *Catena Librorum Tacendorum* (London: Privately Printed, 1885), 345. Ashbee indicates that *The Pearl* sold for £25. *The Catalogue of Curiosa and Erotica* (1892) priced it at £18; and *Catalogue of Rare Curious and Voluptuous Reading* (n.d) sold one of its numbers for two guineas. These catalogues are held in *Album 7: Catalogues and Prospectuses* (1889–c.1908), unpublished.

36   *The Cremorne; A Magazine of Wit, Facetiae, Parody, Graphic Tales of Love, etc.* (London: Privately Printed [Lazenby?], 1851 [1882]). Page references appear in parentheses. For more information about Cremorne Gardens, see Donald Thomas, *The Victorian Underworld* (London: John Murray, 1998), 89–90; and Lynda Nead, *Victorian Babylon: People, Streets and Images in Nineteenth-Century London* (New Haven: Yale University Press, 2000), 109–46.

37   Ashbee, *Catena Librorum Tacendorum*, 357.

38   Mendes, *Clandestine Erotic Fiction*, 201.

39   [Harriet Jacobs], *Incidents in the Life of a Slave Girl. Written By Herself*, 1861, ed. Jean Fagan Yellin (Cambridge, MA: Harvard University Press, 2000); [Harriet Jacobs], *The Deeper Wrong: Or, Incidents in the Life of a Slave Girl. Written by Herself*, ed. L. Maria Child (London: W. Tweedie, 1862). Further references to *Incidents* appear in parentheses.

40   Rev. of *The Deeper Wrong: or, Incidents in the Life of a Slave Girl*, by Linda Brent, *Athenaeum* (19 Apr. 1862) 529. For other reviews of Jacobs's narrative, see the *Anti-Slavery Advocate* (1 May 1861) 421; *London Daily News* (10 Mar. 1862) 2; *Londonderry Standard* (27 Mar. 1862) 4; *Caledonian Mercury* (31 Mar. 1862) 3; *Anti-Slavery Reporter* (1 Apr. 1862) 96; and *Western Morning News* (5 Apr. 1862) 4. Of these reviews, only the *Caledonian Mercury* referred explicitly to the sexual content of the narrative: 'These pages give many vivid pictures of the

terrible licentiousness which characterise the majority of slaveholders. Thousands of young slaves have Anglo-Saxon blood coursing through their veins.'

41 Yellin, 'Texts and Contexts', 263.

42 Yellin, 'Texts and Contexts', 263.

43 Sánchez-Eppler, *Touching Liberty*; Deborah M. Garfield, 'Speech, Listening, and Female Sexuality in *Incidents in the Life of a Slave Girl*', *Arizona Quarterly*, 50.2 (1994) 19–49; P. Gabrielle Foreman, 'Manifest in Signs: The Politics of Sex and Representation in *Incidents in the Life of a Slave Girl*', in *Harriet Jacobs and Incidents in the Life of a Slave Girl: New Critical Essays* (Cambridge: Cambridge University Press, 1996), 77, 80.

44 Sánchez-Eppler, *Touching Liberty*, 96.

45 Had Lazenby's *The Secret Life* continued beyond its three numbers, I wonder if it would have focused on other passages from Jacobs's slave narrative that recent critics have found sexually coded. Later in her narrative, Jacobs not only alludes to white men crossing the colour line, but also white women who conceive black men's children (52). She also describes the ill-treatment of a slave named Luke by his dissipated master in such terms that lead Foreman to infer homosexual abuse; see Foreman, 'Manifest in Signs', 78. When speaking of Luke, Jacobs suggests terrible depravity, but remains silent about its exact nature, a telling omission considering the link between secrecy and sexual abuse in her world: 'Luke was appointed to wait on his bed-ridden master, whose despotic habits were greatly increased by exasperation at his own helplessness. [...] A day seldom passed without his receiving more or less blows. [...] As he lay on his bed, a mere degraded wreck of manhood, he took into his head the strangest freaks of despotism [...]. Some of these freaks were of a nature too filthy to be repeated' (192).

46 Mendes, *Clandestine Erotic Fiction*, 39.

47 For Home Office and Customs Office correspondence on Carrington's illegal publishing activities from the late nineteenth to the early twentieth century, see HO 151/6/66; HO 45/9752/A59329; HO 144/ 192/ A46657/219 & 231; HO 45/10510/129433; Cust 46/199. For information on Scotland Yard's interest in Carrington, see *Report from the Joint Select Committee on Lotteries and Indecent Advertisements* (London: Vacher & Sons, 1908), 30.

48 Carrington's semi-obscene novels with settings in Africa include the following: Hector France, *The Chastisement of Mansour*, trans. Alfred Allinson (Paris: Charles Carrington, 1898); Hector France, *Musk, Hashish, and Blood* (Paris: Charles Carrington, 1900); John Cameron Grant, *The Ethiopian: A Narrative of the Society of Human Leopards* (Paris: Charles Carrington, 1900); *Human Gorillas: A Study of Rape with Violence* (Paris: C. Carrington, 1901); Jean de Villiot, *Woman and Her Master* (Paris: n.p. [Charles Carrington], 1904); and *A Spahi's Love Story* (Paris: Charles Carrington, 1907).

49 Frederick F. Schauer, *The Law of Obscenity* (Washington: The Bureau of National Affairs, 1976), 13. For more detailed discussions of the history of the American trade in obscenity, see Paul S. Boyer, *Purity in Print: Book Censorship in America from the Gilded Age to the Computer Age*, 2nd edn (Madison: University of Wisconsin Press, 2002).

50 G. Legman, *The Horn Book: Studies in Erotic Folklore and Bibliography* (New York: University Books, 1964), 34.

51 *May's Account of her Introduction to the Art of Love* (London-Paris: n.p., 1904); *The Adventures of Lady Harpur; Her Life of Free Enjoyment and Ecstatic Love adventures related by Herself* (Glasgow [Paris?]: William Murray Buchanan St. [Carrington?],

1894 [*c*.1906]). Lazenby's original publication of *Queenie* has not survived. For the publication history of this novel, see Mendes, *Clandestine Erotic Fiction*, 137.

52   *The Adventures of Lady Harpur*, 42.

53   St John D'Arcy, *The Memoirs of Madge Buford, or, a modern Fanny Hill*, 1892 (New York: n.p. [Carrington?], 1902); *A Town-Bull, or The Elysian Fields* (New Orleans: n.p.: [Carrington?], 1893); *Sue Suckitt; Maid and Wife*, 1893 (New Orleans [Paris]: n.p.[Carrington], 1913); *Maidenhead Stories, told by a set of joyous students*, 1894, 2 vols (New York: Printed for the Erotica Biblion Society [Carrington], 1897); *The Memoirs of Dolly Morton: The Story of a Woman's Part in the Struggle to Free the Slaves* (Paris: Charles Carrington, 1899); and *The Story of Seven Maidens*, 1907 (N.p.: Venus Library, 1972). I have seen a later 1913 edition of *Sue Suckitt*. It appears with a false wrapper with *La Guerre des Balkans* as its title. This reprint was likely circulated among English-speaking First World War soldiers.

54   Mendes, *Clandestine Erotic Fiction*, 35.

55   Catalogues gathered in *Album 7* priced these works in British currency: *Catalogue of Rare and Curious English Books* lists *Maidenhead Stories* at one guinea; *List of Rare and Curious Books* prices *A Town-Bull* at one guinea; and *Privately Printed English Books* lists *Miss Dorothy Morton* at three guineas. *Bibliotheca Carringtoniensis*, a collection of Carrington's catalogues held at the Kinsey Institute, contains a catalogue entitled *List of Mr. Charles Carrington's New and Forthcoming works in English and French* that prices *Dolly Morton* at £3. 3s; see *Bibliotheca Carringtoniensis: Being a Collection of the Descriptive Title Pages of Certain Books Published by Mr. Charles Carrington of Paris*, unpublished. All of these books eventually found their way to America. *Dolly Morton* was the most successful book of this kind. It alone found a French audience.

56   *A Town-Bull* was likely authored by an American: it uses an American setting, reveals familiarity with American institutions (the 'Savings Bank'), and adopts American spelling ('colored'). *Sue Suckitt*, by contrast, is more difficult to place because it blends references to American dollars with allusions to English flagellation ('birchen rods').

57   *A Town-Bull*, 155.

58   *Sue Suckitt*, 41–2.

59   D'Arcy St John, *The Memoirs of Madge Buford*, 75–9.

60   Donovan Kipps, Préface, *Dolly Morton* (Paris: J. Fort, n.d.), 2; Charles Reginald Dawes, *A Study of Erotic Literature in England, Considered with Especial Reference to Social Life* (1943 unpublished), 287.

61   *The Memoirs of Dolly Morton*, 71–3. Further page references appear in parentheses.

62   *Woman and her Slave: A Realistic Narrative of a Slave who Experienced His Mistress' Love and Lash* (Paris: Charles Carrington, n.d.).

63   'British and Foreign Traffic in Girls', *Town Talk: A Journal for Society at Large* (17 Jan. 1880) 1–2.

64   Mendes, *Clandestine Erotic Fiction*, 263.

65   Wilbur H. Siebert, *The Underground Railroad from Slavery to Freedom* (New York: Macmillan, 1898).

66   Mendes, *Clandestine Erotic Fiction*, 363.

67   *En Virginie: Épisode de la Guerre de Sécession* (Paris: Charles Carrington, 1901).

68   Donald Thomas, Introduction, *The Memoirs of Dolly Morton* (London: Collectors Edition, 1970), 11–18.

69   Jean de Villiot was a composite name used by Carrington, especially for his openly published works on flagellation. Hugues Rebell and Hector France may have written for Carrington under this pseudonym; see Mendes, *Clandestine Erotic Fiction*, 364.

70   *En Virginie*, ix. 'There reigns the dangerous maxim that a rigid austerity is the only
     safeguard of virtue. The most innocent word frightens; the most natural gesture
     becomes an indecent assault. Emotions, repressed in this way, extinguish or erupt
     in a terrible manner. All for vice or all for virtue, but nothing in between; some
     characters take pleasure in extremes, and we thus see born immoderate prudery
     and monstrous licence' (my translation).

71   *En Virginie*, 198. 'It is undeniably England that takes the cake in this matter' (my
     translation).

72   '*Flagellation in London* and *The Study of Flagellation* [...] *with a Documentary on
     Flagellation in English Schools and Military Prisons*' (my translation).

73   Don Brennus Aléra, *White Women Slaves* ([Paris: Select Bibliothèque], 1910); Don
     Brennus Aléra, *Barbaric Fêtes* ([Paris: Select Bibliothèque], 1910); Don Brennus
     Aléra, *Under the Yoke* ([Paris: Select Bibliothèque], 1910); and Don Brennus Aléra,
     In Louisiana ([Paris: Select Bibliothèque], 1910). Select Bibliothèque was run by
     the Parisian publisher Massy who specialised in flagellation; see *Dictionnaire des
     oeuvres érotiques*, ed. Gilbert Minazzoli ([Paris]: Mercure de France, 1971), 484–5.

74   Don Brennus Aléra, *White Women Slaves*, 135.

75   *Suburban Souls: The Erotic Psychology of a Man and a Maid* (Paris : Printed for
     distribution amongst private subscribers only [Carrington], 1901); *The Mistress
     and the Slave: A Masochist Realistic Love Story* (Athens [Paris?]: Imprinted for its
     Members by the Erotika Biblion Society [Carrington], 1905).

76   Pauline Réage, [Dominique Aury], *Story of O*, trans. Sabine d'Estrée (New York:
     Grove, 1965), 15–17.

77   Sigmund Freud, 'A Child is Being Beaten', *The Standard Edition of the Complete
     Psychological Works of Sigmund Freud*, vol. 17. (London: Hogarth, 1955), 180.

78   Georges Bataille, *Erotism: Death & Sensuality*, 1957, trans. Mary Dalwood (San Fran-
     cisco: City Light, 1986).

79   Lynda Hart, 'To Each Other: Performing Lesbian S/M', in *Between the Body and
     the Flesh: Performing Sadomasochism* (New York: Columbia University Press, 1998),
     58, 60.

80   Marquis de Sade, *Justine; ou les Malheurs de la vertu*, 2nd edn (N.p.: n.p., 1791);
     Leopold von Sacher-Masoch, *Venus in Furs*, 1870 (Paris: Charles Carrington,
     1902). De Sade's *Justine* was only translated into English in 1889; see *Opus
     Sadicum: A Philosophical Romance*, trans. [Isidore Liseux] (Paris: Isidore Liseux,
     1889). However, it circulated in French and is referenced frequently in other
     underground works. Sacher-Masoch's *Venus in Furs*, first published in German
     as *Venus Im Pelz* in 1870, was a later and lesser influence on English flagella-
     tion fantasies. The terms sadism and masochism were, of course, coined after
     these authors, revealing how psychological and medical vocabulary were also
     influenced by the overlapping histories of flagellation and slavery.

Chapter 5 Japanese erotic prints and late nineteenth-century obscenity

1   W. S. Gilbert and Arthur Sullivan, *The Mikado, or The Town of Titupu* (London:
    Chappell, [1885]). For a recent study of the Japanese craze in Britain, see Ayajo
    Ono, *Japonisme in Britain: Whistler, Menpes, Henry, Hornel and Nineteenth-Century
    Japan* (New York: Routledge, 2003).

2   Oscar Wilde, *Salome* (London: John Lane, 1894).

3 Linda Gertner Zatlin, *Beardsley, Japonisme, and the Perversion of the Victorian Ideal* (Cambridge: Cambridge University Press, 1997).

4 James Laver, *Whistler* (London: Faber & Faber, 1930), 109.

5 Edmond de Goncourt, *Hokusai* (Paris: Bibliotheque Charpentier, 1896); Edmond de Goncourt *Outamaro: Le Peintre des Maisons Vertes* (Paris: Bibliotheque Charpentier, 1891). For a careful history of the circulation of Japanese goods and prints in France and Britain in the latter half of the nineteenth century, see Zatlin, *Beardsley*, 23–40.

6 Holbrook Jackson, *The Eighteen Nineties: A Review of Art and Ideas at the Close of the Nineteenth Century* (London: Grant Richards, 1913), 109, 118; Henry Mass et al., eds, *The Letters of Aubrey Beardsley* (London: Cassell, 1970), 21.

7 Frank Whitford, *Japanese Prints and Western Painters* (London: Studio Visto, 1977), 98.

8 John Leighton, 'On Japanese Art: A Discourse Delivered at the Royal Institution of Great Britain. 1 May 1863', in Elizabeth Gilmore Holt, ed., *The Art of all Nations: The Emerging Role of Exhibitions and Critics* (Princeton: Princeton University Press, 1982), 376.

9 Timon Screech, *Sex and the Floating World: Erotic Images in Japan, 1700–1820* (London: Reaktion, 1999), 13–14.

10 Japanese Pillow Book, early nineteenth century.

11 Quoted in Screech, *Sex and the Floating World*, 13.

12 Laver, *Whistler*, 111.

13 Edmond de Goncourt, ed., *Journal des Goncourt: Memoires de la vie Littéraire*, 9 vols, (Paris: Fasquelle, 1887–96), 103. 'The conversation turns to Japan, to the obscene images that they tell me no longer come to Europe because when the country was opened to foreigners, they bought, they bought these images with mockery and public contempt for Japanese obscenity, and that the government was offended, gathered these images, and burned them' (my translation).

14 Alfred Julius Meier-Graefe, *Modern Art: Being a Contribution to a New System of Aesthetics*, trans. Florence Simmonds and G. W. Chrystal (London: William Heinemann, 1908), 252.

15 William Rothenstein, *Men and Memories: Recollections of William Rothenstein*, vol. 1 (London: Faber & Faber, 1931), 134.

16 Maas et al., eds, *The Letters of Aubrey Beardsley*, 56–7, 98.

17 Arthur Symons, 'An Unacknowledged Movement in Fine Printing: The Typography of the Eighteen-Nineties', *The Fleuron: A Journal of Typography*, 7 (1930) 98–9.

18 Symons, 'An Unacknowledged Movement', 116.

19 Quoted in Cline Ashwin, 'Graphic Imagery, 1837–1901: A Victorian Revolution', *Art History*, 1.2 (1978) 365.

20 'The New Master of Art', *To-day* (12 May 1894) 28–9.

21 Meier-Graefe, *Modern Art*, 255.

22 Whitford, *Japanese Prints*, 239

23 Jack Stewart, *The Vital Art of D. H. Lawrence: Vision and Expression* (Carbondale: Southern Illinois University Press, 1998), 9.

24 In his illustrations for *Le Morte Darthur* (1893–4), his first major contract, Beardsley incorporates Japanese costumes and ornament. In his illustrations for *Bon-Mots* (1893–4), grotesques and peacock feathers show the Japanese influence, as does his Japanesque signature piece. His unused illustrations for *Lucian's True History* (1894) include Japanese furniture, cherry blossoms, and grotesques, and also make use of the Japanese white-line technique that brings out objects from a dense

black background. In one of these prints, 'Lucian's Strange Creatures' (1894), Beardsley uses his economical line to have elbows double for displaced breasts. A smug Mrs Grundy figure appears at the right of the print, casting a sidelong gaze at the viewer. Her presence titillates or challenges one to see and react to the wanton line. His illustration 'The Mask of the Red Death' for *The Works of Edgar Allen Poe* (1894–5) signals a shift away from his Japanese phase, but still retains a strong line that reveals pert outlined breasts in folds of clothing. To consult Beardsley's prints, see Brian Reade, *Aubrey Beardsley* (New York: Viking, 1967).

25 In February 1883, Wilde wrote Lane to question his decision to advertise the scandal surrounding *Salome*: 'The interest and value of *Salome* is not that it was suppressed by a foolish official, but that it was written by an artist. It is the tragic beauty of the work that makes it valuable and of interest, not a gross act of ignorance and impertinence on the part of the censor'; see Merlin Holland and Rupert-Hart Davis, *The Complete Letters of Oscar Wilde* (London: Fourth Estate, 2000), 328.

26 Stanley Weintraub, *Aubrey Beardsley: Imp of the Perverse* (University Park: Pennsylvania State University Press, 1976), 75.

27 Maas et al., eds, *The Letters of Aubrey Beardsley*, 54, 58.

28 Reade, *Aubrey Beardsley*, 336.

29 In recent years, critics have attempted to show how text and illustration collaborate; see Elliot L. Gilbert, ' "Tumult of Images": Wilde, Beardsley, and *Salome*', *Victorian Studies*, 26 (1983) 133–59; Zatlin, *Beardsley*; Robert Schweik, 'Congruous Incongruities: The Wilde-Beardsley "Collaboration" ', *ELT*, 37.1 (1994) 9–26; and Lorraine Janzen Kooistra, *The Artist as Critic. Bitextuality in Fin-de-Siècle Illustrated Books* (Aldershot: Scolar, 1995). Kooistra also provides an excellent overview of this debate.

30 Maas et al., eds, *The Letters of Aubrey Beardsley*, 58.

31 Quoted in Jean Paul Raymond and Charles L. S. Ricketts, *Oscar Wilde* (Bloomsbury: The Nonesuch Pres, 1931), 51–2.

32 Rothenstein, *Men and Memories*, 184.

33 Chris Snodgrass, *Aubrey Beardsley, Dandy of the Grotesque* (Oxford: Oxford University Press, 1995), 52.

34 Matthew Sturgis, *Passionate Attitudes: The English Decadence of the 1890s* (Basingstoke: Macmillan – now Palgrave, 1995), 153.

35 Snodgrass, *Aubrey Beardsley*, 72.

36 Ernest Dowson, *Verses* (London: L. Smithers, 1896); Reade, *Aubrey Beardsley*, 360.

37 Derek Stanford, *Aubrey Beardsley's Erotic Universe* (London: New England Library, 1967), 17.

38 Richard Ellman, *Oscar Wilde* (London: Hamish Hamilton, 1987); Snodgrass, *Aubrey Beardsley, Dandy of the Grotesque*; Richard Dellamora, 'Traversing the Feminine in Oscar Wilde's *Salome*', *Victorian Sages and Cultural Discourse*, ed. Thais E. Morgan (New Brunswick: Rutgers University Press, 1990), 246–64; and Kooistra, *The Artist as Critic*. Also see Zatlin, *Beardsley*, 250.

39 Jonathan Dollimore, *Sex, Literature and Censorship* (Cambridge: Polity, 2001), 47.

40 Joseph Pennell, 'A New Illustrator – Aubrey Beardsley', *The Studio*, 1 (1893) 14.

41 Pennell, 'A New Illustrator', 18.

42 D. Tinto, 'Pictures and Painters', *London Figaro* (20 Apr. 1893) 13.

43 'The New Master of Art', 29.

44 Rev. of *Salome*, *Times* (8 Mar. 1894) 12.

45 Jane Haville Desmarais, *The Beardsley Industry: The Critical Reception in England and France, 1893–1914* (Hants: Ashgate, 1998), 2.

46   'Salome', *Saturday Review* (24 Mar. 1894) 317.
47   Maas et al., eds, *The Letters of Aubrey Beardsley*, 223.
48   'Salome', *Saturday Review*, 317.
49   'New Publications', *The Studio*, 2 (1894) 184–5.
50   For these reviews of *The Yellow Book*, see Rev. of *The Yellow Book*, *Times* (20 Apr. 1894) 3; Rev. of *The Yellow Book*, *Academy* (28 Apr. 1895) 349; Rev. of *The Yellow Book*, *Dial* (1 June 1894) 335; and Rev. of *The Yellow Book*, *Pall Mall Gazette* (9 Feb. 1895) 4.
51   For Partridge's parodies of Beardsley's art, see 'How It is Done', *Punch* (28 July 1894) 47; and 'From The Queer and Yellow Book', *Punch* (2 Feb. 1895) 58.
52   For information about Punch's illustrators, see M. H. Speilmann, *The History of 'Punch'*, (London: Cassell, 1895), 560, 564.
53   'She-Notes, By Borgia Smudgiton', *Punch* (10 Mar. 1894); 'She-Notes, By Borgia Smudgiton: Part II', *Punch* (17 Mar. 1894).
54   Sturgis, *Passionate Attitudes*, 225.
55   'The Woman Who Wouldn't Do', *Punch* (30 Mar. 1895); Grant Allen, *The Woman Who Did* (London: J. Lane, 1895).
56   Vanessa Warne and Colette Colligan, 'The Man Who Wrote a New Woman Novel: Grant Allen's *The Woman Who Did* and the Gendering of Male Authorship in New Woman Novels', *Victorian Literature and Culture*, 33.1 (2005) 38.
57   Desmarais, *The Beardsley Industry*, 63.
58   Robbie Ross, 'The Eulogy of Aubrey Beardsley', in *Ben Johnson his Volpone* (London: Leonard Smithers, 1898), xxxiv.
59   Jackson, *The Eighteen Nineties*, 121.
60   Symons, 'Aubrey Beardsley', *Fortnightly Review*, 69 (1898) 754, 759–61.
61   Zatlin, *Beardsley*, 149.
62   Elliot L. Gilbert, ' "Tumult of Images" ', 135.
63   Allison Pease, *Modernism, Mass Culture, and the Aesthetics of Obscenity* (Cambridge: Cambridge University Press, 2000), 81.
64   Pease, *Modernism*, 81.
65   Alexander Pope, *The Rape of the Lock* (London: Leonard Smithers, 1897).
66   Maas et al., eds, *The Letters of Aubrey Beardsley*, 158; *Priapeia, or The Sportive Epigrams of divers Poets on Priapus* (Athens [London]: Imprinted by the Erotika Biblion Society For Private Distribution Only [Smithers], 1888 [1889]).
67   Aristophanes, *The Lysistrata of Aristophanes* (London: Erotika Biblion Society, 1896); Stanford, *Aubrey Beardsley's Erotic Universe*, 9.
68   Aubrey Beardsley, *The Story of Venus and Tannhäuser: A Romantic Novel* (London: For Private Circulation, 1897); Aubrey Beardsley, 'Under the Hill', *The Savoy*, 1 (1896).
69   Rothenstein, *Men and Memories*, 244.
70   Jackson, *The Eighteen Nineties*, 122.
71   Jack Smithers, *The Early Life and Vicissitudes of Jack Smithers* (London: Martin Secker, 1939), 28.
72   Maas et al., eds, *The Letters of Aubrey Beardsley*, 439.
73   For Beardsley's illustrations of women consuming obscenity, see 'Girl and a Bookshop' (1893). An unused design for *The Yellow Book* of a woman reaching for a book among titles that include Beardsley's *Story of Venus and Tannhäuser* also speculates about women's reading pleasures; Reade, *Aubrey Beardsley*, 378.
74   Beardsley, *The Story of Venus and Tannhäuser*, 64.
75   See Peter Webb, 'Victorian Erotica', in Alan Bold, ed., *The Sexual Dimension in Literature* (London : Vision, 1982), 174.

76 D. H. Lawrence, *The White Peacock* (London: William Heinemann, 1911), 222.

77 Lawrence, *The White Peacock*, 223.

78 Raymond and Ricketts, *Oscar Wilde*, 44.

79 Philip Hoare, *Wilde's Last Stand: Decadence, Conspiracy, and the First World War* (London: Duckworth, 1997), 91.

80 Sir Henry Norman, *The Real Japan: Studies of Contemporary Japanese Manners, Morals, Administration, & Politics* (London: T. Fisher Unwin, 1893).

81 For reviews of Norman's *The Real Japan*, see *Atlantic Monthly* 68 (1892) 692–3; and 74 (1894) 834–5.

82 Norman, *The Real Japan*, 267n.

83 Norman, *The Real Japan*, 295–6. The last sentence of this passage is awkward, but clearly targets the sex districts of the world's major cities.

84 [J. E. de Becker], *The Nightless City, or The History of the Yoshiwara Yukwaku* (Yokohama: Z. P. Maruya, 1899); J. E. de Becker, *The Sexual Life of Japan: Being an Exhaustive Study of the Nightless City* (New York: American Anthropological Society, n.d.); and Dr Tresmin-Trémolières, *La cité d'amour au Japon, courtisanes du Yoshiwara* (Paris: Librarie Universelle, 1905).

85 [Becker], *The Nightless City*, xii.

86 [Becker], *The Nightless City*, xiv.

87 T. Fujimoto, *The Story of the Geisha Girl* (London: T. Werner Laurie, 1917), 139. Later sociological works on Japanese prostitution include T. Fujimoto's *The Night-side of Japan* (London: T. Werner Laurie, 1914). Like the works by Norman and de Becker, Fujimoto's studies included reproductions of Japanese prints.

88 *Suburban Souls: The Erotic Psychology of a Man and a Maid* (Paris: Printed for distribution amongst private subscribers only [Carrington], 1901).

89 Peter Mendes, *Clandestine Erotic Fiction in English, 1800–1930: A Bibliographical Study* (Hants: Scholar, 1993), 207; *Amorous Adventures of a Japanese Gentleman Related for the Entertainment of his Honorable Friends* (Yokohama: Printed for the Daimo of Satsuma, 1897). All references to *Amorous Adventures* are from the *c*.1911 edition at the Bibliothèque Nationale de France.

90 *Amorous Adventures*, 74.

91 *Amorous Adventures*, 102.

92 *Yoshiwara: The Nightless City* (Paris [Chicago?]: Charles Carrington [Targ?]: 1907). Further page references appear in parentheses.

Coda: the obscenity of the real

1 Robert Mugabe, 'Opening Statement of the Group of Fifteen', 31 May 2001, Department of Foreign Affairs Republic of Indonesia, 13 July 2001 <http://www. dfa-deplu.go.id/world/multilateral/g15/speech-zimbabwe310501.htm>, 3.

2 Mugabe, 'Opening Statement', 3.

3 '2001 World Press Freedom Review', International Press Institute Watch List, <http://www.freemedia.at/wpfr/Zimbabwe.htm>

4 'An Indecent Exhibition', *Vigilance Record* (Sept. 1892) 62–3.

5 Jean Baudrillard, *The Ecstasy of Communication*, ed. Sylvère Lotringer, trans. Bernard and Caroline Schutze (Paris: Editions Galilée, 1988), 32.

6 Baudrillard, *The Ecstasy*, 43.

7 Joan Smith, 'How Could She? Why Would She?' *The Independent Online Edition* (9 May 2004).

Bibliography

Collections and Archives

The British Library, London

Private Case Collection
Rare Books and Manuscripts
India Office Records

The British Museum, London

Prints and Drawings

The British Newspaper Library, London

Nineteenth-Century Newspapers and Periodicals

The British Film Institute, London

Early Twentieth-Century Erotic Films
Early Twentieth-Century Film Catalogues

The Victoria and Albert Museum, London

Milford Haven Postcard Collection
Thomas Rowlandson Prints
Aubrey Beardsley Prints

The Women's Library, London

National Vigilance Association Papers
Vigilance Record

The National Archives, London

British Public Records

The Bodleian, Oxford

Phi Collection

La Bibliothèque Nationale de France, Paris

L'Enfer Collection

The Kinsey Institute for Research in Sex, Gender, and Reproduction, Bloomington

Nineteenth- and Twentieth-Century Erotic Books, Photographs, and Ephemera

The Huntington Library, San Marino

Metcalf Burton Collection of Sir Richard Burton's books, manuscripts, and papers

Michael Goss, London

Delectus Books Collection

Jonathan Ross Collection, London

Nineteenth-Century Erotic Stereographs and Stereoscopes

Statutes and Parliamentary Papers

Copyright Act (1709) 8 Anne, c.19
Stamp Act (1819) 59 Geo. 3, c.39
Vagrancy Act (1824) 5 Geo. 4, c.83
Vagrancy Amendment Act (1838) 1 & 2 Vict., c.38
Metropolitan Police Act (1847) 10 & 11 Vict., c.89
Obscene Publications Act (1857) 20 & 21 Vict., c.83
Hansard's Parliamentary Papers 144–8 (1857).
Whipping Act (1862) 25 Vict., c.18.
Customs Consolidation Act (1876) 39 & 40 Vict., c.36.
Post Office (Protection) Act (1884) 47 & 48 Vict., c.76
Criminal Law Amendment Act (1885) 48 & 49 Vict., c.69.
Indecent Advertisements Act (1889) 52 & 53 Vict., c.18
Cinematograph Act (1909) 9 Edw.7, c.30
Obscene Publications Act (1959) 7 & 8 Eliz. II, c.66.

Cases

R. v. *Curl* (1727) 2 Stra. 788
R. v. *Hicklin* (1868) L.R.3.Q.B.360

Books and Articles

Note: I rely extensively on Peter Mendes's bibliographical research. Articles from daily newspapers are cited in text and notes, but not in the Works Cited.

'2001 World Press Freedom Review', International Press Institute Watch List. <http://www.freemedia.at/wpfr/Zimbabwe.htm>
Abel, Richard, *The Red Roster Scare: Making Cinema American, 1900–1910* (Berkeley: University of California Press, 1999).
'Acid Drops', Rev. of *The Book of a Thousand Nights and One Night*, by Richard Burton, *The Freethinker* (25 Oct. 1885) 339–40.
Acton, William, *The Functions and Disorders of the Reproductive Organs* (London: John Churchill, 1857).
The Adventures of Lady Harpur; Her Life of free Enjoyment and Ecstatic Love adventures related by Herself (Glasgow [Paris?]: William Murray Buchanan St [Carrington?], 1894 [*c*.1906]).
Album 7: Catalogues and Prospectuses (1889–*c*.1908), unpublished.

210   *Bibliography*

Aléra, Don Brennus, *White Women Slaves* ([Paris: Select Bibliothèque], 1910).
——, *Barbaric Fêtes* ([Paris: Select Bibliothèque], 1910).
——, *Under the Yoke* ([Paris: Select Bibliothèque], 1910).
——, *In Louisiana* ([Paris: Select Bibliothèque], 1910).
Ali, Mahsin Jassim, *Scheherazade in England: A Study of Nineteenth-Century English Criticism of the* Arabian Nights (Washington: Three Continents, 1981).
Allen, Grant, *The Woman Who Did* (London: J. Lane, 1895).
Alloula, Malek, *The Colonial Harem*, 1981, trans. Myrna Godzich and Wlad Godzich (Minneapolis: University of Minnesota Press, 1986).
Altick, Richard D., *The English Common Reader: A Social History of the Mass-Reading Public, 1800–1900* (Chicago: University of Chicago Press, 1957).
Amorous Adventures of a Japanese Gentleman Related for the Entertainment of his Honorable Friends (Yokohama: Printed for the Daimo of Satsuma, 1897 [*c*.1911?]). There is also a *c*.1907 edition.
Ananga Ranga; (Stage of the Bodiless One) or, The Hindu Art of Love (Ars Amoris Indica), trans. A. F. F. and B. F. R. (Cosmopoli: Printed for the Kama Shastra Society of London and Benares, and for private circulation only, n.d. [1885]).
Anderson, Patricia, *The Printed Image and the Transformation of Popular Culture, 1790–1860* (Oxford: Clarendon, 1991).
Aristophanes, *The Lysistrata of Aristophanes* (London: Erotika Biblion Society, 1896).
Aristotle's Master-Piece; or the Secrets of generation, 1684, (London: Printed for by F. L. for J. How and sold by Thomas Howkins, 1690).
Appadurai, Arjun, *Modernity at Large: Cultural Dimensions of Globalization* (Minneapolis: University Minnesota Press, 1996).
Ashbee, Henry Spencer [Pisanus Fraxi], *Index Librorum Prohibitorum* (London: Privately Printed, 1877).
——, *Centuria Librorum Absconditorum* (London: Privately Printed, 1879).
——, *Catena Librorum Tacendorum* (London: Privately Printed, 1885).
Ashcroft, John, Remarks, Federal Prosecutors' Symposium on Obscenity, National Advocacy Center, Columbia, SC (6 June 2002).
Ashwin, Cline, 'Graphic Imagery 1837–1901: A Victorian Revolution', *Art History*, 1.2 (1978) 360–70.
Autobiography of a Female Slave (New York: Redfield, 1857).
Barker, Nicolas, 'Bernard Quaritch', *Book Collector: Special Number* (1997) 3–34.
Barrin, Jean, *Venus in the Cloister; or, The Nun in her Smock* (London: [Edmund Curll], 1725).
Barthes, Roland, *Sade, Fourier, Loyola*, trans. Richard Miller (London: Cape, 1977).
Bataille, Georges, *Erotism: Death & Sensuality*, 1957, trans. Mary Dalwood (San Francisco: City Light, 1986).
Baudrillard, Jean, *The Ecstasy of Communication*, ed. Sylvère Lotringer, trans. Bernard and Caroline Schutze (Paris: Editions Galilée, 1988).
Beardsley, Aubrey, *The Story of Venus and Tannhäuser: A Romantic Novel* (London: For Private Circulation, 1897).
——, 'Under the Hill', *The Savoy*, 1 (1896).
[Becker, J. E. de.], *The Nightless City, or The History of the Yoshiwara Yukwaku* (Yokohama: Z. P. Maruya: 1899). Numerous editions.
Becker, J. E. de., *The Sexual Life of Japan: Being an Exhaustive Study of the Nightless City* (New York: American Anthropological Society, n.d.)
Beharistan (Abode of Spring) By Jami, A Literal Translation from The Persian (Benares: Printed for the Kama Shastra Society for Private Subscribers Only, 1887).
Benbow, William, *A Scourge for the Laureate* (London: Benbow, n.d. [1825]).

Bending, Lucy, *The Representation of Bodily Pain in Late Nineteenth-Century English Culture* (Oxford: Clarendon, 2000).

Benjamin, Walter, 'The Task of the Translator', *Illuminations*, ed. Hannah Arendt, trans. Harry Zohn (New York: Schocken, 1968), 69–82.

Bibliotheca Carringtoniensis: Being a Collection of the Descriptive Title Pages of Certain Books Published by Mr. Charles Carrington of Paris, unpublished.

The Birchen Bouquet; or Curious and Original Anecdotes of Ladies fond of administering the Birch Discipline, c.1770 (N.p.: Birchington-on-Sea [Avery?], 1881).

Blann, Robinson, *Throwing the Scabbard Away: Byron's Battle Against the Censors of* Don Juan (New York: Peter Lang, 1991).

Bloch, Ivan, *Sexual Life in England Past and Present*, trans. William H. Forstern (London: Francis Aldor, 1938).

Boccacio, Giovanni, *The Decameron*, trans. John Payne (London: Privately Printed for Subscribers Only, 1895).

Boer, Inge E., 'Despotism from Under the Veil: Masculine and Feminine Readings of the Despot and the Harem', *Cultural Critique*, 32 (1995–6) 43–73.

Bolt, Christine, *The Anti-Slavery Movement and Reconstruction: A Study in Anglo-American Cooperation 1833–77* (London: Oxford University Press, 1969).

Bolter, Jay David and Richard Grusin, *Remediation: Understanding New Media* (Cambridge, MA: MIT, 1999).

The Bon Ton Magazine; or Microscope of Fashion and Folly, 5 vols (London: Printed by W. Locke, 1792 [1791–6]).

The Book of the Thousand Nights and One Night, 9 vols, trans. John Payne (London: Printed for the Villon Society for Private Subscription and for Private Circulation Only, 1882–4).

The Book of the Thousand Nights and a Night, 10 vols, trans. Richard F. Burton (London: Printed by the Kama Shastra Society, 1885–[6]).

The Book of the Thousand Nights and a Night, trans. Richard F. Burton, ed. Leonard Smithers, 12 vols (London: H. S. Nichols, 1894–[7]).

Bourdieu, Pierre, *The Field of Cultural Production: Essays on Art and Literature*, ed. Randal Johnson (Cambridge: Polity, 1993).

Boyer, Paul S., *Purity in Print: Book Censorship in America from the Gilded Age to the Computer Age*, 2nd edn (Madison: University of Wisconsin Press, 2002).

Bristow, Edward J., *Vice and Vigilance: Purity Movements in Britain since 1700* (Dublin: Gill and MacMillan, 1977).

'Britannia à la Beardsley', *Punch Almanack* (1895).

'British and Foreign Traffic in Girls', *Town Talk: A Journal for Society at Large*, 17 (Jan. 1880) 1–2.

Brodie, Fawn, *The Devil Drives: A Life of Sir Richard Burton* (London: Erie and Spottiswoode, 1967).

Brown, John, *Slave Life in Georgia: A narrative of the life, sufferings, and escape of John Brown*, ed L. A. Chamerovzow (London: The Editor, 1855).

Brown, Simon, *Early Erotic Films*. Unpublished.

Brown, William Wells, *Narrative of William W. Brown, an American slave: Written by himself*, 1847 (London: Charles Gilpin, 1850).

[Burgess, George Rev.], *Cato to Lord Byron on the Immorality and Dangerous Tendency of His Writings* (London: W. Wetton, 1824).

Burton, Isabel, *The Life of Captain Sir Richard F. Burton*, 1893, ed. W. H. Wilkins (London: Duckworth, 1898).

——, 'Sir Richard Burton's Manuscripts', *Morning Post* (19 June 1891) 3.

Burton, Richard Sir, 'The Thousand Nights and a Night', *Academy* (15 Aug. 1885) 101.

Butler, Judith, 'The Force of Fantasy: Feminism, Mapplethorpe, and Discursive Excess', *Differences: A Journal of Feminist Cultural Studies*, 2.2 (1990) 105–25.

Byron, Lord, *The Complete Poetical Works: Lord Byron*, 7 vols, ed. Jerome McGann (Oxford: Clarendon, 1980–93).

——, *Don Juan. Cantos I, II* (London: N.p. [John Murray], 1819).

——, *Don Juan. Cantos I to V* (London: Benbow, 1821).

——, *Don Juan. Cantos VI, VII, VIII* (London: J. Hunt, 1823).

——, *Don Juan. Cantos VI., VII., VIII* (London: W. Dugdale, 1823).

——, *Don Juan. Cantos XVII-XVIII* (London: Duncombe, [1823]).

——, *Don Juan. In Five Cantos* (London: Peter Griffin, [1823]).

——, *Don Juan. A Poem* (London: W. Benbow, 1822).

——, *Don Juan. A Poem* (London: Hodgson, 1823).

——, *Don Juan. With a Preface by a Clergyman* (London: Hodgson, 1822).

——, *Three Plays: Sardanapalus; The Two Foscari; Cain*, 1821 (Oxford: Woodstock, 1990).

The Cabinet of Venus (London: Erotica-Bibliomaniac Society [Carrington], 1896).

Caracciolo, Peter, ed., *The Arabian Nights in English Literature: Studies in the Reception of* The Thousand and One Nights *into British Culture* (Basingstoke: Macmillan, 1988).

Carlile, Robert, 'The Defeat of the Vice Society', *The Republican* (19 July 1822) 225–8.

——, 'Letter "To John Herbert Brown" Member of the Society for the Suppression of Vice', *The Republican* (1 July 1825) 801–22.

The Carmina of Catullus, trans. Richard Burton and Leonard Smithers (London: Printed for the Translators, 1894).

Carpenter, Edward, *The Intermediate Sex: A Study of Some Transitional Types of Men and Women* (London: Swan Sonnenschein, 1908).

——, *Intermediate Types among Primitive Folk: A Study in Social Evolution*, 1914, 2nd edn (London: George Allen, 1919).

[Carrington, Charles], *Forbidden Books: Notes and Gossip on Tabooed Literature by an Old Bibliophile* (Paris: For the Author and his Friends, 1902).

Catalogue of Rare Curious and Voluptuous Reading (N.p.: n.p., 1896).

Chew, Samuel C., *Byron in England: His Fame and After-Fame* (London: John Murray, 1924).

Chorier, Nicolas, *Algoisiae Sigeae satyra sotadica*, c.1660 (N.p.: n.p., c.1680).

'Christian Slavery', *Times* (22 Nov. 1822) 2.

Clara Gazul, or Honi Soit Qui Mal Y Pense (London: The Author, 1830).

[Cleland, John], *Memoirs of a Woman of Pleasure* (London: G. Fenton, 1749).

[Clowes, William Laird], *Bibliotheca Arcana Seu Catalogus Librorum Penetralium Being Brief notices of books that have been secretly printed, prohibited by law, seized, anathematized, burnt or Bowderlised. By Speculator Morum* (London: G. Redway, 1885).

Coates, Henry, *The British Don Juan; Being a Narrative of the Singular Amours, Entertaining Adventures, Remarkable Travels, &c, of the Hon. Edward W. Montagu* (London: James Griffin, 1823).

Cohen, William A., *Sex Scandal: The Private Parts of Victorian Fiction* (Durham: Duke University Press, 1996).

Coleridge, Samuel, *Chistabel; Kubla Khan; The Pains of Sleep* (London: John Murray, 1816).

Colton, C. C., *Remarks on the Talents of Lord Byron, and the Tendencies of* Don Juan. London: Longman, 1825).

Cook, Matt, *London and the Culture of Homosexuality, 1885–1914* (Cambridge: Cambridge University Press, 2003).

The Confessional Unmasked; showing the depravity of the priesthood (London: Thomas Johnston, 1851).

Conrad, Joseph, *The Secret Agent: A Simple Tale* (London: Methuen, 1907).

The Convent School: Early Experiences of a Young Flagellant (New York: Erotika Biblion Society [Carrington], 1898).

Cornog, Martha, ed., *Libraries, Erotica, Pornography* (Phoenix: Oryx, 1991).

The Countess of Lesbos; or the New Gamiani (Paris: Under the Galleries of the Palais Royal, 1889).

Craig, Alec, *The Banned Books of England and Other Countries* (London: George Allen & Unwin, 1962).

Crary, Jonathan, *Techniques of the Observer: On Vision and Modernity in the Nineteenth Century* (Cambridge, MA: MIT, 1990).

The Cremorne; A Magazine of Wit, Facetiae, Parody, Graphic Tales of Love, etc. (London: Privately Printed [Lazenby?], 1851 [1882]).

'Critique on Modern Poets', *The New Monthly Magazine*, 12 (1 Nov. 1819) 371–5.

Cross, P. J., 'The Private Case: A History', *The Library of the British Museum, Retrospective Essays on the Department of Printed Books*, ed. P. R. Harris (London: The British Library, 1991).

Dalziel, Thomas, *The Arabian Nights' Entertainments*, 1864–6 (Warne: London, 1866).

D'Arcy, St John, *The Memoirs of Madge Buford, or, a modern Fanny Hill*, 1892 (New York: n.p. [Carrington?], 1902).

Darnton, Robert, *The Forbidden Best-Sellers of Pre-Revolutionary France* (New York: Norton, 1995).

Davenport, John, *An Apology for Mohammed and the Koran* (London: Printed for the Author, 1869).

——, *Curiositates Eroticae Physiologiae; or Tabooed Subjects freely treated* (London: Privately Printed, 1875).

Davis, Tracy C., 'The Actress in Victorian Pornography', *Theatre Journal*, 41 (1989) 294–315.

Dawes, Charles Reginald, *A Study of Erotic Literature in England, Considered with Especial Reference to Social Life* (1943, unpublished).

Deakin, Terence J., *Catalogi Librorum Eroticorum: A Critical Bibliography of Erotic Bibliographies and Book-Catalogues* (London: Cecil and Amelia Woolf, 1964).

Dellamora, Richard, *Masculine Desire: The Sexual Politics of Victorian Aestheticism* (Chapel Hill: University of North Carolina Press, 1990).

——, 'Traversing the Feminine in Oscar Wilde's *Salome*', *Victorian Sages and Cultural Discourse*, ed. Thais E. Morgan (New Brunswick: Rutgers University Press, 1990), 246–64.

Desmarais, Jane Haville, *The Beardsley Industry: The Critical Reception in England and France, 1893–1914* (Hants: Ashgate, 1998).

Devereux, Cecily, '"The Maiden Tribute" and the Rise of the White Slave in the Nineteenth Century: The Making of an Imperial Construct', *Victorian Review*, 26.2 (2000) 1–23.

Deveureux, Captain, *Vénus in India, or, Love Adventures in Hindustan* (Brussels: n.p., 1889).

Dictionnaire des oeuvres érotiques, ed. Gilbert Minazzoli ([Paris]: Mercure de France, 1971).

Dollimore, Jonathan, *Sex, Literature and Censorship* (Cambridge: Polity, 2001).

——, *Sexual Dissidence: Augustine to Wilde, Freud to Foucault* (Oxford: Clarendon, 1991).

Don John; or, Don Juan unmasked (London: William Hone, 1819).

Don Juan, Canto the Third (London: William Hone, 1819).

Don Leon; A Poem by the Late Lord Byron (London: Printed for the Booksellers [Dugdale], 1866).

Donelan, Charles, *Romanticism and Male Fantasy in Byron's Don Juan: A Marketable Vice* (Basingstoke: Macmillan – now Palgrave, 2000).

[Douglass, Frederick], *Narrative of the Life of Frederick Douglass, an American Slave, Written by Himself* (Dublin: Webb & Chapman, 1845).

Dowson, Ernest, *Verses* (London: L. Smithers, 1896).

Dumas, Alexandre fils, *La Dame aux Camélias*, 1848 (Paris: n.p., 1852).

L'École des Filles, ou la Philosophie des dames, 1655 (Fribourg: Roger Bon Temps, 1668).

Edwards, Amelia B., 'Literature', Rev. of *Lady Burton's Edition of her Husband's 'Arabian Nights'*, by Isabel Burton, *Academy* (11 Dec. 1886) 387–8.

*The Elements of Tuition in Modes of Punishment. c.*1830. London: Printed for the bookseller, [*c.*1880].

Elfenbein, Andrew, *Byron and the Victorians* (Cambridge: Cambridge University Press, 1995).

Ellis, Henry Havelock, *Studies in the Psychology of Sex: Sexual Inversion*, vol. 1 (London: Wilson & Macmillan, 1897).

Ellmann, Richard, *Oscar Wilde* (London: Hamish Hamilton, 1987).

En Virginie: Épisode de la Guerre de Sécession (Paris: Charles Carrington, 1901).

English Cartoons & Satirical Prints, 1320–1832 (Cambridge: Chadwyck-Healey, 1978).

*The Exhibition of Female Flagellants, c.*1777 (London: Theresa Berkley [Dugdale?], [*c.*1840]).

The Exquisite: A Collection of Tales, Histories, and Essays, 3 vols ([London]: Printed and Published by H. Smith [Dugdale], n.d. [1842–4]).

Farwell, Beatrice, *The Cult of Images: Baudelaire and the 19th-Century Media Explosion* (Santa Barbara: UCSB Art Museum, 1977).

Favret, Mary A., 'Flogging: The Anti-Slavery Movement Writes Pornography', *Essays and Studies*, 51 (1998) 19–43.

The Ferret. An inquisitive, quizzical, satirical and theatrical censor of the age (London: 1870).

The Festival of the Passions; or Voluptuous Miscellany (Glenfucket [London?]: Abdul Mustapha, [1863]).

Fisch, Audrey A., *American Slaves in Victorian England: Abolitionist Politics and Culture* (Cambridge: Cambridge University Press, 2000).

Flossie, a Venus of Fifteen, by One who knew this Charming Goddess and Worshipped at her Shrine, 1897 (London and New York [Paris]: Printed for the Erotica Biblion Society [Charles Carrington?, *c.*1900]).

Foreman, Gabrielle P., 'Manifest in Signs: The Politics of Sex and Representation in *Incidents in the Life of a Slave Girl*', *Harriet Jacobs and* Incidents in the Life of a Slave Girl: *New Critical Essays* (Cambridge: Cambridge University Press, 1996) 76–99.

Foucault, Michel, *The Archaeology of Knowledge*, 1969, trans. A. M. Sheridan Smith (London: Routledge, 2001).

——. *The History of Sexuality*, 1976, trans. Robert Hurley, vol. 1 (London: Allen Lane, 1979).

Foxon, David, *Libertine Literature in England, 1660–1745* (New York: University Books, 1965).

France, Hector, *The Chastisement of Mansour*, trans. Alfred Allinson (Paris: Charles Carrington, 1898).

——, *Musk, Hashish, and Blood* (Paris: Charles Carrington, 1900).

'From the Queer and Yellow Book', *Punch*, 29 (1895) 58.

Freud, Sigmund, 'A Child is Being Beaten', 1919, *The Standard Edition of the Complete Psychological Works of Sigmund Freud*, trans. James Strachey, vol. 17 (London: Hogarth, 1955) 177–204.

Fruits of Philosophy; or, The Private Companion of Young Married People (London: J. Watson, 1841).

Fryer, Peter, *Private Case—Public Scandal* (London: Secker & Warburg, 1966).

Fujimoto, T., *The Story of the Geisha Girl* (London: T. Werner Laurie, 1917).

——, *The Nightside of Japan* (London: T. Werner Laurie, 1914).

Fulton, Richard D., '"Now only the *Times* is on our Side": The London *Times* and America Before the Civil War', *Victorian Review*, 16.1 (1990) 48–58.

Galland, Antoine, *Les Mille et Une Nuits, contes Arabes*, 1704–17 (Paris: M. Aimé Martin, [1843]).

Gamer, Michael, 'Genres for the Prosecution: Pornography and the Gothic', *PMLA*, 114 (1999) 1043–54.

Garfield, Deborah M., 'Speech, Listening, and Female Sexuality in *Incidents in the Life of a Slave Girl*', *Arizona Quarterly*, 50.2 (1994) 19–49.

Gay, Jules, *Bibliographie des principaux ouvrages relatifs a l'amour* (Paris: n.p., 1861).

Gay, Peter, *The Bourgeois Experience: Victoria to Freud*, vol. 1 (Oxford: Oxford University Press, 1984).

Gibson, Ian, *The English Vice: Beating, Sex and Shame in Victorian England and After* (London: Duckworth, 1978).

——, *Erotomaniac: The Secret Life of Henry Spencer Ashbee* (London: Faber & Faber, 2001).

Gide, André, *Si le Grain ne Meurt*, 1920 (Paris: n.p., 1928).

Giddens, Anthony, *Runaway World: How Globalization is Reshaping Our Lives*, revised edn (New York: Routledge, 2002).

Gilbert, Elliot L., '"Tumult of Images": Wilde, Beardsley, and *Salome*', *Victorian Studies*, 26 (1983) 133–59.

Gilbert W. S. and Arthur Sullivan, *The Mikado, or The Town of Titupu* (London: Chappell [1885]).

Ginzburg, Ralph. *An Unhurried View of Erotica* (London: Secker & Warburg, 1959).

Gitelman, Lisa, and Geoffrey B. Pingree, eds., *New Media, 1740–1914* (Cambridge, MA: MIT 2003).

Goncourt Edmond de, *Hokusai* (Paris: Bibliotheque Charpentier, 1896).

——, *Outamaro: Le Peintre des Maisons Vertes* (Paris: Bibliotheque Charpentier, 1891).

Goncourt, Edmond de, ed., *Journal des Goncourt: Memoires de la vie Littéraire*, 9 vols (Paris: Fasquelle, 1887–96).

Grant, John Cameron, *The Ethiopian, a Narrative of the Society of Human Leopards* (Paris: Charles Carrington, 1900).

Greenhorn [George Thompson], *Venus in Boston: A Romance of City Life* (New York: n.p. [Haynes], [1849]).

Grewal, Inderpal, *Home and Harem: Nation, Gender, Empire, and the Cultures of Travel* (Durham: Duke University Press, 1996).

Grosskurth, Phyllis, *John Addington Symonds: A Biography* (Longman: London, 1964).

The Gulistan or Rose Garden of Sa'di, Faithfully Translated Into English (Benares: Printed by the Kama Shastra Society for Private Subscribers only, 1888).

Gynecocracy. A narrative of adventures and psychological experiences of Julian Robinson, afterwards Viscount Ladywood, under petti-coat rule, written by himself, 3 vols (London: Privately Printed, 1893).

Hall, Radclyffe, *The Well of Loneliness* (London: Jonathan Cape, 1928).

Halttunen, Karen, 'Humanitarianism and the Pornography of Pain in Anglo-American Culture', *The American Historical Review*, 100.2 (1995) 303–34.

Harlow, Barbara, Introduction, *The Colonial Harem*, by Malek Alloula, trans. Myrna Godzich and Wlad Godzich (Minneapolis: University of Minnesota Press, 1986.

Memoirs of Harriette Wilson, written by herself, ed. T. Little, 2nd edn (London: J. J. Stockdale, 1825).

Harris, Frank, *Contemporary Portraits: First Series* (London: Methuen, 1915).

——, *My Life and Loves*, 1922–9, 4 vols (Paris: Obelisk, 1945).

Harris, George W., *'The' Practical Guide to Algiers* (London: George Philip & Son, 1890).

Harrison, Fraser, *The Dark Angel: Aspects of Victorian Sexuality* (London: Sheldon, 1977).

Hart, Lynda, 'To Each Other: Performing Lesbian S/M', *Between the Body and the Flesh: Performing Sadomasochism* (New York: Columbia University Press, 1998) 36–83.

Haynes, E. S. P., 'The Taboos of the British Museum Library', *The English Review*, 16 (1913) 123–34.

Hegel, G. W. F., *The Phenomenology of Spirit*, 1806 (Oxford : Clarendon, 1977).

Heller, Tamar, 'Flagellating Feminine Desire: Lesbians, Old Maids, and New Women in "Miss Coote's Confession", a Victorian Pornographic Narrative', *Victorian Newsletter*, 92 (1997) 9–15.

Herbert, Lord George, *A Night in a Moorish Harem*, c.1896 (North Hollywood: Brandon House, 1967).

Hoare, Philip, *Wilde's Last Stand: Decadence, Conspiracy, and the First World War* (London: Duckworth, 1997).

Hoffman, Frank A., 'The Victorian Sexual Subculture: Some Notes and a Speculation', *The Baker Street Journal*, 35.1 (1985) 19–22.

Holland, Merlin, and Rupert-Hart Davis, *The Complete Letters of Oscar Wilde* (London: Fourth Estate, 2000).

'Holywell Street Literature', *Town Talk* (6 May 1882) 5–6.

'Holywell-Street Revived', *Saturday Review* (21 Aug. 1858) 180.

Hourani, Albert, *A History of the Arab Peoples* (New York: Warner, 1991).

'How it is Done', *Punch*, 28 (1894) 47.

Human Gorillas: A Study of Rape with Violence (Paris: C. Carrington, 1901).

Hunt, Lynn, ed., *The Invention of Pornography: Obscenity and the Origins of Modernity, 1500–1800* (New York: Zone, 1993).

Hyam, Ronald, *Empire and Sexuality: The British Experience* (Manchester and New York: Manchester University Press, 1990).

Hyde, H. Montgomery, *A History of Pornography* (London: Heinemann, 1964).

——, *The Other Love: An Historical and Contemporary Survey of Homosexuality in Britain* (London: Heinemann, 1970).

'Immoral Current Literature', *Town Talk* (12 May 1882) 3.

'Indecent French Novels', *Town Talk* (31 Jan. 1885) 1.

'Is Empire Consistent with Morality?' *Pall Mall Gazette* (19 May 1887) 2–3.

Jackson, Holbrook, *The Eighteen Nineties: A Review of Art and Ideas at the Close of the Nineteenth Century* (London: Grant Richards, 1913).

Jackson, Louise A., *Child Abuse in Victorian England* (London: Routledge, 2000).

[Jacobs, Harriet], *The Deeper Wrong; Or, Incidents in the Life of a Slave Girl. Written by Herself*, ed. L. Maria Child (London: W. Tweedie, 1862).

——, *Incidents in the Life of a Slave Girl. Written By Herself*, 1861, ed. Jean Fagan Yellin (Cambridge, MA: Harvard University Press, 2000).

Le Jardin Parfumé du Cheikh Nefzaoui (Paris: Pour Isidore Liseux et ses Amis, [1886]).

Johnson, Edward Dudley Hume, '*Don Juan* in England', *ELH*, 11 (1944) 135–53.

Johnson, Samuel, *The Prince of Abyssinia: Rasselas, Prince of Abyssinia* (London: R. & J. Dodsley, 1759).

Johnson, Wendell Stacey, *Living in Sin: The Victorian Sexual Revolution* (Chicago: Nelson-Hall, 1979).

Joyce, James, *Ulysses* (Paris: Sylvia Beach, 1922).

Kabbani, Rana, *Imperial Fictions: Europe's Myths of Orient*, 1986 (Pandora: London, 1988).

The Kama-Shastra; or, The Hindoo Art of Love (Ars Amoris Indica), trans. A. F. F. and B. F. R. (N.p.: n.p., n.d.).

Les Kama Sutra de Vatsyayana. Manuel d'Erotologie Hindoue, trans. Isidore Liseux (Paris: Imprimé à deux cent vingt exemplaire pour Isidore Liseux et ses Amis, 1885).

The Kama Sutra of Vatsayana (Benares: Printed for the Hindoo Kama Shastra Society, For Private Circulation Only, 1883).

Kappeler, Susanne, *The Pornography of Representation* (Cambridge: Polity Press, 1986).

Kearney, Patrick J., *A History of Erotic Literature* (London: Macmillan London, 1982).

——, *The Private Case: An Annotated Bibliography of the Private Case Erotica Collection in the British (Museum) Library* (London: Jay Landesman, 1891).

Kendrick, Walter, *The Secret Museum: Pornography in Modern Culture* (New York: Viking, 1987).

Kennedy, Dane, '"Captain Burton's Oriental Muck Heap": *The Book of the Thousand Nights* and the Uses of Orientalism', *Journal of British Studies*, 39 (July 2000) 317–39.

Kennedy, Dane, and Burke E. Casari, 'Burton Offerings: Isabel Burton and the "Scented Garden" Manuscript', *Journal of Victorian Culture*, 2.2 (1997). 229–44.

Kipps, Donovan, Préface, *Dolly Morton* (Paris: J. Fort, n.d.).

Knight, Hardwicke, 'Early Microphotographs', *History of Photography*, 9.4 (1985) 311–15.

Knipp, C., 'The Arabian Nights in England: Galland's Translation and its Successors', *Journal of Arabic Literature*, 5 (1974) 44–54.

Kooistra, Lorraine Janzen, *The Artist as Critic: Bitextuality in Fin-de-Siècle Illustrated Books* (Aldershot: Scolar, 1995).

Kouli Khan; or, the Progress of Error (London: William Benbow, [1820]).

Lady Burton's Edition of Her Husband's Arabian Nights, ed. Justin Huntly McCarthy, 6 vols (London: Waterloo & Sons, 1886).

Lane, Edward William, *The Thousand and One Nights*, 3 vols (London: C. Knights, 1839–41).

Lane, Frederick S. III, *Obscene Profits: The Entrepreneurs of Pornography in the Cyber Age* (London: Routledge, 2001).

[Lane-Poole, Stanley], Rev. of *The Book of a Thousand Nights and a Night*, by Richard Burton, *The Edinburgh Review*, 164 (1886) 166–99.

Lansbury, Coral, *The Old Brown Dog: Women, Workers, and Vivisection in Edwardian England* (Madison: University of Wisconsin Press, 1985).

Laveleye, Emile de, 'How Bad Books May Destroy States', *The Vigilance Record* (1 June 1888) 59–60.

——, Presidential Address, *National League Journal* (1 Nov. 1882) 9–10.

Laver, James, *Whistler* (London: Faber & Faber, 1930).

Lawrence, D. H., *The White Peacock* (London: William Heinemann, 1911).

Lawrence, Malcolm, 'Leonard Smithers—'The Most Learned Erotomaniac', *American Libraries* (1973) 6–8.

Leask, Nigel, *British Romantic Writers and the East* (Cambridge: Cambridge University Press, 1992).

Legman, G., *The Horn Book: Studies in Erotic Folklore and Bibliography* (New York: University Books, 1964).

——, Introduction, *My Secret Life* (New York: Grove, 1966).

Leighton, John, 'On Japanese Art: A Discourse Delivered at the Royal Institution of Great Britain. 1 May 1863', *The Art of all Nations: The Emerging Role of Exhibitions and Critics*, ed. Elizabeth Gilmore Holt (Princeton: Princeton University Press, 1982).

Letters from Laura and Eveline (London: Privately Printed, 1903).

Lew, Joseph W., 'Lady Mary's Portable Seraglio', *Eighteenth-Century Studies*, 24 (1991) 432–50.

Lewis, Matthew Gregory, *The Monk: A Romance* (London: n.p., 1796).

List of Choice English Books (Paris: Charles Carrington, n.d.).

Le Livre d'Amour de l'Orient: Ananga-Ranga, La Fleur Lascive Orientale –Le Livre de Volupté (Paris: Bibliothèque des Curieux, 1910).

Loth, David, *The Erotic in Literature: A Historical Survey of Pornography as Delightful as it is Indiscreet* (London: Secker & Warburg, 1961).

Lovell, Mary, *A Rage to Live: A Biography of Richard and Isabel Burton* (London: Little, 1998).

The Lustful Turk, or Lascivious Scenes in a Harem, 1828 ([New York]: Canyon, [1967]).

Luke, Hugh J., 'The Publishing of Byron's *Don Juan*', *PMLA*, 80 (1965) 199–209.

Maas, Henry, et al., eds, *The Letters of Aubrey Beardsley* (London: Cassell, 1970).

Maidenhead Stories, told by a set of joyous students, 1894, 2 vols (New York: Printed for the Erotica Biblion Society [Carrington], 1897).

Maidment, B. E., *Reading Popular Prints, 1790–1870* (Manchester: Manchester University Press, 1996).

Makdisi, Saree, *Romantic Imperialism: Universal Empire and the Culture of Modernity* (Cambridge: Cambridge University Press, 1998).

Manchester, Colin, 'Lord Campbell's Act: England's First Obscenity Statute', *The Journal of Legal History*, 9 (1988) 223–41.

Marchand, Leslie, ed., *Byron's Letters and Journals*, 12 vols (London: John Murray, 1979).

Marcus, Steven, *The Other Victorians: A Study of Sexuality and Pornography in Mid-Nineteenth-Century England* (New York: Basic, 1964).

Marriage – Love and Woman Amongst the Arabs otherwise entitled The Book of Exposition, Literally translated from Arabic by a English Bohemian (Paris: Charles Carrington, 1896).

Martineau, Harriet, *Society in America*, 1837, 3 vols (London: Saunders and Otley, 1839).

Mason, Michael, *The Making of Victorian Sexual Attitudes* (Oxford: Oxford University Press, 1994).

[Mathias, Thomas James], *The Pursuits of Literature: A Satirical Poem* (London: Printed for T. Becket, 1797).

May's Account of her Introduction to the Art of Love (London-Paris: n.p., 1904).

Mayhew, Henry, *London Labour and London Poor*, 1861, 4 vols (London: Frank Cass, 1967).

McCalman, Iain, *Radical Underworld: Prophets, Revolutionaries, and Pornographers in London, 1795–1840* (Cambridge: Cambridge University Press, 1988).

McLynn, Frank, *Burton: Snow Upon the Desert* (London: John Murray, 1990).

Meibomius, Johann Heinrich, *A Treatise on the Use of Flogging in Venereal Affairs* (London: E. Curll, 1718).

Meier-Graefe, Alfred Julius, *Modern Art: Being a Contribution to a New System of Aesthetics*, trans. Florence Simmonds and G. W. Chrystal (London: William Heinemann, 1908).

Melman, Billie, *Women's Orients: English Women and the Middle East, 1718–1918: Sexuality, Religion and Work* (London: Macmillan, 1992).

Memoirs of a Russian Ballet Girl (London [Paris?]: n.p. [Charles Hirsch?], 1903).

The Memoirs of Dolly Morton: The Story of a Woman's Part in the Struggle to Free the Slaves (Paris: Charles Carrington, 1899).

Mendes, Peter, *Clandestine Erotic Fiction in English, 1800–1930: A Bibliographical Study* (Hants: Scholar, 1993).

The Mistress and the Slave: A Masochist Realistic Love Story (Athens [Paris?]: Imprinted for its Members by the Erotika Biblion Society [Carrington], 1905).

Mitford, Jack, *The Private Life of Lord Byron; Comprising His Voluptuous Amours, Secret Intrigues* [etc.] (London: Printed by H. Smith [Dugdale], [1828]).

Modern Babylon, and other poems (London: n.p., [1872]).

Montagu, Lady Mary Wortley, *Turkish Embassy Letters*, 1763, ed. Anita Desai (London: Pickering & Chatto, 1993).

Montesquieu, Baron de, *Persian Letters*, trans. John Ozell, 2 vols (London: J. Tonson, 1722).

Moore, Thomas, *Lalla Rookh, an Oriental Romance* (London: n.p. [John Murray], 1817).

Morton, Thomas, *Speed the Plough*, 1798, 3rd edn (Dublin: Burnet, 1800).

Moslem Erotism, or Adventures of an American Woman in Constantinople (N.p.: n.p, n.d [c.1906].

Mosse, George L., *Nationalism and Sexuality: Respectability and Abnormal Sexuality in Modern Europe* (New York: Howard Fertig, 1985).

Mudge, Bradford K., 'Romanticism, Materialism, and the Origins of Porno-graphy', *Romanticism On the Net*, 23 (2001) 1–23. <http://users.ox.ac.uk/~scat0385/23mudge.html>

——, *The Whore's Story: Women, Pornography, and the British Novel, 1684–1830* (Oxford: Oxford University Press, 2000).

Mugabe, Robert, 'Opening Statement of the Group of Fifteen', 31 May 2001, Depart-ment of Foreign Affairs Republic of Indonesia, 13 July 2001 <http://www.dfa-deplu.go.id/world/multilateral/g15/speech-zimbabwe310501.htm>

My Secret Life, 11 vols (Amsterdam: Privately Printed, n.d. [c.1888–94]).

Nazarieff, Serge, *Early Erotic Photography* (Berlin: Taschen, 2002).

——, *The Stereoscopic Nude, 1850–1930* (Berlin: Taschen, 1990).

Nead, Lynda, *Victorian Babylon: People, Streets and Images in Nineteenth-Century London* (New Haven: Yale University Press, 2000).

Nefzaoui, Cheikh, *[The Perfumed Garden]*, Traduit de L'Arabe par Monsieur le baron R**, Capitaine d'Etat Major ([Algiers], N.p., 1850 [1876]).

Nelson, James, *Publisher to the Decadents. Leonard Smithers in the Careers of Beardsley, Wilde, Dowson* (University Park: Pennsylvania State University Press, 2000).

'The New Master of Art', *To-day*, 12 May (1894) 28–9.

'New Publications', *The Studio*, 2 (1894) 183–5.

Nichols, Charles H., 'Who Read the Slave Narratives?', *Phylon*, 20.2 (1959) 149–62.

Norman, Henry Sir, *The Real Japan: Studies of Contemporary Japanese Manners, Morals, Administration, & Politics*, 3rd edn (London: T. Fisher Unwin, 1893).

O'Connell, Sheila, *The Popular Print in England, 1550–1850* (London: British Museum, 1999).

O'Toole, Laurence, *Pornocopia: Porn, Sex, Technology and Desire* (London: Serpent's Tale, 1999).

'Occasional Notes', *Pall Mall Gazette* (24 Sept. 1885) 3.

The Old Man Young Again or The Age-Rejuvenescence in the Power of Concupiscence Literally translated by an English Bohemian (Paris: Charles Carrington, 1898–99).

Ono, Ayajo, *Japonisme in Britain: Whistler, Menpes, Henry, Hornel and Nineteenth-Century Japan* (New York: Routledge, 2003).

Oriental Stories (La Fleur Lascive Orientale) (Athens: Erotika Biblion Society, for private distribution only, 1893).

Ovenden, Graham and Peter Mendes, *Victorian Erotic Photography* (New York: St Martin's, 1973).

Owen, Alex, 'The Sorcerer and His Apprentice: Aleister Crowley and the Magical Exploration of Edwardian Subjectivity', *Journal of British Studies*, 36 (1997) 99–133.

Paine, Thomas, *The Age of Reason*, 1793 (London: Carlile, 1819).

Pakenham, Thomas, *The Scramble for Africa, 1876–1912*, 1991 (London: Abacus, 2001).

Pamphlets Relating to Q. Caroline, unpublished.

Pattinson, John Patrick, 'The Man Who Was Walter', *Victorian Literature and Culture*, 30 (2002) 19–40.

Peakman, Julie, *Mighty Lewd Books: The Development of Pornography in Eighteenth-Century England* (London: Palgrave Macmillan, 2003).

The Pearl, A Journal of Facetia Voluptuous Reading, 3 vols (London: Printed for the Society of Vice [Augustin Brancart], 1879–80 [c.1890]).

Pearsall, Ronald, *Public Purity, Private Shame: Victorian Sexual Hypocrisy Exposed* (London: Weidenfeld & Nicolson, 1976).

——, *The Worm in the Bud. The World of Victorian Sexuality* (London: Weidenfeld and Nicolson, 1969).

Pease, Allison, *Modernism, Mass Culture, and the Aesthetics of Obscenity* (Cambridge: Cambridge University Press, 2000).

Pennell, Joseph, 'A New Illustrator – Aubrey Beardsley', *The Studio*, 1 (1893) 14–19.

Penzer, N. M., *The Harem*, 1936 (London: Spring, 1965).

The Perfumed Garden of the Sheik Nefzaoui or, The Arab Art of Love (Cosmopoli: For Private Circulation Only, 1886).

The Perfumed Garden for the Soul's Delectation (Paris: The Kamashastra Society [Charles Carrington], 1907).

Peterson, M. Jeanne, 'Dr. Acton's Enemy: Medicine, Sex, and Society in Victorian England', *Victorian Studies*, 29 (1986) 569–90.

Phallic Miscellanies (N.p. [London]: Privately Printed [Hargrave Jennings], 1891).

Phallic Objects, Monuments, and Remains (N.p. [London]: Privately Printed [Hargrave Jennings], 1889).

The Phoenix of Sodom, or the Vere Street Coterie (N.p.: n.p., 1813).

Pope, Alexander, *The Rape of the Lock* (London: Leonard Smithers, 1897).

Pope-Hennessy, James, *Monckton Milnes: The Flight of Youth 1851–1885* (London: Constable, 1951).

Porter, Roy, and Lesley Hall, *The Facts of Life: The Creation of Sexual Knowledge in Britain, 1650–1950* (New Haven, CT: Yale University Press, 1995).

Presley, John Woodrow, 'Finnegans Wake, Lady Pokingham, and Victorian Erotic Fantasy', *Journal of Popular Culture*, 30.3 (1996) 67–80.

Priapeia, or The Sportive Epigrams of divers Poets on Priapus (Athens [London]: Imprinted by the Erotika Biblion Society For Private Distribution Only [Smithers], 1888 [1889]).

Priapeia, or The Sportive Epigrams of divers Poets on Priapus (Cosmopoli: Printed for Private Circulation [Carrington?], 1890).

[Prince, Mary], *The History of Mary Prince, A West Indian Slave* (London: n.p., 1831).

Prospectuses (N.p.: n.p., n.d.).

Quincey, Thomas de, *Confessions of an English Opium-Eater* (London: Taylor & Hessey, 1822).

The Quintessence of Birch Discipline (London: Privately Printed [Lazenby], 1870 [1883]).

The Rambler's Magazine; or, Annals of Gallantry, Glee, Pleasure, & the Bon Ton, 2 vols (London: Pub. by J. Mitford, [1827–9]).

The Rambler's Magazine; or, the Annals of Gallantry, Glee, Pleasure, & the Bon Ton, 7 vols (London: n.p., 1783–90).

The Rambler's Magazine; or, Fashionable Emporium of Polite Literature (London: Benbow, 1822 [–5]).

Randiana; or Excitable Tales; being the Experiences of an erotic Philosopher (New York [London]: n.p. [Avery?], 1884).

Rare Unusual Books (N.p., n.p. : n.d.).

Raymond, Jean Paul, and Charles L. S. Ricketts, *Oscar Wilde* (Bloomsbury: The Nonesuch Press, 1931).

Reade, Brian, *Aubrey Beardsley* (New York: Viking, 1967).

Reade, Rolf S., [Alfred Rose], *Registrum Librorum Eroticorum*, 2 vols (London: Privately Printed, 1936).

Réage, Pauline [Dominique Aury], *Story of O*, 1954, trans. Sabine d'Estrée (New York: Grove, 1965).

Report from the Joint Select Committee on Lotteries and Indecent Advertisements (London: Vacher & Sons, 1908).

Report of the Proceedings of the First General Meeting of the Subscribers to the Oriental Translation Fund (London: n.p., 1828).

Rev. of *Autobiography of a Female Slave*, by Anonymous, *Athenaeum* (4 Apr. 1857) 134–5.

Rev. of *The Book of a Thousand Nights and One Night*, by Richard Burton, *Standard* (12 Sept. 1885) 5.

Rev. of *The Book of a Thousand Nights and a Night*, by Richard Burton, *Bat* (29 Sept. 1885) 875–6.

Rev. of *The Book of a Thousand Nights and One Night*, by Richard Burton, *Echo* (12 Oct. 1885) 2.

Rev. of *The Book of a Thousand Nights and a Night*, by Richard Burton, *Saturday Review* (2 Jan. 1886) 26–7.

Rev. of *The Deeper Wrong; or, Incidents in the Life of a Slave Girl*, by Linda Brent, *Anti-Slavery Reporter* (1 Apr. 1862) 96.

Rev. of *The Deeper Wrong; or, Incidents in the Life of a Slave Girl*, by Linda Brent, *Athenaeum* (19 Apr. 1862) 529.

Rev. of *The Deeper Wrong; or, Incidents in the Life of a Slave Girl*, by Linda Brent, *Caledonian Mercury* (31 Mar. 1862) 3.

Rev. of *The Deeper Wrong; or, Incidents in the Life of a Slave Girl*, by Linda Brent, *London Daily News* (10 Mar. 1862) 2.

Rev. of *The Deeper Wrong; or, Incidents in the Life of a Slave Girl*, by Linda Brent, *Londonderry Standard* (27 Mar. 1862) 4.

Rev. of *The Deeper Wrong; or, Incidents in the Life of a Slave Girl*, by Linda Brent, *Western Morning News* (5 Apr. 1862) 4.

Rev. of *Don Juan*, by Lord Byron, *Blackwood's Edinburgh Review*, 5 (1819) 512–23.

Rev. of *Don Juan*, by Lord Byron, *Blackwood's Edinburgh Review*, 14 (1823) 282–93.

Rev. of *Don Juan*, by Lord Byron, *British Critic*, 12 (Aug. 1819) 197.

Rev. of *Don Juan*, by Lord Byron, *Eclectic Review* 12 (Aug. 1819) 149–50.

Rev. of *Don Juan*, by Lord Byron, *Gentleman's Magazine* 89 (1819) 152.

Rev. of *Don Juan*, by Lord Byron, *Gentleman's Magazine* 93 (1823) 250–2.

Rev. of *Lady Burton's Edition of her Husband's 'Arabian Nights'*, by Isabel Burton, *Academy* (31 Dec. 1887) 438–3.

Rev. of *The Library Edition*, ed. Leonard Smithers, *Athenaeum*, 23 (Feb. 1895) 247–8.

Rev. of *Linda; Incidents in the Life of a Slave Girl*, by Linda Brent, *Anti-Slavery Advocate* (1 May 1861) 421.

Rev. of *Narrative of the Life of Frederick Douglass*, by Frederick Douglass, *Chambers's Edinburgh Journal*, 5 (1846) 56–9.

Rev. of *The Real Japan*, *Atlantic Monthly*, 69 (1892) 692–3.

Rev. of *The Real Japan*, *Atlantic Monthly*, 74 (1894) 834–5.

Rev. of *Slave Life in Georgia*, by John Brown, *Athenaeum* (31 Mar. 1855) 378.

Rev. of *The Yellow Book*, *Academy* (28 Apr. 1895) 349.

Rev. of *The Yellow Book*, *Dial* (1 June 1894) 335.

Rev. of *The Yellow Book*, *Pall Mall Gazette* (9 Feb. 1895) 4.

Rev. of *The Yellow Book*, *Times* (20 Apr. 1894) 3.

Reynolds, George W. M., *The Mysteries of the Court of London* (London: John Dicks, 1849–56).

Richardson, Alan, 'Escape from the Seraglio: Cultural Transvestism in *Don Juan*', *Rereading Byron: Essays Selected from Hofstra University's Byron Bicentennial Conference*, ed. Alice Levine and Robert N. Keane (New York: Garland, 1991) 175–85.

Roberts, M. J. D., 'Making Victorian Morals? The Society for the Suppression of Vice and its Critics, 1802–1886', *Historical Studies*, 21.83 (1981) 157–73.

——. 'Morals, Art, and the Law: The Passing of the Obscene Publications Act, 1857', *Victorian Studies*, 28 (1985) 609–29.

Robertson, George, *Obscenity: An Account of Censorship Laws and Their Enforcement in England and Wales* (London: Weidenfeld & Nicolson, 1979).

Robinson, Douglas, *Translation and Empire: Postcolonial Theories Explained* (Manchester: St Jerome, 1997).

Rochester, John Wilmot, *Sodom; or, The Quintessence of Debauchery*, 1684, ed. Patrick J. Kearney ([London: P. J. Kearney, 1969]).

The Romance of Chastisement or, Revelations of the School and Bedroom (N.p. [London?]: n.p. [Lazenby?], 1870 [1883]).

The Romance of Lust; or Early Experiences (London: N.p., 1873–6).

The Romance of Lust; or Early Experiences (Rotterdam: Berge, *c*.1895).

Ross, Robbie, 'The Eulogy of Aubrey Beardsley', *Ben Johnson his Volpone* (London: Leonard Smithers, 1898).

Rothenstein, William, *Men and Memories: Recollections of William Rothenstein*, vol. 1 (London: Faber & Faber, 1931).

Sacher-Masoch, Leopold von, *Venus in Furs*, 1870 (Paris: Charles Carrington, 1902).

Sade, Marquis de, *Justine; ou les Malheurs de la vertu*, 2nd edn (N.p.: n.p., 1791).

——, *Opus Sadicum: A philosophical romance*, trans. [Isidore Liseux] (Paris: Isidore Liseux, 1889).

Said, Edward, *Culture and Imperialism*, 1993 (New York: Vintage, 1994).

——, *Orientalism.*,1978 (New York: Vintage, 1979).

'Salome', *The Saturday Review* (24 Mar. 1894) 317.

Sánchez-Eppler, Karen, *Touching Liberty: Abolition, Feminism, and the Politics of the Body* (Berkeley: University of California Press, 1993).

Satirical Songs and Miscellaneous Papers, connected with the Trial of Queen Caroline, unpublished.

Saunders, David, 'Copyright, Obscenity and Literary History', *ELH*, 57.2 (1990) 431–44.

——, 'Victorian Obscenity Law: Negative Censorship or Positive Administration', *Writing and Censorship in Britain*, ed. Paul Hyland and Neil Sammells (London: Routledge, 1992) 154–70.

The Scented Garden of Abdullah, the Satirist of Shiraz, trans. Aleister Crowley (London: Privately Printed, 1910).

Schauer, Frederick F, *The Law of Obscenity* (Washington: The Bureau of National Affairs, 1976).

Scheick, William J., 'Adolescent Pornography and Imperialism in Haggard's *King Solomon's Mines*', *English Literature in Transition*, 34.1 (1991) 19–30.

Schueller, Herbert M., and Robert L. Peters, eds., *The Letters of John Addington Symonds*, 3 vols (Detroit: Wayne State University Press, 1969).

Schweik, Robert, 'Congruous Incongruities: The Wilde-Beardsley "Collaboration"', *ELT*, 37.1 (1994) 9–26.

Screech, Timon, *Sex and the Floating World: Erotic Images in Japan, 1700–1820* (London: Reaktion, 1999).

Sedgwick, Eve Kosofsky, *Between Men: English Literature and Male Homosocial Desire* (New York: Columbia University Press, 1985).

The Seducing Cardinal's Amours with Isabelle Peto & Others, 1830 (London: Published as the Act directs, by Madame Le Duck [Lazenby and Avery?]; and to be had by all respectable booksellers, 1830 [*c*.1886]).

Sellon, Edward, 'On Phallic Worship in India', *Memoirs Read Before the Anthropological Society of London, 1865–1866* (London: Trubner, 1866).

Seville, Catherine, *Literary Copyright Reform in Early Victorian England: The Framing of the 1842 Copyright Act* (Cambridge: Cambridge University Press, 1999).

'She-Notes, By Borgia Smudgiton', *Punch* (10 Mar. 1894) 109.

'She-Notes, By Borgia Smudgiton: Part II', *Punch* (17 Mar. 1894) 129.

Sheaves From an Old Escritoire, London: Printed and Published by Henry Robinson [Carrington ?], 1896).

Shore Leave, or Amorous Japanese Tales (N.p: n.p, n.d.).

Siebert, Wilbur H., *The Underground Railroad from Slavery to Freedom* (New York: Macmillan, 1898).

Sigel, Lisa Z., 'The Autobiography of a Flea', 8 Feb. 2001 <http: //eserver. org/cultronix/sigel/>

——, *Governing Pleasures: Pornography and Social Change in England, 1815-1914* (New Jersey: Rutgers University Press, 2002).

Sigma [John Morley], 'The Ethics of Dirt', *Pall Mall Gazette* (29 Sept. 1885) 2.

——, 'Pantagruelism or Pornography?' *Pall Mall Gazette* (14 Sept. 1885) 2–3.

Silverman, Kaja, *Male Subjectivity at the Margins* (New York: Routledge, 1992).

The Sins of the Cities of the Plain or the Recollections of a Mary-Anne with Short Essays on Sodomy and Tribadism, 2 vols (London: Privately Printed [Lazenby?], 1881).

Stisted, Georgina M., *The True Life of Capt. Sir Richard F. Burton* (London: H. S. Nichols, 1896).

Smith, F. B., 'Labouchère's Amendment of the Criminal Law Amendment Bill', *Historical Studies*, 17 (1976) 165–75.

Smith, Joan, 'How Could She? Why Would She?' *The Independent Online Edition* (9 May 2004).

Smithers, Jack, *The Early Life and Vicissitudes of Jack Smithers* (London: Martin Secker, 1939).

Snodgrass, Chris, *Aubrey Beardsley, Dandy of the Grotesque* (Oxford: Oxford University Press, 1995).

Society for the Suppression of Vice (London: S. Gosnell, 1825).

Southey, Robert, 'The Vision of Judgement', *Don Juan*. Cantos VI–VII (London: Printed and Published by W. Dugdale, 1823).

[Southey, Robert?], 'Art IV.—Cases of Walcot V.Walker', *Quarterly Review*, 27 (1822) 123–38.

A Spahi's Love Story (Paris: Charles Carrington, 1907).

Speilmann, M. H., *The History of 'Punch'* (London: Cassell, 1895).

Stanford, Derek, *Aubrey Beardsley's Erotic Universe* (London: New England Library, 1967).

Stedman, John, *Narrative, of a Five Year's Expedition Against the Revolted Negroes of Surinam, in Guiana, on the Wild Coast of South America: From the Year 1772, to 1777*, 2 vols (London: n.p., 1796).

——, *Curious Adventures of Captain Stedman, during an expedition to Surinam* (London: Thomas Tegg, [c.1805]).

Stewart, Jack, *The Vital Art of D.H. Lawrence: Vision and Expression* (Carbondale: Southern Illinois University Press, 1998).

The Story of Seven Maidens, 1907 (N.p.: Venus Library, 1972).

Stowe, Harriet Beecher, *Uncle Tom's Cabin, or Life among the Lowly* (London: H. G. Bohn, 1852).

Sturgis, Matthew, *Passionate Attitudes: The English Decadence of the 1890s* (London: Macmillan, 1995).

Suburban Souls: The Erotic Psychology of a Man and a Maid (Paris: Printed for distribution amongst private subscribers only [Carrington], 1901).

Sue Suckitt; Maid and Wife, 1893 (New Orleans [Paris]: n.p.[Carrington], 1913).

Sultan Sham, and the Seven Wives: An Historical, Romantic, Heroic Poem, in 3 Cantos by Hudibras, the younger (London: Printed and Published by W. Benbow, 1820).

Supplemental Nights to the Book of The Thousand Nights and a Night, 6 vols, trans. Richard F. Burton (London: Printed by the Kama Shastra Society for Private Subscribers Only, 1886–8).

Swift, Jonathan, *Lemuel Gulliver's Travels into Several Remote Nations of the World* (London: [Henry Curll], 1726).

Symonds, John Addington, 'The Arabian Nights' Entertainments', *The Academy* (3 Oct. 1885) 223.

[Symonds, John Addington], *A Problem in Greek Ethics* ([N.p.]: Privately Printed for the Author's Use, 1883).

——, *A Problem in Modern Ethics: Being an Inquiry into the phenomenon of Sexual Inversion* (London: n.p., 1896).

Symons, Arthur, 'An Unacknowledged Movement in Fine Printing: The Typography of the Eighteen-Nineties', *The Fleuron: A Journal of Typography*, 7 (1930) 84–119.

——, 'Aubrey Beardsley', *Fortnightly Review*, 69 (1898) 752–61.

'A Talk with a Slave Woman', *Anti-Slavery Advocate*, 2.3 (1 Mar. 1857) 102–3.

Tardieu, Ambroise, *Etude medicale-legal suer les attentats aux moeurs*, 1857, 7th edn (Paris: n.p., 1878).

Thomas, Donald, Introduction, *The Memoirs of Dolly Morton* (London: Collectors Edition, 1970) 11–18.

——, *A Long Time Burning: The History of Literary Censorship in England* (London: Routledge & Kegan Paul, 1969).

——, *The Victorian Underworld* (London: John Murray, 1998).

Thomas, Helen, *Romanticism and Slave Narratives: Transatlantic Testimonies* (Cambridge: Cambridge University Press, 2000).

Thompson, Roger, *Unfit for Modest Ears: A Study of Pornographic, Obscene, and Bawdy Works Written or Published in England in the Second Half of the Seventeenth Century* (London: Macmillan, 1979).

Thompson, William, *Appeal of One Half of the Human Race* (London: n.p., 1825).

Thorburn, David, and Henry Jenkins, eds., *Rethinking Media Change: The Aesthetics of Transition* (Cambridge, MA: MIT Press, 2003).

The Thousand and One Quarters of an Hour, ed. L. C. Smithers (London: H. S. Nichols, 1893).

Tinto, D., 'Pictures and Painters', *London Figaro* (20 Apr. 1893) 13.

A Town-Bull, or The Elysian Fields (New Orleans: n.p.: [Carrington?], 1893).

The Transmigrations of the Mandarin Fum-Hoam, ed. L. C. Smithers (London: H. S., 1894).

Tresmin-Trémolières, Dr, *La cité d'amour au Japon, courtisanes du Yoshiwara* (Paris: Librarie Universelle, 1905).

Trollope, Frances, *Domestic Manners of the Americans*, 2nd edn (London: Whittaker, Treacher, 1832).

Trudgill, Eric, *Madonnas and Magdalens: The Origins and Development of Victorian Sexual Attitudes* (London: Heinemann, 1976).

Turner, Mark W., *Trollope and the Magazines: Gendered Issues in Mid-Victorian Britain* (Basingstoke: Macmillan – now Palgrave, 1999).

Untrodden Fields of Anthropology: Observation on the esoteric manners and customs of semi-civilised peoples, 2 vols (Paris: Librairie des Bibliophiles, 1896).

Venette, Nicolas, *Conjugal Love, or The Pleasures of the Marriage Bed* (London: Garland, 1984).

Venus School-Mistress, or, Birchen sports, *c*.1808–10 (Paris: Société des Bibliophiles [Carrington?], 1898).

Villiot, Jean de, *Woman and Her Master* (Paris: n.p. [Charles Carrington], 1904).

Warne, Vanessa, and Colette Colligan, 'The Man Who Wrote a New Woman Novel: Grant Allen's *The Woman Who Did* and the Gendering of Male Authorship in New Woman Novels', *Victorian Literature and Culture*, 33.1 (2005) 21–46.

Watkins, John, *Memoirs of the Life and Writings of the Right Honourable Lord Byron* (London: H. Colburn, 1822).

Watson, Sophie, *Memoirs of the Seraglio of the Bashaw of Merryland* (London: S. Bladon, 1768).

Webb, Peter, 'Victorian Erotica', *The Sexual Dimension in Literature*, ed. Alan Bold (London: Vision, 1982).

Weeks, Jeffrey, *Coming Out: Homosexual Politics in Britain from the Nineteenth Century to the Present*, 1977 (London: Quartet, 1990).

——, *Sex, Politics, & Society. The Regulation of Sexuality Since 1800*, 1981, 2nd edn (London: Longman, 1982).

Weintraub, Stanley, *Aubrey Beardsley: Imp of the Perverse* (University Park: Pennsylvania State University Press, 1976).

The Whippingham Papers (London: n.p. [Avery?], 1888 [1887]).

'The White Slave Trade in Constantinople', *The Vigilance Record* (1 Apr. 1902) 31.

Whitford, Frank, *Japanese Prints and Western Painters* (London: Studio Visto, 1977).

Wickwar, William H., *The Struggle for the Freedom of the Press 1819–1832* (London: George Allen, 1972).

The Wild Boys of London (London: Farrah, [1873?]).

[Wilde, Oscar], *Teleny, or the Reverse of Medal. A Physiological Romance of To-day*, 2 vols (Cosmopoli [London]: n.p. [Smithers], 1893).

Wilde, Oscar, *Salome* (London: John Lane, 1894).

——, *Teleny, Étude Physiologique* (Paris: Édition Privée [Charles Hirsch], 1934.

Wilkes, John, *An Essay on Woman* (London: Printed for the Author, [1763]).

Williams, Linda, 'Corporealized Observers: Visual Pornographies and the "Carnal Density of Vision"', *Fugitive Images: From Photography to Video*, ed. Patrice Petro (Bloomington: Indiana University Press, 1995) 3–41.

——, *Hard Core: Power, Pleasure, and the 'Frenzy of the Visible'*, 1989 (Berkeley: University of California Press, 1999).

Wolf, John B., *The Barbary Coast: Algiers Under the Turks 1500 to 1830* (New York: Norton, 1979).

Wolfson, Susan J., '"Their She Condition": Cross-Dressing and the Politics of Gender in *Don Juan'*, *ELH*, 54 (1987) 585–617.

Wollstonecraft, Mary, *A Vindication of the Rights of Woman* (London: n.p., 1792).

Woman and her Slave: A Realistic Narrative of a Slave who Experienced His Mistress' Love and Lash (Paris: Charles Carrington, n.d.).

'The Woman Who Wouldn't Do', *Punch* (30 Mar. 1895) 153.

Wood, Marcus, *Blind Memory, Visual Representations of Slavery in England and America, 1780–1865* (Manchester: Manchester University Press, 2000).

——, *Slavery, Empathy, and Pornography* (Manchester: Manchester University Press, 2003).

Wright, Thomas, *The Life of Sir Richard Burton*, 2 vols (London: Everett, 1906).

Yeazell, Ruth Bernard, *Harems of the Mind: Passages of Western Art and Literature* (New Haven: Yale University Press, 2000).

Yellin, Jean Fagan, Introduction, *Incidents in the Life of a Slave Girl*, by Harriet Jacobs, ed. Jean Fagan Yellin (Cambridge, Mass.: Harvard University Press, 2000) xvi–xxxii.

——, 'Texts and Contexts of Harriet Jacobs' *Incidents in the Life of a Slave Girl: Written by Herself'*, *The Slave's Narrative*, ed. Charles T. Davis and Henry Louis Gates Jr. (Oxford: Oxford University Press, 1985) 262–71.

The Yellow Room., or Alice Darvell's Subjection (London [Paris?]: Privately Printed [Carrington?], 1891).

Yokel's Preceptor; or, More sprees in London! (London: H. Smith [Dugdale], n.d [*c*.1855]).

Yoshiwara: The Nightless City (Paris [Chicago?]: Charles Carrington [Targ?]: 1907).

Young, Wayland, *Eros Denied* (London: Weidenfeld & Nicolson, 1965).

Zatlin, Linda Gertner, *Beardsley, Japonisme, and the Perversion of the Victorian Ideal* (Cambridge: Cambridge University Press, 1997).

Index

Abu Ghraib   172
Acton, W.   93
Adventures of Lady Harpur, The   116
age of sexual consent   190
Alcock, Sir R.   127
Aléra, D. B.   122
Ali, M. J.   58
Allen, G.   148, 149
Allen, M.   162
Alloula, M.   16
American Civil War   97
anal penetration (not penile)   113
anal sex   80, 82, 86, 114, 193
   see also homosexuality
Anthropologia   187
Anthropological Society of London   187
anti-sensualism   5
Anti-Slavery Society   99
anti-sodomy laws   184
Appadurai, A.   3
Arab and Indian texts   7, 8, 56–95
   Arab sexuality   57, 74, 77, 78, 79, 82,
      85, 86, 93
   British sexual inadequacy   58
   homosexuality   57, 58
   public literary debates on
      pornography   57
   as sexual guidebooks   86–7
   see also Arabian Nights; *Marriage – Love
      and Woman Amongst the Arabs*;
      Old Man Young Again; *Perfumed
      Garden, The*; *Scented Garden, The*
Arabian Nights (Burton)   8, 56, 58–73,
   82, 87–8
   Arab sexuality   59, 61, 64, 65–8, 72
   Athenaeum Club   63, 66–7, 190
   British prudery   61–2, 66, 67, 68, 73
   Carrington's involvement   91
   censorship   68, 70
   censure   64
   footnotes   58
   French translation   192
   imitations of original works   90

Kama Shastra Society   58, 60, 64
   limited accessibility of translation   61
   pornography   59, 60, 64–70, 72, 73,
      75, 76
   reviews   63–5
   sexual violence   58
   Stisted's defence of   191
   'Terminal Essay on Pederasty'   72–9,
      82, 85, 89, 91, 188
   'Terminal Essay on Pornography'
      67, 72
Arbuthnot, F. F.   56
Aristophanes   157
art nouveau   8, 145
Ashbee, H. S.   7, 57, 93–4, 98–9, 175,
   182, 184, 188, 198
Ashcroft, J.   1–2, 9
Athenaeum Club   57, 63, 66–7,
   75, 190, 194
Aury, D. (pseudonym Pauline
   Réage)   123
Australia   12
auto-eroticism: Beardsley   152
Avery, E.   75, 191, 200

Bacon, F.   129
Barlow, C. E.   15–16
Barrin, J.   10
Barthes, R.   24
Bataille, G.   124
Baudelaire, C. P.   146
Baudrillard, J.   3–4, 171
Bayros, F. von   160, 161
Beardsley, A.   8, 9, 125, 126–8,
   129–62, 166, 168, 170, 204–5
   auto-eroticism   152
   Bons-Mots illustrations   204
   bookplate design for
      Pollitt, H. J.   159
   Burial of Salome (*Salome*)   134,
      143, 152
   censorship   144
   censorship, evasion of   152, 157

Beardsley, A. – *continued*
  Climax, The (Salome)   149, 151, 160
  curvilinear line/linear style   130–1,
      134–5, 145, 149, 156–7
  decadence   147, 156
  desire and sexual disgust, oscillation
      between   144, 147
  Enter Herodias (Salome)   133, 135
  exoticism   146, 147, 156
  Eyes of Herod, The (Salome)   134, 140
  female sexuality   149–50, 152
  grotesque, emphasis on   130
  J'ai Baisé Ta Bouche Iokanaan,
      J'ai Baisé Ta Bouche   131–2, 145
  japonisme   129, 152
  Kiss of Judas   152, 154
  Lawrence, D. H.: use of Beardsley's
      drawings   160–1
  'Lucian's Strange Creatures'   205
  Lucian's True History illustrations
      (unused)   204
  Lysistrata   157–8
  'Mask of the Red Death, The' (for *The*
      Works of Edgar Allen Poe)   205
  miscegenation   145
  Morte Darthur, Le   204
  Peacock Skirt, The (Salome)   134, 141
  photomechanical line block
      process   130–1, 145
  Platonic Lament, A (Salome)   134, 138
  pornographic coding   134, 152
  Rape of the Lock, The   157, 160
  Salome   144, 145–6, 149,
      152, 157, 160
  Savoy, The   157–8
  sexual perversions, eccentricities
      associated with   149
  sexual rebellion   144
  sexuality   143
  shunga   143
  social implications of aesthetics   143
  Stomach Dance, The (Salome)   134, 137
  Story of Venus and Tannhäuser, The
      157–8
  Toilet of Salome I, The (Salome)   133,
      134, 136
  Toilet of Salome II,
      The (Salome)   134, 142, 147
  Under the Hill   157–8
  Verses, cover for (Dowson, E.)   144

  visual parodies of in *Punch*   145,
      148–9, 156
  white-line technique   204–5
  Woman in the Moon, The (Salome)
      134, 139
  Yellow Book, The   144, 147, 148
Becker, J. E.   163, 164
Benbow, W.   26, 29, 31, 34, 37,
      38, 45, 180, 182
Bending, L.   98
Benjamin, W.   60
Berkley, T.   198
Best, S. G.   115, 116
bestiality   58, 83, 117, 157, 164
Bibliothèque Nationale (Paris)   175
Blake, W.   100
Blore, R.   183
Boccaccio, G.   10
Bodleian Library (Oxford)   175
Boer, I.   181
Bolter, J. D.   3
book clubs   9
Boulton, E.   194
Bourdieu, P.   7
Bracquemond, F.   126
British Film Institute library   178
British Home Office   20, 88–9, 115
British Library   175, 195
British Museum   175
British sexual inadequacy   58
British sexual prudery   61–2, 66, 67,
      68, 73, 93–5
Brodie, F.   70, 73, 83
Brontë sisters   58
Brooks, J. B.   45, 48
brothels:
  male   193, 194
  specializing in flagellation   198
Brown, J.   103, 108, 120
Brown, S.   178
Brown, W. W.   103
Burgess, Rev. G.   41–2
Burton, I.   60–1, 68–9, 71–2, 82–4,
      86, 189, 191–2
Burton, Sir R.   5, 7, 9, 56–95, 170, 195
  Anthropological Society,
      founder of   187
  Ashbee, acquaintance with   188
  Carmina of Catullus, The   73, 81, 83
  esoteric pornography   147

imitations of his works 8
and National Vigilance Association
   surveillance 192
Old Testament, reference to 191
Penzer's reliance on his works 181
political importance as contributed by
   Harris, F. 189–90
'Porter, The and the Three Ladies of
   Baghdad' 188
Priapeia, The 73, 81, 82–3, 192
'rent-boy' scandal and sodomy
   report 194
*see also Arabian Nights; Perfumed
   Garden, The; Scented Garden, The*
Butler, J. 124
Byron, Lord 9, 182, 183, 184
see also Don Juan

Campbell, Lord 11
Canada 12
Cannibal Club 187
Cannon, G. 9, 45, 98
Carey, Rev. P. D. 86
Carlile, R. 46, 180
Carmina of Catullus, The (Burton Sir R.)
   73, 81, 83
Caroline, Queen 33
Carpenter, E. 74, 85, 193
Carrington, C. 9, 89–91, 115, 117,
   123, 191, 201
   Dolly Morton 119–20, 121, 122
   English works with American
      settings 116
   flogging and female slaves 115
   Japanese prints and texts 164
   Lazenby's works 116, 118, 119
   Lustful Turk, The 53, 185
   Marriage and *Old Man* 196
   Moslem Erotism 54
   Perfumed Garden, The 195
   see also Villiot
Catnach, J. 29
Catullus 10, 93
censorship 10–11, 115, 170
   Arab and Indian texts 82, 83, 84
   Arabian Nights (Burton) 68, 70
   Beardsley's illustrations 144,
      152, 157
   Don Juan (Byron) 24
   Japanese erotic prints 125

censure 26, 30, 37, 64
Child, L. M. 108–9
child prostitution 190
Chorier, N. 10
circulation, limited 73
Cleland, J. 10, 74, 94, 98
Cleveland Street Scandal 76, 194
clitoridectomy 58
Clowes, W. L. 94
Coates, H. 42
Cobbett, W. 37, 46
Cockburn, Justice A. 176
Coleridge, S. T. 58
Colton, C. C. 42
Comstock Act 1873 12
Confessional Unmasked, The 176
Congress of Vienna 51
'Conjugal Nights' 188–9
Conrad, J. 21
Comstock, A. 115
Cook, M. 74–5
coprophilia 157
copulation 16
Copyright Act 1814 38
Copyright Act 1842 38
copyright and *Don Juan* (Byron) 23, 28,
   38, 39–41
copyright infringement 26
corporal punishment 98
Crary, J. 16
Cremorne, The 104–5, 108–14, 117
Criminal Law Amendment Act 1885
   190
criminality 4
Crowley, A. 79, 85–6, 87
Cruikshank, I. R. 43, 44
cultural forces 4
cunnilingus 16, 83
Curll, E. 10, 98
Customs Consolidation Act 1876 12,
   176
Customs Office 20

Dalziel, T. 58
D'Arcy, S. J. 117
Darnton, R. 3, 6
Davenport, J. 93
Dawes, C. R. 117, 175
De Villers 21
Dellamora, R. 143, 195

Desmarais, J. H.   146, 155
Devereux, C.   120
Diamio of Satsuma   164
digital images   169
Dingwall, E. J.   175
Dollimore, J.   87, 144
Dolly Morton   117–22
Don Juan (Byron)   7, 23, 24–45, 46
   Canto 2   30
   Canto 3   30
   Canto 4   30
   Canto 5   30
   Canto 6   30, 31, 37–9, 40
   Canto 7   38–9
   Canto 8   38–9
   censorship   24
   censure   26, 30, 37
   copyright   28, 38, 39–41
   harem cantos   30
   imitations of original   24, 27, 28–9,
      32, 38, 42
   piracy of original   23, 24, 26, 28–9,
      32, 33, 38
   radical politics and press   33, 34, 37
   working-class readership   26, 27–9
Don Leon   184
Donelan, C.   31
Douglas, Lord A.   86
Douglass, F.   97, 102–3, 108, 120
Dowson, E.   143, 144
Dugdale, J.   45
Dugdale, W.   9, 14–15, 26, 38–42,
   44–6, 53, 182–4
Dumas, A.   11
Duncombe, E.   45
Duncombe, J.   9, 26, 45

Eastern obscenity *see* Arab and Indian
   texts; harem fantasies
Edwards, A. B.   69
Egerton, G.   148
Elfenbein, A.   26, 41, 44–5, 182
Ellis, H.   74, 75, 85, 86, 92, 193, 196
Ellmann, R.   143
empire, expansion of   4–5, 20
empiricist movement   57
En Virginie   203
Erotic Society of Japan (Paris)   164
eroticism   4, 8–9, 125

Erotika Biblion Society   21, 71, 72,
   83, 157, 192
eunuchism   58
evangelists   97
exoticism   169, 171
   Beardsley   146, 147, 156
   global   23
   Japanese erotic prints   145, 163–4
   lurid   182
   oriental   38
   see also sexual exoticism
Eyre, Lord Chief Justice   28

Fairburn, J.   46, 47
Fanny Hill   10, 22
Favret, M.   99, 100, 104
fellatio   16
female erotic licence in the harem   54–5
films and obscenity   4, 6, 19–20,
   169, 170
Fisch, A.   97, 103, 197
flagellation, fixation with   8,
   97–104, 188
   see also transatlantic slavery
Flaubert, G.   86
Foreign Office   20
Foreman, P. G.   110
Foucault, M.   2, 193
Foxon, D.   10
France   5, 6, 10, 12, 13, 19
France, H.   202
Freud, S.   6, 98, 124
Fulton, R.   97

Galland, A.   58, 60, 65, 66
Garfield, D.   109
Gay, J.   94
Gay, P.   5
George III, King   10
George IV, King   33–4, 37
Gibson, I.   97–8
Gide, A.   86–7
Gilbert, Sir W.S.   125
globalisation   3, 7, 16, 20
Goncourt Brothers   127–8, 146, 204
Goss, M.   164
Gosse, E.   76
Grewal, I.   48
Griffin, J.   42
Grolier Society   89

Grosskurth, P.   76
Gruisin, R.   3

Hall, L.   10
Halttunen, K.   97
Hankey, F.   21, 57, 187
harem fantasies   7, 19, 23–55
    Cabinet of Venus, The   53
    female erotic licence in the
        harem   54–5
    Lustful Turk, The   48–53
    Monk, The   48, 52
    Moslem Erotism   54–5
    Night in a Moorish Harem, A   53, 54
    orientalism   23
    Perfumed Garden, The   54
    piracy, abolition of   51, 54
    relocation of harem property to
        English girl's boarding schools
        50–1
    Scenes in the Seraglio   48, 53
    Seducing Cardinal's Amours, The   48,
        52–3
    sexual violence against
        women   48–9, 52
    slavery, abolition of   51, 54
    sodomy   49–50
    Venus School Mistress, The   50
    see also Don Juan
Harlow, B.   181
Harris, F.   189–90
Harris, G. W.   86
Hart, L.   124
Harunobu, S.   127
Haynes, W.   115, 199
Hegel, G. W. F.   124
Heller, T.   198
Hendlemen, L.   20
Herodotus   77
heterosexual fantasy   111–12, 113
Hiroshige, A.   126
Hirsh, C.   9
Hodgson, W.   29
homoeroticism and transatlantic
    slavery   98, 100, 110–14, 115
homosexual communities   193
homosexual identity   8, 73–4, 75
homosexual rape   78–9
homosexuality   57, 58, 193

Arab and Indian texts   57, 58,
    76, 77, 78, 82, 84, 85, 86
    transatlantic slavery   98, 117
    see also pederasty; sodomy
Hone, W.   27, 33
H. S. Nichols & Co.   72
humanitarianism   97
Hunt, J.   30
Hunt, L.   6
Hyam, R.   5, 63
Hyde, H. M.   76

imperial politics   82
imperialism   5, 62–3
incest   105, 116
Indecent Advertisements Act
    1889   12, 176
India   12
intergenerational sex   116
    see also pederasty
international conferences   12
Internet pornography   4, 5, 169–70
Italy   10, 13

Jackson, H.   126, 156, 158
Jackson, L.   194
Jacobs, H.   108, 109–11, 113–14, 117,
    119, 199, 201
James, H.   76
Japanese erotic prints   125–68
    censorship   125
    eroticism   8–9, 125
    exoticism   163–4
    geisha   162
    Nightless City, The   163,
        164, 165–6
    photographic media, advance of
        166, 167, 168
    pillow books   127
    shunga ('spring pictures')   127–8,
        152, 162, 164, 166, 168
    Yoshiwara (red light districts)   125,
        162–4
    see also Art Nouveau; Beardsley;
        japonisme
japonisme   129, 152
*Jardin Parfumé du Cheikh Nefzaoui,
    Le*   195
Johnson, S.   58
Jones, B.   145

Jones, P. 85, 86
Joyce, J. 6
Judge, H. 9, 21
Juvenal, D. J. J. 10

Kabbani, R. 181, 188
Kama Shastra 187
Kama Shastra Society 56, 58,
　　60, 64, 73, 187
Kama Sutra 187
Kearney, P. 6, 107
Kelly, G. 128
Kendrick, W. 59
Kennedy, D. 59, 60, 65, 78
King's and Queen's Bench
　　trials 177
Kinsey Institute 175, 195
Knipp, C. 60, 75, 78, 188
Kooistra, L. J. 143
Krafft-Ebing, R. von 86, 158

Labouchère Amendment to Criminal
　　Law Amendments Act 76
Labouchère, H. 76, 194, 195
*Lady Burton's Edition of her Husband's
　　Arabian Nights* 69
Lane, E. 58, 65, 66
Lane, F. S. 6
Lane, J. 129–31, 133, 145,
　　148, 157, 205
Lane-Poole, S. 66–7
Lansbury, C. 198
Laveleye, E. de 59, 67
Laver, J. 126, 127
Lawrence, D. H. 6, 160
Lawrence, T. E. 79, 87
Lazenby, W. 9, 115, 116, 118–19,
　　200, 201
　　Birchen Bouquet, The 104
　　Lustful Turk, The 53
　　Queenie 116
　　*Quintessence of Birch Discipline,
　　　　The* 104
　　Romance of Chastisement, The 104
　　sodomy featured in published
　　　　works 74–6
　　see also Cremorne, The; Pearl, The
League of Nations 12
legislation and the print trade in
　　nineteenth century 10–12

Legman, G. 94, 115
Leighton, J. 127
lesbianism 105, 124
　　see also tribadism
Lew, J. 181
Lewis, G. 52, 189
Leyland, F. R. 126
Liberty, A. 127
Licensing Act (1557–1695) 10
Liseux, I. 79, 81, 82, 195
Livingstone, D. 97
Lord Campbell's Act (England's First
　　Obscenity Statute) 176
Lovell, M. 71–2, 81, 84
Luke, H. J. 26, 27, 29
Lustful Turk, The 48–53, 185

McCalman, I. 6–7, 9, 24, 33, 45, 98
McLynn, F. 73, 78, 79, 83
magazines 15
mail-order postal trade 9, 12, 53
male brothels/prostitutes 193, 194
Marcus, S. 2, 5, 6, 48, 49, 57, 98, 193
Marks, J. L. 34, 35, 36
*Marriage – Love and Woman Amongst the
　　Arabs* 56–7, 90–1, 92, 93, 94
Martial 10
masochism 203
　　see also sado-masochism
Mason, M. 5
masturbation 16, 83, 157
Mayhew, H. 13
Maylor, V. 70
Meibomius, J. H. 10, 98
Meier-Graefe, A. J. 128, 131
Melman, B. 48, 181–2
Memoirs of Harriett Wilson 183–4
Memoirs of Madge Buford, The 116, 117
Mendes, P. 6, 9, 54, 57, 75, 90, 107,
　　115–16, 194
Metropolitan Police Act 1847 11, 176
miscegenation 58, 106, 145
Mitford, J. 44, 182
Molly Houses 193
Monckton Milnes, R. 56, 57, 75,
　　187–8
Montagu, Lady 42, 181
Montesquieu, Baron de 181
Moore, G. 71, 127, 133
Moore, T. 24, 30, 32

morality laws (France) 1898 and 1908   12
Morley, J. (pseudonym Sigma)   64–5
Morris, W.   130, 131
Mosse, G.   67
Mudge, B.   6
Mudie's Circulating Library   102
Mugabe, R.   169–70
Murray, J.   26, 27, 38–9
My Grandmother's Tale   105–6, 108, 116
  'Kate's Narrative'   105–8, 110
My Secret Life   193

Napier, Sir C.   73
National League Federation   59
National Vigilance Association   121,
    177, 178, 192
Ncube, T.   170
Nead, L.   6, 11, 14
Nelson, J.   71, 88
New Zealand   12
Nichols, C.   199
Nichols, H. S.   9, 71–2, 75, 191
Nonconformists   97
Nordmann, G.   107
Norman, Sir H.   162–3
Numantius, N. (Karl Ulrichs)   81

Obscene Publications Act 1857   11,
    60, 71, 92, 176, 189
Obscene Publications Act 1959   176
Obscene Publications Bill 1580   10
Offences Against the Person Act 76
Old Man Young Again, The   57, 90–1,
    92, 93, 94
orgies   164
  see also threesomes
Oriental Lascivious Tales   192
Oriental Stories   192
Oriental Translation Fund   56
orientalism   3, 4, 7, 8, 23, 26, 42, 59, 73
O'Toole, L.   4, 6
Ovid   10, 93
Owen, A.   87

Park, F. W.   194
Partridge, J. B.   148
Pasolini, P. P.   172
paternal incest   105, 116
Payne, J.   58, 60, 66, 70–1, 75, 91, 188
Peakman, J.   6, 10, 98

Pearl, The (Lazenby)   17, 22, 105–8, 110,
    113, 116, 193, 200
Pease, A.   6
pederasty   83, 157
  see also Terminal Essay on 'Pederasty'
    under Arabian Nights
Pennell, J.   145
Penzer, N.   181
Perfumed Garden, The (Burton)   8, 54–7,
    70, 73–4, 79–82, 87–8, 195
  Carrington's edition   195
  Carrington's involvement   91
  twenty-first chapter, omission of
    80–2, 85, 195
Peterloo massacre   24, 179
Phoenix of Sodom, The   193
photographic media, advances in   16,
    19, 166, 167, 168, 169, 170, 171
photography   19–20
piracy, abolition of   51, 54
Pitts, J.   29
Poe, E. A.   129
political arousal   100
Pollitt, J.   158, 159
Pope, A.   157
pornography   8, 169
  Arabian Nights   59, 60, 64–70, 72,
    73, 75, 76
  public literary debates   57
  Wood's definition of   199
port cities, immorality of   15–16
Porter, R.   10
post   4, 5
  see also mail-order
Post Office   20
Post Office Act 1893   12
Post Office Act 1908   12
Post Office (Protection) Act
    1884   12, 176
Post and Telegraph Act 1901   12
Priapeia, The (Burton, Sir R.)   73, 81,
    82–3, 192
Prichard, G.   12–13, 185
Prince, M.   103
print trade in nineteenth century   4,
    6, 9–22, 169
  book clubs   9
  censorship   10–11
  containment   26

print trade in nineteenth century –
    continued
  empire, expansion of   20
  erotic films   19–20
  French and Italian translations   10
  globalisation   16, 20
  harem fantasy   19
  international conferences   12
  legislation   10–12
  mail-order postal trade   9, 12
  photographic media, advances
      in   16, 19
  photography   19–20
  port cities, immorality of   15–16
  sex manuals   10
  Society for the Suppression of Vice
      12–13
  subscriptions   9, 16
  technologies   179
  women and families, participation of
      in trade   14
Private Case collection   175, 190
Proclamation Society   11
prostitution   125, 162–4
  child   190
  male   193, 194

Quakers   97
Quaritch, B.   88

R v. Hicklin   176
Rabelais, F.   10
radical politics and press   33, 34, 37
railway   4, 5
rape   78–9, 116
  see also sexual abuse; sexual violence
Reade, B.   133, 143
real, obscenity of   169–72
realism, extreme   170, 171, 172
reality, virtual   172
Rebell, H.   202
Reddie, J. C.   194
Reed, E. T.   148–9, 150, 152, 153, 155–6
Reid, G.   170–1
'rent boy scandal'   194
Report from the Joint Select Committee   178
Richardson, A.   31
Ricketts, C.   162
Robson and Kerslake   79, 195
Rochester, J. W.   10

Romance of Lust, The   193
Rops, F.   131, 146
Ross, R.   133, 156
Rossetti, D. G.   126
Rothenstein, W.   128–9, 133, 158
Rowlandson, T.   32–4, 182
Royal Asiatic Society   57
Royal Geographic Society   57

Sacher-Masoch, L. von   124, 203
Sade, Marquis de   2, 7, 105, 122, 124,
      147, 158, 188, 203
sadism   203
sado-masochism   78, 124
Said, E.   4, 52, 79, 86, 87, 188
Salome (Wilde)   8, 125, 131–2, 136–7,
      144, 145, 157, 162, 205
  French version   146
  reviews   147
  see also particular illustrations for
      under Beardsley, A.
Sánchez-Eppler, K.   109, 113, 199
Sanger, Dr W. W.   163
Santa Cruz   200
Sargent, J. S.   128
Scented Garden, The (Burton)   8, 56, 57,
      73, 74, 81, 82, 85
  Isabel Burton's burning of   83–4
schools, obscenity infiltrating   185
Screech, T.   127
sea travel   5
Secret Life of Linda Brent, The   108–11,
      113–14
Select Bibliothèque   115, 122
Seville, C.   38
sex between different classes   105
sexual abuse within transatlantic slavery
      108–10, 114, 119
sexual curiosity   97
sexual exoticism   63, 68–9, 73
sexual expression, freedom of   87
sexual identities   9
sexual migration   86–7
sexual violence:
  Arabian Nights   58
  harem fantasies   48–9, 52
  and slavery   96, 97, 102–4, 110, 118,
      119, 199
sexuality   8, 169, 171
  abrogation   6

and Beardsley's illustrations 143
disciplining of 4, 5
female 149–50, 152
see also Arab sexuality *under* Arab and
Indian texts; *Arabian Nights*
Shakespeare, W. 62
Sheaves from an Old Escritoire 185–6
shunga ('spring pictures') 127–8, 152,
162, 164, 166, 168
Siebert, W. H. 120
Sigel, L. 6, 9, 20, 44, 49, 52,
57–8, 63, 187
Silverman, K. 87
Sins of the Cities, The 194
Six Acts 24, 179
slavery, abolition of 51, 54, 96
slavery imagery 8
Smith, F. B. 76
Smithers, J. 158, 191
Smithers, L. 75, 90, 191, 192
Arabian Nights 68–9, 71–2
and Beardsley 129, 158
Carmina of Catullus, The 81, 83, 88
Priapeia, The 81, 82–3
Scented Garden, The 84–5
Smyth Pigott, E. T. 131
Snodgrass, C. 133–4, 143
Society for the Reformation of
Manners 10
Society for the Suppression of Vice 11,
12–13, 177, 180, 183, 185, 192
Don Juan (Byron) 26, 29
harem fantasies 50, 67
New York 115
sodomy 49–50, 58, 67–8, 193
Arab and Indian texts 73–4, 75, 76,
78, 79, 80, 81, 82, 86, 87
and blackmail, association
between 184
Boulton and Park trial 194
harem fantasies 49–50
transatlantic slavery 99, 105,
110–14, 117
Somerset, Lord A. 76, 194
Sotadic Zone of Vice 77
Southey, R. 28, 45
Soye, Madame de 126
Stamp Act 179
Stanford, D. 143
Statute of Anne 1709 38

Stead, W. T. 6, 66, 68, 76, 91, 190
Stedman, J. 100, 108, 198, 199
Sterne, L. 62
Stewart, J. 131, 160
Stisted, G. 84, 191
Stockdale, J. J. 42, 183
Story of Seven Maidens, The 116, 117
Stowe, H. B. 97, 124
Sturgis, M. 133, 149
subscription, private 9, 16, 73
Sue Suckitt 116, 117, 202
Suetonius 77
Sullivan, Sir A. S. 125
Supplementary Nights: 'Reviewers
Reviewed' (Burton) 76
Swift, J. 62
Swinburne, A. 57, 76, 187
Symonds, J. A. 73–4, 75, 76, 81, 85,
193, 195
Symons, A. 129–30, 156–7

Tardieu, A. 75, 77
technological media 6
telegraph 5
telephone 4
Thomas, D. 10, 121
Thompson, G. (pseudonym
Greenhorn) 199
Thompson, R. 10
threesomes 16, 105
Tinto, D. 145
Town-Bull, A 116, 117, 202
transatlantic slavery 8, 96–124
anal penetration 113, 114
flagellation, preoccupation with 96,
97–104
genital endowment of Black slave
man 106, 116
interracial sex 99
Memoirs of Madge Buford, The
116, 117
My Grandmother's Tale 105–8,
110, 116
*Narrative of the Life of Frederick
Douglass* 102–3
racial domination 115
racialised sexuality 106, 117
Secret Life of Linda Brent, The 108–11,
113–14
sexual domination 115

transatlantic slavery – *continued*
  Story of Seven Maidens, The   116, 117
  Sue Suckitt   116, 117
  Town-Bull, A   116, 117
  visual representation of
      flogging   100
  white woman as slave and
      eroticisation of whiteness   119,
      120, 122
  White Women Slaves   122
  whitewashing of slave woman   108,
      114, 119
  Woman and her Slave   119–20
  *see also Cremorne, The; Dolly Morton;
      Pearl, The*
transvestism   99
Tresmin-Trémolières, Dr   163
tribadism   75, 80, 99
Trollope, A.   71
Turner, M.   71
Tweedie, W.   108

Ulrichs, K.   86, 195
Uncle Tom in England   197
Uncle Tom's Cabin   97, 117, 124, 197
Utamaro   163, 164, 166

Vagrancy Act 1824   11, 176
Vagrancy Act 1838   11, 176
Vaux, H.   14
Venette, N.   10
Venus in Furs   203
Victorian Customs Act 1883   12
video   4
Villiot, J. de (composite name used by
      Carrington)   121–2, 202

Vizetelly, H.   92, 196
voyeurism   105

Warne, V. K.   149
Watkins, J.   29
Watson, S.   182
Weeks, J.   73, 76, 193
Weintraub, S.   133
Wetherell, I.   170
Whipping Act 1862   98, 197
Whistler, J.   126, 134
White Women Slaves   122
Whitford, F.   127, 131
Whitman, W.   77
Wilberforce, W.   11
Wilde, O.   86–7, 117, 161, 205
  trial   130
  see also Salome
Wilkes, J.   10
Williams, L.   6
Wolfson, S. J.   31
Woman and her Slave   119–20
women and families, participation
      of in obscenity trade   14–15, 177
women's exposure to obscenity   70
Women's Library (London)   177
Wood, M.   100, 104, 108, 199
Wright, T.   81, 188

Yeazell, R.   31, 52, 53, 181
Yellin, J. F.   109

Zatlin, L. G.   125, 131, 143–4, 157
Zimbabwe Censorship and
      Entertainment Control Act   170
Zola, E.   127, 196